2020 WIPEOUT
A New Terror

Stuart Holland

2020 WIPEOUT
A New Terror

AUTHOR'S FOREWORD

This book is a work of fiction and any resemblance to actual persons, living or dead, is purely coincidental. Some of the organisations mentioned in this fiction story actually exist, or existed in recent history, others are entirely fictional. The locations mentioned throughout this story are not fictional, though their descriptions have been changed in certain places to fit this story.

Stuart Holland, 2019

PROLOGUE

The world is a dangerous place. When they killed the leader of al-Qaeda, the politicians told everyone it would make the world a safer place. But, it hasn't. All it's done is to drive the fanatics and the members of the networks underground. Now, instead of a few central locations for the authorities to watch, each of these groups of just a few people or even lone wolves, is capable of acting on their own. They've got smarter, act more intuitively, and are becoming progressively more dangerous.

For example, take this new plant we have discovered in Syria. Heaven only knows what it's for or who funded its construction. It could well be for legitimate purposes, but it could equally be highly dangerous. We just don't know, because the world has changed, so finding out its true purpose is next to impossible.

Any of our sleeping targets, and we have hundreds of them, could wake up tomorrow and decide it's the right day to create mayhem on the mainland or elsewhere. We have reached the point where we simply don't know what resources they have to hand, or how they intend to use them, or when. In truth, apart from the usual array of knives and guns that are so prevalent on the streets these days, we have no idea what other types of weapons they may already have access to.

But, our greatest fear is that the greatest threat to our security may well not be the targets who are known to us. The world has changed, because we now have to worry about the have-a-go type lone wolf who we know nothing about. Add to that we have to worry about organisations like Braddock. We have to worry about them because they could be a threat, not because they are already known to be a threat.

With this in mind, I would suggest we will need more and more resources to endeavour to at least stay on a level playing field with the threats we may well be facing.

Selena Preston
Projects Manager
ATRIUM, March 2020

CHAPTER ONE

Tuesday 23rd June 2020

The market at Yalvac was already bustling when the white van arrived. The temperature was already over eighty degrees and would certainly reach ninety by mid-afternoon. The van had no air conditioning and its driver mopped his forehead with a grubby handkerchief as he pulled the vehicle into the dusty side of the road. It was a journey Daniel Newton had made many times before. Yalvac was one of his more regular destinations and Newton had long since decided on the best day of the week to make his visit, the best time of the day to arrive and the best place to try and park. He was a couple of hundred yards from the marketplace and the side road in which he had parked was almost deserted. A woman in traditional Turkish dress was busy mopping the step that led into her humble dwelling. She ignored Newton as he alighted from the van, carefully locked it and began the short walk to the market. As he walked, Newton glanced at his watch and smiled to himself.

Newton walked casually, trying hard not to look like a tourist. He reached the first of the market stalls and stopped to look at the array of fruit and vegetables. He picked out some oranges and held them up to attract the stallholder's attention. Two minutes later he was walking away with a brown paper bag tucked under his arm.

He browsed through a couple of stalls that sold leather belts and bags. The marketplace was already full of American tourists. Summer had arrived. The coaches that bussed in the flocks of willing, eager tourists had already begun to arrive for the day and Newton knew some serious haggling would be taking place at most of the stalls. The local people relied heavily on the tourist trade and with the ruins of the Biblical city of Antakya, or Antioch, no more than a short journey away, Yalvac

9

attracted some heavy tourist traffic in season. It was the beginning of the season and Newton knew the marketplace would soon be heaving. It was so different to the quieter, winter months.

Newton found the street café he had frequented so many times before and took a seat at a roadside table. The coffee was strong and ice cold, a refreshing drink on what was already a scorching, summer's day. Newton sipped the coffee carefully, watching the flow of shoppers with some amusement. He'd spent six days on the road getting here. Now he had a couple of days to pick up the consignment before his journey home would start. He'd use the afternoon to make contact with his supplier. As always, he knew the orders would not be ready. They never were ready, which was why he always allowed a couple of days in the area. It was Tuesday so most probably he'd be kicking his heels until Thursday or possibly Friday. There was no rush, there never was. As always he had all the paperwork in the van. The import licences, order manifests, the lot. He could account for everything he transported, he always could. He was meticulous and fastidious as to detail, which was why he had been chosen.

It had all started years earlier when Newton had been involved in the mercy dashes to take aid to Syria and other countries. He hadn't had the white van then but had hired one for the trip. It had been an experience he would never forget and it had opened his eyes to the opportunities that were presented by travelling around Europe and beyond. After a while he'd made some contacts and had orders to import various kinds of goods. All he'd done was hire another van, travelled around Europe picking up the various goods he was to import, and taken them back to England.

Somewhere along the way, and he couldn't remember when, he'd been approached by two well-dressed businessmen. They owned a string of shops and needed to bring the goods they sold into Britain on a

regular basis. Their proposition had been a good one. They bought Newton his white van, supplied him with the orders once every two months and he did all the travelling and collecting of products. Everything was legitimate, above board and covered by immaculate paperwork, licences and the necessary travel documents. He was paid two thousand pounds for each journey together with all his travelling and accommodation costs.

For a single man who'd just been made redundant it had been like a dream come true. Newton had begun the journeys, visiting the towns mentioned by his employers, picking up the orders as they directed him. At first he'd been eyed by the various authorities with a good degree of suspicion but he'd learned how to handle them. Helped by the immaculate paperwork he'd never been held up for more than a few hours. The products were mainly rugs, linen, leather goods and other miscellaneous gift items. There was never any cause for concern at any border crossing.

He'd made over twenty journeys before he'd been introduced to Dieter Zussman. Zussman was a jeweller, a small time trader with Eastern connections. Like the two businessmen Newton worked for, he needed certain products brought into the country. Again it was all legitimate, paperwork was provided and the contacts seemed authentic. It was easy for Newton to accept the additional business, especially as his new contacts were all in the same areas he was already covering. The extra thousand pounds a trip also helped Newton, and to the people behind Zussman it was a price worth paying.

Newton began collecting the cheap bracelets, bangles, watches and other, more expensive, items of jewellery he had on his order sheets. He'd now made well over a dozen such collections. They were always almost the same in terms of quantity. There'd be a few hundred bracelets, twenty to thirty watches, a couple of trays of rings of various types, some strings of necklaces and various other items.

Newton watched the tourists as they flocked to the marketplace, seeking out the ultimate bargain, in much the same way a bird of prey seeks out its next victim. Newton smiled to himself as he sipped the second iced coffee. The Mediterranean area was hot by this time of year and the rugged Turkish coast was only a few miles away. If, as he knew would be the case, he was going to be delayed for a few days, he'd take the van off down to the secluded cove he'd discovered. There he'd be able to relax a bit and catch a few hours of sunshine. The marketplace was busy now with the numbers of tourists that had swooped on it. Newton stood up, reckoned the temperature was fast approaching ninety, and joined the bustling crowd.

***

Dieter Zussman was a small man, stocky and balding. He wore silver-rimmed half-spectacles that perched on the end of his somewhat ruddy nose. The dark blue pinstripe suit sported a clean, neatly pressed handkerchief in the top pocket. He looked what he claimed to be, a displaced Jew who was building his own business in a foreign land. He stood diminutively behind the counter. On the customer side of the glass-topped counter stood a woman. Taller than Zussman by some four inches, she had long, blonde hair that flowed down over her shoulders. She was attired in a simple frock and the bulge in the lower part of the dress revealed the later stages of her pregnancy.

'Gavin,' she said, 'that's my husband, insisted I came to look for an eternity ring. I think the diamond and sapphire band you have in the window looks absolutely gorgeous. Do you mind if I try it on?'

'Of course you must try it on, Madam. We do actually have a number of designs, if Madam would like to look at some others for comparison purposes.'

'Oh, that would be splendid.'

'Sandra,' he called out into the back of the shop, 'could you bring out the diamond and sapphire rings please?' Zussman smiled and walked over to the shop window. He unlocked the glass panel and withdrew the tray containing the ring from the display.

'Now, Madam, this contains seven diamonds and on the top part of the band there are five sapphires.'

'What a strange design,' she commented.

'Yes, Madam, it is a ring from the East of Europe, one that we import especially for our more discerning clients. Ah, Sandra, thank you my dear.'

The pretty, dark-haired twenty-something had opened the door behind the counter and handed Zussman a tray containing about twenty rings of various designs.

'Now, Madam, I have to say that because it is a special ring, this is reflected somewhat in its value.' Zussman coughed delicately as if somewhat embarrassed by the price tag.

'I should hope so too. Oh look, are those angels?' She'd been looking at the tray of rings and swooped on one of them. Tiny figures appeared to have been carved into the gold band on either side of the central, top diamond. Further diamonds and sapphires covered the majority of the rest of the band.

'I believe they are love birds or some such. They are rather delicate, aren't they?'

'Yes, absolutely delightful. Can I try it on?'

'Of course you may, Madam.' The woman offered the finger on which she already displayed a rather ostentatious diamond engagement ring and a plain band of gold for her wedding ring. Zussman delicately placed the ring on her finger. It fitted easily.

'We can adjust the ring in about an hour if Madam wants us to,' Zussman offered.

'Oh, it's gorgeous. How much is it, please?'

'Three thousand two hundred pounds,' Zussman replied. He noted the woman did not flinch or react to the sum of money. She held her finger up to the light, admiring the beauty of the creation. As she did so, Zussman recognised the design marks on the engagement ring. They told him it was one of his own. 'We could, of course, give you a ten percent discount seeing as you are a regular customer,' he hastily added.

'That is very kind of you, Mr Zussman. You know, I think Gavin will be delighted with this. It's to celebrate our third child you know. Yes, I'll take it, but it will need to be made a bit smaller I think.'

'Yes, I would agree with you. Do you know what size your wedding band is?'

'No, I'm afraid not.'

'It doesn't matter. We can fit you very quickly.'

Ten minutes later the size had been determined, the ring paid for in cash, which surprised Zussman, and the woman was walking back down the road with the receipt in her handbag and an hour to wait before she could make the collection. The ring was in the backroom, the band size being skilfully adjusted by the young woman who Zussman had employed as an assistant jeweller. She was showing promise, a great deal of promise and Zussman considered she would be more than capable of doing the job he had planned for her if he expanded the business to a third shop in a few months' time.

The man had been standing nonchalantly at the back of the shop, his face turned away from Zussman as he looked at a display case, while the customer was being served. Now, as she closed the door behind her, he stepped forward.

'Yes, sir,' Zussman was still closing the window display cabinet, having replaced the ring. The tray of rings was under the counter out of view.

'Mr Zussman, how are you today?' The voice was heavy, thick set and heavily accented. The man was thin and sporting a short, grey beard. His eyes were heavy set, and his breath stank of garlic.

'Very well, thank you.' Zussman started to sweat slightly as the man took one step towards the counter.

'That is good, very good. Our friend asked me to drop in to see if you had heard anything about the goods yet, so I can assure him everything is okay.'

'I've heard nothing yet, but as the driver is not due back for another eight days, it is likely the contact has not been made yet. Phone me in a few days and I will tell you if I have any news. Now, to avoid suspicion, I suggest you don't come back here. Use the method we agreed before. We don't want anything to go wrong, do we?'

'No, Mr Zussman, we do not. That would be most unfortunate for everybody. Let us hope the driver is as astute on this journey as he always has been before.'

'He will be. Your people have been using him for several years. Has he ever let you down?'

'No, but some of our people are just a bit nervous seeing as this journey is, how shall we say, a bit special.'

'He'll be fine. The paperwork is as good as ever. I am sure everything will go smoothly for all of us. Now, before my assistant hears anything untoward, I will bid you good day.'

Zussman came from behind the counter and escorted the other man to the door. Zussman held the door open politely and quietly ushered his visitor back onto the street. With the door closed behind him, Zussman took the neatly folded handkerchief from his top pocket and padded the top of his forehead.

'Sandra,' he called, 'I am going out for some coffee. I will lock the door on the way out so you won't be disturbed. You have the ring we just sold to adjust and after that the carriage clocks need to be polished. If there are any phone calls, please take messages.'

He'd barely finished speaking before the door behind the counter opened and the young woman appeared.

'Okay, Mr Zussman. How long will you be?'

'About forty minutes. You can wait that long for a break until I get back?' He framed it as a question but the woman knew it was really a statement.

'Of course I can.' She disappeared into the room behind the shop and closed the door. Zussman turned the shop sign to display 'Closed' and, locking the door behind him, walked briskly down the High Street of Reigate in Surrey. It was early for coffee, barely ten o'clock, but Zussman had much on his mind. So much depended on a chain of events taking place several thousand miles away, events he could not control, events that would severely affect his future if they went wrong. Yes, Dieter Zussman was a troubled man.

***

Most people think of an Operations Room as being a place bustling with activity. Selena Preston was different. Her Operations Room consisted of a single desk on which sat a solitary telephone and a laptop computer. The room contained the usual filing cabinets and bookcase, two sofas and half a dozen chairs that were arranged in waiting room fashion around the walls. The building in which the Operations Room was housed was not ostentatious. In fact it hardly merited attention at all. The room was on the second floor of the building. Some obscure firm of city lawyers occupied the first floor and a chain store owned the street level premises. The room suited Preston perfectly. It gave her the solitude she liked, yet at the same time she was never more than a phone call away from the team. The team, she laughed to herself on occasion, was almost anything but a team. The mere word, 'team', implied some kind of bonding, unity, working together, yet she had eight disparate individuals who worked mostly on their own, without contact, unless it was through her. They were, in Selena Preston's opinion, almost like shadows.

Selena Preston was a unique woman. Now in her late thirties, she had often been paraded as the high flier she had proven to be. She was attractive, with short-cropped blond hair and a disarming smile. Her credentials were, of course, visibly impeccable. They had to be for she was entrusted with one of those jobs that required utter, unswerving loyalty to the Crown. She'd been vetted, checked and double checked by just about every intelligence agency and she had come through them all. She had no known boyfriend or other baggage in her life and she was totally devoted to her job. Her rise through the essential departments and the necessary training programs had been meteoric and at some point she had been shown to have an IQ that would make most MENSA members blush with envy. She had a razor sharp mind, an almost photographic memory that absorbed details like a sponge and she was one of the rare breed of people who had remained totally calm and clear thinking during every crisis that had been thrown at her during training. She deserved the job and she worked at it for up to sixteen hours a day. Some people reckoned she even slept with the job.

Preston looked out of the window of her office across the waters of the river Thames and scratched the top of her head. The London Eye was rotating as it always did, the sun glistening off the capsules as they continued on their unending journey. Even though the wheel was some distance away it still dominated her line of sight when she looked upstream.

It had been quiet, too quiet, since the team had been put together. The aftermath of the Twin Towers disaster, the reprisal actions in Afghanistan, the dismantling of a number of terrorist networks, and the death of Osama bin Laden, once leader of al-Qaeda, were all in the distant past. Other terrorist factions had arisen, including ISIS, but they had not caused the formation of this particular team. What had caused the formation of the team was a new threat that had risen, or at least there was fear that it could be about to rise. From the smouldering remains of the original factions and the more recent ones still in distant lands, some Mandarin in

Whitehall had conceived the possibility of a new, even more deadly, force being formed.

Five years earlier a top-secret laboratory deep in the Nevada desert had been breached by what was believed to be a lone assailant. It had taken months for the news to leak out to the relevant authorities in allied countries and then the threat had been categorised as small though the suspected assailant had never been captured. A single phial containing the deadly Marburg virus could not be accounted for after the breach and after a while it had been attributed to a possible accounting error. The boffins who worked at the top-level laboratory had suggested that a single phial would not be able to pose a significant threat and as there had been no outbreak of the deadly virus that could be attributed to the phial, it was widely considered the virus would have died given the phial in isolation gave the virus a life-expectancy of just a few months. But it was this breach that had caused the first elements of the team being assembled in the UK.

More recently, incidents in the UK involving nerve agent poisonings, Paris, Belgium and elsewhere on Continental Europe had also influenced the minds of the relevant people. As a result, the machinery had been put in motion because no possible risk to National security could be ignored. Moreover, the Mandarin in Whitehall carried a good track record and a great deal of influence in the right circles. He was not a member of the Old Boys club of influence but he had certainly gained the respect and more importantly the ear of certain members of the club over the past twenty or more years.

ATRIUM (Anti-Terrorist Research, Infiltration and Undercover Manoeuvres) had been formed as part of the strategy to unearth plans any terrorists might be making, as well as provide a separate layer of protection against this new, perceived threat. That had been well over a year ago and for all their contacts, all the targets they had followed and watched closely, they'd come up with nothing. Of course, the eight members of ATRIUM, nine if you included Preston, had been assisted greatly. New Scotland Yard, the Intelligence Services and the various authorities all around the country had played their part, watching and following the known suspects and sympathisers. They'd all reported back through the lines of command until the disseminated information arrived back on Preston's desk. Then it was filed, meticulously.

Preston looked out of the window and wondered if the time had come to call it a day. ATIUM had unearthed nothing that the other intelligence services did not know about. They had uncovered nothing of a specific terrorist threat, not even an inkling of any activity, for the past year and it was costing a great deal of tax payers' money. Questions were already being asked in certain quarters and if the existence of the group were to become known outside of those quarters the disaffection would rise rapidly. Preston was keen to avoid the public condemnation of yet another Quango, for that is how people would doubtless see ATRIUM.

After a few minutes looking out at the London Eye, Preston turned back to her desk and picked up the plain, manila-coloured folder. In it were the eight sheets of paper that comprised the latest reports from the team. She read them again, looking for signs of something, though she didn't know what. She looked at the report from Travis Marshall. He'd spent the month watching a couple of known fanatics but had nothing to report other than the observation that one of them had either walked past or visited a jeweller's shop south of London on three separate occasions within a period of ten days. The visits seemed innocuous but Marshall deemed them worth including in his report if only because there was nothing else to include.

Preston turned to the next report which was from Brian Keeley. Based around Newbury he'd been keeping a watching brief on a small group of known activists. There were five of them, all of Arabic extraction. They visited the local Mosque regularly, and met at a café on the outskirts of the town centre twice a week. Other than that they either spent much of their time in the local snooker hall which was owned by a past star of the game, or they spent their days out and about. None of them appeared to have employment but that was nothing unusual and nothing to get excited about.

The other six reports were equally as unimpressive as Keeley's and Marshall's. Preston banged the folder down on her desk and paced around the room seeking inspiration. She came to the coffee maker sitting on top of the filing cabinet next to the door to her office and poured a cup for herself before returning to her desk. She picked up the phone and pressed a speed-dial button.

'Marshall, this is Preston, are you secure?'

'Yes Ma'am.' Marshall spoke with a deep, strong, military tone of voice.

'Good. I've read your latest report. Like the rest there isn't much going on. Are you sure the chap you're watching is who we think he is?'

'I'm one hundred percent sure. I've even been into his flat and had a look round. There's stuff confirming his identity but absolutely nothing to suggest he's involved in anything at the moment.'

'There wouldn't be. Since what happened to bin Laden the new factions have taught their people to act independently and to be smart, smarter than we anticipated, but that may be their downfall. I've been thinking. All the listed targets are doing exactly the same as your chap, or in other words, nothing. Not since I joined the Firm as a rookie have things been this quiet and that is what is worrying me. Travis, I think these guys are putting us to sleep, letting us believe the whole thing has gone away but deep down, hidden from view, something is going on. I can almost smell it. I can almost believe they are waiting for something, some sort of trigger to bring them all back into action.'

'Yes Ma'am.' Marshall sounded weary. He'd heard the same message several times over the past ten months since he joined the team but somewhere deep inside him his instincts told him she was right. There was something going on, as his boss said, it was just too quiet. Of course no-one knew if they were looking in the right places – all they could do was follow their instincts and any known leads, which were few and far between.

'Travis, I want you to check out that jewellery shop. It's probably nothing but then again it might be something.'

'I'm already onto it, Ma'am. I've also started checking on the owner, one Dieter Zussman. He wasn't born in this country but has been here for a number of years according to the immigration registers. I've put out some enquiries to try and find more. It may take a day or two. I know where he lives and will be paying him a visit in the next few days. I'll also be doing a check on his shops.'

'Good work, Travis. On top as usual. Let me know immediately if anything comes up.' Her voice was calm, authoritative. Yet she wondered why her conversations with Marshall usually managed to get her heart beat raised by a few beats a minute.

'Thank you, Ma'am, I will.'

The phone went dead and Preston reclined in her leather-upholstered swivel chair. She pointed her index fingers together and placed them under her chin before closing her eyes. The stillness of the room matched the level of activity her team had uncovered.

CHAPTER TWO

Newton mingled with the crowd of tourists. He walked past the stalls of fruit and vegetables, past the tables piled high with various exotic linens and fabrics and past the counters offering leather goods to the tourists. He found the small artefacts stall in its usual place. The young woman attending to a customer recognised him immediately. She was petite with long dark hair and an olive complexion. Her pretty, dark eyes opened wider when she saw Newton. Barely perceptibly she nodded her head in the direction of the small tented area behind the counter and Newton walked behind her. Not a word had been spoken – the words would come later.

The old man was sitting on an apology for a canvas camping chair. His long grey hair was unkempt, as were the clothes he wore. The white gown had gone a strange yellow and grey colour with age and lack of care. He sat there with the brown sunhat pulled down almost to his eyes. In his mouth was a simple pipe from which came a thin stream of smoke from the burning briar within. It smelled slightly sweet.

Newton was accustomed to the sight and the fact the relic of a bygone era remained seated was a mixed blessing. It certainly meant the goods were not yet ready for him to take away. On the other hand it also meant he had time to bathe in the Mediterranean and possibly avail himself of the dark-haired beauty serving just out of sight.

'Mr Newton, is it that time again already?' The old man smiled and his accent was heavily Turkish in origin.

'Arken Saltig, it's good to see you again too.' Newton knew the ritual and held out a hand of greeting. It was taken and Newton used the contact to help the old man out of his chair. 'Fancy an iced coffee?' Newton was hoping the answer would be in the affirmative. The heat was almost unbearable in the tent, that and the sweet stench of the tobacco.

'That would be nice. Shall we go?' For an old man he suddenly became very agile. 'Sheera, we are going to talk business,' he called out.

She replied in Turkish, a language Newton had no knowledge of. She talked Turkish to her Uncle when she wanted to let Newton know she was available. If she'd talked in English, a language in which she was fluent, it would have meant there could be no contact. With a light heart, Newton led the old man back to the street café.

The iced coffee tasted even better in the sweltering heat of the early afternoon sun. Arken Saltig continued to smoke his pipe while he sipped the drink. Only when they had sat in silence for five minutes did he start to converse with Newton.

'You had a good journey, no?'

'Yes thanks, pretty good. It's starting to get hot in the days now and the van has no cooling system, so I have to take longer than in the winter. The Bosporus was calm at least. Now, you received the order from England, didn't you?'

'The order,' there was a twinkle in his eye. It was going to be bad news. 'Ah, the order,' he suddenly seemed to recall. 'Yes, the order, it is almost ready. The leather and the linens are all ready for you to take but I have not received the jewellery yet.'

Newton looked concerned. This was the part of the order he really needed to have ready. The rest of the consignment he was due to pick up could wait if it wasn't ready within the next couple of days, but the jewellery was a different matter. He'd been left in no doubt what the consequences would be if he returned without the jewellery. He'd also been assured the consignment would be ready for him to collect. It always had been before. The routine was simple. Zussman placed the order four weeks before Newton was due to make a trip. The contacts were always the same and the delivery point in Yalvac never changed. After a few teething troubles in the early days, the system had worked perfectly for more than fifteen trips. Newton had never been held up by the jewellery.

'Have you heard when it will arrive?' It was a pointless question because Arken Saltig never knew anything. Saltig looked with a degree of scrutiny at Newton and shook his head.

'Perhaps a day, perhaps two, I can't say. Do you not have the contact's number?' Saltig seemed unconcerned.

'No, that's all handled from London. I'm just the delivery boy.'

'Then, my dear Mr Newton, I suggest you contact London if you are concerned.' Saltig may have known nothing but he was rarely lost for a suggestion, so long as the suggestion didn't require him to do anything personally.

'Yes, I will do.'

Newton fished his mobile phone out of his pocket and checked the time on his watch. It was just after one o'clock, making it about ten o'clock in London, he reckoned. Newton noticed there was no signal available to make the connection he needed.

'I'll have to try later on. Either I'm out of range or there is a problem with the connection.'

'You see all this technology and there are still problems and delays. Do not worry, Mr Newton, your precious jewellery will turn up, just have patience.' Saltig poked Newton's mobile phone and laughed slightly as he spoke.

'I guess you're right, Arken, perhaps it will arrive tomorrow. You will be in your shop then?'

'Of course, there is no market tomorrow.'

'If the jewellery arrives I can pick up everything on the order?'

'Of course, now I had better get back to my niece. She does tend to worry if I am away from the stall when we are busy.'

'Of course.' Newton smiled and the two rose to once again join the thronging masses as they carved out a fresh path to Saltig's own stall. It took them a good five minutes to battle their way through the crowds. Newton knew the market would be busy but it was the only way he could hope to see the beautiful enigma that was Sheera. It was the only way they could secretly arrange to meet later that day.

Newton walked the old man back to the front of his stall, noticed Sheera was just passing a customer his change and said quite loudly,

'I will see you tomorrow then. I think I'll take the rest of the afternoon off and go down to the sea to get away from this heat.'

'Very well, Mr Newton, I will see you again tomorrow.' The men shook hands briefly and Newton turned to walk away from the stall. As he did so, the siren behind the counter nodded slightly.

Newton finally made it back to his van. He noticed the woman washing her step had finished her task and presumably gone inside. The locals all shopped early at the market, long before the tourists packed the narrow streets, so she was unlikely to be at the market. Only the tourists who treated the heat and the stench of the market as part of the culture would be milling around the stalls at this time of day. It was good news for the stallholders and bad news for anyone who seriously thought they could pick up a bargain. Newton had watched the market on several occasions and admired the business acumen of the native people. They always made money in season and lots of it, the tourists saw to that. The past had been harder for them but not dire, what with the terrorist attacks in New York and the resultant fear of flying, a fear that seemed to have largely dissipated now, judging by the masses in the marketplace that day. Newton smiled to himself as he took up his position in the driver's seat.

He pulled the van out onto the dusty road and headed for the coast. Pisidian Antioch and the ancient ruins were nearby. Newton drove past them, ignoring the directions leading to the car parks and tourist area. He drove slowly past the place where the disciples in the Holy Bible were first called Christians. To a religious man it would have been like driving past a shrine but Newton was not a religious man and he had little time for what he considered were little more than piles of rubble. Newton was more interested in the sea, a place where the air stirred and the temperatures seemingly dropped. He'd spent many visits exploring this part of the coast and he'd found the cove he loved the most. It was isolated and it was his trysting place with Sheera.

He pulled up by the side of the track, picked up a bag containing what he needed for the beach and locked his van. He walked slowly down the dusty pathway until he reached the rocks at the edge of the small expanse of sand. The hot sun beat down from the azure blue sky, but a cool breeze was blowing in off the water and it made Newton happy. He changed into bathing trunks, applied the high-factor skin protection cream he used, put on sunglasses and lay down on his towel on the sand to read the book he'd brought with him. He was into detective fiction and he'd picked up the book while waiting for the ferry at Dover. He'd already read two other books on the way to Yalvac and he had another couple of books in the van to read on the way home.

Newton read for twenty minutes before the heat of the sun forced him to turn over. He put the book down now, closed his eyes and began to dream of his imminent meeting with the lovely Sheera.

As his thoughts returned to the delay he was suffering, he picked the mobile phone out of the bag he'd brought with him. He turned it on and breathed a sigh of relief when the little aerial lit up showing three bars – a good signal. Newton punched the number on the keypad, pressed the green 'connect' button and waited hopefully.

***

Dieter Zussman sat alone at the small table in the café. He looked forlorn, a deeply troubled man. The chicken and salad sandwich he'd bought with the coffee for breakfast, had barely been touched even though he had been looking at it for twenty minutes. He sat there motionless, looking out of the window of the café onto the activity in the street. He wondered how many of the people who walked past his window had ever suffered a similar dilemma to his own. He wondered what they would do in his situation, but he could not ask them. He'd been told to stay silent, to stay away from the authorities, to avoid mentioning what had happened. When the packages arrived safe and sound he had been promised everything would be all right.

He'd placed the order as usual even though he didn't need the stock. Actually, the level of stock he'd accumulated over the past year was crippling him financially, but he had no choice. He was a single man with his only living relative, a brother, being abroad. Syria was not his favourite country to live in, it was worse still to be held prisoner there. His brother was being held until such time as he, Dieter Zussman, had completed the tasks required of him. Zussman knew he could not reveal the truth or ask for help. The reprisals would be too severe for him to cope with.

Dieter Zussman sat and looked miserably out of the window. His mind took him back to the beginning of the chain of events that had brought him to London, England. At first it had been exciting to be offered a fresh start, now it was worrying him. He'd spent the last few years building up a solid business. There were two shops now, one in Reigate, the other in Dorking and he had plans for a third one, probably in Sutton. He'd never been allowed to forget the mission all the time he'd been building up the legitimate business he owned, at least on

27

paper, and for that reason he knew it could all be taken away from him in an instant. It was the mission that was worrying him because he knew the time was near. Perhaps, over the last few years, his allegiances had changed somewhat but he knew deep down inside he had no choice. The business was of secondary importance after all that had happened. There were other, more pressing, priorities.

The shoppers and business people passing the window had no idea as to the extent of his woes and worries; they couldn't have. The world had been told it had become a safer place after the death of the al-Qaeda leader. Though the threats remained, the authorities stressed the intelligence services were mostly one step ahead of the terrorists and periodic arrests seemed to prove this was indeed the case. So the average man in the street was lulled into believing the world was indeed a safer place, at least in the United Kingdom. It was what the politicians needed people to believe and the propaganda had worked so far.

If just one of those passers-by could have looked into Zussman's eyes and read his thoughts as he sat there, they would have known the propaganda contained little in the way of reality. The relative silence since 3rd May 2011, and then the eventual, perceived collapse of al-Qaeda, and even the rise and the subsequent fall of ISIS was, Zussman considered, nothing more than the lull before the storm, and the storm was coming. The countdown to that storm had begun.

His thoughts were brought to an abrupt halt with the ringing sound of the mobile phone in his pocket. Almost without thinking he put the phone up to his ear and made the connection.

'Zussman.' His single word was spoken softly.

'Dieter, its Daniel Newton. I have a problem.'

'Go on,' Zussman's heart sank even lower at the sound of Newton's voice.

'Your consignment of jewellery has not arrived at the pickup point. I only arrived this morning and can hang on a couple of days, but my travel plans will not work if I don't move after that.'

'I see,' Zussman was thinking fast. 'I will contact the supplier to see what is happening. If you phone me back in two hours I will see what I can do.'

'Thanks, Dieter. What is the weather like in England? It's ninety and sunny here.'

Zussman longed for the warmth of the land he had grown up in. He hated the snow, the frost and the rain. He hated the months of cold and the shortness of the British summer.

'It is colder than I would like, though the sun is shining. Are you well?'

'Yes, Dieter, and I'm sitting on the beach at the moment. It is good to relax after a long journey. I will let you go and sort out the order. I'll call back in a couple of hours.'

Newton hung up and Zussman took a bite of the unappetising sandwich. Ten minutes later he was back in the shop. He didn't carry the contact numbers around with him. That was forbidden and far too risky. They were securely locked away in the shop safe and there was only one copy. If he lost that copy there would be no more contact. Upon his return he allowed his assistant to take her break. Leaving the shop door displaying the 'Open' sign, Zussman went into the office at the back and opened the safe. The well-thumbed document was folded neatly at the bottom of a pile of documents. Zussman unfolded it and placed it on the workbench. He dialled the number he wanted and spoke briefly to the person at the other end. He spoke rapidly, softly, in a language that was of some Arabic extraction. The conversation finished and Zussman, having obtained the information he required, replaced the receiver.

As if the conversation had been of no consequence, Zussman went to inspect the ring that had been adjusted for the early morning customer and admired the skill with which his assistant had effected the changes. She really was good and if everything worked out she'd do well running her own shop, a shop Zussman had already hinted at to her.

***

Travis Marshall was not a man to waste time. It was part of the reason he had been asked to join the team. It was part of the reason, but only a tiny part. His true credentials lay elsewhere, a background of secrecy that made him ideal for ATRIUM. Marshall had spent the morning in front of his computer. The information was beginning to arrive. Zussman had arrived in England just over four years earlier, according to the immigration people. The shop had been purchased using cash and the business was registered in Zussman's name. Tax Returns had been correctly filed, taxes paid, nothing untoward or of concern about the volume of business except for the observation the accounts indicated a slightly higher level of stock than might have been expected. That could be offset by the fact Zussman had opened a second shop just over a year ago, so there was nothing concrete to be concerned about.

The enquiries confirmed what Marshall already new concerning Zussman's home. Again it had been paid for in full, again in cash. Zussman lived there alone. The house was not ostentatious and was exactly the kind of house a reasonably well-to-do businessman would live in. Marshall noticed the date on the transfer of deeds for the property occurred exactly two weeks before Zussman arrived in the country. Marshall assumed Zussman had bought it while living abroad so he had somewhere to live once he arrived in the country. Possibly, thought Marshall, Zussman had a contact in this country, someone who had helped him to make the purchase. It was likely but not necessarily the case. It was still a point he needed to include in his next report to Preston, however unpromising it may seem.

The overseas enquiries indicated Zussman did not, as Marshall had presumed, originate from Germany. He'd travelled through Germany on his way to England but it was clear his origins were from further East. Marshall rubbed his chin as he read the results of the enquiry. He knew the further East he had to look the harder it would be to get co-operation, with the possible exception of the Israelis. He'd already filed that enquiry and expected the results at any time. If he drew a blank there, he'd have to start again.

Dieter Zussman had no criminal convictions in England, not even a speeding ticket or parking violation. He was, so far as Marshall could tell, squeaky clean, perhaps a bit too clean. While he waited for the reply from the Israeli connection he had made, Marshall picked up the thin file containing the reports he'd filed on the two Iraqis he'd been following. Known Islamic fanatics, following a tip off in 2006 from Interpol, Marshall had to concede they had continued living exemplary lives since their arrival in England. They had become part of the Muslim community in South London, attended the local Mosque regularly and during the five months they had been under scrutiny, Marshall and the group of professionals he used to carry out such duties had never observed them either contacting other known activists nor causing any disturbance. Like Zussman, they were squeaky clean, and like Zussman, something didn't feel quite right even though Marshall had spent a great deal of time and effort, both in his former job and his current one, trying to discover if they were up to anything. It seemed as if they were reformed characters living blameless lives. For a moment, Marshall wondered if the death of Osama bin Laden had shocked them so badly that they had turned from their known pasts, but his thoughts only lasted for that moment.

The fax printer was working again while Marshall read the last 'nothing to report' report he'd filed. It was what he was waiting for. When the page had been ejected from the printer he looked at it, read the sentences three times, screwed up the paper and tossed it into his wastepaper bin with the solitary word,

'Blast.'

Dieter Zussman did not originate from Israel, at least not the Dieter Zussman who now lived in South London. There were, of course, a number of D Zussman's that had originated from Israel during the past fifty years but Dieter was not found amongst their first names. Marshall knew he had to look further into the matter. That would take time and not a little bit of luck.

Marshall looked again at the picture of Zussman he'd procured a few days previously. Zussman was stepping out of his Dorking shop in the picture Marshall had taken. Marshall had a preconceived idea what a Jewish jeweller should look like and Zussman fitted the generalisation perfectly. It did not, of course, make him Jewish, but the name added weight to the supposition. Marshall needed to know for sure, if only because he was curious. There was something about the jeweller that intrigued him. It was not usually difficult to trace somebody who had a trade but despite all of his enquiries in the past couple of days it seemed that Dieter Zussman literally stepped onto planet earth about four years ago. Of course that was when Zussman had first arrived in England, so there would be nothing on him from the English authorities before that date but Marshall had expected something to show up from some of the International enquiries. There was nothing.

Marshall rubbed the back of his neck while his thoughts sank in. It was something Marshall did a lot of – thinking. Perhaps Dieter Zussman did literally step onto planet earth four years ago. What, he thought briefly, if he was really someone else? What if he was part of the veil of silence that had fallen in the last few years? Marshall had to stop himself abruptly before his imagination ran wild. If Dieter Zussman was a Jew then there'd be no question of him having anything to do with the silence, such a notion would be absurd.

Having looked at the results of the various enquiries, Marshall thought it would be extremely useful to know a little bit more about the man whose picture he now held in his right hand.

CHAPTER THREE

The sea was warm and the sand hot to walk on. Daniel Newton had bathed in the Mediterranean on many occasions and now, as he walked from the water, the sand felt almost as if it was burning. He ran quickly up the short beach to his towel and stood on the cloth which felt cooler to the touch. The water had been invigorating and had helped to relax the muscles that were still tired from the days of driving.

Newton applied a fresh layer of sun screen and sat down on the towel. He faced towards the water watching the waves lap gently at the shore. He took the mobile phone from his pocket once again and called Zussman.

'Dieter, this is Daniel, do you have any news for me yet?'

'Hello, Daniel, I have made contact. The consignment left the factory two days ago, so it should arrive either tomorrow or the next day but it all depends on whether there are any delays at the borders.'

'Sure, Dieter, that is encouraging news. I will wait here for as long as possible, but I do not want to let the papers expire as it would cause a lot of trouble.'

'I know, Daniel, but I really do need the packages this time around. There are some special items in the order and I have customers who are getting anxious about the delays. It really is important to me so I'd be very grateful if you could wait until the last possible moment for them.'

'You know I will do that, Dieter, I always do. I didn't know the order was so important to you. Look, the latest I can leave it is four days, if I then drive long hours to get through the borders before my papers expire.'

'Four days should be plenty. Hopefully they will arrive tomorrow anyway.'

'Let's hope so, Dieter. As usual, I'll ring you when I have them.'

'Thanks, Daniel, have a nice evening.'

'I will, Dieter. Goodbye now.' The line went dead. Newton replaced the mobile in his bag and continued to look out over the deep blue sea. The news from London had been better than he'd been expecting and it put him in a good frame of mind.

Up on the rocks behind him, Daniel Newton was being watched. The woman watched as he took the mobile phone out of the bag, she watched while he talked into it and she watched when he put the phone back in the bag. Then she picked her own mobile phone out of her bag, typed in the message 'he is here' and pressed send, before replacing the phone in her bag. Then she clambered down the rocks. She padded across the ten feet of sand to where Newton sat looking in the opposite direction. Suddenly Newton felt the coolness of her hands as they covered his eyes. She was close to him, very close, and he smelled the perfume she was wearing. It was Eastern perfume, pleasing and aromatic. He reached up and grabbed her arms before pulling her on top of him. She laughed and pulled away from him, preferring instead to sit on the damp towel beside him.

'You have been swimming?' Her bright, dark eyes looked straight at his.

'Yes, it was time to cool off.'

'And you are feeling good after your swim?'

'Yes, Sheera, I'm feeling very good. How are you?'

'Much better now that you are here. It has been a long time, or at least it has felt that way.'

Sheera Ganzagha was just twenty years old. She was beautiful, vivacious and full of the life someone that young should have. She had first met Newton when she had been in her mid-teens. He had been an enigma to her teenage senses; strong, athletically built, a Westerner who chose to visit her land, and in those early days she dreamed often about him taking her back with him. She'd met him because she often helped out on her uncle's market stall. At first Newton had treated her with courtesy, bringing her cheap gifts from England, watching her grow into the fine young woman who now sat beside him.

The relationship had started only a year earlier and it had been at her instigation. She'd made the first approach, making Newton feel very awkward at first. She'd assured him it was okay and she had enticed and ensnared him until he had been like putty in her sexually charged hands. Sheera had her reasons for instigating the relationship, reasons that had helped her ensure things had happened very quickly indeed on that particular visit when they had first discovered each other's bodies. It had taken less than two days from the first approach to the first act and her vivacity had stunned Newton. She knew what she wanted and her culture clearly left her yearning and longing for something she could not obtain locally. She was fiery, passionate and almost wanton in her desires for Newton. On that first occasion he had brought her to the beach and it had since become their regular spot. She'd learned to drive and had access to her father's car. They never used it for their acts of passion for fear of leaving evidence. They had used his van on occasion, especially on the winter visits, but the beach was their favourite location, the beach and the warm Mediterranean Sea.

Newton looked into her eyes and stood up, holding her hand.

'Come, let's cool you down.'

He pulled her to her feet and waited while she undressed. Together they ran into the water, both eager to further explore their mutual passion.

***

The late afternoon sky was dark and overcast. Lighting up time had not yet arrived but the majority of vehicles on the road were now using sidelights. The forecast was for rain and the leaden skies indicated the forecasters were going to be right. Travis Marshall adjusted his rear view mirror to stop him being dazzled by the car behind, a vehicle where the driver had switched on the full beam. Marshall flicked the indicator stick on his red Ford Fiesta to signal his intention to turn left. He was travelling at forty miles an hour and had begun to brake when the car in the fast lane decided, without notice, to pull in front of him. Marshall applied the brake firmly and at the same time sounded his car's horn. The driver ahead of him seemed oblivious to what was happening. Either that or he was feigning ignorance. The silver-coloured Mondeo continued on its journey as Marshall took the left junction. He was used to the madness on the roads. Something like the incident he'd just been part of happened almost every day.

Marshall was also acutely aware he was preoccupied and he could not be sure his own reactions were up to scratch. Perhaps, he thought, as he came to a halt by the side of the road, it hadn't been a real incident after all. Perhaps his attention had been diverted as he was driving and the car had really indicated after all. Perhaps it had actually pulled in further ahead of his own car than he'd imagined. Perhaps, but he doubted it. Marshall was a man who, at the moment he had pulled off the main road, had been preoccupied with his thoughts.

He spotted the house he was searching for, not that he was looking for it for now, but he needed to know where it was for the next day. He had a habit of finding out where properties were before he visited them. He liked to know where they were, what they looked like, what the surrounding area was like, and he needed to find out all of this while the house was still visible in normal light. He'd nearly been too late for this house. The afternoon match had lasted longer than he'd expected and he'd not been able to get away from the snooker hall as planned. The snooker was all part of Marshall's cover and over the past few months it had come in useful. The extra frame had been a nuisance, if only because it delayed him by half an hour. It wasn't the half hour that had been the problem. It was the extra delay he'd suffered due to the increased traffic as the rush hour approached. Now he sat in the car and thanked his good fortune that darkness had not yet descended.

Leaving the car, he strolled down the road in the manner of a resident walking home at the end of the day. He noticed the driveway, still empty. Zussman hadn't returned yet, which was interesting to Marshall. He'd expected the jeweller's car to be in the drive. He noticed the porch leading to the front door was constructed from brick and there was no outer door. It didn't matter because he didn't plan to use the front door, but it was still information. The downstairs windows at the front of the house all looked to be some kind of replacement double-glazing, set into the typical white uPVC the window companies so liked to use. It made the windows secure but not impregnable, though Marshall preferred not to interfere with such devices. His gaze took him to the first floor. Here the windows had not been replaced, though they all appeared to be locked shut. This whole process took Marshall less than ten seconds and he carried on walking. It didn't look promising but there was still opportunity.

He walked up the road, stood on the corner for a few seconds and then retraced his steps. This time he could see the side of the house. Halfway up the brickwork was a solitary window, probably the landing window, he conjectured. It was too small for his purposes and anyway it was halfway up a vertical wall without even a drainpipe or ivy creeper nearby. Marshall walked back past the house and turned the corner of the road. He walked fifty yards, stopped and withdrew a handkerchief from his trouser pocket. As he pretended to wipe his nose he turned to look at the back of the house and breathed an almost audible sigh of relief when he found what he was looking for. The location wasn't perfect as it was visible from the main road, but Marshall doubted anyone would be looking up at the house at the time he was thinking of visiting it.

Having seen what he wanted, he returned to his car. He drove around for a few minutes checking for clubs, pubs or anything that might affect his plans. There were none, except for the small country pub a couple of hundred yards away and it did not look like it was the life and soul of the area. The run-down building in desperate need of repair and the battered red pick-up in the car park clearly showed the owners struggled to exist let alone make a living. It did not look as though a crowd of revellers would suddenly pass down the road. Marshall smiled to himself. This would be easy. He loved soft targets and, apart from having to climb up to the first floor, this was about as soft as they came.

Once back on the main road, heading for home, Marshall turned on the radio. Home was a flat in South London, very South London. It wasn't a large flat and it wasn't well appointed. Sparsely furnished and functional was a more accurate description and it suited Marshall perfectly. He wasn't a team player, he never had been really. He was much happier as a loner. Now, for the past ten months he'd been very much alone, having only essential contact with most of the team. At the best of times Marshall disliked the team spirit, so the past few months had been welcome to him. Knowing others were on hand if he needed them made his job easier, though he'd never had to call on them for assistance. Sure, he had to file the usual weekly progress report, but it was a report that was only ever read by Preston, assuming she hadn't already stopped scanning the weekly nil report.

Marshall had so far undertaken four operations like the one he'd been planning this afternoon and so far he'd got precious little to show for his efforts. He had also undertaken countless hours of careful surveillance on various targets, again without any significant results. Not that he was aware any of the rest of the team had fared any better – they hadn't.

Now, with the overall project running for nearly a year, there was growing pressure to cut back, to assess, reduce the size of the team and, above all, to get results. It was results that counted, but there had been few of those. Of course it didn't help any of the team that the targets they had been allocated were apparently living ordinary lives. It really gave the team little chance of success.

Marshall and others in the team lived with the hope that one day something of interest would come to life, for then they would be hailed as heroes, as successes, as being worth all the training and outlay that had been lavished on them. There were eight of them in all, a select band of the very best the department could find. Eight team leaders each with their uniquely formed teams.

Marshall wondered where the others were and what they were doing. He hadn't seen any of them since the monthly briefing almost three weeks previously. He had no regular contact with them and didn't even know about their individual assignments. He didn't need to know and it was safest he didn't. They almost certainly knew as little about his activities as he did about theirs – it was team policy. Only those attached to a team leader knew what was going on in the team and only one woman, Preston, knew everything that was going on. Even then she only knew what the team members told her. Much of that was retrospective information. For example, Marshall hadn't actually mentioned what he was planning, he'd report the outcome afterwards – he had to do that even though he wished he didn't.

The clouds were thickening and the first few drops of rain began to fall. It was just after six in the afternoon. Marshall drove carefully with his mind once again focused on the ever-growing volume of early evening traffic.

***

He went by the name of Simon Hart, and he was a wealthy man. He never attracted media attention and was definitely not one of those self-proclaimed superstars, but he lived more than comfortably in a rambling seven-bedroom country mansion which was surrounded by five acres of mainly wooded grounds. He loved the seclusion and had gone to great lengths to keep unwanted people off his land.

Hart had the appearance of a true Brit. His CV indicated he'd been educated at two of the finest schools in the country and then trained as an architect. He had built up a solid business but behind the scenes he had a more than passing interest in computers. In his spare time he made his money online, trading, dealing, and promoting. He had discovered quickly he was good at all these things. So good he had acquired a portfolio of properties in the UK and a few villas overseas. At least that is what anyone looking into his affairs would discover. But there was much more to Simon Hart than anyone who passed him in the street would ever know.

Now, he looked out of the large double-glazed patio doors onto the croquet lawn that was lit only by the light from the lounge. Darkness had descended and a light drizzle was falling.

Hart's newspaper, not one of the tacky tabloids, sat neatly folded on an occasional table next to the empty cup of coffee. With an apparent degree of difficulty, Hart raised himself from the plush armchair and, with a perceptible limp, walked over to the doors. He looked beyond the croquet lawn to where the tennis court remained invisible in the night time gloom, and beyond that to the wooded area and the stream that ran through that part of his property. He smiled to himself and decided there was work to be done before his guest arrived.

The work, as he called it, required little more than answering a half-dozen emails and it took him less than half an hour. His businesses effectively ran themselves.

For twenty four hours a day, seven days a week, fifty two weeks of the year, the punters paid him money. He had others that did the real work, the web site designs, the content and the support work. He just creamed the top off the revenue and enjoyed life to the full. It had taken him nearly five years to get to this point, five years during which he had planned, waited and hoped. Now his labours were about to bear fruit. He drew the plush gold curtains across the patio doors and walked slowly into his study.

The safe was discreetly hidden behind a large oil painting. The painting was of no great value but it looked attractive. Two walls of the study were lined with bookshelves on which a collection of paperbacks and leather bound hardback editions reposed. Hart was not a great reader but loved acquiring fiction stories. They were almost an obsession with him and he especially liked to collect the tomes of virtually unknown authors in the belief that one day just one of them might make him even richer.

Hart opened the safe and extracted a bundle of papers. There was a collection of small sheets on the top of the bundle and these were tied to a larger sheet that had been folded a number of times. Hart untied the string and deposited the smaller documents on one side of the desk. Then he opened the larger sheet, a piece of A3 paper and laid it flat on the desk top. Although he'd drawn the plan and studied it a hundred times he still checked it again for any minute flaw. He looked at the map of Great Britain which occupied the central part of the sheet of paper. It was a tracing of the coastal outline. On the land mass had been drawn a number of large black dots, some major cities and other places of interest. To these dots were drawn lines that extended to the edges of the sheet of paper. There, where each line ended, was a number and some other information printed in tiny hand writing, so small that it was virtually illegible.

Hart paid particular attention to the dot that represented Dover. He checked the number and picked up the smaller sheet of paper that bore the same number at the top of the page. He read the information carefully and smiled. The operation was now just a few days away.

The phone on the left side of the desk rang and Hart picked it up.

'Hello,' he said softly.

'Is that you, Simon?' The voice was female and foreign.

'Yes.' Hart was still speaking softly.

'Did you get my text? The courier is here but the goods have not yet arrived at this end. I can't speak for long. Our friend has just gone to the boy's room and will be back in a minute.'

'Okay, let me know when they turn up.' Hart smiled again. It had been a stroke of genius on his part to be warned four days before the operation could begin. It allowed him to put all the essential parts of the operation into motion at precisely the right time. She had been a real find, though it had not been a coincidence, and getting her on his side and working for him had been easy. Once he'd known how the chain of contact worked it had been a simple matter. That winter just over eighteen months earlier, which combined improving her education with providing him some creature comforts as they sailed around the Mediterranean, had been a most enjoyable way to spend three weeks. Hart had been watching Newton for over two years before he met up with Sheera. He'd found Newton through the contacts he'd made, contacts who were not particularly savoury, though they were necessary and had become embroiled in his business. He'd figured there had to be more to Newton than the simple delivery boy, so he'd kept a close watch on the company Newton kept, watching until he knew he was right.

Sheera Ganzagha was eighteen at the time, bright, friendly and looking to move away from her native town of Yalvac. Hart was rich, well-connected and offered the girl the freedom she was looking for. She had come complete with a chaperone for her protection, not that she wanted it. The chaperone had spent the first week on board the yacht in her cabin suffering the effects of 'mal de mer', or at least it had seemed that way. The emetic mixed in the chaperone's food was probably more responsible for the woman's illness than any motion of the yacht but it suited Hart to have the woman kept out of the way. It gave him access to Ganzagha.

Hart knew Ganzagha was already friendly with Newton. Hart had simply used a mind-control drug to brainwash the girl into working for him in return for generous funding. Essentially, Sheera contacted Hart whenever Newton went to Yalvac on one of his business trips. She told Hart what he picked up and any other information she could glean. In return, Hart maintained a decent offshore bank account balance for her and visited her at least twice a year, ostensibly to show her the increased balance on the account. Sheera also had the promise that when the time was right, Hart would take her away from Yalvac and offer her a new life in the UK.

She'd kept to her side of the bargain, as had Hart, and phoned him every trip Newton undertook. Hart already knew the current trip was different, his contact had told him so, and Hart was ready. Ganzagha simply had to confirm the jewellery had arrived in Yalvac and tell him when Newton started the return journey. She didn't need to know why it was so important and he hadn't told her. She simply longed to see Hart once again, to see the nest egg and to hope that this would be the time when she could leave Yalvac and find the freedom she had always dreamed of.

Hart replaced the receiver and drummed his fingers on the table. He'd been this route five times before, the waiting, the preparation and the watching. He'd known they were practice runs. The unsavoury characters with whom he had forged a temporary alliance had kept him well-informed and he had paid them well. This time, though, the stakes were high, incredibly high. This time it was his opportunity, his moment. Everything he had secretly longed for since his childhood – the dreams that made him a megalomaniac with incredible wealth and power - were about to become reality. Hart was, in effect, a mad man, but no one would ever diagnose his condition. Now the bullying and injustices in his childhood would finally be avenged. He had but a few days to wait. The clock was ticking.

Carefully he refolded the map of Great Britain and placed it back under the pile of documents. He returned the bundle to its place in the safe and locked the door, spinning the wheel to ensure only someone who knew the combination would be able to open it.

Then Hart made a phone call of his own. For some minutes he talked softly to the person on the other end.

'And I think it would be useful if I could show you exactly what I want before we draw up too detailed a plan.'

'Okay,' said the other person.

'I'm frightfully busy for the next few days but could you come round on Thursday 2nd July at the end of the day – say about five o'clock. It shouldn't take long but I'd like to get things started with the planning people.'

'Let me check my diary.' There was a pause. 'Yes, that looks okay to me. I'll book that in my diary now. Let me just double check your address.' And he read back the address which Hart confirmed.

'2nd July, five o'clock it is then.'

Hart ended the call and smiled thinly to himself.

The black Saab sports car pulled off the road and came to a halt at the double full-sized wrought-iron gates that protected the drive to Hart's estate. The driver, a young woman with dark, flowing hair, alighted. Dressed in a pinstripe suit she walked briskly over to the intercom. She pressed the buzzer and waited. Even though she was expected and it was raining gently, the gates were not open, they never were. It was all part of Hart's desire for solitude.

'Hello,' the voice sounded from the speaker above the buzzer.

'Hi, it's Christine and it is raining.'

'Okay.' A motor sounded and the wrought-iron gates slowly began to open. As they did so, the woman walked back to her car. When the gates had opened sufficiently she gunned the engine and roared down the driveway. After a few seconds the gates clanged shut behind her. She screeched to a halt outside the front door to the mansion, the shingle on the driveway being flung in all directions from the severe braking of the car.

She alighted and slammed the door of the driver's door shut and marched determinedly up to the front door. It was not locked. She pushed it open and disappeared indoors, slamming the door shut behind her. In her hand she carried a black bag, not unlike a large handbag.

She found Hart in the living room, sitting in his favourite armchair.

'Hi, Simon, I wish you'd leave the gates open for me when you're expecting me. I got quite wet buzzing you.'

'Sorry, I forgot, and anyway you are fifteen minutes early.'

'Fair enough, but please remember in future.' She knew her plea would get forgotten, she'd asked many times before but to no avail.

'You're dressed in black tonight, and formal. Does that indicate what kind of mood you're in?'

'No, it was what you asked for. I hope it pleases you.'

'Oh, it does. Three hours wasn't it?'

'Yes. Where do you want to start?'

'Mmm,' Hart looked at the woman he'd used from the Escort Agency a number of times. Now they kept their dealings private and he paid her well for her time. 'I think to begin with you can give me a massage, I'm feeling a bit tense in the neck, shoulders and in my lower back.'

'Where do you want to do it?'

'Let's go to the gym. There's a couch I use for weights that's suitable.'

'Lead on,' she said.

'Fancy a bottle of champagne as usual?' he enquired.

'Oh, go on then, why not!'

He took the bottle of real champagne out of the ice bucket, selected two crystal glasses from the dresser and led the woman out of the living room, up the stairs and into the well-equipped gymnasium. He undressed to the waist, poured the drinks and lay down on the couch while she prepared herself.

She came ready for most eventualities. She'd got used to what he liked and disliked and she knew that the gymnasium indicated they were in for an athletic evening after she had given him the massage. She also knew the next fifteen minutes would set the tone for what happened later. If she pleased him, soothed him and relaxed him, it would be a very pleasurable way to earn the eight hundred pounds they had agreed. If she failed, she'd still get the money but would not find him so pleasant. It was all part of the job. She had to take the rough with the smooth. This particular evening she sensed he was more tense than usual so she set about preparing the best massage she knew.

Fifteen minutes later he ordered her to undress whilst he discarded his remaining vestments. He was not in a hurry and it was his turn to have fun. After all, he was paying for it, so he wanted to enjoy himself as much as possible. His touch could be gentle and tonight it would be electrically so. It excited him to know she could never tell what mood he was in, so she was never sure what was going to happen. Tonight he would take her to the place where the angels sing, somewhere between heaven and cloud nine.

CHAPTER FOUR

Dieter Zussman arrived home just after six thirty. It was dark and the rain was falling when he pulled into his driveway. The business of the day was over and Zussman remained as troubled as he had been that morning. He took his attaché case and the bag containing his evening meal off the passenger seat and as quickly as possible let himself into his house. He left the brown paper bag containing his evening meal on the kitchen table while he went upstairs to change out of his pinstripe suit. When it was neatly hanging back in his uncluttered wardrobe, Zussman turned his attentions to the food. It looked unappetising but then again, Zussman was in no mood to eat.

As he ate the food he flicked through the channels on the television and decided there was nothing worth watching. He wondered why, for the first time, the jewellery was late. The answer was obvious – there had been a problem in Syria. Perhaps the courier had experienced border delays, perhaps he'd been arrested. The possible reasons for the delay grew in Zussman's mind until he was convinced the whole plan would go wrong and he'd be the one who took the blame. Five practice runs had been executed without fault, without suspicion and without delay. Now, with the mission taking place for real there was a delay. Of course, if the courier had been caught then the whole mission was off before it had got started. Surely, thought Zussman, he could not be blamed for that. Of course, if the delay lasted for more than a couple of days and Newton had to leave without the jewels then Zussman would be blamed. He imagined the consternation that would be caused if they had to delay by a few months. All the teams would be kept on hold, it would cost thousands in extra funds and he, Dieter Zussman, would be seen as the one to blame.

No one doubted that Zussman was loyal to the cause, the training camps and other events had made sure he was. Neither did anyone in the organisation doubt Zussman was a clever man. For that reason he was being watched carefully. He was the contact and until the cargo had been delivered, he was going to be watched. In fact, though he didn't know it, Dieter Zussman was being watched twenty four hours a day by a team of members loyal to the cause. If he picked his nose, it was reported. When he went to lunch that was reported too. The time he left his house in the morning and the time he arrived back were also observed and his telephone had been tapped and every call made both at home and in the office had been transcribed. Those watching him knew far more about the office assistant, Sandra, than he did. They knew too of the promises she'd made to her boyfriend on various occasions.

Dieter Zussman knew very little of the wall of surveillance that surrounded him, but he was a cautious man so his plans remained where they could not be touched, in his head. He turned off the television and settled back to complete his plans, plans he would activate if anything went wrong.

While he thought to himself, he reflected on the size of the organisation and the effort that had been put into obtaining several dozen of a particular type of jewellery box, both for the trial runs and now, the real event. He had long since imagined that he knew what the boxes contained and he didn't want to be part of the second phase of the operation, which was why he had started to make his own plans.

He also had worked out in his own mind how the main plan hung together. Newton picked up the boxes and brought them back to England. They'd be delivered to his shop, along with some other merchandise he'd ordered. Then, with the shop shut, he would be visited by the same two men who'd helped him when he'd first arrived in the country. He'd hand over the boxes and a few days later his brother in Syria would be freed unharmed. That part of the plan was simple.

What came afterwards was down to the network and he had no involvement, other than he had his own plan to get as far away from any of the boxes as he possibly could. He'd seen the drawings and he'd seen similar devices in the training camps. He had a very good idea what was about to arrive and he didn't intend to find out but he knew it would be capable of far greater human destruction than flying an aeroplane into a skyscraper could ever be. Times had changed and a new, more subtle, approach was being adopted. It had taken a long time to perfect and two nomadic tribes had been all but wiped out by the tests. Now, the product was perfected and it was coming to Great Britain.

Dieter Zussman was afraid, very afraid, but he knew one word, one tiny leak of information, would mean certain death for his brother and probably for himself too. He sat in his armchair with his eyes closed, planning his future. If all went well, he'd be putting those plans into action a few days from now.

Later that evening, across the road and behind the curtains of an upstairs room, the observer noted the fact that Zussman turned on the upstairs lights, turned off the light in the front room and then, after a period of about ten minutes, extinguished the remaining light, plunging the house into darkness.

***

It was two o'clock in the morning and the street was deserted. The jewellery shop was shrouded in darkness, the nearest street light being some distance away. Marshall was careful to park his car a hundred yards from the shop in a designated parking bay. There was no need to attract attention from any passing police car. As was his habit, Marshall noted the time on the car's clock and also recorded the date as Wednesday 24 June.

The front of the shop was protected by a steel mesh shutter and Marshall knew any attempt at entry, other than using some kind of ram raid technique, was futile. He wandered down the road to the side alley and gained access to the small courtyard behind the shop.

By the light of his torch he worked the locks on the back door. There were four of them in all, a Chubb lock, a Yale type and two large, heavy duty padlocks. It took Marshall less than a minute to relieve the padlocks from their duty and a further minute to unlock the Chubb. The Yale type lock posed no greater obstacle and within a further minute, Marshall was standing in the little back office of Zussman's jewellery shop in Reigate.

Having checked the door between the office and the shop was closed, Marshall turned on the lamp sitting on the worktop, being careful to point the beam of light away from the door to the shop. He worked quickly, passing over the boxes that contained various screws, springs, and other parts used in the trade. He came to the filing cabinet and rifled through the lists of receipts, invoices and orders.

'Damn,' he cursed softly when a staple cut into his finger. He withdrew his hand from the filing cabinet and looked at the finger. A tiny blob of blood had oozed from the puncture. He sucked the finger for a moment, waiting for the blood to clot.

From the filing cabinet he walked over to the floor safe. Marshall was not surprised to discover it was locked. The safe was easy enough to crack and in less than five minutes of working in silence with his stethoscope, Marshall heard the lock click as it was released. He pressed the lever and the door opened for him. The safe contained trays of jewels, watches, rings, bracelets and earrings. The safe itself was divided into two sections, a small section at the bottom and a much bigger one above it. The trays of valuable jewels sat in the larger section. In the lower section was a bundle of papers. Marshall took the bundle out of the safe and unfolded the top document. It contained a number and the name Sidar Hassani. The document was well thumbed but clean. Marshall took the tiny camera out of his pocket and took the required picture before carefully refolding the document. The remaining paperwork contained little of interest and in a couple of minutes Marshall was relocking the safe.

Ten minutes later he left the building the same way he had entered it, being careful to leave no trace of his presence, or so he hoped. He started the car and headed for Dorking. At that time of the night, it was just over a ten minute journey during which he met one vehicle coming in the opposite direction.

The Dorking shop was not on the High Street but down one of the narrow alleys. Like the Reigate shop it was shuttered. Marshall knew it would be, having already checked the place a few days earlier. Again the little parade of shops had rear access. The path behind the shops led onto the alley, but was protected from sight by means of a sturdy wooden gate. The gate at the end of the alley posed no threat to Marshall who climbed over it with consummate ease. He back-tracked down the path to the shop and gained access through the back door, much as he had done in Reigate.

This was a smaller shop and the office at the back was little more than a work area cordoned off by a curtain from the shop floor. Again there was a safe which took Marshall just a few minutes to crack. His efforts were in vain for the safe contained nothing but the trays of jewels he expected to find.

Marshall closed the safe and spotted the display box that had fallen under the workbench. He picked it up and examined it. The box was about four inches square and two inches tall. The lid was hinged and opened easily. Outside, the box was a dark red colour. Emblazoned on the lid in gold was the name 'Zussman Jewellers'. Inside, the box and lid were both lined with green velvet. In the bottom part of the box was some kind of support structure, also covered in green velvet. The structure was about one and a half inches in diameter, two inches long, and was shaped like a cylinder lying on its side.

Marshall lifted the cylinder out of the box, looked at it more closely and decided it was probably used to hold either a bracelet or the strap of a watch in place. He replaced the cylinder, closed the lid and put the box back on the worktop.

The inspection of the rest of the shop took just a few minutes. Everything seemed exactly as he had expected it to, nothing out of place. It really did seem as though Zussman was a legitimate businessman, nothing more and nothing less. Marshall left the building, locked the door carefully and made his way back to his car.

As he drove home, he surmised the number on the document he'd photographed was probably just one of Zussman's contacts overseas, possibly someone he imported from. He concluded that his searches had turned up nothing of interest. It was looking like he was going to have to file another 'nil' report to Preston.

***

Preston was in the office early the following morning. She always was an early riser anyway, but it had been a restless night due to the humidity so when dawn arrived she got dressed and began her day. The office was air-conditioned and quiet and it gave her space to think. She pulled out the last set of reports that the team had filed and read them again. Her conviction that the Intelligence Services were being put to sleep grew. There simply wasn't enough activity considering the known number of fanatics who lived in the country. Something was wrong - her sixth or seventh sense told her that. Her instincts told her it was not going to be easy to work out what that something was. She ran her hand through her close-cropped hair and poured a second cup of coffee. She knew Marshall had been engaged on activities the previous evening and knew his report would be forthcoming during the course of the morning. The fact he hadn't phoned her was a bad sign as it indicated he'd found nothing of particular interest.

The other members of the team were all carrying out their usual activities which meant they would only write a report at the end of the week unless something of importance happened – which seemed more unlikely with each passing week. Preston sipped the coffee and looked out of the window.

After a minute she picked up Keeley's last report. He and a team of Special Branch officers had been tasked with keeping a watching brief on five known fanatics, all from the Middle East. They were known to be fanatics because during the nineties they'd been active. In 2008 they'd gone to ground and since then had done nothing. The same was true of the people the rest of the team were watching. Preston read the report again. There were five known fanatics, all living on benefits, all without jobs, all just passing the time of day, day after day. What, thought Preston, were they up to?

One thing she knew for certain, people didn't change in the way this particular group of people had changed without reason. It had to have been an order from on high, a command from the highest point of leadership in the group they belonged to. She was convinced it wasn't al-Qaeda but Preston had no doubt some of the few remaining leaders from that organisation were behind whatever was being planned. She felt it deep inside her, something was about to happen. She agreed with the Whitehall Mandarin who had confirmed her position, something was about to happen and it left an extremely bitter taste in her mouth, a taste that would linger long after the coffee had been finished.

There were now nearly five hundred people involved in the team, one way or another. For sure the team officially comprised just eight people, but they had first call on any resources they needed for any activity that could be, however remotely, deemed as being associated with the prevention of terrorism. Those eight people had drawn in the groups of watchers they needed and they had been keeping a close eye on dozens of suspects.

Dieter Zussman had not been on the list until Marshall had trailed one of their suspects to his shop and Marshall had decided to take a closer look. Until Marshall was convinced the visits had been a coincidence, Zussman would be watched carefully, though he would never know it.

As the early morning light filtered into Preston's office the phone rang.

'Preston,' she answered the call.

'Hi, this is Marshall. I have a report for you. It's not much but there may be something. I visited the jeweller's shops last night, both of them. The Reigate shop has a safe with some paperwork in it. There was one sheet of paper with an overseas phone number and a name on it. I've checked the name but he's not on our files. The number, though, comes from somewhere in Syria. I don't expect we'll get much help from them on actually finding a location.'

'I see,' Preston sounded alert. 'What do you think, Marshall?'

'Probably just a supplier but I want to check out Zussman's house first. I should be able to do that today while he's at work. I know where it is and I think it's a soft one to crack.'

'A thought for you. If you imported jewellery, would you get it from Syria?'

'I'm British so no, but our friend has other allegiances so I guess he might do.'

'I want him watched, Marshall. I want to know what kind of jewellery he's importing from there. It may be nothing, but it might give us a clue as to what my instincts tell me is about to happen.'

'Yes, Ma'am, but apart from the shops we don't have much else to go on. We may just have to wait until he gets some more supplies in and take another look.'

'Did you find anything else?'

'No, ma'am, just the kind of things you'd expect to find in that kind of shop. He sells fairly upmarket products mostly, so quite a lot of the gear was locked up in the safes in both shops.'

'I see, well let me know if you come across anything at his house, though I don't think you will. Like the rest of the people we've been looking into I have a feeling that this Zussman is not worth too much more effort. What else do you have going on at the moment?'

'A couple of other Middle Eastern types we're keeping our eyes on, but they're sitting quietly at the moment. I've got a couple of chaps watching them but it is all routine stuff.'

'Okay, stay on Zussman until you're sure where he stands. I'll try and dig out something else for you to get stuck into in a day or two.'

'Thanks, ma'am,' Marshall sounded tired. The phone line went dead and Preston returned to drain her cup of coffee. It had gone cold but she didn't seem to notice. The link between Zussman and a contact in Syria was intriguing, unexpected and probably totally innocent.

While Marshall and Preston had been talking about him, Dieter Zussman had breakfasted and set off for work. As he backed down the driveway to his house, his every move was observed from behind the closed curtains across the road. Zussman's routine was just that, routine, and the observer knew he had nothing to do until the evening. He made the usual phone call to tell his colleague that Zussman was off in his car and then he lay back on the couch. The night of wakefulness, waiting just in case Zussman did anything nocturnal, had a late night visitor or even tried to make a run for it, were all things the observer had been trained to expect. He'd watched and waited dutifully until Zussman had left in the usual way that morning. Now, with ten hours before Zussman would return, the observer closed his eyes and in a few minutes had fallen asleep, his period of duty over.

Dieter Zussman drove to the usual side road where he left his car. The walk to the Reigate shop was barely five minutes long but it gave the diminutive man a chance to take in some of the fresh, cool, morning air. He arrived at the shop invigorated and ready for the day's business. As usual, and without Zussman being aware of what was happening, he was watched from a distance for the whole length of his walk.

Zussman entered his shop via the front entrance, rolling up the shutters as he did so. He locked the door behind him, opening time was not for another half an hour, and went into the little office at the back. He opened the safe and began to take the display cabinet trays of jewellery and rings from where they had been placed for security reasons the evening before. It took him ten minutes to place the various trays in the display cabinets.

The jeweller was about to shut the door to the safe when something distracted him. There was something about the bundle of papers in the bottom of the safe that concerned him. Something did not feel quite right for some reason. He took out the small bundle of papers and examined them. There was something about the way he had put the bundle of documents into the safe the previous evening that did not now seem to be quite the same. It might have been his imagination, or the onset of paranoia, but he was sure something was different. He unfolded the top sheet and immediately his heart froze. He felt the pounding in his chest as the surge of fear-generated adrenalin kicked in. There, on the top left corner, was a tiny brown stain. He was sure it had not been there the day before. He was more than sure – he was positive. He'd taken great care of that piece of paper since the day it had been given to him and it had never been stained before.

Several miles away, Travis Marshall looked again at the photograph of the piece of paper. The number and the name were clear and he'd already made the possible enquiries concerning those pieces of information. There was something else in the top left corner, something slightly blurred and too small to make out. Perhaps it was a fault in the picture, a spec of dirt, or something that had been on the lens. Marshall put the photograph back in the folder and prepared for his day's work.

CHAPTER FIVE

Marshall was looking out of the window of his flat wondering about Zussman. In particular, the contact number and name on the piece of paper troubled him. It seemed odd that someone with such an obviously Jewish sounding name should have dealings with a person from an Islamic country such as Syria. It worried Marshall greatly that the contact was in Syria; almost anywhere else in that part of the world would have caused Marshall to be less concerned.

It was ten o'clock according to the radio playing softly in the background. Marshall had been up for two hours, already filed his report with Preston and was sipping his third cup of coffee of the day. He'd not heard from any of his personal team yet. Assuming any of them had anything to report, which was unlikely, he'd get to hear about it in an hour or so.

Marshall made the decision to change his plans. He'd been prepared to go to Zussman's house later that day. Still worrying about the Syrian connection, Travis Marshall decided to pay the house a visit immediately.

The morning traffic was relatively light and Marshall took just over twenty minutes to reach the road where Zussman lived. He drove past the house, checking that Zussman's car was not there, and parked fifty yards further down the road. Marshall walked back past the house, turned the corner and found the small gate that led to the back garden. It was not locked and Marshall passed into the relative safety of the garden unnoticed.

As he opened the gate a buzzer sounded in the house opposite the one in which Zussman lived. The man next to the buzzer was sleeping but the sound of the buzzer woke him from his dreams. In an instant he was behind the curtains peering out. He could see nothing. From his position the back of the house was invisible.

'Damn,' he said, and then in some Arabic dialect continued to curse the fact that he'd have to go outside and check the gate. The rules said to wait ten minutes, which was what it would take for him to dress and make his way over to the gate. Continuing to mutter to himself in his native dialect, he moaned about the likelihood that it was probably a false warning anyway. Perhaps the wind had shaken the gate and temporarily broken the connection that caused the alarm to sound. It wouldn't be the first time something like that had happened. The man started to dress slowly.

Marshall moved quickly to the back of the property and tested the downstairs windows. They were all locked. He noticed with some surprise that the kitchen door onto the garden was of the old kind. It had not been replaced, which was a stroke of luck, provided it wasn't bolted inside.

Marshall was in luck that morning. He picked the lock in less than two minutes and was relieved when the door opened. He passed inside and shut the door carefully. A second buzzer sounded across the road at the moment the back door opened. The man, still dressing, stopped in his tracks. Something was definitely happening. The buzzer sounded the same as the first one, but the little, red, flashing light indicated the alarm had been triggered by the back door and not the garden gate. The observer finished dressing and withdrew the Magnum six shot from beneath the mattress he'd been lying on. He checked the magazine and ensured the safety catch was on.

Marshall moved quickly once inside the house. The kitchen was of little interest to him. He checked the drawers and cupboards but they contained nothing out of the ordinary. The dining room was similarly disappointing. The living room was typical of a semi-detached house. It contained all the usual items of furniture and a few ornaments. Marshall ran silently up the stairs. There were three bedrooms. The smallest was unfurnished, just a simple cream carpet on the floor. The second bedroom contained a double bed that had not been made up. There was also a standalone wardrobe which Marshall checked. It was empty.

The third bedroom was clearly Zussman's. Marshall found what he was looking for. The picture in the frame was evidently of importance to Zussman. The silver frame indicated it was valuable to him and its position on the table beside the single bed gave it greater importance. The picture was of two children, young teenage boys. They were dressed in simple white flowing robes and smiling. Marshall rifled through the drawer under the table and found Zussman's passport, a driving licence and some other paperwork, all of which identified the owner as Dieter Karsten Zussman, born in Frankfurt nearly forty one years previously. Marshall already knew that was not the case.

He continued his search. He found a letter to Zussman written in English. It came from Syria and was dated six months previously. The signature was difficult to read but looked like Ahmed Ali Burgansa. Marshall copied the name into his notebook and looked out of the bedroom window. He was overlooking the garden and instantly saw the man trying the gate he'd used a few minutes previously. Marshall stopped in his tracks, still holding the letter. The man opened the gate and walked up to the kitchen. Marshall lost sight of him and very carefully began to refold the letter. He put it back where he'd found it and padded silently to the bedroom door. He heard the kitchen door being rattled and then silence returned. Whoever was out there did not seem as intent on entering the house as Marshall had been.

Marshall padded back into the bedroom and looked out of the window. The man was walking back up the garden. Marshall breathed a sigh of relief. He turned and knocked the picture frame off the side table. His reactions were like lightning. He dived forward and grabbed the picture before it hit the floor. He didn't need to do it because the frame would have made little noise on the carpet but his reaction was spontaneous.

He held the picture in his hand and looked at the back of it. He'd not noticed the two names etched into the backing mount. The names were faint but discernible as 'Ahmed' and 'Mohammed' and there was a date, '1994'. Marshall noted the names and the date and turned the picture round. He guessed the boys were about fourteen and twelve years old. If the date was right that would make them about forty and thirty-eight years old now, if they were still alive.

Travis Marshall found nothing else of interest in Zussman's bedroom. The house was as clean as the shops. In fact, thought Marshall as he padded back down the stairs, the whole set up was a little bit too clinical. Sure, the house was lived in, but it contained so few personal possessions that it was almost unlived in. There was something about the place that unnerved the man from ATRIUM. His training and his experience told him something was wrong but at the moment it was something intangible. He took one final look around the ground floor, decided he'd seen all there was to see and returned to the kitchen.

Carefully he opened the door and let himself back into the garden. He locked the door behind him again, leaving no trace that he had ever been there. The garden gate was on the latch and Marshall passed through it easily.

Whoever had been in the back garden had disappeared. Marshall considered it likely the man had been some sort of opportunist thief. After all, the garden gate offered no security, but the locked kitchen door required someone with a bit more skill and determination than the average opportunist to breach it.

Across the road, the buzzers sounded again. The observer returned to the curtains, cursing the fact that the alarms were going off while he was technically off duty. He watched as Marshall appeared round the corner, focused the camera with the powerful lens and captured Marshall's image on film. He had no idea if the man he'd pictured had come from the house or whether it was coincidence. As a member of the network he could not afford to take chances. Security had to be maintained at all costs. It would be up to others to decide if the man in the picture warranted further attention.

***

Brian Keeley was also a member of ATRIUM. He had been based in Newbury for the past six months. The unit he was primarily tasked with watching had become what the business called sleepers. There were five of them in all and Keeley had acquired a small army of officers to help him in his mission. This was one of the largest known groups of fanatics left in the country. The powers that be considered this group were the most likely to coordinate or lead any future actions in England. Keeley was the most experienced member of the team so the task had been assigned to him.

Like Marshall and the rest of the ATRIUM team, Keeley had a military background of some description. The details of his training, service, background and experience were probably more securely guarded than a Top Secret government file and definitely more secure than the government anti-terrorist strategy, or at least the various versions that had fallen into media hands at various points over the past few years. Keeley was an enigma, a solitary man, like Marshall, a man who had learned how to exist in far harsher conditions than those that surrounded him in Newbury.

At the moment Marshall was triggering the kitchen door alarm at Zussman's house, Keeley sat back in his black, leather upholstered chair and began to address the eight officers who sat around the oval table with him.

'Thank you for coming, gentlemen, I know we are all busy people so I won't waste time. With the exception of Gary Peterson,' Keeley gestured in the direction of a man in his early thirties sitting half way down one side of the table, a man who half-smiled in response, 'we all know each other so we won't waste time in introductions. I've already told Gary about you guys. For those who are interested, Gary is a web specialist. He can probably get you into more computers than you care to imagine and he is what I'd call an information specialist. He's been working for SB4 for the past four years but he's just been assigned to us because of something that's happened. He'll tell you about that in a minute. For now, though, I'd like your updates on what's happening.' Keeley looked at the man on his left, a look that indicated he was the first to give his report.

The man cleared his throat and began to speak.

'Jamal Al'Makir has been a prime target since he came to Britain in the late nineteen nineties as a youth. As you all know, he entered the country from France as an alleged refugee. He got asylum, they did in those days, and was then pictured at the scene of various riots during the early part of the new millennium. He was arrested three times but never charged. Since 2010 he's been dead quiet. He's spent the last week swimming at the sports centre, he's done some shopping but nothing of interest and spent a lot of time sitting in one or other snooker hall. He's also been to the Mosque twice, staying about twenty minutes each time. In short, as always, this guy has either gone to sleep or he's lost interest.'

'Thanks, Roger. Steve, have you anything to tell us?' Keeley looked at the next face round the table.

'Brian, as you know my chaps are keeping an eye on Ali Benadri. Came to the UK much as Al'Makir and was active during the first decade of the new millennium. Since then he's been quiet but we've been keeping an eye on him. He does quite a lot of jogging, has been doing it for the past few months, and also chills out at the local gym. He spent a couple of hours at the boxing club and has also been to the Mosque. Has met with Al'Makir and the others on a couple of occasions, but it all looks pretty innocuous, and there's never been more than three of them together at any one time.'

'Thanks, Steve. That may be about to change but it's interesting to hear what these guys do with all their spare time.' Keeley had been making a few notes and had decided to keep the ace he held firmly up his sleeve until the end. 'John, have you got any news for us?'

'Not really, Brian. Mahar bin Aldre, as you all know came here in two thousand and two and soon made contact with the other guys. We've been watching him on and off since then, with increased surveillance over the past four months. He's a gambling man and spends hours in the Coral shop every day. He doesn't place too many bets but studies form and chats with all and sundry. He's not into fitness things but is more your terrorist turned couch-potato. I think the guy is a sleeper with no immediate plans to wake up. If any of our overseas chaps got into his condition they'd be recalled to go through some more training. I think he's looking forward to the long haul. As always, I've got nothing of interest to report this week.'

The man called Dave was next to deliver his report. Like those before him he had little to brief the group on. Mohammed Gantala had come to the UK at the very end of the nineteen nineties. Britain had been warned about him by the Germans. He had tenuous links with the remnants of the Bader Meinhoff group, so he was considered a threat. He was, according to Interpol, a munitions expert, a bomb-maker of note, and was probably at least partly responsible for a huge action against the Israelis during the late nineties, though he'd never been charged with it. From the moment he'd arrived he had been watched closely. Like the others he'd simply gone to sleep, that euphemism used for people that suddenly switched off, like robots that needed recharging, until they were re-activated at some point in the future. Gantala, like the others was biding his time at the expense of the tax payer. Dave, the rugged man at the bottom of the table, was sure of that.

The final report was given by Bob. Bob Green had cold, green eyes and like the others wore a military style haircut. He was never one given to many words and his report was as short as it was succinct.

'Saleem Masra has done sod all this week other than his daily run round the block and some shopping. He's made contact with Al'Makir and Gantala but both were short encounters and seemed innocuous. He's another sleeper.'

'Thanks Bob,' said Keeley, warming at the thought of what was about to be revealed. 'Okay, so that's our regulars dealt with. Now, we come to the reason for Gary's presence here today. Gary, the floor's yours. Tell us a bit about what you do.' Keeley sat back and watched while the man in his thirties, who was sitting half-way down the right side of the oval table, stood up.

'Gentlemen, what I am going to tell you today is based on several years of work, as many years of analysis and is the probable reason why your targets are all sleeping. First, though, you need to know a bit about me. I'm part of SB4 and have been for over four years. My background is computer espionage and fraud and, well, we rather stumbled across something we've been keeping an eye on for a while. A little over three of years ago an offshore company called Braddock Holdings was set up in the Bahamas. It has bank accounts there, in the Scilly Isles, Switzerland and three other countries around the world. The combined accounts, as of yesterday, contained funding in the region of one hundred and forty eight million pounds sterling. We, err, kind of stumbled across Braddock Holdings when we were looking at one of your chaps, Al'Makir. We were watching his UK bank account for sudden, unexplained movements. He received fifty thousand from Braddock Holdings just less than two years ago. Since then, though they're all smaller amounts, he's received more than another hundred thousand.'

The others round the table were watching the new boy intently. Instinct told them this could be what they had been waiting for.

'We've discovered that Braddock Holdings has also put up the money for what we think is some kind of operation that's being funded in South London, all legitimate businesses, all with links to Middle Eastern countries. Actually, we've tracked all kinds of money movements across the world, though there are loads of gaps in the picture thanks to the countries that refuse to help us.'

There were nods of agreement from some of the men before Peterson continued.

'From a purely business point of view, we reckon that Braddock Holdings has a financial interest in just about every terrorist cell we know exists in this country, including your five targets.'

'Sorry to butt in, Peterson,' Steve interrupted, 'but where is all this leading?'

'Ah, you want the short version.'

'It would help,' Steve responded.

'Well, the reason your targets are asleep is because they are waiting for something to happen from the Middle East, we think. That's where a large chunk of the recent funding has mostly been going. Braddock Holdings have invested over twenty million, we estimate, in something in Syria. All by the back door, all very illegal and hushed up. We can't prove much of it because of the lack of co-operation, but the movements indicate this is what has been happening.'

A low whistle went up from a couple of the men around the table.

'Our theory,' Peterson continued, 'is that something will happen in the Middle East that will trigger these people into action. At the moment, apart from the State benefits, Braddock Holdings is funding their lifestyles.

Whatever is going to happen, based on the size of Braddock Holdings, it will be big.'

'And who the hell runs Braddock Holdings?' Dave was writing fast as he spoke.

'It's a nominee company with signatories in various countries. To date we've identified eight bank accounts and from what we've hacked out of the system so far, each account has a different signatory. What we have established is that the signatories are all bogus and virtually all the movements happen electronically over the World Wide Web. It is, to put it mildly, a sod of a problem to find out who the real people behind Braddock Holdings are.'

'What about the company registration?' Dave enquired.

'Registered in the Bahamas and so far we've had no luck tracing the owners because of their privacy laws.'

'So,' Keeley intervened, 'we have some organisation funding these guys. Whatever they need they get and the indications are that something is going on in the Middle East and more particularly in Syria. At some point, gentlemen, we have to assume our targets will receive instructions to become active again. From what Peterson has told me privately, the SB4 people think it will be sooner rather than later, simply because the funding volumes have increased dramatically over the last few months.'

'Christ,' said Roger, 'why didn't they tell us about this before?'

'Because they didn't know about us until some Whitehall knob got hold of our reports and the SB4 report. He put two and two together and decided to alert each of us about the other's existence. That's when we got told what SB4 were doing. Because you guys were doing such a great job, I got allocated the task of checking things out with SB4 and hence today's meeting. Now, I have to take this higher, much higher, but for now I want the targets watched twenty four, seven, is that understood?'

'Braddock Holdings, Brian, who's going to work on that?' Roger knew it wouldn't be him. He was already occupied with a prime target.

'SB4 have done what they can. They have a team monitoring the appropriate accounts, as best they can. We'll know if funds get moved, so it may give us a warning.'

'Assuming the funds haven't already reached their destination,' Dave said soberly.

'Of course, but with account balances of over one hundred million that we know about, we expect them to be using some of that money in the near future.'

'Where's the money come from, guv?' Brian had sat quietly throughout Peterson's presentation.

'Internet businesses feeding straight through bogus and sometimes temporary email accounts into the Braddock accounts. It's all very easy to set up. The adult industry alone is worth about thirty five billion dollars a year, so one hundred million doesn't seem that much really.'

'Have we no idea who's behind all of it?'

'None, but when he makes a move the SB4 team will be onto him very quickly indeed.'

'I hope you're right,' Brian shook his head with a degree of disbelief at what had been revealed.

'So do I,' Keeley said evenly. 'Now, gentlemen, unless there's anything else, I think we all know what we have to do. I will be trying to increase the available manpower on our particular targets.'

Keeley knew those gathered around the table thought he was a department head, it was how ATRIUM had been set up. In reality, Keeley knew his next conversation with Preston would place a huge demand on manpower from the security forces, a demand that would probably be unparalleled since the early days after the destruction of the Twin Towers in New York. His next conversation with Preston would almost certainly result in every known terrorist living in the United Kingdom being placed under continual surveillance. It was going to cost a fortune and Keeley hoped the information from Peterson was accurate.

Keeley waited until his office was empty before he placed the call to Preston. She was sitting in her office looking out at the London Eye when Keeley's call came through. At first she just sat there listening to the reports of inactivity amongst the targets. She was used to those. Her interest was roused when Keeley got to the bit about SB4's deductions. Keeley knew the head of SB4, though that person did not know of Keeley's involvement in ATRIUM, it was something very few people knew. Because the head of SB4 thought Keeley was working directly for a Whitehall guru, he'd contacted Keeley and asked him to speak with Peterson. That had been two days before and Preston had sanctioned the meeting without speaking to SB4 first – it would have aroused too much interest from SB4. Now she listened to the information that made her sit on the edge of her seat. Still she was looking at the London Eye, but she'd stopped counting the number of capsules, her mind focusing hard on what she was being told.

After ten minutes she closed the call with Keeley and called her superior. This was what they'd been waiting for, Preston was sure, and damn SB4 for keeping things quiet for so long. Her controlled anger subsided once she had the full attention of her superior. She knew, as always, he would back her, he had no choice. When she'd relayed the information she asked for a favour. It was granted.

Preston terminated the call and smiled slowly to herself. She now had control over all the relevant departments. She would coordinate whatever was needed to ensure the targets they were watching remained impotent. The meeting was arranged for four o'clock. They'd all be there and doubtless there would be some objections to her leading them, such objections were inevitable. The fact was, she now had the authority to do what was needed and that was precisely what she intended to do. Preston figured that by five o'clock what could turn out to be the largest ever intelligence operation mounted on mainland Britain would have begun.

***

It was nearing the end of the business day in Yalvac. Daniel Newton had spent much of the day sitting idly on the beach in his favourite cove. The sun had been hot and the breeze from the sea had been welcome. At four o'clock local time, Newton parked his van outside the small shop owned by Arken Saltig. He walked through the door and smiled at the young woman behind the counter.

'Is Arken around?' He asked her quite simply.

'Yes, in the back. Your boxes have turned up, by the way.'

'Oh, that's good, but it's too late to start back today. Not only that but I fancy one more evening by the sea.' He winked at her and she looked back at him.

She called out to the back of the shop in Turkish and Newton took the hint. He was still smiling when Saltig appeared from behind the rush curtain that divided the shop from the back room.

'Ah, Mr Newton, I have some good news for you.'

'Your niece told me. As I was telling her, it is too late to start back today, but I can load my van up now and get an early start tomorrow.'

'Very well then, I take it you have all the paperwork?' Saltig suddenly sounded very business-like. Newton returned briefly to his van and returned a couple of minutes later carrying the relevant documents. He laid them on the counter and waited while Saltig checked them against his own documents.

'All is correct,' he said after a minute. 'The merchandise is in the garage at the rear. Take your van round there and I will show you which pile is yours.'

'Thanks Arken, I'll meet you round there.' Newton smiled at the young woman and Sheera Ganzagha smiled back politely.

It took Newton ten minutes to load the merchandise onto the back of the van. The last consignment he loaded were the jewellery boxes that had caused him the delay. As he stored them carefully, he observed there were two dozen of them, but the observation passed him by and he thought no more of it.

'Well,' Newton said finally, 'I take it the payment has been made as usual.'

'Of course, it is much safer than carrying great bundles of cash around with you. When will you be coming back?'

'About two months I should think. It all depends on the people I work for, when they need more products. You know the score, Arken, it is so difficult to guess what the market will do, especially now that the UK has officially left the European Union.'

'That is true, so very true. Anyway, I hope you have a safe journey back to England. No doubt we will see you soon.'

'Thanks, and good luck to you too.' Newton swung the driver's door closed and started the engine. It roared into life and he was soon disappearing down the dusty track that led to the main road and his final encounter with the Mediterranean and later, the delightful Sheera.

CHAPTER SIX

It was quarter past five and Preston had concluded her meeting with the department heads. As she already knew would be the case, the surveillance effort on the known fanatics, activists and potential terrorists had been stepped up. Even as she looked back out at the London Eye, she knew the various departments were already struggling to work out how the extra demands could be handled. She had control but it did not thrill her.

Preston had started the meeting by berating the fact the teams had not been working together. There'd been the expected grumbles that nobody even knew about ATRIUM so how the hell could they have co-operated. The groans turned to silence when Preston revealed the information from SB4. The intelligence heads from MI5 and MI6 looked askance and the security heads went pale at the thought of what might be happening. This was no theoretical scenario that was being enacted, real money was moving in extremely frightening directions, funding God knows what.

Preston had been given the resources, promised co-operation and her own superior had been there to offer her the kind of backing she had never received before. She looked at the London Eye and was oblivious to the rather small man in the pinstripe suit who knocked gently on her half-open door.

He knocked again, a little louder. Preston turned.

'Miss Preston, sorry to disturb you but the head of MI6 thought you ought to have a copy of this report following his conversation with you earlier.' The man offered her a manila folder on which were stamped in red the words 'Top Secret'. She took it from him, thanked him for bringing the report from the MI6 building and showed him out of the room. The folder was sealed using red wax and a string. Preston sliced the string with a penknife and opened the folder.

'Christ, I thought he looked sheepish,' she exclaimed. 'Now I know why.' Preston looked again at the report, muttered a few more words under her breath and then regained her composure. She dialled a number and waited for the head of MI6 to be put on the line.

'Gareth, I got your file. Why didn't you mention this at the meeting?'

'Sorry, Selena, but the latest intelligence only started coming in this morning and the report hadn't been typed when I left. Once I got back to the office and read it I knew you should see it immediately.'

'How confident are your chaps about this?'

'About ninety percent I'd say. The aerial and satellite pictures have shown there has been construction of some kind going on there for a couple of years or more but there has been increased activity in the area over the past several months and a lot of whatever they have been building now seems to be underground. To be honest, it could have been going on for years without us knowing anything. At first we thought it was going to be some kind of factory or manufacturing plant, which of course would be a legitimate construction. Then we considered the other possibilities. I have to say that it looks more probable it is some kind of underground laboratory as opposed to anything else.'

'Not oil or plastics then?'

'No. Those towers in the picture are dummies, made to make the plant look like something it isn't. We haven't seen a puff of anything come out of them since they were constructed about two years ago, and the Infra-Red shows they're constantly at the same temperature as the ground.'

'So what are they producing?'

'Well, we put a team in on the ground a couple of weeks ago, and it took them four days to get near the site, past a lot of what was ostensibly Syrian security, and another three days to get out of the country. From what those guys could tell, it looks like they are hiding a laboratory under the sand. If you want a guess, I'd say they're breeding something, germs probably.'

'Shit,' said Preston. 'What should we do? Tell the Americans?'

'They already know. We told them this afternoon. They want to send in a patrol to take the plant out but that could cause political problems. Until we know for sure what's in there, we simply can't just walk in and destroy it – it would cause uproar amongst the rest of the Arab world, especially after the last weapons of mass destruction fiasco.'

'True, well we can't just do nothing and sit on our hands. How about we make a formal request for information through NATO?'

'They wouldn't tell us if we asked, so what's the point?' The head of MI6 sounded weary – he was.

'Okay, Gareth, I know it's the end of the day. Have you got any idea how they've funded it?'

'None at all, I'm afraid. They certainly haven't used their usual suppliers for this. We've been keeping a close watch on those organisations for a long time. They could have gone further a-field but with their credit rating there aren't too many options open for them.'

'What about neighbours?' Preston's brain was working flat out on the information she'd read in the report. It was a bold, audacious project that must have, initially at least, been carried out right under the nose of the British and Americans, and she found it hard to believe that nobody knew anything about it when it had all started.

'Possible, but the intelligence teams haven't noticed anything remotely suspicious over the past year or so.'

'Well, they got the money from somewhere, and the equipment. You can't just create a plant like this in the middle of the desert out of nothing.' Preston was beginning to sound exasperated.

'No, I agree with you there. One thought, though it's a long shot. You mentioned an organisation this afternoon. What was it called, something like Bradcock Holdings?'

'Braddock Holdings,' she corrected him, 'what of it?'

'Could they, whoever they are, have funded it?'

'It's possible, I suppose, but until we have a better idea of who the hell is behind Braddock Holdings, it doesn't really make sense.'

'Okay, Selena, let me put this past you. What if the owner of Braddock Holdings is an Arab? Let's say he's in cahoots with a group of terrorists and he wants to do something horrible to the West, something that would outstrip the Twin Towers for sheer spectacle. What if he was behind this plant, would that make sense?'

'Yes, but we don't know the owner is an Arab.' Preston was sitting in her chair looking out of the window.

'It doesn't really matter if he is or not. What if he just sympathises with the aims of these people and happens to have the finances to make things happen?'

'It's a thought,' she said. Silently, she considered it was a damn frightening thought and it would also explain why the targets they'd been watching for so long simply did nothing. They did nothing for the very reason that there was nothing to do. All the time the plant in the Syrian desert was being built, commissioned, tested and put into operation, there was nothing to do, so that is what the network did – nothing. It made perfect sense, horrifyingly perfect sense. All it needed was the link from Braddock Holdings to the plant and one or more of the targets to be established and it would all fit frighteningly well into place.

'I'll leave it with you,' the head of MI6 responded.

'Thanks, Gareth. I take it you have some chaps keeping an eye on things?'

'You bet we do.'

'Good, in which case I'll step up the pressure from my end and see what I can get the boys at SB4 involved

77

in. I'll talk to you again just as soon as anything comes in.'

'Good night, Selena,' the man offered with the kind of resignation that indicated he still had an evening's work ahead of him.

Preston bid him farewell and hung up the receiver. A minute later she picked up the phone again and dialled a number.

'Keeley,' he replied.

'Preston, can we talk?'

'Sure.'

'Brian, we've discovered what we think is an underground laboratory in Syria. Actually, MI6 discovered it a while ago but only chose to tell me about it today, damn them. We don't know exactly what it is for sure but the scant intelligence they have managed to obtain suggests it could be some kind of laboratory. I want you to talk to your chap from SB4 and see what you can do to take Braddock Holdings apart. I need to know if they're involved and also, if possible, what the plant is for.'

'But surely the intelligence gatherers should be able to tell you that,' Keeley protested.

'I know, I know. They sent a team in, got some pictures and then two of them got killed getting away. The pictures don't say much and they didn't get close enough to find out much. The Syrians, or some other party, have put some pretty impressive security round the place so the best we've got are some long range photos which are pretty inconclusive.'

'What about reconnaissance craft, or drones?'

'They still don't show much. The aerial shots show what the plant definitely isn't and not what it is.'

'Okay, I'll get Peterson to take another look at the data.'

'Thanks. Also get him to look into places that could supply the kind of equipment needed to make biological weaponry. I want to know of any sudden increases in business on anything, no matter how remotely it might be connected.'

'Yes, ma'am, but it'll have to be tomorrow. I'm involved in some surveillance tonight.'

'Okay, let me know when you get anywhere.' It was phrased as 'when', not 'if'. Preston had confidence in Keeley, the same confidence she had in all the team members, but Keeley was one of the senior players in ATRIUM.

The line went dead as Preston broke the connection.

***

Simon Hart waited patiently by the front door while his guest parked his car. The driver was a cautious man and the car looked like it should have failed its road worthiness test some years earlier. The car spluttered to a halt and the driver alighted.

'Mr Hart,' the voice contained a Jamaican lilt, 'it is good to see you.'

'Come in Justin. Still driving the death trap, I see.' Hart smiled as the two men shook hands.

'She goes,' the tall Jamaican offered in mock defence. The two men walked indoors, out of the night air and out of sight of anyone who may have been watching, not that anyone was.

'So,' Hart continued once they were sipping brandies in the drawing room, 'how did the trip go?'

'Very well indeed, everything is fully operational and phase one production is complete as you already know.'

'Good, Justin, that is very good. Did you give them the final payment?'

'Yes, they confirmed we will have the phase one product in a few days. Phase two will be ready for shipping in a month. I have to say it all looks very impressive and from what I am told they have completely fooled the intelligence gatherers in the West.'

'Excellent. It seems like it is time for some real action. Have you any idea where you'd like to go when this is all over?'

'Back to Jamaica, I think, or possibly somewhere else around there, maybe Tobago and a long, cool, cocktail or two.' Justin Pritwick laughed over the glass of brandy he was holding.

'Five million is a lot of cocktails,' Hart said evenly.

'I know, I know. How long do you think it will take?'

'A few days after I take delivery.'

'That quick?' The Jamaican sounded surprised. 'So, where are you going?'

'Somewhere where you won't have to worry about me!' Hart smiled back. 'The phase two product is something I will be able to use on my own, I think, so you'll just have to watch where my share of the money goes if you want to find me.'

'I won't be doing that. So far as I'm concerned it's the high life once I leave these shores. How sure are you that they will pay up?'

'They don't have a choice and they won't have time to develop plans, so they'll pay up. If they don't then I have other ways of ensuring my colleagues get paid, and that includes you. So even if phase one doesn't work as I expect it to, you won't be out of pocket. Now, Justin, there's just one more thing we need to worry about.'

'The network?' Pritwick suddenly sounded sober.

'The network,' Hart confirmed the observation. 'They're not going to like this one little bit.'

'Yeah, five years of following what they think are orders from their esteemed leaders, followed by the biggest rip off they've ever suffered. I can imagine it's going to piss some of them off.'

'Yes, and you must be prepared for them to come looking for you.' Hart's voice sounded serious.

'But they don't know who we are. Tell me they don't know who we are?' Pritwick sounded nervous.

'No, they don't know who we are yet, but they will try to find out. You can be sure of that.'

'Okay, so I'll take precautions,' Pritwick now sounded resolute. Nothing was going to stop him enjoying his millions.

'And that means you don't flash the money around for a few months at least. Take it easy and make sure you blend into wherever you go.'

'Okay. What's going to happen to the business?'

'It'll continue to run itself. The coffers will get deeper and deeper and I'll keep administering it from wherever I go. Everything is on the laptop so it shouldn't be a problem. You and the other guys will get paid as agreed so there's nothing to worry about for anyone and from now on I will be taking all the risks. Eventually things are likely to tail off but I figure it will take a couple of years at least.'

'So, that should be enough time to achieve any additional goals you may have.'

'Right, now I have to set up the final plans. There's a lot of work to be done over the next few days and we can't afford any mistakes. The targets have all been selected and the devices are waiting for their cargoes. I'll phone you if I need any deliveries to be made, and for God's sake get a better crate than the one outside in the next few days just in case I do need to use you for anything more. A hire job will do.'

'Sure, Simon.' The brandy glasses were empty and the meeting was coming to an end.

'Fancy a game of snooker before you go?' Hart stood and limped in the direction of the games room. It was a well-rehearsed limp and it served him well.

'Okay.'

Two hours later the rust heap in the driveway staggered into life and Justin Pritwick drove back down the driveway, the thought of twenty million pounds weighing lightly on his mind. The months of work, the risks and the trips abroad he'd endured were about to pay off, big time, he thought.

Simon Hart closed the front door once the car had gone, pressed the button on the control panel that opened the wrought-iron gates and waited until the sensors indicated the car had crossed the security beam. Then he pressed the button again. Pritwick had left Hart's home for the last time. Everything was going nicely to plan and Hart returned contentedly to his living room.

The phone call was short. Christine Matthews was busy with another of her clients when her mobile phone sounded. She apologised profusely for the break in the massage she was giving and picked up the device.

'Christine, its Simon, I'm sorry if you are busy but something has come up. I need to change our next arrangements as I will be away for a few days.'

'Can I phone you back later and talk about it?'

'If you can make it Friday evening at about nine o'clock, we can make some future arrangements then.'

'Okay, Friday at nine it is. Look, I must go, I'm in the middle of something.'

'Fair enough, see you then.' Hart replaced the receiver. Everything was going very, very nicely now.

Christine Matthews replaced her mobile phone in her bag and turned her attentions back to the man lying on the couch. He was in his mid-forties, slightly balding, somewhat overweight but not obese. He turned and looked up at the woman.

'Who was that?' He enquired politely.

'Just someone I know. Some big businessman who wants to take advantage of my services. Now, where was I?'

'You were doing my shoulders. So, this businessman, what does he do?'

'Something to do with computers I think – I don't really know, any more than I know what you do, or any of my other clients.'

'It's probably best that way.' The man certainly didn't want Christine Matthews to know what he did for a job. Strictly, according to the ATRIUM rules, he should not have contacted her in the first place but she'd been clocked visiting one of his targets on a number of occasions and when he'd finally got pictures of what was happening behind the closed doors the temptation was too great. Alan Green had met with the woman three times now. He'd spent some time searching out the Escort Agency that employed her and then he'd made a specific request based on the alleged recommendation of a friend. It was fiction but it had worked. It wasn't the first time in his secret career that he'd been down this route, claiming it was all in the line of duty. Now, he lay back and allowed her to earn the money he was paying her. She was good, very good and he knew the best was yet to come.

***

Dieter Zussman had finished his evening meal and was sitting watching the television as usual. The stain on the document in his shop's safe was troubling him and he wasn't paying much attention to the peak time program being broadcast. He was more concerned with his own plans, plans which he would be activating very soon. He was still concentrating on his plans when the phone in the hallway began to ring. Reluctantly he rose from his chair and went to answer it.

'Hello,' he answered the call with as little interest as possible.

'Mr Zussman, you do not know me, but I know you and I have your interests at heart. I thought you would like to know your house was visited this morning after you had gone to work.' The caller let the news sink in for a moment before continuing. 'We want to be sure that you have nothing of value to our group in your house.'

'No, nothing, and there's nothing that could reveal my true identity either. All I have is a contact number for my man in Syria and I keep that in a safe in the office.'

'That is good. Would you please go and check round your house to make sure everything is in order? I will phone you back in ten minutes.' The line went dead.

Zussman was shaking. His own private space had been violated and he had not been aware of it. What was he supposed to check? He'd been home for two hours, changed, cooked a meal and noticed nothing. Perhaps whoever had visited him had found his secret place. He must check that but not now, only when the curtains were drawn and the lights were turned off. He'd often suspected he was being watched. The phone call confirmed his worst fears. Executing his plan would be more difficult if they were watching him, which he now knew they were. Still, he had to execute it if only because it was of paramount importance to his continued survival.

The phone rang again.

'Dieter, its Daniel Newton.' Zussman breathed a sigh of relief – a friendly voice to soothe him.

'Daniel, I take it you have some news for me?' Zussman's voice sounded urgent.

'Yes, it is good news, Dieter. The boxes have arrived. I will be leaving first thing in the morning. With luck I will be back in five days.'

'That is good news, Daniel. I look forward to seeing you again. When you get back could you bring the boxes straight round to my Reigate shop. They are very valuable and I will want to put them straight into the safe.'

'Sure thing, Dieter. If they are so valuable why not use a registered courier instead of me?'

'Because I trust you, Daniel. Now, make sure you keep an eye on them!' Zussman tried to sound casual but he failed miserably. His heart was pounding from the news, he had less time than he'd expected before his plans would need to be enacted.

'Let me know when you get to Munich, Daniel. I will know you are only two days away then.'

'I will do, Dieter. I'd better go now, there's a dark-haired lass trying to attract my attention.'

'Good luck, Daniel and goodbye.' The line went dead as Zussman hung up. He ran through the house checking the various rooms. Everything seemed in order but he already knew that would be the case. He'd just reached the hallway again when the phone rang.

'Mr Zussman, have you had time to check?' The voice was cold, dispassionate.

'Yes I have. Everything is in order, nothing missing. Are you sure the person came into the house?'

'Positive. I wouldn't worry too much though. It is unlikely he will come back. It was probably an opportunist burglar who got disturbed. Anyway, please don't be alarmed. Have a good evening.' The caller terminated the conversation abruptly. Zussman replaced his receiver and returned to his chair. He spent the next hour sitting uncomfortably, sure he was being watched, desperate to check his secret place, yet not daring to break with his evening rituals, just in case whoever was outside had worked out what his pattern of movements would be.

At ten o'clock, Dieter Zussman began his nightly ritual of checking the property's security, locking and bolting doors and switching off lights. At quarter past ten the last light was extinguished and the observer across the road knew Zussman had gone to bed.

Zussman waited ten minutes in pitch darkness before he turned the torch light on. Shielding the faint light from the window, across which he'd pulled the thin drapes, he lifted the corner of the carpet and unscrewed the floorboard he'd spent so long cutting and shaping. It took him nearly ten minutes to take out the four screws. He worked slowly and silently, just in case they had listening devices in the room. Finally he lifted the board and pulled out the small, metal tin. Inside were the papers he treasured. He held the last two letters from his mother, written shortly before she had been shot by a dissident faction. He held the new passport, driving licence and birth certificate. He'd long ago figured that if the network could procure such documents then so could he. They'd given him a Jewish identity, well he'd take it one stage further with yet another identity and then he'd disappear. The concept was simple but therein lay its brilliance. In just a few days' time Dieter Zussman would be gone and it would be as though he had never existed, which he hadn't. Zussman caressed the documents lovingly before placing them back in the tin. He replaced the tin in its hiding place, screwed down the board and replaced the carpet before climbing back into bed. He felt happier now he knew his private possessions were as safe as his plan.

**

Simon Hart was thinking quietly to himself as the strains of a Mozart Sonata wafted benignly around his living room. It was the end of the day and Hart was unwinding using his second most favoured technique. The first involved Christine Matthews and her digital dexterity and in reality Mozart was a poor second. The Sonata was in the mid-section when Hart was interrupted by the phone.

'Hi, Simon, sorry it's so late but I haven't had the chance to get to the phone until now.' The woman was speaking softly, as if she did not want to disturb someone close by.

'Hi there, Sheera, how are you?' Hart was immediately fully awake.

'I am well but very tired. Our mutual friend has quite an appetite which is why I could not contact you earlier. The boxes you wanted to know about have arrived and he will be leaving with them in the morning.'

'Good work, Sheera and thanks for the call. Say, would you like to meet up in Munich in a few days' time? Only I have to be over there on business.'

'I would love to, Simon, but it costs so much.'

'Forget about the cost, I'll get the tickets sorted out. If you fly from Ankara, would that be okay?'

'Yes, it would be fine. I can get the train to Ankara. Where will I meet you?'

'At Munich airport I would think. Let me sort out the details tomorrow morning. Give me a ring tomorrow afternoon when you get a chance and I'll tell you what I've arranged. I can't wait to see you again.'

'Nor can I wait to see you. Until tomorrow then,' her voice became softer, even more conspiratorial.

'Until tomorrow, Sheera,' Hart blew a kiss down the mouthpiece before gently returning the receiver to its cradle. He turned up the volume on the Hi-Fi system and listened to the concluding section of the Sonata. If Simon Hart was worried about the future it didn't show but he now knew one thing – the countdown had begun.

CHAPTER SEVEN

He was four hours into the surveillance operation and Brian Keeley had already put in a day's work for ATRIUM. Now, he was feeling tired and hungry. The man who'd just joined him in the back of the van was younger, fresher and had only just come on duty. Police Constable Darren Fretton was new to this game, having been acquired by Keeley from the local force when the orders went out to increase manpower. Fretton had relished the prospect of working with the professionals and was suitably impressed when not only had Keeley come and interviewed him at Newbury station but had then had him assigned to himself.

'Right, Fretton, some things you need to know about these guys. They're all Islamists to start with. Now, I don't have anything at all against Muslims but these guys are not your average law-abiding, peace-loving religious kind, they're what we call fanatics, so they're dangerous.'

'Yes, guv, I've read their MOs.'

'Good for you, Fretton. Did the reports tell you what this particular group of people have done in the past?'

'Some of it, guv.'

'Some of it, eh, well you can take what you've read and probably multiply it by ten. In that house,' Keeley pointed out of the back window of the van in the vague direction of the house they were watching, 'are two of Britain's potential greatest threats. They have been trained to kill in large numbers and they are prepared to die for their cause if necessary. In short, Fretton, they will stop at nothing to achieve their aims, so we take care, very great care.'

'Yes, guv, but what are their aims at the moment?'

'We don't know, yet, which is why we're keeping a close eye on them.'

'And who exactly is in there at the moment, guv?'

'Al'Makir is there for sure. The early shift watched him go home from the snooker hall, and Mohammad Gantala. He's been there since yesterday evening. Who else might be there, we can't be sure, except it isn't any of the other prime targets we're watching at the moment.'

'I see. Who's our back up, guv?' Fretton was looking out of the darkened window. A pedestrian walked past the van and had no idea he was being observed.

'When we need someone, if we need someone, I have a team on standby. They can get to where we need them in less than ten minutes. Hello, something's happening.'

The house they were watching was suddenly plunged into darkness. It was just after ten o'clock and, if the surveillance reports of the previous few nights had been accurate, it was far too early for the occupants to be retiring for the night.

'Tango Alpha One Nine, this is Tango Control, come in.' Keeley spoke softly but with a degree of urgency.

'Tango Alpha One Nine, reading you loud and clear. The back of the house is in darkness, what about you, over?'

'Confirm darkness. Any sign of movement?'

'That's negative Tango Control, no sign of targets.'

'Keep watching, they're up to something.'

'Yes, guv. Hang on, the Infra-Red shows there's movement in the back garden. We're picking up two heat sources. They could be our targets.'

'Confirm, two heat sources from your end. There's nothing at the front. We're ready to move when you get sight of them.'

'Roger Tango Control. We now have targets in sight. We can positively identify target T1 and target T4. Do you copy, Tango Control?'

'Roger that.' Keeley put the handset down. 'That's Al'Makir and Gantala to you, Fretton. They're on the move.'

'Yes, guv.' Fretton eased himself away from the window at the back of the van and climbed into the driver's seat. Finally he called back to his superior. 'Ready to move off when you are, guv.'

'Thanks, Fretton.' Keeley held up the handset again. 'Tango Alpha One Nine from Tango Control, what's happening?'

'They're walking off down the road away from us, heading south, that's away from the town.'

'They're probably heading towards their usual haunt. Do you want us to follow?'

'Negative, control, we can watch them for now.'

'In that case, we'll go and take up position where we think they're heading.'

'Roger, control, we'll follow them and keep you informed.'

The conversation was ended and Keeley gave directions to Fretton. The car park was only a couple of minutes' drive away, but it would take the men on foot over fifteen minutes to walk there. The car park was shared between a café and public house and Keeley had spent many uncomfortable hours crouched in a van watching the various customers of both establishments.

Fretton parked the van at the back of the car park. There were no lights here and from the road the van would look as if it had been there for some time, possibly abandoned and definitely unoccupied.

Across the road from the café and pub was a row of houses, three storey affairs. All six dwellings were in darkness. Keeley noted the observations in his pocket book, writing by a carefully hooded torch-light. The van had been parked for nearly ten minutes and no one had entered or left either establishment.

'Tango Control this is Tango Alpha One Nine, come in, over.' The handset crackled quite loudly in the stillness of the van. Keeley responded.

'Tango Control, what's up?'

'Targets are walking towards Café Richard as expected. We're following on foot and by car. They are estimated to be with you in about five minutes.'

'Thanks Tango Alpha One Nine, we're watching for them.'

'Any sign of the others?'

'That's negative, no other news in from the team.'

'Looks like another routine visit then, guv,' the voice sounded weary.

'Probably One Nine, but we have to be sure.'

'Roger that, Tango Control. We're removing the foot patrol to avoid suspicion. We'll continue to watch by vehicle.'

'One Nine, I can see the targets coming down the road now. You can leave them to us.'

'Roger, Tango Control, we'll head back to the house and establish surveillance there.'

'Confirmed, One Nine. We'll follow them back for you when they leave.' The handset went dead. Keeley motioned for Fretton to join him in the back of the van.

'Which will it be, Fretton, the pub or the café?'

'The café, guv, it's virtually empty.'

'So is the pub, if the car park is anything to go by. Still, I agree with you.'

The two watchers didn't have long to wait. A minute later the targets entered the front door of the café and disappeared inside.

'What next, guv?' Fretton asked using a very soft voice.

'We wait.'

'Yes, guv.' Fretton sounded as if he knew the next part would be boring. He was hungry too and the thought of sitting outside in a cramped van while the people they were watching sat inside in the warm, probably with plates of hot food, irritated him.

'Don't worry, Fretton, another four hours and we get relieved.'

'Yes, guv.' Fretton was watching through the rear, tinted window of the van. 'Guv, there's some more guys out there.

Keeley looked up and peered into the gloom.

'Christ, why weren't we told?'

'Guv?' Fretton sounded confused.

'They're all here, Fretton, the whole set. That tall guy is Ali Benadri, target three. The bloke on his left is Bin Aldre, target two, and the other chap is Masra, target five. How the hell have they slipped their watchers?'

The question was rhetorical which was just as well because Fretton could not have supplied a helpful response.

'Tango Control, to Tango Bravo Four, come in.'

'Tango Bravo Four, reading loud and clear.'

'Where are you, Tango Bravo Four?'

'Outside the residence of target three. There's no movement to report, guv.'

'There wouldn't be. The bloody target has just walked past my window.'

'Guv?' The voice contained a tone of disbelief.

'Did you check the target was in residence?'

'Yes, guv, at the start of the shift.'

'So how did he get out?'

'No idea guv. Where are you?'

'Café Richard. More importantly the whole group of prime targets are here.'

'Guv?' The person identified as Tango Bravo Four sounded totally confused. 'So they've all slipped the net?'

'It appears so, Tango Bravo Four.'

'Shall we come and join you?'

'Negative. The car park is almost empty. If three or four cars suddenly turned up it would be a bit suspicious.

Stay where you are. Also, alert the rest of the Bravo team that they're watching empty houses and tell them to stay away from here too.'

'Roger that, guv. Anything else?'

'No, Hamilton, there's nothing else. Just be more careful next time, and you can pass that on to the rest of your team too.'

'Yes guv,' the airwaves crackled again as Hamilton broke the connection. Six months of routine surveillance with no alerts, nothing unusual, had put the team of watchers to sleep.

Inside the café, the five men ordered fish and chips and bottles of beer. The café wasn't licensed but the owner knew the men and always had a small stock of their favourite tipple. He could always claim it was a private party. Indeed, the men wouldn't pay for their food and beer but would leave a generous donation in the bogus charity box that sat on the grubby counter.

After fifteen minutes Keeley asked Fretton to go and walk past the café window to see what was happening. The group of five men were sitting round a circular table. The bottles of half-emptied beer mingled with the cigarette butts and the half-empty plates. Fretton could see the five men had Arabic complexions. They had beards of varying lengths and their hair was long and unkempt. They wore tracksuits and trainers as if somehow that would make them blend into their surroundings. The café they sat in was small and dirty. The café owner appeared to be making some futile attempt to clean up the place. The five men were deep in conversation and the owner's presence went unnoticed.

'Okay, so Mahar and Ali will go and collect the goods in six days, as soon as they arrive in the country. You will also deal with the delivery boy and the person you collect them from. There can be no chance of anyone upsetting our plans. Once you confirm you have the goods we will activate our network.' Al'Makir flashed a signet ring when he gesticulated with his right hand as he spoke.

'Sure.' Ali replied.

'And you have the directions for where to take the goods after you collect them?'

'Sure.' Ali replied again. They'd had this conversation a dozen times before, but now it was for real.

'That is good. We must act carefully over the next few days. We have waited a long time for this and we don't want to lose this opportunity to strike a blow for justice and liberty.'

'To justice and liberty.' The quietest of the group held up his beer bottle in mock salute and the toast was taken up by the others in the group.

The owner of the café had seen it all before and was not surprised. He couldn't understand a word being spoken, it was always the same and it all sounded like Greek. It wasn't – the language came from further East, an Arabic dialect native to the men who were holding the conversation.

'Justice and liberty,' Mahar pondered the words for a moment. 'So much rests on this, so much we can do. Jihad is nearly fulfilled.' Mahar was not a philosopher but he made a valiant effort to act the part of one as he repeated the words, 'justice and liberty.'

Ten minutes later and Fretton was back in the van reporting his observations to Keeley. The group stood and left the café, leaving the owner to clear their table as part of his half-hearted effort to tidy up the establishment. The five men had been gone for three minutes and were still visible, walking down the main road. Keeley ordered Fretton to follow their targets, and concentrate on Al'Makir if they parted company. Having given the instruction, he opened the back door of the van and went into the café. As he did so, Fretton started the van's engine and prepared to follow the targets.

'Coffee please.' Keeley made the request in a calm, unhurried voice. He leaned on the counter in a casual, unassuming manner. He was a tall man, lean, fit, middle-aged and the kind of person who could melt almost unnoticed into a crowd. He would never attract attention, despite his height.

The coffee was served and Keeley went and sat at one of the smaller, grubby tables. He and the owner of the café were quite alone. He sipped the coffee, remembered that it was rude to spit the revolting liquid out, and swallowed the mouthful with as little fuss as possible. It was amazing the health people hadn't closed this place down but then it was unlikely any of its clientele would raise any issues with the relevant department.

Brian Keeley was one of life's observers. He'd visited this particular café several times over the past few months and each visit had been for a purpose. He took an active role in the surveillance team and had been keeping his eyes open. When he'd found what he was looking for he figured it was best to do what he was good at – observe. That's what he'd put in his report and, after some discussion, his approach had been agreed by Preston. At first all he'd done was watch. He'd already been watching the man called Ali, target three, for some months. It was Ali who'd led him to the café and Keeley was curious as to why they had picked this particular café. Perhaps it was because it was unobtrusive, perhaps because the group could feel safe that no one would understand their conversation.

Keeley had watched the group come together. Ali Benadir and Mahar Bin Aldre spent much time together, as did Al'Makir and Gantala. Masra was the loner of the group, possibly because of his past. They all visited the Mosque on occasions and spent much time travelling around Berkshire. Al'Makir and Gantala had rented a flat in Newbury, just off the town centre, and within forty-eight hours of them moving in, Keeley had been there. They were out at the time of Keeley's visit. He'd made sure of that. The listening devices had been planted, one in each of the bedrooms and a third in the living area. They were well hidden and unlikely to be discovered by the two men who seemed to spend only a few hours there each night. Keeley had rented a room nearby for use by the team. It was within reception range of the devices he planted and he set up his equipment. For six months Keeley had kept his listening post active and in that time the team had heard nothing of interest. During that same period he watched as the group of five men met on various occasions. Benadri and Bin Aldre were evidently old friends and did a lot together. After six fruitless months Keeley was getting restless, yet he'd known for some time that something was up – call it an instinct, if you like, but something was about to happen.

'I saw those chaps leaving again as I drove up,' Keeley offered by way of conversation. 'They're a funny group to visit this kind of place.'

'So, they're business.' The café owner was disinterested in Keeley's observations.

'Yeah, but they're hardly your usual sort of customer.'

'I don't care. They eat five meals and buy drinks. It's how I earn my living.'

'Yeah, I guess so.'

Keeley was tired with the usual games he had to play to get information from the owner. He'd been playing the game for several weeks, ever since he decided to fish for information.

'So, twenty says you didn't hear anything of use today,' Keeley suddenly came directly to the point of the conversation. As he spoke he held out the twenty-pound note. The café owner took the piece of paper, pocketed it and rubbed his chin thoughtfully.

'That one you showed me the picture of,' he began.

'Ali Benadri,' Keeley interrupted him.

'Yeah, well I think that he and that pal of his are planning to go somewhere in a few days. Most of what they talk about is in Greek or some such language but you could tell Ali and his pal are up to something. I'd say by their excitement it is going to be soon, very soon.'

'Yeah?' Keeley tried not to sound too excited himself. 'Anything else?'

'Oh a lot of praising God for Jihad or something, and they drank a toast to some gibberish they were talking about. Then they got up and walked out.'

'Good.'

'So, what's this all about?'

'I don't know. My boss just pays me to watch them.' Keeley lied, something else he was good at. Keeley had a nagging worry about what Benadri and Bin Aldre were up to and within twenty minutes of leaving the café he'd have the alarm bells ringing in the right quarters and security stepped up to an even higher level. Keeley returned to the grimy table and finished his coffee. Finally, after about twenty minutes, he stood up and turned to face the serving counter.

'Right, thanks for your help. You've got my number if anything else comes up, though I doubt it will. I'd best be off.' Keeley opened the door to the café and stepped outside. As the door closed behind him, Keeley began to take the mobile phone out of his coat pocket, preparing to make contact with Fretton, to find out what was going on.

He never heard the single bullet that entered his head just above the place where his eyebrows met. He fell backwards, his body crashing against the door he'd just closed, his life breath rapidly deserting him.

Assad Veltharma watched from his vantage point across the road from the café. Keeley had been good but not that good. The group had known they were being watched for some time. It was why they never spoke of business in the flat in Newbury. It was why they'd paid cash to rent the flat across the way from the café. The barrel of the rifle was still warm and the acrid smell of the discharge still wafted through the room. Veltharma watched and waited. He heard the sirens in the distance and began to pack away his few belongings.

Outside the café, the pool of blood was growing larger. It seeped from the head of the corpse slumped in the doorway. Veltharma finished packing and left the single-roomed flat. He descended the stairs and flung his bag into the back of the battered, white Escort. He pulled out onto the road, turning away from the sound of the sirens, his job completed. He would now become a sleeper until called upon by the network for their next enterprise. He was, and would remain, unknown to all except those who provided him with his daily needs. He was, so far as ATRIUM and the combined intelligence services were concerned, the genuine, invisible man.

The sirens grew louder and the first of the police cars roared into the car park. The officers could see the body lying against the café door. Carefully they approached the scene. There had been a spate of gangland killings in the area and on more than one occasion the police had been drawn into a booby trap resulting in a number of officers being injured.

It took them ten minutes to secure the area, by which time the paramedics had arrived. The body was examined and laid on a stretcher. Then a black, unmarked car arrived. A man with black, shiny shoes and a dark, neatly-pressed suit stepped out from the rear door. He marched crisply over to the officer in charge, showed him his credentials and handed him a mobile phone. The officer spoke briefly to his superior who confirmed the identity of the man. Finally, the officer in charge returned the mobile phone, saluted smartly and walked off to give instructions. Behind the black car was a hearse bearing the name of a funeral director.

In less than ten minutes, Keeley's body had been transferred to the hearse. Three black, unmarked cars had now arrived and a team of black-suited men had taken charge of the situation. It took them an hour to examine the area, meticulously searching for any clues as to the assassin. They knew the bullet was still lodged in what remained of Keeley's brain. It would be retrieved within the hour and it would probably be their biggest clue. Once they had that information and the angle of entry of the bullet, they'd be able to start working out where the shot might have come from. It would all take a couple of hours at most, then they'd launch the enquiry in full.

Two hours later the results from the pathology unit were through. It was a single entry and judging by the brain tissue that had been destroyed it had been fired at an angle of about twenty-five degrees above the head.

Forty minutes later the café owner had been interviewed and the dark-suited men knew the assailant had not been waiting outside. They made their calculations and worked out the shot could have come from one of three properties across the road. A further ten minutes elapsed before the team leader broke down the door to the flat that had been used by Veltharma. The spent cartridge lying below the window confirmed they had the right room. It would be sealed off and a thorough search instigated in the morning. Meantime the team leader carefully placed the cartridge in a clear plastic bag, sealed it and handed it to the man behind him. He left the room and within two minutes was being driven to the pathology laboratory.

The team knew that Preston would want the report, containing as much information as they could muster, sitting on her desk first thing the following morning. It would be a long night. She'd already been told what had happened and was preparing for a long night of her own. The network, it seemed, was about to come to life.

CHAPTER EIGHT

Thursday 25th June

Preston's office was buzzing with activity. The seven team leaders had been called during the night and, for some, that had meant they had spent the past six hours travelling. Preston sat behind her desk looking round at the assembled group. These were the best in Britain and though Keeley's demise was one of the risks of the job, something they all accepted, they were nonetheless in a state of shock. The news of Keeley's death had been met with a degree of surprise mixed with a growing certainty that the targets were about to be activated, either of their own volition or from some external influence.

'Ladies and gentlemen, if I could have your attention,' Preston started. 'As you all know, Brian Keeley was killed last night. The intelligence shows we have a problem. First of all, he was following his own target. This person happened to be with another target his team were watching. Keeley was with a local Police Constable by the name of Fretton. It seems that the two targets met with three others that Keeley's team were supposed to be watching. That was the first breakdown. These three men had all slipped past their watchers unnoticed. Now, we know from Fretton that he followed all five men down the main road for a period of ten minutes. From the timings and the direction the shot was fired, and the fact that we've discovered the place from where the gun was fired, the team investigating the incident assure me that it's not possible for any one of the five to have got back to the scene to pull the trigger. You will appreciate that this means there must be a sixth member of the Newbury group, someone who is either not known to us or who is part of one of your operations. The scene was clear of anything that might have helped us identify the gunman so for now we must assume there is a sixth operator in Newbury. I've put Roger Harding in charge of that area. He was Keeley's second in command and knows the state of operations. For obvious reasons he can't be with us this morning.'

'Ma'am,' Marshall interrupted his leader, 'can I ask why you've called us all in here?'

'Because, Marshall, we collectively have a problem. If three known 'A' listed targets can simply walk away from their observers like these people did yesterday evening, then we are all potentially at risk from the same thing being repeated. I know resources are tight but we have all simply got to remain vigilant. I called you all in to see if there is anything we can do to make sure this doesn't happen again.'

'Double the team sizes.' Amanda Whiting was in her late thirties. She was every bit as tough as Preston and had spent over five years in the field watching suspects.

'Doubling the team sizes is not practicable. We don't have time to train new people in our methods and we can't draw on any more people from the forces. They're already stretching to help us with what they can.'

'I understand Keeley was using a lot of locals on the surveillance last night. Perhaps we're over using them.' Phil Langton spoke softly. He was older than most of the others in the room and knew that in a couple of years he'd be able to quit, not that he hated the work, he just wanted to retire to spend more time on his beloved fishing.

'Yes, most of the teams were locals, but we can't help that. They've all done some training and they knew what their targets looked like.' Preston looked at Langton calmly before continuing. 'Which didn't matter seeing as the targets all got away from them.'

'Which means,' Marshall spoke up, 'they know we, or at least someone, is watching them. That being the case, any one of us could be next. We know them, they know us. Only we don't know all of them and they don't care whether we're local cops, intelligence or ATRIUM. To them we are all the same, all legitimate targets.'

'Exactly.' Preston knew she could rely on Marshall, it was why she had picked him for the team in the first place. 'Now, does anyone have any other ideas?'

'We could combine teams, Ma'am.' Marshall looked around the room as he spoke. He knew at least half the people there had soft areas, just one or two targets to watch and resources to do their work for them.

'How do you mean, Marshall?'

'We look at where the greatest threats are. I'd suggest Newbury is one and London another. Then we look at any areas where there is minimal threat. We can leave a skeletal force in those areas, just enough to keep tabs on the targets there, and move the rest into the high risk areas.'

'It's an idea,' Preston scratched her head as she thought it through. Marshall was good, very good.

'Okay, I like that. Anyone got any other ideas?'

'I guess Marshall would consider my area to be a lower risk area seeing as we've only currently got three targets in the area, but I don't know how anyone could say they are in any less danger than anyone else right now.' Langton hated the idea of having to relocate at short notice. He also hated the idea that he might be placing himself and some of his team in greater danger than they had been before.

'Well, Ma'am,' Marshall intervened, 'I'd have to say the Newbury lot are the greatest threat at the moment. We know from the last few reports, and from what happened last night, that this group of five are planning something. Okay, we don't know what, but they are up to something. Speaking for my own region, South London, I'd have to say the targets there are also gearing up for something. Hopefully I'll know more about that later today. All I can say for sure is there's a South London jeweller who has connections with a couple of targets. This jeweller is not who he says he is.

I found that out yesterday, but it's too early to say what his connections are, or where his loyalties lie, but I'm pretty sure the targets in my area are preparing for something. If anyone wants my opinion I'd say the targets in the South are getting ready for some kind of activity.'

'I agree, Marshall, there's definitely been a shift in activity in the Southern regions over the past few days. Okay, here's what we are going to do. I want each of you to go back to your areas and work out the minimum configuration you need to maintain an effective watch on your designated targets. Then I want you to work out what surplus resources you have at your disposal. Ignore the local cops and people like that. You can use them to shore up your teams for the kind of operations they can help you with. I want to know how many people in your actual teams are spare right now. When you have that information, I want to see your figures. By the end of today, please. I will talk to each of you this evening and issue a new plan sometime early tomorrow. If there are any questions ...' her voice trailed off.

There was a pause of some fifteen seconds. Langton and one other clearly felt ruffled by the demands being placed on them. Langton went red in the face at the thought of reassigning his team and even having to do some work of his own. Alan Green was sitting next to him and muttered something about relocation expenses. Certainly, Green did not want to be relocated. Though he was already in the South of England, his Hampshire based team were only watching two 'A' listed targets. Green was happy with his assignments, they gave him time for the massages he had grown to love and he did not want to be isolated from the very attentive Christine Matthews. Green most definitely did not relish the thought of being relocated, even the short distance to Newbury or South London. He would do his utmost to make his patch look important, to beef up the significance of the two targets he was already assigned to. He would, if necessary, fabricate some kind of activity, just so long as he could avoid relocation.

'Very well, I won't detain you any longer. I expect those reports to be e-mailed to me by five this afternoon. Marshall, if I could just have a private word,' Preston stood as she spoke, the meeting over.

It took just a couple of minutes for her office to empty. She turned, closed the door and looked out of the window as she walked back to her desk. The London Eye was still turning, almost imperceptibly slowly.

'Thanks for your support, Travis,' she said when she'd sat down.

'That's okay. I just said what I thought needed to be said.'

'I know you did. I'm going to get a hard time over this from Langton and Green, aren't I?'

'Langton is just biding his time until he can retire. He's been involved in security things for twenty years and has basically had enough. I'd suggest you leave him where he is and move some of his team away. It might be worth getting him to call his team together and then you go and talk to them personally. As for Green, he's just a lazy sod.'

'He's also becoming a liability, Travis.' Preston shoved the folder across the desk. 'This is confidential by the way.'

'Of course,' Marshall opened the folder, read the contents quickly and passed it back across the desk.

'Do we know who she is?'

'She's a prostitute, a high class one but still a prostitute. She got picked up about a month ago and Green's mobile number was in her diary. The police have only just passed the information along. It took them three weeks to find out who he was and who he worked for. That's when the wheels started turning.'

'Is it enough to kick him out?'

'Most certainly it is. Technically he's a liability and a security risk. But the fact is, Travis, we've already had someone chat to the woman and she hasn't a clue who Green is, or most of her other clients for that matter. She claims she just has the client's first name and a number. She rings them when she's quiet to see if they want to avail themselves of her services. In reality I think Green has been lucky this time.' Preston looked evenly at Marshall as she spoke.

'Yeah, I guess so. Still, you will have to talk to him won't you? Show him the error of his ways and make him promise not to do it again.'

'Yes, I think that's all that is needed this time, unless anything else comes to light.'

'You mean he might have been daft enough to be doing it with more than one of them?' Marshall sounded annoyed that a trusted member of the team could so flagrantly break the rules.

'Who knows, Travis, who knows? I know you're up to your eyes in it at the moment but I've told Harding he can contact you if he needs any help or advice.'

'Thanks for letting me know, Ma'am. I don't know Harding well but he seemed a capable chap from what Keeley told me once.'

'Yes, he is, very capable, but if this South of England theory holds any water, you and he might have to pool resources in the near future so I thought it wise to have the communication channels already opened so to speak.'

'Very good, Ma'am, now is there anything else?'

'Two final things, Travis. Firstly I don't need a report from you on resources. I've told Harding the same. You're both in the active zone so I don't want to waste your time.'

'Thank you, Ma'am.'

'Secondly, if you're not busy this evening, I know a rather good restaurant by the river if you fancy dinner.'

'As it happens, I'm not busy this evening, Ma'am.'

'Excellent, in that case I'll pick you up from your flat at about eight thirty.'

'Yes, Ma'am, what are we celebrating?'

'Us, Travis, us, and for the record, I do have a name which I'd prefer you use when we're on our own – it's Selena.'

'Yes Ma'am, I mean, Selena. Eight thirty it is then.'

'Well, Travis, you'd better go and do whatever you have to do.' He'd made no fuss, no protestations at being busy. It had all gone very smoothly. Preston smiled to herself as Marshall closed the door softly behind him. He walked away from the building still wondering why his boss would want to take him out for dinner, especially now things looked like they were about to happen.

**

Daniel Newton started out early. He checked the white van before he left the guest house he had been staying at and found everything to be in order. He'd made the same journey on several occasions and knew at this time of year the heat of the middle of the day would make driving intolerable, especially as his van didn't have air conditioning. For two summers he'd been promising himself a new van, a modern one with air conditioning and as many gadgets as his budget would allow.

The roads were dusty. They always were at this time of year. The early start meant Newton was well into the countryside before the locals started their daily routines. He always allowed himself two full days to cross the mainland of Turkey, with hopes he would be able to catch a crossing across the Bosporus before the night fell on the second day. He then allowed himself three more days to reach Munich, with the intervening nights being spent in Romania and Hungary. From Munich it was a day's journey through Germany to a rather nice GastHaus he knew on the German French border and then on the final day he'd reach Calais, cross to Dover round about lunchtime and make his destination early that evening. All told, Newton knew he faced the next seven days on the road, seven days and six nights meeting up with his old friends, some older than others.

He had plans for a fiery-tempered redhead in Istanbul, if he could make the journey in time. That was for the next day. For tonight he had hopes for a dark-haired thirty-something who lived on the outskirts of Konya. Newton had these compensations lined up all along his route, ensuring his evenings were never filled with dull moments. He'd spoken to Rebeka on the phone the previous evening and she had promised him a comfortable bed in her apartment on the outskirts of Konya. It helped Newton concentrate on the journey ahead of him, a journey through the spectacular mountains of southern Turkey.

He passed through Adana at eleven o'clock and decided to take an early break for lunch. On the road to Konya he took the turning to Tarsus and in a few minutes came across the tranquil lake he had discovered on a journey the previous year. The boats were out on the lake now and Newton found a sheltered spot under a tree where he could watch them. He popped a can of Cola and sipped it slowly. The temperature was already in the nineties and the driver's compartment of the van was beginning to feel very hot indeed. The window was already wound down so Newton could take advantage of the cooling breeze when he was driving. Now he rested his elbow on the window ledge and watched the boats floating gently on the water. His memories took him back to the beautiful Sheera and their evenings of passion just passed. Newton already wanted to return to her. He wondered how long the gap would be this time and hoped it would be no more than two months.

After half an hour, Newton started the engine again. His break was over and he still had a long way to go. The mountain section of the day's driving was the slowest. The winding road became little more than a track at times and on more than one occasion Newton had to crawl behind a local lorry making its deliveries.

Once over the mountains the journey progressed more quickly. Newton was in good spirits and stopped to take a further break at two o'clock. The heat was overwhelming now and Newton decided to head for the shelter of a small wooded area he knew. He'd wait there until the heat of the day had passed and then set out on the final hundred miles to Konya. He'd be there early evening, have a cool bath, sample some good home cooking and enjoy the evening with the exquisite Rebeka.

***

Roger Harding had a miserable day ahead of him. He'd been up half the night, ever since news of Keeley had broken. Preston had spoken to him at some unearthly hour and now he faced his first day in charge of the team. Being an efficient man and wanting to impress, Harding had been over to Keeley's flat, broken in, picked up the relevant folders and other paperwork and then spent the next four hours familiarising himself with the team assignments, supplementing his existing knowledge. He read the copies of the reports Keeley had sent to Preston and at six o'clock in the morning he phoned her back with a strategy. The approval had been given almost instantly and now, at ten o'clock in the morning, Harding had assembled the team in the inauspicious office on the outskirts of Newbury.

'Thanks for coming at such short notice,' he began by addressing the seven. 'For those of you that don't know, Brian Keeley was killed last night by a sniper.'

There were several gasps around the room but Harding was sure everyone already knew why the meeting had been called.

'Now, for whatever reason, I've been put in charge of this area which is why we're here today. Brian's funeral will be in four days' time and will be a small family affair. For those of you who are interested in attending please ask me in a couple of days for the details. Right, to business. Last night's operations were a shambles. Between us,' and Harding felt guilty as he spoke, 'we managed to lose three of our prime targets. Fortunately we know where they went, Café Richard, and who they met. What we don't know is what they talked about, other than the café owner thinks they are planning something for the near future. There was talk of 'Justice and Liberty' and the word 'Jihad' was mentioned a number of times. Most of the time the group talked in Greek, or so the owner said when he was interviewed after the shooting. Actually it was probably an Arabic dialect. Now, without knowing what they talked about we have to take the words the owner did understand as some kind of threat. So, I want extra vigilance and we must be sure we don't lose our targets again.'

'But, Roger,' Steve started, 'we're so damned dependent on the locals to provide cover, and they don't have the training.'

'I know, Steve, but we have to do our best. We're sitting on a real hot bed here. For whatever reason these five people have all settled down here and it's our job to keep an eye on things, with or without the help of the local forces. Ultimately we take responsibility for any lapses in security.'

'Yeah, I know, but it sure would be less complicated if these guys were actually trained in what they're being asked to do. I mean, Brian was with a rookie last night for God's sake.'

'I know, and it would have made no difference, even if he'd been with one of us. The recordings show Keeley had already instructed him to follow the targets and in particular Al'Makir, so Fretton was not at fault, he was just following orders. I don't think it would have made a blind bit of difference if we'd had the whole team there, it was our operational procedures that were at fault.'

'So, what are we going to do?' John didn't particularly like Harding, a feeling that was mutual.

110

'For a start, I've asked for more trained personnel, in particular armed response personnel, to be made available to us. That's going to take about forty eight hours to put into place. We will also have to move in some people from the quieter areas. The boss has that in hand today. Next, there will be no more spontaneous contact. We follow the procedures to the letter and we make damn sure things are secure before we make a move. The procedures might not have saved Brian but they would have made it possible for us to have captured or eliminated the sniper. The clean-up team are still working on that, so the area around Café Richard is strictly off limits for the next forty eight hours, which brings me to another point. We know the five main targets were heading towards Newbury at the time. Fretton was following them. That means there is a sixth member, the killer, someone we know nothing about. We need to find this guy and quickly, before he takes another pop at one of us.'

'Where do you want us to start?' Steve spoke softly as if the reality of the events of the past twelve hours was beginning to sink in.

'Primarily we keep hard on the backs of the five prime targets. It's likely they'll be contacting the sixth person at some point. We already have wires in their houses, what we need to do now is up the surveillance on them and keep a record of everyone they meet. Also, David and Bob, I want you to go over the contact reports for the last couple of months and see if there's anything we might have missed before?'

'Sure, Roger,' Bob replied. 'When do you want that done?'

'Today. I'll help you get started after this meeting. Okay, one more assignment and that's for you, Gary. We really need to know all we can about Braddock Holdings. Get your team to redouble their efforts, see if you can find out anything more. What would be really useful are the names of the guys behind it. If they are our

111

existing targets we need to know because it means they've got far greater funding than we'd previously supposed. If Braddock isn't linked to these guys we need to know who it is linked to and what they are about.'

'Sure, Roger, I've already got three shifts working on the information. We're basically being held up by the Bahamas and offshore establishments, but we'll crack them somehow.'

'Okay, gentlemen, we all know what we're up against. Unless there's any other business I suggest we get back to the task in hand.'

The meeting broke up and the team dispersed. Bob and John waited until the last of the team had gone before they accompanied Roger Harding into the back office. The folders containing the months of surveillance reports, photographs and miscellaneous documents, receipts and orders were piled high, having long since outgrown the filing cabinet next to the pile.

John looked at the pile with a degree of astonishment.

'I suppose we'd best get started.'

CHAPTER NINE

The sun streamed into the living room at Simon Hart's mansion. He'd been awake for some hours, excited by the prospect of what lay ahead and though he was still dressed in his bathrobe he'd already started work. He'd checked his emails and read the major items of news. He wondered exactly what the press would be printing just over a week from then.

Hart had checked on the flights to Munich, both from London and Ankara and had made all the reservations in accordance with the plans he'd made the previous day. He looked out of the window onto the croquet lawn, the tennis court and the gardens beyond and smiled. It was a warm day, the perfect day to start the ball rolling.

Hart sat back in his favourite armchair, sipped the cup of hot tea he'd poured a few minutes previously and picked up the newspaper again. He opened it at the ninth page and perused the article concerning the shooting in Newbury the previous night. The police had put it out that they were looking for a gangland killer and had even issued a reasonably detailed description of the supposed attacker. There were few factual details in the report, a sure sign, Hart thought, that there was something not quite right about the shooting, something the authorities wanted to keep hidden. He picked up the phone.

'Andy, hi it's Simon, how are you?' Andy McKinter was an old acquaintance of Hart's, the kind of acquaintance who dealt with the darker side of life.

'Fine, how are you?' If McKinter was surprised to receive a call from Simon Hart at this time of the day, it didn't show in the tone of his voice.

'Actually I'm feeling very well at the moment. Say, are you up to speed on what's happening in the Newbury area?'

'Are we talking about the shooting last night?'

'Yeah, I was just wondering if there was any truth in the gangland theory.'

'Not a chance, Simon. Newbury isn't exactly what I'd really call gangland territory. Yes there are pockets of trouble, every town or city has them, but it's not what I'd consider to be real gangland territory.'

'What's the word on the street then?'

'I don't know. All I can tell you is some government body or other had a half-mile area sealed off within a couple of minutes of it happening. Other than that I haven't heard anything and I don't expect to either. If it's that important to seal off the whole area then you can be pretty sure nothing will leak out.'

'You're probably right. So, do you think it was a terrorist related incident?'

'It could be, but equally it could just have been a revenge attack. If I hear anything more I'll let you know.'

'Thanks, Andy. Now, I'm going abroad for a few days the day after tomorrow so when I get back I'll get back in touch with you.'

'Okay, Simon. Are you going anywhere nice?'

'Only Munich, I've got a spot of business to attend to.'

'I see, have a good time.'

'I will and thanks, Andy.' Hart replaced the receiver. If McKinter had not received any word from the lowlifes on the street then it wasn't gangland based. That still left a lot of possibilities but Hart reckoned the fabrication in the press indicated it was more sinister than the authorities wanted people to believe. Hart smiled again as he wondered what cover up stories would be printed in the days ahead.

***

After leaving Preston's office, Marshall travelled south. He'd been sitting on a piece of information he'd received over five weeks previously and decided today was the right time to check it out. The information he'd received related to a female by the name of Helen Darling. She was in her thirties and had a history of working in computers. Marshall had discovered that through his initial enquiries. The piece of information that had caught his interest was the fact she'd had contact with one of ATRIUM's targets on more than one occasion. There would probably be a logical reason for the contact but Marshall had to check it out.

The surveillance team in Horsham had kept tabs on the woman for the past five weeks. She'd met with Assan Hirala on four separate occasions, all of them in pubs and all the meetings had lasted just a few minutes. Hirala was on the 'B' list of targets. He wasn't considered a huge danger to security in his own right, but was known to associate with other targets. He was also known to have previously been active abroad and to have passed through the Afghan training camps. He was, in terrorist terms, small fry, expendable. It was believed that he had been conditioned to act without question when given orders and he was the kind of product of such training who believed it was noble to die for the cause. He was regarded as being a fanatic and he was being watched. Since her contact with him on the first occasion, Helen Darling had also been watched, not by the ATRIUM team but the local police. Marshall had read their reports and felt uneasy. The woman needed the ATRIUM touch, as he liked to call it.

Marshall drove carefully down to Dorking and picked up the Horsham road. Forty minutes later he'd found the woman's home. He knew she'd be at work. He knew the place where she worked, the time she arrived there that morning and the colour of the clothes she was wearing. He knew what car she drove and the mileage on the clock. The phone call he'd made just after leaving Preston's office had given him all this and alerted the watchers in Horsham that Marshall was on his way. They'd give him cover and at the same time make sure his investigation went unhindered. If necessary, they could delay Darling on her way home that evening, though Marshall intended to be long gone by then.

The house was detached with a small garden. It had single–glazed windows that looked like they needed a coat of paint. The driveway was empty and the integral garage suggested there would be a door between the garage and hall.

Marshall walked up the driveway and rang the doorbell twice. As expected, there was no answer. He walked across to the garage door and tested it. It was locked but Marshall took only ten seconds with something that looked a bit like a toothpick to unlock it. The door swung open and a few seconds later Marshall pulled it closed behind him. The door was where he'd reckoned it would be and it was not locked. Marshall smiled to himself as the door opened softly.

Marshall gained access to the house proper and began a meticulous search of the premises. The kitchen was tidy, just a dirty plate and cup from breakfast sitting on the sink drainer. The pile of papers on the shelf comprised mainly of bills. There were a couple of letters that were of no consequence and some flyers that had been posted through the door at some point. Marshall made sure he replaced the pile of documents exactly where he had found them before starting on the lounge.

The pictures on the mantelpiece were presumably family, probably the woman's elderly relatives. The rest of the room yielded nothing of interest so Marshall looked in the cupboard under the stairs. It contained a vacuum cleaner, some old boots, a tap for bleeding radiators and a few other items that Marshall had expected to find. He closed the half-size door and looked briefly at the pile of post lying on the front door mat. Marshall recognised the familiar credit card statement, a couple of items of junk mail and a handwritten pink envelope that looked like it contained a card of some description. Marshall already knew the woman's birthday was less than a week away so the pink envelope did not excite him.

The house contained three bedrooms. The first one Marshall examined was clearly a guest room. The two single beds were neatly made up and the room contained a wardrobe, chest of drawers and two bedside tables. The drawers of the table and the chest were empty and the wardrobe contained a couple of spare pillows, a couple of blankets and three winter coats on hangers.

Marshall proceeded to the master bedroom and found what he was looking for. The woman's passport was in the bottom of the underwear drawer on the right hand side of her dressing table. The passport was three years old, had no visa entries and looked virtually unused. On top of the passport was the woman's driving licence, inserted in a plastic wallet. Both items confirmed her name, age and address, all things Marshall already knew. Underneath the passport was a neatly folded payslip made out to the woman, dated a couple of months previously and bearing the name of Braddock Holdings. Marshall's interest was immediately aroused. The name was familiar from something Preston had said that morning. The gross payment was just over eight thousand pounds. The entries on the slip for tax and insurance were all set to zero. Carefully, Marshall laid it out on the top of the dressing table and photographed it. Payment had been made by BACS transfer so Marshall hoped the SB4 team would be able to trace the transaction back to its origins.

Having taken three pictures to be sure, Marshall refolded the document and returned it to the underwear drawer. He checked the other drawers and under the mattress but found nothing of further interest. The final room was clearly used as Darling's study. It contained shelves of books on various subjects and boxes containing ornaments still wrapped in newspaper and a hundred other objects. It would have taken Marshall a couple of days to complete an inventory of them all, a proposition which did not appeal to him.

He closed the door and took out his mobile phone.

'Preston,' the reply was short and the woman sounded as if she was busy.

'Hi, it's Marshall. I've found a link to Braddock Holdings.' He went on to describe where he was and what he'd found. 'Basically, Ma'am I'd like her pulled in for questioning.'

'Why?'

'Well, there's Braddock Holdings for a start and also the fact we have her on camera talking to a 'B' list target.'

'That doesn't give us grounds for arrest.'

'I know it doesn't. I was hoping more to go down the route of her helping with enquiries for now. I'm not interested in her, per se, but her contacts could prove to be of interest.'

'And if she doesn't co-operate and simply goes back to those contacts it will put them even more on their guard than they already are thanks to Keeley's incident.'

'Yes, Ma'am,' Marshall was defeated and knew it.

'You can still get SB4 to trace the transaction, though. It might give them something to work on.' Preston knew Marshall well and she sympathised with his desire to pull the woman in for questioning. She also knew it would break the rules and a half-decent solicitor would have her released before they'd even asked her for her date of birth. It was the rule and for now the rules had to be obeyed.

'I'll give Harding a ring and let him get his chap onto it.'

'See you later, Marshall.' Preston hung up and left Marshall to make good his exit from the house. An hour later Marshall was at home, the Polaroid pictures in his hand, relaying the information on the payslip to Harding. It took Harding half an hour to get through to Peterson, who let out a soft 'Yes' when Harding relayed the information Marshall had given him. Within five minutes of putting down the phone to Harding, Peterson had a team of three sitting in his office awaiting instructions.

***

The nerve centre of SB4 was a building that looked like a warehouse. The outside of the building had the appearance of coarsely corrugated metal, painted in a dark grey. The walls had a series of windows all glazed with dark glass, and there was a double entrance door, again in darkened glass. The window, door and roof trims were painted in bright yellow. To the casual passer-by the use of the building would have remained a total mystery. Just inside the main doors was a small, aluminium-coloured plaque bearing the inscription 'SB4 HMG'.

Beyond the outer doors were inner ones, leading to a small lobby. The reception desk was manned by an armed guard in military uniform. Security was clearly important. The door leading into the building proper was solid metal, actually as strong as a safe door, alarmed and protected by a system that required each user to swipe a card and then place a finger on a pad for the fingerprint to be checked against the information stored on a database.

The office beyond the security screen was a hive of activity. Thirty people worked in the building at any one time and the various offices and work areas contained a mass of electronic equipment. In one corner of the office area was a partitioned office with accommodation for four people. There were four computer screens, a mass of wires and other devices hooked up along one wall. To one side was a desk and behind the desk sat Gary Peterson. In front of him sat three men, all younger than Peterson, all having passed the most stringent of security clearance procedures. Peterson looked out at his protégés and smiled.

'Gentlemen, we have a mission. You have all been involved in the investigation of the company called Braddock Holdings. We, for reasons I can't divulge, have now been asked to urgently locate those who run that company. Now, I know,' Peterson continued quickly before anyone had time to protest, 'that we've been down this route before and got nowhere and that the company is offshore and technically hidden but it is of very great importance we do our best. This request comes from the top so it will do us all a lot of good to come up with the answers. I want you, Simmonds and Rawlings, to go back over all the old transactions and data we've collated. Harrison, I want you to try pushing again on the various banks that Braddock has accounts with.'

'Yes, guv,' Harrison was young, enthusiastic and had a strong sense of duty about him.

'Okay, we have one new piece of information to put into the melting pot. She's a female by the name of Darling, Helen Darling. One of my contacts has discovered she has a payslip originating from Braddock Holdings.' Peterson waived three sheets of photocopied typescript in the direction of the three men sitting opposite him. 'The details of the account are here. I want you, Harrison, to check this woman's account out. Go back to the point where Braddock was formed and see if you can find out how many payments she's received.'

'Yes, guv,' Harrison took a copy of the typescript and examined it. 'It shouldn't take too long. If she's involved, why don't they just pull her in on the anti-terrorism act, or something?'

'Because they have no evidence she's involved with anything other than a casual contact with a known suspect. Also, they don't know what this payment was for. She may be an innocent outsider who simply provided some kind of service. We need to find out and frankly, at the moment, a decent brief would get her released before they got her to give her middle name.

That being the case, if she's involved, she'd put the targets on their guard. If we're right in what we think, that would put Braddock Holdings on guard and make our job even more complicated. So, for the next forty eight hours or so, the powers that be don't want her touched.'

'Yes, guv, is there anything else?'

'No, not for now. I want you all to let me know the minute anything comes to light. I'll be doing some checks on some of the other information we've sifted in the past. Can we meet back here tomorrow at one o'clock for a review on what we've achieved?'

'Guv,' the men responded one by one. The meeting broke up and the team left the office for their desks. Peterson sat alone, looking at the blank walls of his partitioned office and the array of electronic equipment mounted on the wall opposite his desk. He stood, walked over to one of the consoles and started typing.

***

It was approaching eight thirty in the evening and Marshall sat waiting for the knock on the door of his flat. He'd not been asked out for dinner by Preston before though they had taken lunch together on a couple of occasions. Marshall had spent some time wondering what Preston's motive was, what she was going to ask of him. For a wild moment he wondered if she had other intentions. He dismissed the idea as preposterous and got back to the work he was involved with.

Preston found the flat, knocked three times on the door and indicated they were already running late. Marshall followed her back to the car, a dark-blue, mid-range BMW and sat in the passenger seat while Preston made her way back onto the main road.

'How has today gone?' Preston broke the silence once they were on the main road.

'Not too bad. I still think there's more to Darling than we realise at the moment and I've relayed the account information to Harding. I expect he's passed it on to his chap at SB4, so we may get some news in a day or two.'

'As I said, I don't want to pull her in until we're certain we have a connection she can't wriggle away from.'

'Yeah, I know, but all the same Ma'am,' he was immediately interrupted.

'Selena, please, we're not in the office now.'

'Sorry, Selena, force of habit,' Marshall smiled. 'Where was I, oh yes, whatever she did for Braddock Holdings she got paid eight grand for over a period of a month, so it must have been valuable to them.'

'Yes it must have been, or she might have been doing work for someone else and they got Braddock to pay for it.'

'True, but if that's the case I can't believe SB4 haven't picked up on it before now.'

'Unless they missed it simply because they weren't looking in the right direction. In which case your find could be of great interest to them.' Preston paused for a moment before continuing. 'Right, Travis, we have a problem now that Keeley's dead, what with Green's liability to security and Langton's indifference. I've been chewing things over, and it's not what this evening is about, but I want to reorganise the group. I want to cut out the dross, the baggage, or whatever you call it and tighten things up. We're sitting around waiting for something to happen and quite frankly, in one or two areas of our network, something could happen before we were even aware of it and that would be bad news for all of us. So, if you're agreeable, I'd like to split the network into three areas, South, Midlands and North.'

'It's your call of course but yes, that would make sense. Who do you have in mind?'

'I thought about Amanda Whiting for the North. She and Mark Winters both come from there so they know the area and also they make a good team. For the Midlands I was thinking about Richard Fairmile and put

Phil Langton in with him. That would prevent us having to relocate Langton too far. For the South I was thinking about you and getting Roger Harding in alongside if only because he knows what Keeley was doing.'

'Sounds pretty much what people would expect. What are you going to do with the others?'

'I'm going to have a chat with Green tomorrow afternoon. I want to find out just what kind of a risk he is but provisionally I'm going to make him a spare resource for your area.'

'Thanks,' Marshall sounded less than pleased with the idea. Alan Green was a loner, like Marshall, and the thought of having to keep an eye on him for security reasons did not appeal. Still, Preston was in charge so it was her decision.

'Fern Brooks is my only real worry. I don't quite know what to do with her.'

'Well, why not give her the Welsh area on her own. We all know it's quiet there, but it's a big patch and she will need a team of half a dozen working directly for her.'

'I knew you'd have the answer. Thanks, Travis, it should suit her well.'

'While we're talking about reorganising, can I mention a concern about the sub-team sizes?' Marshall had been looking through the various reports that had been circulated.

'Sure, what is it?'

'Well, whilst I consider the eight people who work directly for me to be about right, and Harding has about half a dozen I seem to recall, I can't understand why Langton and Green had teams of fifteen and eighteen reporting to them. It all seems a bit excessive.'

'A fair comment, but what do you recommend we do with them?'

Well, if Langton is staying pretty much in the same area, I'd suggest his team is limited to ten and the rest are relocated to the South. We're going to need some extra manpower if the Newbury lot or the lot I'm watching get active. As for Green's team, I don't know what to suggest. It's probably best to see what your meeting with him turns up.'

'I agree. Right, we've arrived. Hope you don't mind but the restaurant I wanted to go to was booked so I thought we'd try here. I hope you like French.'

For a moment Marshall paused before he worked out what she had said.

'French is fine by me. So, is that the business over with?'

'Not quite. I'll tell you more once we've ordered.'

Marshall opened the door to the restaurant and allowed Preston to lead the way indoors. They were fussed over, coats taken from them and then they were shown to their table, a table that was set to one side of the main part of the restaurant, affording them a degree of privacy. They ordered drinks and scanned the menu while they waited. Finally the order was placed and Preston continued.

'The world is a dangerous place, Travis. When they killed the original leader of al-Qaeda the politicians told everyone it would make the world safer but it hasn't. All it's done is to drive the fanatics and the members of the networks underground. Now, instead of having a few central places to watch, each of these groups is capable of acting on its own. They've got smarter, act more intuitively and they are getting progressively more dangerous. For example, take this new plant we've discovered in Syria. Heaven only knows what it's for and it might be perfectly legitimate, but it could equally be highly dangerous. We just don't know any more because the world has changed. Any one of our sleeping targets could wake up tomorrow and decide it's the day to create mayhem on the mainland or elsewhere. They could even hop on a boat or come in via the tunnel and we'd probably not know until it is too late. We don't know what resources they have or when they plan to activate them. Hell, we don't even know what weapons they have access to, and these days they may well be able to get hold of a lot more than guns and bomb making materials. Not only that but our biggest threat now probably isn't from the known targets. It's changed, Travis, because now we have to worry about the have-a-go type who we know nothing about. Add to that we have to worry about organisations like Braddock. And we don't know how many organisations like Braddock are out there or what they are involved in. We have to worry about them because they could be a threat, not because we actually know they are a threat.'

'I agree, but where is this leading?' Marshall had listened carefully to every word and agreed with the woman he sat opposite.

'It's leading to the fact that we spend all our time thinking the worst, worrying about what might happen and not actually living. Do you understand what I am saying, Travis?' She smiled at him as she spoke.

'I think so Ma'am, I mean, Selena. You want to live a little before it's too late.'

'Exactly, and I want to start doing that tonight with someone I can trust, someone I don't have to worry over spilling the beans, someone who knows the Official Secrets Act as well as I do, someone who knows the implications if they get caught.'

'Sorry, you've lost me, Selena.'

'Damn it, Travis, I've been your boss for nearly a year now and you have no idea?' She raised her voice slightly as if hurt.

'No idea about what?' Marshall sounded confused.

'I fancy you, you daft man. I've fancied you since the night I accompanied you on the Sidral surveillance operation, the night when you pushed me out of the way of the van that was about to run me over. Now do you understand?'

'You want to start something with me, something romantic?' Marshall had changed to sounding flattered.

'Yes, if you're willing. God knows how long we can keep it under wraps, or whether it's practicable, or what will happen, but I fancy you rotten and would like to give it a try.'

'Well, I have to confess I've often thought about you and yes, I've fancied you, but I never thought anything would come of it. Okay, if you're game, so am I, but we will have to be very careful.'

'We must absolutely and definitely be very careful.' She giggled like a young girl who was plotting something very naughty indeed. 'No-one must get a whiff of it or we're both finished. The waiter's coming so let's change the subject.' She smiled and blew Marshall a swift kiss. While the waiter placed the starter course in front of them a million thoughts flashed through Marshall's mind. Was this really happening? How far would it go? How far could it go? He'd find out later on.

CHAPTER TEN

Friday 26th June

The early morning sun penetrated Marshall's bedroom. He'd slept the best sleep he'd had in several months. Beside him the naked body of Selena Preston stirred. She opened a bleary eye and raked her fingers affectionately down Marshall's back.

'Good morning,' she whispered. 'Did you sleep well?'

'Yes, did you?'

'Yes, what time is it?'

Marshall looked at his bedside clock.

'Half past six.' He groaned, knowing he had another hour before he needed to rise.

'I must be going, Travis. I've got to get home and change before heading off to see Langton and his team.' As she spoke she rose from the bed and started to dress. She was, thought Marshall, a very attractive woman and one who had completely surprised him. She was soft to touch unlike the hard exterior she portrayed in the office. She was warm, sensuous and athletic in bed and she had completely exhausted him before they had rolled over and fallen asleep. It had been the best six hours sleep he'd ever had and despite the early hour, he felt refreshed.

Marshall watched the woman dress for a minute and then asked her, 'Do you want coffee or anything before you go?'

'Better not, Travis, but thanks for asking. Are you happy to do this again sometime? I mean, you're okay about things, aren't you? You didn't think it was too much like me pulling rank, did you?'

She'd been dominant and persuasive the previous evening but Marshall had been more than pleased to cooperate with her demands.

'No, everything was fine. Actually, it was bloody good. My only concern is keeping it under wraps.'

'Yeah, but it's not a problem if we're careful and watch how we are when others are around us, others who already know us, that is.'

'Yeah, I suppose so. So, when do you want to meet up again?'

'It's probably a good idea to leave it a couple of days. Today's Friday so what about meeting up on Sunday?' Preston was almost dressed.

'Yeah, Sunday's okay for me. What do you fancy doing?'

'How about I come over to you for the evening again?'

'That sounds good to me.'

'I'll come over about eight then, if that's okay?'

'That's fine, now are you sure I can't get you anything?'

'No, I'd best be on my way.' Preston reached over the bed and kissed Marshall on his cheek before letting herself out of the flat. It was going to be a difficult day but the night before gave Preston a new sense of purpose and belief in herself.

Three hours later Preston arrived at Langton's office. Like the others, it was functional in nature as most of the work involved being out of the office. The rush hour into Birmingham had started by the time Preston had travelled up from London and the traffic was heavy for the last few miles. Edgbaston was an area Preston knew quite well, having dated someone from the University when she'd been a student. Preston had spent many weekends on campus and roaming around the various Halls of Residence, before they had finally split up when she'd discovered what he did while she was away at her own college. In Preston's mind, infidelity led to untrustworthiness which in turn meant it was a bad idea for her to remain involved. She came off the motorway at Northfield, and headed towards Selly Oak before turning just past the University and heading for Edgbaston.

Langton's office was just on the borders between Edgbaston and Harborne. Preston parked in a side road and walked into the building. It looked like a house that had been converted for business use and Preston noticed the small, aluminium plaque by the door with the initials ATRIUM etched into it. She pushed the door open and identified herself to the security guard at the desk. He ushered her up the stairs where the two main offices were.

'Phil, good morning,' she said on entering his private, smaller, office.

'Good morning, Ma'am. I've got the team next door as requested.'

'Good, but I'd like a quick word with you first. I've read the report you sent me on staffing levels and operations. It strikes me that there isn't much going on here at the moment.'

'No, but it could flare up at any time.'

'Yes, yes, I know, but listen, Phil, hear me out. I'm not proposing to close this place down for the moment. To do that would be irresponsible, just in case, as you say, something did flare up. What I'm going to do is some resource manipulation. I'm teaming you and Fairmile up to cover the whole of the Midlands, broadly from Oxford up to Manchester. Now, Fairmile already has the North end of it and a team of eight working for him and you have fifteen working for you. I simply can't justify having twenty three operatives sitting on their hands at the moment, so I'm going to have to reassign some of your team. I'm merging the Southern teams of Marshall and Harding into a cohesive force which should do well seeing as it's Newbury and South London that are showing signs of some activity at the moment. I want five of your team relocated to the Newbury area with effect from the end of next week. I'll leave it up to you as to who goes.'

'But, they all have families and they are all on assignments at the moment,' Langton protested.

'I know, so pick the ones already in the South of your patch. They can commute to Newbury and the area for a while, it's not that far. The chances are it will only be for a month or so anyway, and if things pick up round here you can have them back.'

'I see, Ma'am, but the chaps aren't going to take it very well, I don't think.'

Preston thought they probably wouldn't take the news at all well, especially as Langton had no doubt been priming them for the eventuality.

'Okay,' she said, 'I'd better talk to the team.'

Langton led her into the adjoining office and introduced her for the sake of those who'd not met her before. Preston spent twenty minutes carefully outlining the structure of ATRIUM, the current resource levels and the problems they were experiencing. Then she moved on to the reassignment issues. As expected, there were protests but Preston managed to handle most of the questions with her usual professional aplomb. Finally she told the team that Langton would be talking things over with each of them and the decision on who to reassign would be his as the team leader. She fielded questions for a further ten minutes and then made her apologies. Langton had ten days to organise the changes.

***

Dieter Zussman looked more worried than usual as he stood nervously behind the counter of his Reigate shop. It had been a quiet morning. Friday's always were, though the lunch period usually picked up. The man standing at the counter was a ditherer, or at least that was the way Zussman perceived him. In fact, Travis Marshall was acting the part with commensurate ease.

'It's for an office colleague who's retiring next week,' Marshall explained.

'Yes, sir,' Zussman had been told this several times now.

'Well, some of the team want to go down the traditional carriage clock route but others have asked me to be a bit more original, so I'm not quite sure what to do. You've got some nice clocks in the price range, but I was wondering whether some kind of bracelet or a watch would be a better idea.'

'Well, sir, if you are talking about a nice watch then to be quite frank with you, one hundred and forty pounds won't take you very far, certainly not into the realms of the better quality timepieces. On the other hand you could get a sterling silver bracelet, engraved with a short inscription for about that price. It really depends what your retiring colleague would appreciate.'

'Look, I hate to be a pain, but could I see the kind of bracelet the budget would allow me to buy?'

'Certainly, sir, I have some out the back. If you'll excuse me for a minute I'll just fetch them for you to look at.' Zussman didn't wait for the response. He dived into the little back office. While he was gone, Marshall scanned the shop carefully, looking for something, anything that would tell him a little bit more about Dieter Zussman. There was nothing. Zussman was out of the shop for less than two minutes. He returned carrying a dark red jewellery box, similar to the one Marshall had spotted in the Dorking branch. Zussman opened it to reveal the silver bracelet sitting neatly on the supporting cylinder.

'This one costs one hundred and twenty pounds and of course it comes with the display box. We could engrave a small inscription on the underside if sir wanted us to. If we did it at the time of purchase we'd make no extra charge for that.'

'It does look nice. How long would the engraving take?'

'If you could leave it with us for about an hour, it would be done by then.'

'That's fine. I've got a few other things to do. Yes, all right then, I'll take it. One twenty, wasn't it?'

'Yes sir.' Zussman closed the box and placed it to one side of the counter. 'Now, what inscription would you like?'

'If you have a piece of paper, I'll write it down.' Marshall took the pad that was offered him and wrote down the words, 'Alan Green, 25 years of service, Happy Retirement' and the date underneath it.

'Is that okay?' Marshall asked when he'd finished.

'Yes, sir, that is fine and a very nice gesture I think.'

'If you don't mind me saying it, Mr Zussman, but that is an extraordinary accent you have. Let me guess where it's from. I've travelled the East quite a lot. I'd say it is somewhere like Israel.'

'Why do you think that, Sir?'

'Oh, your name sounds like it belongs from Israel and there are some memories I have of that country from a few years back. Am I right?'

Zussman was thrown off guard, and coughed nervously, twice.

'No, Sir, not quite. I actually come from Syria, but it is a neighbour, so you were close.'

'Oh, I'm sorry, I'm usually quite good with accents. Syria, I haven't been to Syria. Is it a nice country to live in?'

'Not really,' Zussman sounded miserable, 'which is why I came to England some years ago.'

'Oh, I'm sorry you didn't like your homeland. Still, I guess we can't all like where we live.' Marshall wanted to change the conversation. 'Anyway, I have to get on. I didn't mean to upset you or anything it's just that I have this thing about accents and where they come from. I'll have to remember yours – Syria. Right, here's the one twenty.' Marshall handed over a wad of notes, all small denominations.

'Thank you, Sir. Actually it's quite nice to have a customer take an interest in where I come from – not many do, you know. Now, the bracelet will be ready in one hour.'

'Thanks, Mr Zussman, I'll be back for it.' Marshall turned and walked out of the door. As he closed it behind him the little bell rang somewhere inside the shop. Once outside the shop, Marshall paused to look in the window. As he did so, he saw Zussman mopping his forehead with the immaculate white handkerchief that had been tucked into the breast pocket of his suit jacket. Marshall smiled to himself. Zussman was clearly worried, troubled and nervous about something and Marshall intended to find out what it was. An hour later, Marshall returned and collected the bracelet.

***

Peterson's office was occupied by the same four men who had met there the previous day. It was one o'clock and a tray of sandwiches sat to one side of Peterson's desk. All the men held plates and were eating.

'Right, gentlemen,' Peterson started as soon as they were all settled. 'Let's have the updates. Simmonds, Rawlings, anything come to light?'

'Not really, guv. Nothing more than we'd found out before. As you know, there is a lot of money changing hands. Most of it arrives, in the accounts we've been able to crack, in small amounts, but that might not be true of the off-shore accounts we haven't been able to penetrate. Evidently there is also quite a lot of movement of cash around the accounts, or at least we think there is. We've still got quite a lot of transactions to recheck but it looks like we were pretty thorough the first time we looked at the material.' Simmonds helped himself to another sandwich having delivered the report.

'Okay, keep at it for now. Harrison, have you got any news?'

'I'll deal with Helen Darling, first off, guv. Managed to trace the transaction back to Braddock – it comes from one of their Swiss accounts so it wasn't too difficult to confirm the origin. Darling's own account is more interesting. She's been paid for the past six months by Braddock, a total of forty two thousand. Looking at the pay slip your contact sent us I'd say those payments are probably all gross of tax and National Insurance, like she is a freelancer, or contractor or something. What is also interesting is there is nothing going out of the account that would even get close to National Insurance payments, let alone payment of Income Tax. I did a credit check on the woman. She has two credit cards, both paid off every month, and over the last six months at least she's basically used them for food shopping, the odd rail ticket and at some petrol stations. Darling also has a savings account that has twenty thousand in it, slightly over, and no other debts that I could find on the system. I could find no evidence of any tax payments that would relate to the Braddock payments.'

'Interesting,' said Peterson as he made a note of the observation on his pad of paper. 'Go on.'

'I've tried pushing on the doors of the offshore banks where Braddock have accounts. Not too much luck there, I'm afraid, but I've still got a couple more to try this afternoon. It's a matter of time zones. Do you object if I use some sort of potential terrorist angle on them, guv?'

'No, if you think it helps. Our objective is to get results. So far as I'm concerned if they won't co-operate then you can do what you have to do to get the information out of them, only don't break the law.' Peterson smiled. Harrison was a good man, methodical and genial, perhaps a little too genial. The thought of Harrison using strong-man tactics amused Peterson.

'Thanks, guv. That's about it really.'

'Good work on the Darling matter. Right, gentlemen, since yesterday I've persuaded our lords and masters to let us in on what is happening. Basically they think Braddock is funding something and that something could well be linked to some terrorist groups they know about. These people are, I might add, all living peaceful lives in this country, so the anti-terrorist agencies have no legitimate reason to pull them in at this time. Our lords and masters would like us to try and trace these chaps and see if any of them have dealings with Braddock. I have a list of the suspects, their current locations and details of their residency. Most of them are on benefit of some kind so it shouldn't be too difficult to track them down. Remember, for now, we're not interested in any fraud or anything, just on a potential link to Braddock. If you come up with any fraud though, on a personal note, I'd keep a record of it. You never know what might be useful in the future.'

Peterson handed round the list of suspects. The list contained all the targets being watched in the Newbury area, together with a couple of names from Marshall and one from Langton's team. The tray of sandwiches was rapidly becoming depleted. The three men who were sat around Peterson's desk looked at the list of names, names that were meaningless to them.

'Any of these chaps got aliases?' Simmonds asked after a minute.

'Not that we're aware of and you can be sure the people who are watching them have done their homework thoroughly and checked with immigration and the other groups. You can assume these people are living, working, or whatever, using these names.'

'Okay, I'll run them through the computer this afternoon, if you want.' Simmonds did not like going over old ground. He was ambitious, a star seeker, and he sniffed the opportunity for glory with the names in front of him.

'Fair enough, but don't waste time on them. Our main concern is still with lifting the lid on Braddock Holdings.'

Simmonds was the first to leave the office. With a flurry of activity he fairly ran to his work area and started typing in the names on the list. The number crunching and searches would take time and the analysis of the results would occupy him into the evening. He didn't care, just so long as he finally got noticed and promoted so he could do more important things. He was a driven man, driven forward by the thought of success. He did the mundane work because he had to, and he was happy to go the extra mile if it meant one day he'd have his own office and a team of people doing things the way he wanted them done.

***

Daniel Newton had spent most of the day behind the wheel of his van. He'd found Rebeka the previous evening just the way he'd remembered her and they had spent a quiet evening together. She was not one of his paid hosts, rather someone he'd met on a journey a few years previously, a person he genuinely found attractive and someone who evidently liked him too. The previous evening they had been intimate as usual and she had been as gentle as she always was. It had been the perfect memory to take with him as he drove from Konya to Izmit. If anything, the day was warmer than the previous one and he'd found the dust and the heat suffocating by lunch time. The Sakarya River just south of Eskisehir offered him a welcome break in his journey. He found a shaded spot down a dirt track and pulled in. He had a view of the river and the mountains in the distance formed an attractive backdrop. Lunch was a cheese roll and some fruit washed down with tepid bottled water. Newton knew he still had one hundred and fifty miles to the crossing and he needed to be there before dusk.

On the far side of the Bosporus was Istanbul and in Istanbul, Newton had a redhead waiting for him. He'd called Korchina the previous day and she had booked his hotel room for him. She'd be along later that evening after he had bathed and dined. She sounded sultry on the phone, her dark, mysterious voice, luring Newton with promises that she would be there for him. With what he paid her, she could hardly afford to resist, though she found Newton to be a strangely nice person to be with.

136

It was late afternoon when Newton first glimpsed the shimmering waters of the Bosporus. He drove carefully down to the shore and the carport. He'd made good time and managed to fit onto the boat that was waiting at the quayside. The crossing itself was an opportunity to relax a little before the bustling city of Istanbul would demand his complete concentration. It was nearly the end of the office day in Istanbul and Newton knew the usually busy streets would be filled with the traffic of workers keen to get home, drivers who seemed to care less about their own personal safety than they did about their desire to get home early. The roads would be chaotic and dangerous. With luck, Newton thought, he'd make it to the hotel intact. At least a vehicle the size of his white van would deter all but the most reckless of drivers from getting in his way.

The Bosporus was calm and the afternoon sun helped Newton to unwind as he walked around the upper deck. He was more relaxed than he had been a couple of days earlier, when he was waiting for the boxes of jewellery to arrive. Now, as he crossed the Bosporus, he knew for certain he'd cross the borders before his paperwork expired. It was a great weight off his mind and it helped Newton to look forward to the evening of Turkish delight that awaited him.

CHAPTER ELEVEN

It was late afternoon in England and Preston had returned to her office after the meeting with Langton. She'd expected the protestations over her plans and the complaints at the time schedule, Langton was just one of those people who resented and opposed change. The drive back to her South London office had taken a couple of hours and the motorway traffic had been mercifully light. Preston had scheduled in her meeting with Green for four o'clock, so she'd had time to think, time to consider the options open to her and time to look out of the window at the London Eye in the distance.

During the course of the afternoon Harding had called her to let her know there had been little progress from SB4 but they were going to be working the entire weekend in an attempt to crack the Braddock case. The one ray of hope was the result of the enquiries into the financial affairs of Helen Darling. If nothing else, Preston had decided, they could get the Inland Revenue people onto her for tax evasion. For now, though, she wanted no action to be taken. Harding was to do nothing that might warn the woman she was being investigated. It was imperative she did not realise what was happening so she could not warn others to be on their guard. Preston had already decided that if Helen Darling was involved in something it would only be a matter of time before they found out what it was.

The military intelligence units had provided no more information on the plant in Syria, she hadn't expected them to. Any further information on that line of enquiry would need a team to be put in on the ground, something that would not happen unless a dire emergency arose. Even then it would probably mean air strikes first and to do that would require a coalition of the allies to be strengthened with some excuse to warrant the attack on the perceived enemy. The excuse simply didn't exist at the moment so the plant in the Syrian desert would remain a mystery. Selena Preston had absolutely no idea that she was already too late to stop what was being created in that plant from coming in the direction of her own country.

The knock on her door was gentle and polite.

'Come in,' Preston called out. It was five minutes to four and if nothing else, she had to give Green credit for being punctual.

'You wanted to see me, Ma'am?'

'Yes, Alan, come in and take a seat.'

Green looked nervous but clearly did not consider his private activities were about to be brought into question.

'How are you?' Preston asked him once he'd taken the seat that was waiting for him next to the desk.

'Not so bad. Frustrated like the rest of the team that nothing much is happening.'

'Yes, I see. Actually I meant, how are you getting on in Hampshire? Are you settling in okay?' It was a fair question.

'Yes, thank you, Ma'am.'

'And are you making a social life for yourself?'

'Sorry, Ma'am, I don't think I understand?'

'Well, Alan, you can't be working all the time. I just wanted to know if you'd managed to make any friends out of the office.'

'Oh, I see, well it does take time. I've joined one of those amateur dramatics societies, which has been quite interesting. They're doing a play in a couple of months' time. I'm backstage for now but I hope to get a part in the future.'

'Well, it's a start. Now, I'll be frank with you, Alan, I have a problem.'

'Ma'am?' If Green knew what was coming he didn't show it.

'The police down your way picked someone up a few weeks back, someone who had your private telephone number in her address book. Do you understand me, Alan?'

'Not Christine Matthews?'

'Who is she, Alan?'

'Just someone I know. She's part of the drama group. I give her lifts to rehearsals sometimes, seeing as she lives close by. I can remember giving her my number, but I can't see why that should be a problem.'

'Oh, well no, it wasn't this Matthews woman I was thinking about. I take it you've had her screened, as per your contract.'

'Well, not exactly, but I'm sure she's okay.'

'You can't be too careful, Alan, just as you weren't with Julie Henderson.'

Green started to grow hot and was clearly flustered by the mention of the woman's name.

'Who the hell is she?' He blustered.

'A prostitute, Alan, a high class one who charges a lot for her services, but a prostitute none-the-less.'

'And you say she has my number?'

'Yes, Alan. You know it's against the rules to use these people. They are open to being used by our targets and could easily set you up. So, who is she?'

'Just someone from an agency I've used a couple of times.' Green knew he'd been found out. The best he could hope for now was a severe reprimand. If Preston had already gone to the lengths of explaining why the rule stood, she was obviously taking the matter seriously.

'Tell me more.'

'She offers things that a man needs. I found her through a glossy magazine. Actually I found the agency, phoned them up and asked for a certain kind of escort. They took my number and passed it onto Julie. She phoned me back about an hour later, as I recall, and we set up a meeting, which was in a travel lodge room and not at my place.'

'I see, so she doesn't know where you live?'

140

'I doubt it, unless she's got round directory enquiries, which I doubt seeing as my number is unlisted.'

'I see, in which case the possible damage might have been limited. Are you still seeing her?'

'No, I haven't seen her for a couple of months now.' Preston sensed Green was lying. His forehead was glistening with perspiration.

'So does that mean you are using someone else, or have your needs changed?' Preston was still relaxed, sitting back in her chair, talking casually as if to a friend.

'My needs have changed. I've got the drama group now, so I don't have as much free time for other things.'

'I see. Well, of course we'll be checking out your group and its members. It's standard security procedure. We'll also be checking out Christine Matthews. Until we have done so and are satisfied there is no security risk either to you or the team, I have no choice other than to suspend you from duty. If things don't check out, you know what will happen, don't you?'

'Yes, Ma'am.'

'Okay, if you could write down the name of your group and what you know of Christine Matthews.' Preston pushed a pad of paper in front of Green. He wrote a few details and handed it back to her.

'Now, Alan, I suggest you take a holiday for a week or so. You look like you need one and it will give us time to sort this mess out. It will also give me time to effect the reorganisation of the teams and will help you to avoid contact with other members or your own people, something which you know must not happen while you are suspended.'

'Yes, I know that, Ma'am.'

'Well, Alan, unless you have anything else to say, I suggest we leave it at that.' Preston sat forward as if indicating she suspected Green might want to divulge everything, save people time and effort and above all make a clean breast of it all. He chose not to.

'No, there's nothing else, Ma'am.' Green knew it was the end of the road for him. The checks would show there was no such group and that both Matthews and Henderson before her had visited his pad. Henderson would talk, if only to save herself from prosecution. He doubted that Matthews would react any differently under pressure. So, with the termination of his contract imminent, Green saw no reason why he should assist the investigators. It would give them something to do, tracking down his social life. They did precious little else at the tax payers expense, so they could spend a few days really earning their money.

'In that case, let me know if you plan to go anywhere, just in case we need to contact you.' Preston knew she'd have Green back within seventy-two hours and in all likelihood she'd be terminating his secret service career. He'd been a fool and he would have to pay the price of his folly.

'Ma'am,' Green said as he rose wearily from his chair and turned to the door. 'I may go down to Cornwall for a few days. I'll let you know.'

'Thank you, Alan. Have a good holiday.' The door closed behind Green and Preston picked up her phone. The searches on Matthews would start immediately and she could get Henderson's local force to interview her again. The call relating to Henderson lasted five minutes.

'Marshall, are you secure? It's Preston.'

'Yes, Ma'am.'

'Good, I have a job for you to do. I've had a chat with Alan and there are a few loose ends to tie up. I want you to take a look at a woman called Christine Matthews. Apparently she belongs to the Hantley Players drama group.' Preston continued to read out the details Green had given her.

'How urgent is this, Ma'am?'

'It's fairly urgent. Alan's taking a few days off but we need to get the facts as soon as possible.'

'I'll start on it this evening.'

'Thanks, Marshall. I have to go now, there's a call coming through that I have to take.' There was a subtly softer lilt to her voice as she spoke the last sentence.

'Very good, Ma'am.' Her tone of voice had not been lost on Marshall.

The phones went dead and Marshall turned his attention to the pad of paper he'd scribbled the information on.

'Well, Alan, it looks like you've finally blown it,' he muttered to himself. Marshall still knew nothing about Green's previous liaisons with Julie Henderson.

It was six o'clock when Marshall set out to investigate Christine Matthews. He'd spent just over an hour checking out the details Preston had given him. He'd confirmed her address and telephone number from the information Green had divulged. The database, not surprisingly, held no information for a drama group called Hantley Players. Marshall knew that Matthews would be able to confirm the accuracy of that piece of information.

His journey into the heart of Hampshire took him just over an hour and a half and he found the woman's house with ease. The house was a semi, located in the middle of a row of such houses. Marshall noticed the black Saab sports car in the drive. If the electoral roll details he'd checked were accurate then Christine Matthews lived alone. With the car in the drive, Marshall assumed she was at home. He was right. At the moment when Marshall parked his car down the road from Matthews' house, Christine Matthews was in the master bedroom on the top floor applying the final touches to her makeup. She had already guessed at why her client wanted her to dress as a business woman, and it had excited her. Simon Hart paid her well for her to satisfy his many and varied desires, and she was happy to oblige his fantasies.

Christine Matthews was in a good mood. Hart had called her during the afternoon and confirmed their arrangements for the evening. She'd been happy to agree to his wishes. He was a short drive away and the time of her departure was drawing close.

Sat outside in his car, Marshall was busy on his mobile phone. He'd called up one of his contacts, someone in the force, and asked for a car search. Without question the request had been processed and it confirmed what Marshall had suspected. The car belonged to Christine Matthews. Marshall saw the upstairs light go out and put the mobile phone back on the passenger seat. He waited five minutes before the woman appeared. It wasn't what he was expecting and it gave him a choice. He could either wait until she was out of the way, and then conduct his search, or he could follow her. He chose the latter option and started his engine just as she reversed her car onto the highway.

Keeping a respectable distance behind her, Marshall followed her to the gates and driveway that marked the entrance to Hart's estate. The woman pulled into the small off-road area outside the gates and Marshall carried on driving. He had to drive nearly half a mile before there was anywhere to turn round and by the time he'd returned, the woman's car was disappearing down the driveway as the gates closed behind her. Marshall noted the address on the side of the gate and decided to return to Matthews' house. He figured if she was visiting such a grand place and they were going to be rehearsing a play, she would be gone for some time, long enough for Marshall to check out where she lived and find out who the owner of the estate was.

It took him nearly ten minutes to return to the road in which Matthews lived and five minutes later he was standing outside the kitchen door in the back garden. He could not be seen from here as that part of the garden was not overlooked. At half past eight there weren't going to be too many people around anyway so Marshall could work without any real likelihood of being disturbed.

It took him less than five minutes to gain entry through the kitchen door. Although the lock would have deterred the average burglar, Marshall had received special training and the lock posed no serious threat to him. He took off his boots and left them on the outside of the door. The garden was damp and he didn't want to leave a mud trail around the house.

The house stank of perfume. It reminded Marshall of a Boudoir, somewhere he'd once had to visit in France as part of some operation. The house was also clean and tidy. Using his torch light, shielded by his hand from any window, Marshall progressed slowly through the house. The lounge was comfortable and clean. The telephone sat neatly on a table. Under the table top was a drawer. Marshall pulled the drawer open and discovered the address book. He thumbed the pages until he found Green's entry. The woman knew Green's address and his phone number, a fact that made Marshall mutter to himself, 'We've got you, hook, line and sinker, Alan.'

Carefully he placed the book on the floor and took two snapshots on his mobile phone of the opened page. It was the evidence Preston needed. It proved Green was a liar.

Marshall thumbed the pages more slowly, looking for the address Matthews had just led him to. He found it on the page after Green's entry. Simon Hart, address, contact number, it was all there in black and white. Who, thought Marshall, was Simon Hart? Two more snapshots captured Hart's entry for posterity.

Marshall thumbed the rest of the book, photographing every page. He found no entry for anything that was obviously a drama group and then replaced it carefully in the drawer.

He checked the rest of the lounge and found nothing of interest. The upstairs rooms were equally unforthcoming except for the row of uniforms and outfits Marshall found hanging in one of the two wardrobes in the spare bedroom. They were intriguing and they indicated what the woman was involved in. Marshall photographed them, just for the record.

Fifteen minutes after entering the house, Marshall was back in the kitchen. He'd found nothing to indicate the woman was involved, as Green claimed, in a drama group. There were no copies of any plays lying around, and most of the uniforms he'd found were hardly theatrical costumes, though Marshall had to concede some could have been used as such. Marshall closed the kitchen door behind him and carefully locked it. There was little more he could gain by sitting outside the house waiting for the woman's return and equally, he didn't fancy the prospect of trying to get inside Hart's estate, so Marshall decided to call it a day and started his journey back to South London.

He was back at his flat just after ten o'clock and decided to prepare his report for Preston. The pictures from his smartphone camera spoke for themselves really but Marshall was thorough so he wrote down the details on the standard report form. Having done this he printed the report off and then pinned the pictures to the report and sealed the whole lot in a manila envelope. It could all be handed to Preston when they met on Sunday or he could courier it to her if she needed it sooner. He picked up his telephone and dialled her number.

'Hi, it's Marshall, are you free to talk?'

'Yes, how are things going?'

'Fine, I've just got back in after going over to Green's patch and checking out the Matthews woman.'

'Oh, is that how you spend your evenings, Travis?'

'Only when my boss asks me to.'

'So, I take it you've found something out.'

'Yes, a couple of things. First, Green is lying. Christine Matthews may be many things but there is absolutely nothing in her house to suggest she belongs to a drama group.'

'You got into her house?'

'Yes, she was out.'

'Did you have a warrant?'

'No, there wasn't time to arrange one.'

'Oh, go on.' Preston sounded intrigued.

'As I was saying, there was nothing in her house to indicate she is involved in amateur dramatics. There are some costumes, but I'd say they're more the kind of things she'd wear for her clients than on a stage.'

'You think she's on the game?'

'Yes, no doubt about it. She went out soon after I arrived and I followed her to a house. A big house with double gates and a long drive, I might add. She was dressed as a business woman but with high heels, a short skirt, that sort of thing. I reckon she was visiting a client, who happens to go by the name of Simon Hart, according to her address book which I found at her address. I've run him through the computer since I got back, but I came up with a big fat zero, so I'll spend some more time on him tomorrow.'

'Good work, Marshall. Do you think Christine Matthews is dangerous?'

'Probably not, but it depends on just who her client list extends to. Green's name, address and number all appear in her address book, as do quite a lot of other names. I didn't notice any of our more prominent targets in the book, but there's always a risk.'

'What do you think I should do about Green, Travis?'

'I don't know Ma'am. You could place him under surveillance while he's on suspension. See what he gets up to, whether he poses a risk to us. You could also ban him from the various liaisons he has going, though I doubt he'd take heed of that and even if he did it would only be a matter of time before another one came to light.'

'I think I agree with you. For now I'll give him a couple of weeks to sweat over things and to give us time to check his contacts out properly. Do you have a complete list of Matthews' clients?'

'Yes, Ma'am, I photographed the entire address book. I can spend time tomorrow looking into the details if you want, but I want to check out our jeweller friend first thing in the morning. There's something about him that continues to gnaw at me and I need to find out what it is.'

'Very well, Travis, I'm contactable tomorrow, if you need me, and I'll see you at eight if that's still okay with you.'

'That's fine, Ma'am, unless Zussman gives me any problems, which I doubt will be the case. We can get some food in when you arrive.'

'Okay, Travis, I'll see you at eight tomorrow. Take care, Travis, and good luck with Zussman.' Preston terminated the call. She rubbed the back of her neck and wondered just how big a risk Green had become.

**

Christine Matthews went through her usual ritual of berating Hart for not having had the gates open for her, then she casually mentioned that she thought she had been followed to his house that evening. Hart froze momentarily as she told him this. He was lying on the couch in the gymnasium, stripped to the waist, her cool hands massaging the back of his shoulders, so she could not see the change in the expression on his face.

'Are you sure?' He asked, slowly.

'No, not really, I just had a feeling. Does it matter?'

'Probably not, but you can't be too careful. Did anyone pull in either behind you or in front of you when you stopped at the gates?'

'No, but a red car, I think it was a small Ford, passed me when I'd stopped.'

'Did you get the index number?' Hart sounded more relaxed, he wasn't, but there was no point in worrying the woman. 'Oh, that's good, just there,' he added as she applied some firm pressure on his left shoulder.

'No, Simon, I didn't think about that, though I'm pretty sure it began with an 'X'.'

'It doesn't matter. This red car carried on going down the road?'

'Yes, it disappeared round the corner.'

'As you say, it was probably a coincidence. Argh! That's cold.'

The woman had applied a small blob of white cream to his neck just as he spoke and now she used her fingertips to work it into his neck.

'Sorry, Simon, but if you're to get the best out of this massage I suggest you try and relax.'

'I will. One more thing, though. Who were you with when I called you last Wednesday?'

'You know I don't discuss my clients with other people.'

'I'll bet he doesn't pay you like I do?'

'No, he doesn't, but then again he can't afford to. He doesn't live in a mansion like you do. Actually he lives in little more than a studio flat.'

'My heart bleeds for him. Do you know what the poor chap does? I might be able to help him.'

'Not really, he's always kept his business life and, come to think of it, his social life too, very quiet. Actually I know very little about him, except that he drinks too much and has fairly similar tastes to you.'

'Really, now that is interesting. What else do you know about him?'

'As I said, I don't discuss my clients with other people.'

'Yeah, I know, I didn't mean to pry. I just wanted to know what the guy wanted. You know it turns me on.'

'Oh, that! He had me dressed as a young girl. You know the kind of thing. I was wearing a tight white blouse, school tie, skirt, short white socks, and pigtails. It's what gets him going. Then I massaged him like I'm trying to do to you and then we got on with things.'

'What did he talk about?'

149

'Not a lot really. He wanted to know about you, after you'd phoned. Other than that he seemed to be a bit preoccupied until I helped him to relax.'

'What did you tell him about me?'

'Nothing, Simon, now will you just lie still and let me get on with things?' Matthews began to feel as if she was being interrogated and it annoyed her.

'Sure.' Hart relaxed and allowed the waves of pleasure to ripple through his upper body as she continued with his back massage. One hour and a half later she was finished. Hart lay on his double bed, totally relaxed, and Matthews put her clothes back on. It had been an athletic session once Hart had received his massage. It was a little ritual with him, feeling the sensuous touch of the woman on his flesh before he turned his attentions to whatever he fancied that evening. Now it was over and she had earned her fee. The money as always was in a brown envelope.

As Hart stirred, Matthews checked the envelope.

She whispered. 'Was that good for you, Simon?'

'Excellent, Christine, as always. Now, if you'll give me just a minute to get up, I'll let you out.'

'Sure, Simon, I'll wait for you downstairs.'

Hart was on the edge of the bed, sitting up, his naked body protected only by the black, satin sheet. The woman closed the bedroom door behind her and went down to the lounge. Hart took less than five minutes to follow her. He watched as she drove back down the drive and then closed the front door behind him. The gates at the end of the drive opened, allowing the woman onto the road.

Hart turned his television on and watched the woman as she roared off down the road, her black Saab disappearing swiftly against the darkness of the night. Hart pressed a button on a handset and the picture froze before it started rewinding at speed.

Hart stopped the recording at the point where the woman pulled into the area just outside his gates. He watched as the red Fiesta passed her and continued on down the road. He watched the gates open and start to close again. Suddenly the car came back into frame. It slowed right down and then sped off down the road in the same direction that Matthews had just gone. Hart stopped the tape and replayed it. This time he froze the film on a frame that showed the slightly fuzzy picture of a man in the driving seat. Hart played a few more frames and stopped it again when the index number of the car was in view. He noted the number on a piece of paper. Christine Matthews had been right about the 'X' starting the registration, but she had been totally wrong about being followed.

'Damn it,' Hart muttered to himself.

CHAPTER TWELVE

Saturday 27th June

Saturday dawned cloudy with light drizzle. Travis Marshall had risen early and driven down to the road where Dieter Zussman lived. He wanted to catch the diminutive jeweller leaving home, so he'd set his alarm for six o'clock and driven straight down to where Zussman lived.

He drove past Zussman's driveway, noted his car was still parked there, and turned the car round a hundred yards further up the road. Marshall sat back and waited, knowing Zussman would have to leave home by eight o'clock if he was going to open the shop up personally. It was just after half past seven. Marshall lifted the thermos flask off the passenger side foot-well and poured himself a cup of coffee. The drizzle was becoming progressively harder and Marshall had to clear the windscreen periodically.

With the coffee in his hand he looked up the road, both at Zussman's house and the house opposite. He stared for a moment at the house opposite Zussman's and was sure he saw the curtains in the front bedroom twitch. Perhaps the occupant was getting up, Marshall thought, taking another sip of the steaming liquid. Five minutes passed and the curtains twitched again, though they did not open. Five more minutes and the curtains moved again though there was still no sign of them being opened.

'Christ,' thought Marshall suddenly, 'Zussman's being watched.' He muttered to himself, a thousand thoughts suddenly flooding his mind. Did Zussman know? Why was he being watched? Who was watching him? These and countless other thoughts suddenly crossed Marshall's mind.

Ten minutes later Zussman opened his front door and made his way to the driver's door of his car. A moment later he was reversing out of his driveway. Marshall had his engine running and noticed there was more movement from the window across the road from Zussman's house. Zussman was, thought Marshall, almost certainly going to work. He decided to wait. To have followed Zussman immediately would only have aroused suspicion if the person in the bedroom was indeed watching Zussman. Marshall checked the number on the house across the road from where he was parked and calculated the number of the house where the curtains were moving. He made a note of it and decided to make some enquiries later on.

Five minutes after Zussman had disappeared up the road, Marshall followed him. He drove to Reigate and parked a safe distance from the shop. Leaving his car, Marshall walked swiftly into the town centre. It was still not half past eight and there was an almost surreal calm about the place. Marshall walked past Zussman's shop without looking in the window and continued on to the end of the one way traffic system. He looked in the antique shop and the pine furniture shop. They were both closed but they gave Marshall the chance to take a careful look around him. If Zussman was being watched at home, Marshall figured it was likely that his shop was also being watched. Perhaps, Marshall thought, whoever was watching Zussman, had seen him enter the shop a few nights previously. Perhaps they had, but it was not very likely. After all, reasoned Marshall, why watch an empty shop late at night unless you were planning to turn it over.

Marshall spent a few minutes looking in the shop windows and then retraced his steps to Zussman's shop. This time he did look through the window. The displays were still partially missing and the shop was closed and Zussman was coming out of his office at the back of the shop. Marshall carried on walking. Having purchased a bracelet the previous day he did not want Zussman to recognise him loitering outside the shop at this early hour, it would have been too suspicious. Across the road and above the shop window, the curtains moved and a camera clicked. Marshall's visit to the closed shop had been duly recorded. The man behind the camera smiled to himself. If Zussman was becoming a liability then he could be disposed of, much as they would dispose of anyone who got in the way when the time was right.

Marshall returned to his car. As he did so, Simon Hart placed his suitcase in the boot of his silver Mondeo and set out for Gatwick airport. His flight wasn't until early afternoon but what with the check-in procedures and the fact he liked to look round the shops at the airport, Hart had decided to set out early. It would take him nearly an hour to get to the airport, probably half an hour to complete the check-in and then he'd have time for a look round and a meal before going through to the departure area.

Simon Hart pulled out of the driveway to his mansion and drove smoothly towards the main road leading to the motorway network. He was not in a hurry and was in buoyant mood. Years of meticulous planning were about to pay off. Years of wrong were about to be righted and all because he'd had the foresight to be careful and plan with the meticulous precision he had once been taught. Now, he was on the way, now things were about to happen, Hart felt strangely confident, as if a new surge of power had begun to flow through him. The delectable Ganzagha would be arriving in Munich the following day, giving Hart plenty of time to make his preparations. It was vital that everything went smoothly in Munich. The success of the entire plan depended on Munich. Hart smiled, knowing no one else had a clue. Even the delectable Ganzagha had no idea what her trip to Munich was all about. Most certainly Christine Matthews had no idea what Hart had planned for her. In Hart's grand scheme of things she was little more than a distraction. She would play her part in his grand plan, just as Ganzagha would.

The traffic was light and Hart drove slowly as if he had all the time in the world. He felt relaxed thanks to the presence of Matthews the previous evening. He knew the countdown had begun. It thrilled him, excited him, and invigorated him.

***

Gary Peterson had decided to work the Saturday. He was a conscientious person and often spent a few hours in the office at the weekend. This particular Saturday the office was quiet. It had been a busy week and the team members were all spending time with their families.

Peterson had a feeling that something was about to break. He felt that somewhere, something would come to light concerning Braddock Holdings. As he sat at his desk he looked at the half dozen sheets of paper the computer printer on his desk had generated overnight. The sheets of paper were the transaction movements relating to the Braddock Holdings accounts SB4 had been monitoring. There were the usual lists of movements that seemingly went into black holes. Peterson had formed the view that they were probably movements to other Braddock accounts in countries SB4 hadn't been able to penetrate. Then, on the fifth page, a transaction caught Peterson's eye. The amount was not large, twenty thousand pounds. What caught Peterson's eagle eye was the fact it was paid directly into a UK bank account. It was the breakthrough he'd been waiting for. Slowly he re-read the transaction details, afraid the information would change before his eyes. It didn't.

Peterson walked over to the computer by the far wall of his office and typed in the sort code and account number where the twenty thousand had been deposited. In a moment the screen showed the full account details. The account transactions clearly showed the money being paid in as cleared funds, and then a few minutes later the whole balance of the account was withdrawn and the account closed. According to the transaction coding, everything had happened electronically. Where the money had gone to was not shown, but it was still the breakthrough Peterson had been hoping for. There, at the top of the page was the account holder and his address.

'Hi, can I speak to Selena Preston, please?'

'Speaking?'

'Oh, good morning Ma'am, I'm sorry to trouble you on a Saturday but there's something you should know?'

'Sorry, who am I speaking to?' Preston sounded her usual, composed self.

'I apologise, Ma'am, my name is Peterson, from SB4.'

'Gary Peterson?' Her query came from the surprise that a member of SB4 should contact her directly.

'Yes, Ma'am,' he responded.

'Shouldn't you go through Harding first?'

'I can't raise him on his home or mobile numbers and this is important.'

'How did you get this number, Peterson?'

'Harding gave it to me in case I couldn't get to him.'

'I see, so what is so important you felt you had to call me this morning?'

'We've had a breakthrough, during the night. I don't know how much you know about what we do, but we have been monitoring Braddock for some while now, and last night someone got careless.'

'Go on,' Preston now gave her undivided attention to the caller.

'We picked up a transaction from Braddock for twenty thousand that was paid straight into a UK Bank. That money was then immediately withdrawn, electronically, and the account closed.'

'Why does that make the matter urgent? People close accounts every day.'

'We couldn't trace where the money has gone to. It has to be another account somewhere, and almost certainly overseas. What makes this special is it finally gives us a name.'

'Who is it?' Preston was ready to write the details name.

'It's a chap by the name of Justin Pritwick. His address is,' and Peterson rattled off the address in Surrey.

'Thank you, Peterson. I think we'll arrange to have a little chat with Mr Pritwick. Could you fax the evidence over to me at ATRIUM?'

'Yes, Ma'am.'

'Good work, Peterson.'

'Thank you, Ma'am.' Peterson genuinely sounded thrilled that someone had deigned to praise his efforts. It was a rare thing to happen indeed. For some reason, the powers that controlled the actions of SB4 rarely heaped praise on the diligence of the team even when they achieved quite remarkable results from their endeavours. For someone in Preston's position to offer thanks and praise was rare.

Preston ended the call and immediately dialled a new number.

'Preston, are you secure, Marshall?' her voice sounded urgent.

'Yes, Ma'am.' Marshall was just about to start back home from Reigate when the call came through. He switched off the engine and out of habit locked the doors from the inside of his red Fiesta. The car that was waiting for his parking space sounded its horn in frustration when Marshall switched off the engine. Marshall ignored the ranting of the furious driver.

'I have a job for you, Marshall. The boys at SB4 have come up with a name that might be associated with Braddock Holdings. I want you to visit the guy and if necessary pull him in for questioning. The sum of twenty thousand pounds was transferred from Braddock to his UK account last night. A couple of minutes later the whole balance on the account, nearly thirty thousand was transferred out to God knows where and the account closed.'

'Sounds suspicious,' Marshall offered.

'Yeah, it is. The guy's called Justin Pritwick and I'll give you his address too. I want him talked to. Anything, and I mean anything, suspicious and I want him hauled in for questioning. Take the police with you and make it official. We're going to lay this Braddock thing to bed once and for all.'

'Yes, Ma'am.' Marshall was delighted at the thought of some real action and a chance to put his interrogation skills to use. He wrote down the name and the address before reading it back to Preston. He also wrote down the other information Preston had dug up on Justin Pritwick. It wasn't much, but it was better than nothing.

'I'll see you later, Marshall,' Preston continued, 'and you can tell me how it went.'

'Yes, Ma'am, will do.' Marshall terminated the call on his mobile and picked up the Surrey street map. It took him two minutes to locate the address and decide the best route to get there.

Pritwick's house was not ostentatious. Located on the fringes of Godalming, the house was a standard nineteen thirties semidetached affair, without a garage. Marshall found the road with ease and sat outside the house waiting for the local police to arrive. He'd been waiting for ten minutes before the marked car made its presence known. Two fresh-faced uniformed officers alighted and Marshall met them just up the road from where he'd parked. He showed them his identity card which the taller of the men in uniform took some time to scrutinise. ATRIUM was an outfit he'd never heard of, but the orders had come down from the Chief Superintendent that Marshall was to be afforded every possible courtesy and assistance.

'I've been watching the place for about ten minutes,' Marshall began when his identity card had been returned, 'and I can't see any signs of life. I suggest one of you goes round the back, just in case, and then we'll knock on the door.'

'Okay, Rogers, I'll take the front.' The taller man was clearly more senior in rank. Wearing the three stripes of his rank, Sergeant Andrews was intrigued by the call they had been given. Now, to let Marshall know he was in charge of the situation, he looked straight at the Constable standing beside him. By way of reply, Rogers grunted something and then started to walk round the block of houses to the alley way at the back.

'We'll give him two minutes and then see what happens.' Marshall waited quietly for the seconds to pass then strode purposefully up the drive and banged loudly on the door three times. He waited one minute and while he did so, he bent down and pushed open the letterbox. The house was in silence. Marshall knocked again and called out through the opened letterbox to see if anyone was in. Again there was no reply.

'Okay, we need to gain entry. Officially you don't know I can do this.' Marshall grinned as he extracted the relevant tool from his pocket. The door was double locked but it took Marshall less than two minutes to gain entry.

'Thank God you're on our side. You are on our side, aren't you?' The Sergeant was impressed and somewhat taken aback that the man he'd been ordered to assist was breaking just about every rule in the book.

'More than you will probably ever know, Sergeant. Now, I think we can go in.' Marshall led the way into the house and Sergeant Andrews followed him, closing the door quietly behind them. The house was eerily silent. Marshall made a quick inspection of the ground floor, found no one and ran up the stairs. The rooms upstairs were empty too.

'Damn, the bird has flown.'

'You are sure this is the right house, Sir?'

'Positive, we got it from his bank account.'

Marshall was in the main bedroom and quickly opened the wardrobe. It was bare, as were the drawers in the chest under the window.

'Look! He's flown, Sergeant. We're too late. All his clothes have gone, and I'll wager all his personal effects have gone too. The question is where has he gone?'

'It could just be a dump address. He could just use this as a place to have mail sent to. All he has to do then is come by every now and again and pick it up.'

'Of course, if he's involved in what we think he's into, then it makes sense!' Marshall was thinking quickly. The uniformed person may not have been trained in the same way Marshall had been trained, but it didn't mean he couldn't spot the blindingly obvious. 'Good thinking, Sergeant. Now, there was no mail on the doormat when we arrived, which means there has been no post since he last visited this place. That's assuming he doesn't live here and he's simply done a runner.'

'I'm sorry Sir, but you've lost me.'

'It doesn't matter, Sergeant. I'll bet your theory is right. He doesn't live here. Look, there are things you don't know that I'm afraid I can't tell you, but you are probably right. Tell you what, when we go outside, could you just knock on the neighbour's doors and see if they know anything about the chap who lives here?'

'Yes, Sir.' Andrews suddenly realised the call out was of far greater importance than he had imagined it would be.

'Excellent. If you're right Sergeant, then the neighbours will know very little about the person who is supposed to live here. Well, there's not much else we can do here. I suggest we go and call your Constable in and then get on with things. I'd like someone to watch this place for the next forty eight hours. If anyone turns up I want them to be taken in for questioning and I want to be contacted on this number immediately.' Marshall handed the officer a business card. 'Believe me when I say it is of the utmost importance I get to talk quickly to anyone who has a key to this place.'

'Yes, Sir, I understand.'

'Good. Right, let's get out of here.'

The Sergeant took one neighbour while the Constable took the other. Five minutes later they were back with Marshall. Neither of the neighbours knew anything about the person whose house they had just visited. Indeed, his adjoining neighbour thought nobody lived there. He'd only ever seen a dark-skinned gentleman, possibly of Caribbean origin, drive up in a battered old car on a couple of occasions and even then he'd not stayed more than a few minutes. When Constable Rogers relayed this piece of information, Marshall knew Pritwick didn't live there.

Ten minutes later, Marshall was driving back home. It had been a busy start to the day, what with Zussman to follow and now this failed raid. As he began the journey, Marshall wondered exactly where Pritwick lived and more importantly, why he needed a dummy address for his mail to be sent to. Setting up such an address was not something the average person would do but was more the action of someone with something to hide.

CHAPTER THIRTEEN

Daniel Newton crossed the Bulgarian border just south of Elkhovo. It was mid-morning and the weather was mild and grey. His route would take him up the east side of the country, crossing the Romanian border at Ruse where the river Danube formed a natural frontier. Once in Romania he would skirt round the south of the country, stopping overnight at a hotel he had discovered in Alexandria. He called it a hotel but in reality it was little more than a guest house. It had one outstanding quality which was the hospitality offered by the owners of the establishment. Newton had formed a close friendship with them and always took them something from England. In return they afforded him the most comfortable room in the house, a room which was isolated in the roof of the building.

The rain started falling as he drove through the mountains leading to Sliven. It was lunchtime when he arrived at the town and Newton was glad to be able to park the van outside the hostelry he had frequented on many occasions. As was usual, he had scarcely entered the almost deserted public bar when the man standing behind the counter came running from behind it to shake Newton's hand profusely. The men embraced in the customary ritual for the country and the barman led Newton to a table.

Newton spoke no Bulgarian and the bartender spoke only a few words of English. Fortunately the grubby menu was written in both languages so Newton made do by gesticulating with his finger at what he wanted. The beer took just a couple of minutes to arrive and the food followed shortly afterwards. Newton spent twenty minutes eating and drinking before returning to his van. As he did so, the face and upper body of a young woman dressed in black appeared in one of the upstairs windows of the hostelry. Newton did not notice her watching as he

162

strolled casually back to his vehicle. The rain had stopped and the sky was breaking.

Newton knew he still had a long way to go that day and the next twenty miles would be slow. Passing through the mountain passes was always a tricky business with anything larger than a simple cart and Newton knew the van would find some of the hairpin bends almost impassable. He thanked his luck that the rain had stopped. It made the going easier for him. He was, by nature, a cautious driver. His many excursions around Europe had taught him that it simply didn't pay to rush or attract attention from any of the countries authorities. The military police, secret police, and a host of other organisations could make the life of a travelling tourist sheer hell if they wanted to. Newton had long since adopted a strategy of remaining as inconspicuous as possible. His strategy worked.

It was mid-afternoon when Newton arrived at the border crossing into Romania. Mercifully the traffic at the border was light and Newton waited only a few minutes while his passport was checked. He waved the import documentation in front of the Customs officer who ignored it. The visas and stamps in his passport showed Newton was a regular traveller. As such he was almost certain to have his paperwork in order and there was nothing about Newton's demeanour that would have aroused suspicion. In less time than he would have imagined possible just a few years ago, Newton was across the river Danube and making his way to Alexandria.

Once across the Romanian border, Newton still had thirty miles to go and knew he would arrive well before sunset. The day had gone remarkably smoothly for him and the ease of the border crossing left him with some time to spare.

In the back of his van the various goods he was importing lay waiting for their destination. Newton had learned the art of stacking and packing them so they did not get damaged or thrown around. At the back of the van the jewellery boxes sat firmly wedged into position. It was the one thing Zussman had stressed before the journey. The contents of the boxes were delicate, and required the utmost of care when being handled. If Newton had had any idea what the boxes contained he would have refused to carry them, but Newton had no idea that his life and the lives of millions of people through whose towns he travelled were in the gravest of danger from the contents of the boxes. Newton travelled on blissfully unaware of the deadly cargo he was carrying.

***

Dieter Zussman closed up the shop at five o'clock precisely. It had been a quiet day, doubtless partly due to the persistent drizzle that had been falling for much of it. Unaware that he was being watched, Zussman returned to his car and began the journey home. The roads were wet which made Zussman drive more cautiously than usual. When he arrived home he seemed to the observer across the road that he was more agitated than usual. Zussman fumbled with the front door key before disappearing into his home. The envelope was lying on the doormat behind the door. He picked it up and noticed it came from a town in Iraq, the name of which he recognised. It had been mentioned once in a telephone conversation with his contact there. It was the same conversation when Zussman had decided to reveal his address. Both men had reservations about what they were being forced to do so they had agreed to keep in touch. Clearly, the arrival of the letter indicated something of great importance had happened or was about to happen.

Zussman closed the front door, took off his coat and shoes and took the envelope into the lounge. He examined it carefully to check it had not been unsealed and then resealed. There were no tell-tale marks of the envelope having been tampered with so Zussman carefully slit the envelope along its seam. He extracted the single, thin sheet of paper and read it.

'My dear Dieter,' he read quietly to himself, 'forgive this intrusion but I have a concern I must share with you. The last batch of jewellery you ordered was delayed by two days because the boxes were delayed in getting to my shop. I have a friend who is a security worker at the Al'Sendara plant. He contacted me yesterday because he recognised your boxes at the plant a few days ago. It is his belief that your boxes have been used to transport a deadly package. Two dozen phials of a virus coded as Wipeout-V1 have been taken out of circulation according to the register at the plant. These phials are just under two centimetres long and a few millimetres in diameter. The virus is contained in an orange liquid form, but the virus itself is meant to be used in the air once released. The virus has a life of about seventy two hours before it is oxidised and each phial contains enough of the virus to destroy a town the size of London, or New York, if it is dispersed properly. I do not know for sure that your boxes have been used to transport the phials but I urge you to take great care when you take delivery. Your friend, Sidar.'

Zussman slumped in his chair. He'd known the boxes were of importance to the people who'd brought him to England and he'd been told to handle them with great care and not to open them other than to remove the jewellery. Under no condition were the boxes to be passed on to members of the public. His brother's life depended on Zussman doing everything he had been told to do. He'd had no choice and anyway he would only have the boxes in his shop for a few hours, so it had seemed a relatively simple thing to agree to, not that he'd had any choice. Now, the news from Iraq made Zussman nervous, very nervous. The reality of the training camps in Afghanistan came flooding back to him as he sat gazing at the sheet of paper. Zussman remembered the pictures of the nomadic tribes that had been wiped out by the forerunner of Wipeout-V1 and it made him feel sick to the stomach. He could still see the whole villages of motionless bodies, seemingly untouched, yet each face bearing the hallmark of the anguish the virus under development had caused.

They were distant memories but memories he would never forget. Now, the reality of the whole set up dawned on him and he knew what was going to happen very soon. He was glad he would not be directly involved but it meant he could not continue to look forward to opening the third shop. Dieter Zussman now knew he had just a few days before he would be gone for good. His plans needed to be completed and quickly, if only because the letter from Sidar showed him things were far more sinister than he had dared to think they would be.

The letter had left a nasty taste in Zussman's mouth and he had lost his appetite. The meal he had brought home with him lay unopened on the kitchen table. It would be much later before Dieter Zussman would even remember he had brought it home with him.

***

Travis Marshall was a man with a good appetite. He'd spent the afternoon tidying up his flat and attending to a few items of official business. By the time Selena Preston rang the doorbell at precisely five minutes past eight, Marshall was ready. They took a couple of minutes to agree on having a curry and Marshall rang the take-away establishment he'd used on many occasions. The fact they provided a delivery service was one of the reasons Marshall used them. He placed the order and gave the delivery directions.

'Right, I've got a bottle of white in the fridge, red if you'd prefer or lager. The food will be about half an hour.'

'Well, in that case I'll start with a glass of white wine.' Preston was dressed casually but still carried with her an air of authority. She didn't particularly mean to, it

166

was just her demeanour. She sat on one end of the sofa and waited for Marshall to fetch the drinks from his kitchenette.

'White wine,' he said as he handed her a glass. 'It's a Chardonnay so I hope you like it.'

Preston sipped the drink and nodded her head approvingly.

'So,' she said, 'how did it go today? Did you get anything out of Pritwick?'

'I didn't even get Pritwick. The address was just being used for post deliveries. Either that or he's already flown the nest. My gut feeling is he's never lived there but goes round to pick up the post occasionally. I've left orders for round the clock surveillance to be maintained for the next few days to see if anyone turns up.'

'Mmm,' said Preston, 'and Zussman?'

'Oh, he's not who he claims to be. That's not totally unexpected. He's running a respectable business with no hint of any underhand dealings. His accounts are impeccable, taxes paid, a right model citizen, except for one thing.'

'Go on,' Preston took a swig of wine.

'Well, when I took a look in his house, it was almost as if he had too few personal possessions. Then there was a picture of two lads taken in 1994, names of Ahmed and Mohammed. Those lads were in their early teens then, so they'd be about the same age as Zussman is now. Also, Zussman had a letter from someone called Ahmed Ali Burgansa. It might not be the same Ahmed, but it came from Syria about six months ago, so it could be. I don't know if all of this adds up to anything but it wasn't what I was expecting to find in his house. Also, I'm fairly sure Zussman is being watched, not by us, but some other group. I'm fairly sure I triggered some kind of alarm system when I broke into Zussman's house. Someone came and checked the kitchen door and back gate while I was in the house. Again it could have been an opportunist thief, but the timing was just too coincidental. If he is being watched then we have to ask the question, why? What is so significant about Zussman that someone wants to keep tabs on him?'

'A good thought, Travis. I think we should consider having a little chat to Mr Zussman. I think perhaps we should pay him a visit tomorrow. If he is involved in anything it may make him talk or at least take some kind of action.'

'It might, but what if he's involved with our targets? Don't forget he's already had one of them visit his shop.'

'If he is, then it will tell them we are still on their tails. It will make them think twice before becoming active again.'

'Unless they've already got a plan they're working to. I had this idea last night. You know the contact Zussman has in Iraq, what if Zussman is planning to bring something into this country other than jewellery or, more likely, what if the people who are watching him are forcing him to bring something in with his jewellery. They just sit there and wait until it comes and then they take it off him. We've seen the same kind of thing before you know.'

'They could be, but surely they have enough contacts and resources not to need to use some Jewish businessman as a go-between?' Preston took another mouthful of wine.

'What if he's not Jewish?'

'Not Jewish, with a name like Zussman? Come on, Marshall!'

'It's not his real name, I'm sure of it, unless he was born in some obscure country we can't get any assistance from. I've made loads of enquiries over the past week or so and they've all drawn blank. Whoever he is, even if he is Jewish, he was not born Dieter Zussman.'

'Well, Travis, we can ask him tomorrow, can't we. Now, I don't want to spend the whole evening talking shop. Life is too short for that.'

The conversation turned to more personal matters and eventually the doorbell rang. The curry was eaten and the evening turned into night. At half past ten one of Marshall's operatives called his mobile number to update him with the news Zussman had gone to bed for the night. The operative had been set to watch Zussman's house earlier in the day and knew Zussman was being watched by some, as yet unknown, person or persons. The operative was skilled at undercover work, specially trained for this kind of situation and had gone unnoticed throughout the evening since he'd followed Zussman home. Marshall thanked him politely for his report and suggested he went and got some sleep. A relief would pick up the operation early in the morning. Marshall switched the mobile back to standby and returned to the needs of the dominant female who was lying beside him.

CHAPTER FOURTEEN

Sunday 28th June

The hotel, a dozen or more kilometres from the southern outskirts of Munich, Germany was not ostentatious. The early morning sun played across the front of the building, filtering into the bedrooms that occupied the upper floors. It was Sunday and church bells were sounding in the distance.

Simon Hart had arrived the previous afternoon on a direct flight from London. He'd used the hotel before and had hired a car from the airport to drive there. The car was small, functional and unlikely to attract attention. Hart had selected the hotel a year earlier once he had established Newton's habits meant he always spent a night at a travellers rest place a few kilometres away. It was perfect for Hart's intentions. The attractive Sheera Ganzagha would be arriving on a plane from Ankara that was due to land at lunchtime. Hart had told her he would collect her from the airport. He had an evening of fun planned for them both. It was an evening he hoped would throw the woman off her guard. She was too valuable a prize to let go of right now.

Hart showered and dressed before going down to the restaurant for breakfast. He was not in a hurry that morning. Taking the car he travelled to the Grassvelde hypermarket just half a kilometre away. He'd been there before and had considered the place ideal, especially as it was located right on the outskirts of Munich. It was a large building with air conditioning and like most such shopping complexes, it was always busy. Even this Sunday morning the car park was filling up with shoppers. Hart parked his hire car and ambled into the shopping area. It was a complex that housed not only the main hypermarket store but also an array of smaller shops. Hart wandered round for half an hour, satisfying himself that this would be the chosen location. He singled out a shop selling wooden artefacts and picked up the beautifully crafted elephant. It was not particularly large or heavy but it attracted Hart's attention.

He replaced the animal after checking the price tag and walked on. The shopping mall was becoming progressively more busy, something which pleased Hart. He looked round casually and noticed many of the stores were still holding their sales. They would not be for much longer but then that didn't bother Hart.

The morning wore on and eventually Hart decided it was time to head for the airport. He didn't want to be late for Ganzagha's arrival. Tardiness would get things off to a bad start, the last thing he wanted.

Half an hour after he'd parked his car and ambled into the arrivals hall, Ganzagha appeared from behind the security screen. She saw Hart and waved enthusiastically. He waved back and walked round to meet her. They kissed and hugged briefly before walking back to the car park. She had only a small bag with her, enough possessions for a couple of days.

'It's good to see you again, Simon,' she purred as they walked to the car.

'And it's good to see you again. What has it been? Six months or more, I think. I really must make more effort to come over and see you more often.'

'It's all right. If you came any more often you would probably go off me. I like it this way, because we never have time to argue so everything is always good.' She snuggled into his arm as they walked.

'True, but you must come over to England and stay at my place. It's only modest but it's comfortable.' Hart put an arm round her shoulders affectionately. 'Are you hungry?'

'Yes. I haven't eaten since quite early this morning.'

'Good, well I know a rather good restaurant where we can have some lunch and then I'll take you into

171

Munich and we can do some shopping. I hope you don't mind but I've booked us into a little restaurant I know in the country. They specialise in Bavarian food and are very good. Then, I thought we could have a romantic walk through the beautiful gardens the restaurant is set in before retiring for the night.'

'It sounds wonderful.'

'Good, I hoped you'd like it. Now, here is my car.'

Hart opened the passenger door and waited for Ganzagha to take her seat. He closed the door gently and then put her bag in the boot before taking up his place in the driver's seat. The drive to the local Bier Keller took barely twenty minutes and in another ten they had ordered lunch.

***

Dieter Zussman woke early on the Sunday. He had much on his mind and the letter he'd received the previous day had only served to convince him the time was rapidly approaching for him to leave the country. He knew he had to wait for the jewellery boxes to be delivered and passed on to the people who controlled him, but after that he would run and run as fast as he could, anything to get away from what he knew was going to happen. Zussman decided to take a drive. He needed to book tickets and wanted to book them some way from where he lived. If, as he suspected, he was being watched, then he had to go some distance away to be sure of losing anyone who was following him.

At nine o'clock Zussman opened his front door. It triggered the alarm across the road, causing the observer to twitch the bedroom curtains. Zussman didn't notice, his mind was preoccupied with the drive ahead of him. He'd spent half an hour telling himself to keep one eye on his rear view mirror, watching for any pursuer.

So he set off, and drove south. He picked up the motorway at Reigate and headed east. After one junction he turned off onto the connecting motorway and headed south towards the airport. He kept his eye on the rear view mirror but could not tell if he was being followed. The traffic was light and there was nothing immediately behind him. He had, in fact, surprised the observer across the road from where he lived, by his change in habits and had set off before any kind of surveillance operation could be mounted. It was Sunday, after all, and Dieter Zussman had never shown his face before mid–afternoon before today and even then his ritual walk round the block was nothing for the watchers to get excited about.

Dieter Zussman was not alone, though. The operatives working for Travis Marshall were more organised. Almost the first thing they had done after Zussman finally went to bed the previous evening was to approach his car. They secured two homing devices under the engine compartment and a third behind the rear bumper. The operative who did this had remained unseen by the watcher across the road. Now, as Zussman sped down the motorway, he was being followed at some distance so as not to alarm him. Zussman headed for Crawley, a town just a few miles from the airport, and parked his car. The dark green Zafira pulled into the car park nearly two minutes later. As it did so, one man alighted. Brad Chatson was a tall, thin man. He saw Zussman ahead of him, heading towards the flight of stairs that would eventually lead to the shopping centre. Chatson was a seasoned surveillance operative and knew if he was going to lose Zussman it would probably be in the next few minutes. While his team mate, Don Gratton, parked the Zafira, Chatson followed Zussman.

Zussman clearly felt confident he was not being followed for he didn't look round once. He walked directly to the travel shop and attracted the attention of one of the members of staff. They sat down next to a computer screen and after twenty minutes Zussman stood up, shook the other person's hand and left the shop. He took a quick look at his watch and decided it was time for coffee.

Chatson had remained outside the shop, talking quietly into his radio to Gratton. Gratton had found Zussman's car and moved the Zafira to be near to it. He concurred with Chatson that he should remain in the vehicle, just in case Zussman made a sudden move. Zussman was clearly not in a hurry. He took his time drinking his coffee, looking out of the window at the shoppers as they passed by. After half an hour he decided to make a move and started back for the car. Chatson was waiting for him, sitting on a bench outside the café, ostensibly reading a Sunday paper. He let Zussman walk away from him, told Gratton to be ready to move and only then did he shuffle the paper together and start to make his own way back to the car park. Gratton picked Chatson up at the exit as arranged and they followed Zussman at a discreet distance back onto the motorway. They followed him like that until Zussman reached his driveway. The Zafira turned into the road nearly a minute after Zussman and the two operatives were just in time to see him unlock his front door. The Zafira drove past and parked where it had been earlier that morning.

'Marshall, it's Chatson, we've just followed the target back to his house from Crawley. There's nothing more to report. He only visited the travel agents and had coffee.'

'Did he pick up a ticket or anything at the agents?' Marshall asked patiently.

'No, nothing we could see. He spent about twenty minutes in there and left. We're up the road from where he lives now, and he's inside. What do you want us to do?'

'Keep watching. I'll be coming to have a chat with him in a bit. After that it may be he decides to do something, so I want you to stick around and see what happens. Chatson, don't forget the watcher at the window over the road. We don't want to set too many alarm bells ringing just yet.'

174

'Yeah, we remembered. There's no way he, or she, could see us from there. We can only just see Zussman's house ourselves so we must be invisible from across the road.'

'Good, well now I know he's home, I'll be about an hour.'

'Okay.' Chatson turned off the mobile phone and relayed the gist of the conversation to Gratton. When he'd finished they pulled out the Thermos and poured a couple of cups of hot, dark coffee.

An hour later a red Fiesta pulled up outside Zussman's house. Marshall jumped out of the driver's seat as Preston opened the passenger door. Together they marched up to Zussman's front door and pressed the buzzer. Inside, Zussman was startled by the intrusion and made his way slowly to the door. He left the chain on and opened the door the few inches the chain permitted.

'Yes, who is it?' He enquired

'Mr Dieter Zussman?' Preston enquired.

'Yes, who are you?'

'Detective Chief Superintendent Selena Preston,' she began and showed him the warrant card that came as part of her credentials. 'Could we have a word, please?'

'What about?' Zussman was still examining the warrant card and seemed unsure what to do next.

'It's a delicate matter. Now, we can either talk here where everyone can hear us, or we can come inside.'

'Have you got a warrant?'

'We don't need one.' Preston remained calm though the delay was beginning to annoy her.

'Yes you do.'

'No we don't, we only want a chat, not a search.'

'Okay then.'

Zussman opened the door fully and allowed Marshall and Preston into his residence. He took them into the front room and offered them a seat. Preston sat down while Marshall decided to stand near the doorway.

Zussman sat in his armchair and looked intently at Preston.

'What do you want?' He questioned her.

'You are Dieter Karsten Zussman?'

'Yes.'

'And you live here alone?'

'Yes. Look, what do you want to know?'

'I'll ask the questions, Mr Zussman. You own a jewellers shop in Reigate and another in Dorking, don't you?'

'Yes, but if you know these things, why ask me?'

'You import a lot of your jewellery, don't you?'

'Yes.' Zussman sounded tired.

'Where do you import it from?'

'Mostly from Eastern Europe, I have some business connections out there.'

'And how do you import it, Mr Zussman?'

'What do you mean?'

'How does the jewellery get from Eastern Europe into your shop?'

'I have someone who goes out there and brings it back for me. He imports things for a few businesses in the south of England I believe.'

'What is his name?'

'Daniel Newton. I believe he's self-employed but seeing as I pay him a fixed fee for each trip it doesn't really matter to me what his business practice is. What is this all about?'

'I said I would ask the questions. Where is Mr Newton now?'

'Somewhere in Europe I think. He's on a journey to pick up products at the moment. He should be back in a few days' time.'

'Presumably he drives around Europe, or does he fly, Mr Zussman?'

'He drives. He's got one of those middle-sized white vans.'

'Do you know the registration number?'

'No.'

'I see, and where does Mr Newton live?'

'I don't know. I have a mobile number for him and when I have an order to be collected I simply call him. He comes round to the shop to pick up the paperwork and his payment and the next I see of him is when the goods arrive. It usually takes about four weeks.' Both Marshall and Preston were watching the man carefully. If he was lying, he was a good actor. Preston made him write down the mobile phone number he used to make contact with Newton.

'Now, Mr Zussman, we know you have a contact in Iraq called Sidar Hassani. Who is he?'

'I don't know what you're talking about.' Zussman's protest was feeble and he began to show perspiration on his forehead.

'Come, Mr Zussman, we know he is your contact. Answer the question please.'

'I've never heard of him before.'

'I see, so you have never made any calls to Iraq from your Reigate office? We can check the phone records to make sure.' Zussman developed a faint quiver at the corner of his lip.

'All right, yes I have a contact in Iraq. He supplies some of my jewellery, what of it?'

'What else do you know about Mr Hassani?'

'Not much. I was put in touch with him some years ago by another of my business contacts. Hassani was looking for an opportunity to supply his jewellery in Europe. I believe he also has his produce on sale in Germany, France and Spain. I simply phone him when I need to order some more of his goods and he prepares the order. For convenience he arranges for it to be transported from Iraq, through Syria and into Turkey where Newton picks it up.'

'Very good, Mr Zussman, now we are getting somewhere. Where did you live before you came to this country?' Preston pursed her lips for the response.

'Frankfurt. It's where I was born.'

'No, Mr Zussman, it is not where you were born. I've checked.' Marshall stepped forward from the doorway as he spoke. 'Answer my colleague. Where were you born?'

Zussman was starting to shake. He was alone, unprotected and afraid.

'All right, all right, I was born in Syria. My parents were both killed when I was in my teens. I had my younger brother to look after and we stayed with an uncle. Then, when I was in my thirties I was offered a chance to come to Europe. It took some years to learn English and to set up a business.'

'Who set you up, Mr Zussman?' Preston smiled thinly at Marshall.

'I don't know, I swear it. They gave me identity papers, a passport and some money. When I arrived in England I was brought here to this house and shown where my shop was. I only had one to start with. I spent a few years building up the business, using the skills I had gained in Syria. Then a couple of years ago two men appeared in my shop, late one afternoon and said it was payback time. I honestly don't know who they are.' Zussman was almost crying now and Preston could not be sure he'd told her the whole truth.

'Thank you Mr Zussman. Now, we know you are in this country under an assumed name. What is your real name?'

'Mohammed Ali Burgansa. I was born in Alepp, in Syria, forty six years ago.' Zussman sighed as if relieved the truth was finally coming out.

At this point Preston decided to take a gamble. If Zussman was telling the truth then he could be of use to her, if not then she would take responsibility for the fallout.

'Mr Zussman, do you recognise any of these people.' Preston opened her handbag and took out a dozen pictures. They were the faces of the various targets ATRIUM had been watching intently for some while. Zussman looked at each picture in turn. He did not rush and his eyes showed no sign of recognition.

'No, I do not recognise any of them. Who are they?'

'That doesn't matter. Well, thank you for your time. I hope we haven't kept you from anything?'

'No.' Zussman sounded relieved. It was over, at least for now.

'There is just one final thing. You're not planning on going away anywhere, are you? It's just in case we need to talk to you again.'

'I am planning to take a small holiday at the end of next week. It's just a few days away, and then back to work as usual.'

'Are you going anywhere special?'

'No, no, just a few days down to the New Forest. There's a little hotel I stay at occasionally. The food is good and I can walk over the forest and relax. It is all I need, just a few days at a time.'

'I see, well I think we're done. Marshall, we'd best leave Mr Zussman in peace. It is Sunday, after all.'

'Ma'am,' Marshall replied, leading the way back to the front door.

'By the way, Mr Zussman, how do you get on with your neighbours?' Marshall asked him just before he opened the front door.

'Fine, thank you. It's a quiet road.'

'And the people over the road, how do you get on with them?'

'I never see them actually. Why do you ask?'

'Oh, just interested in the neighbourhood. I have a liking to understand how communities knit together. It's kind of a hobby. Well, we won't keep you and thanks for your time.'

Marshall opened the door fully and he and Preston marched back to his car. The interview was over and the tape machine he'd left running would have picked up everything that had been said. Marshall started the car, reversed it up the road and turned it round. As he did so, he spotted the curtains across the road twitching.

'Well,' Marshall began, 'I'd say he's running scared of something. I'd also say he's note very observant. He didn't recognise me from going to his shop the other day, the day when I purchased a retirement bracelet for Alan. I must give it to you before you sack him. So, if Zussman is one of them then he's in a whole pile of trouble once they find out about us. If he is part of the team then God only knows how much of that was lies. We'll have to check out Newton, of course, but the number is one of those pay as you go types so I doubt we'll get any joy from trying to trace it back to an owner. I'll get someone to look into Newton first thing tomorrow.'

'Yes, okay, you do that Travis. I'll get the intelligence people to do what they can on Hassani. Also, tomorrow, I want you to check out the flight schedules and bookings for the next two weeks. I want to see if either Zussman or someone by his real name is booked on any flight out of a UK airport. If there is, I want to know what plane he's on and when it leaves. Whatever else happens, until we've finished our enquiries into Zussman I don't want him leaving the country. I want twenty-four, seven surveillance on him and I want our chaps to be aware there are others watching him too, though God knows who they are.'

'We could break the door down and ask the person at the window,' Marshall offered.

'We could, and if he has links to our targets it would only make them go even more under cover. No, we know he's there, so we can leave it at that for the moment. What are you doing this afternoon?'

'I hadn't got anything planned after our chat with Zussman. Why?'

'Fancy a walk somewhere?'

'Yeah, I could do with some fresh air after that.'

'Oh, and that's a nice touch, about Alan.' Preston smiled conspiratorially.

* * *

Daniel Newton spent Sunday on the road. Being the weekend, the traffic was light and the often narrow roads were virtually empty. He knew the day would require a lot of driving so he set out very early. By the time the residents of Timisoara were waking up, Newton was sitting at a street-side table with a cup of dark coffee in his hand. The morning was warm for the time of year and Newton knew the temperature would rise further as he approached the Hungarian border.

He crossed the border with relative ease just before half past eleven and headed for Szeged on the river Tisza. Just south of Szeged, Newton knew of a hostelry that had gardens overlooking the river. With half the day's journey already behind him, he pulled into the café. The early start had made him hungry and the dusty roads had given him a thirst for beer. The Hungarian pint was cold and welcome as Newton sat in the quiet garden watching a sailing boat glide effortlessly downstream. His objective for the day was to reach the grandly named 'Hotel Zaldinski', a small establishment on the northern banks of Lake Balaton.

Newton had fallen in love with the place when he'd first found it. The hotel was part of a small village, a few miles from Veszprem, and Newton had made friends with a local woman, by the name of Fridaar. She was in her thirties and widowed. She was well educated and spoke fluent English, with a slightly distorted American accent. Newton had met her shortly after her husband had died. She had explained to him that her husband had been a boat owner. He plied his trade across the Balaton and had been involved in an accident which had claimed his life. The boat had sunk and it had been some weeks before the rescue teams had recovered both his body and that of his best friend. Newton and Fridaar had become good friends and he even wrote to her occasionally from

181

England. When he stayed at the hotel, she would stay with him. Decorum and custom dictated he could not stay at her place, so she went to visit him. They had a relationship that had been going on for a few years. Fridaar hoped that one day Newton would take her away from the place that held sad memories for her but Newton had never broached the subject with her.

The boat had sailed past the garden and was making its way quietly downstream. A few locals had joined Newton in the garden but they kept their distance. Newton could hear their heated conversation, though the language was something he knew nothing of so he couldn't tell what the discussion was about. Finally he downed the last mouthful of beer and set about the next stage of his journey. He was running exactly to his own schedule, a schedule he had followed many times before, a schedule other people knew about and had observed on a number of occasions.

As Newton left the hostelry a man sitting in the corner raised his head. He was a small, thin man, painfully thin. He wore a white, loose fitting top, shorts and sandals and sported a closely-cropped beard and short, dark hair. He watched Newton leave in his van and then picked the mobile phone out of his pocket. He dialled a number and waited for a few seconds. In an Arabic dialect he spoke briefly to the person at the other end, telling him Newton had passed through the town that morning. The conversation was short and succinct. It was enough to set the wheels in motion that would ensure the goods in Newton's van reached their intended destination on time. The countdown had been going for a few days. Now, with Newton passing through Hungary, the person on the other end of the phone knew there were just a few days left before the real mission began. Everything was ready and waiting, waiting for Newton to cross the English Channel with his precious and deadly cargo.

CHAPTER FIFTEEN

Hart spent the afternoon ensuring the young woman at his side was content and relaxed. They took luncheon at a Bier Keller just outside Munich and afterwards he drove her into the heart of Munich. They spent the afternoon viewing the sights and walking round the shops. To Sheera Ganzagha it seemed that she had stepped out of her closeted world in Yalvac into a completely new and almost unreal world. It took her some time to come to terms with the scale of Munich and when she had done so she began to enjoy herself.

Ganzagha was attracted to the clothes shops, the fashion shops for women and the array of shops selling perfume and cosmetics. She walked close to Hart, holding his hand for much of the time, scarcely able to believe a world like this actually existed.

They walked for much of the afternoon before Hart took her back to the hotel where they were staying. He took her up to his room and waited while she looked in wonder at the scenery outside the bedroom window. He waited while she unpacked her travel bag, placing her few possessions in a drawer and then they stood together, their lips meeting as they embraced passionately. The sun was beginning to fall towards the horizon as their desire for each other grew. It had been several months since Hart had touched this young, pretty woman and his desire for her was intense.

They undressed and climbed under the duvet. Hart had initially intended to wait until after the evening meal but the woman clearly wanted him now. He knew from past encounters that her appetite would not wane after their first act of passion, indeed it would only add to her desire, a desire which he would fulfil later that night.

Outside, the sun crept closer to the horizon and the streetlights started coming on. At the same time as Hart and Ganzagha were taking their mutual pleasures, Daniel

Newton arrived at the 'Hotel Zaldinski'. It was already dark when he arrived, exhausted from the day's travels. There had been an incident at the crossing over the River Danube, several miles north of Kiskoros. A cart had shed its wheel, toppling the cart onto its side. It had evidently happened during the morning and the remains of the cart were still at the side of the road when Newton finally pulled onto the bridge. The queue of traffic had been quite considerable and with traffic only able to pass over the bridge in one direction at a time, the delay had been considerable. In addition, the afternoon sun had been uncomfortably warm, adding to Newton's misery.

With relief, he parked the white van in the make-shift car park and took his overnight bag from the passenger foot-well. He pushed open the front door to the establishment and smiled when he saw Fridaar waiting for him. She was chatting to the owner of the place, someone she had known for many years. He knew of her affair with Newton but could be trusted to keep news of it from reaching the ears of the village's gossip-mongers. Hart went through the check-in formalities and in less than ten minutes he and Fridaar were in his bedroom.

They kissed briefly before Newton went to fill the bath. He was tired, felt grubby and needed to relax. Fridaar understood his tiredness but had needs of her own. As the water poured into the bath, Newton lay out fresh clothes to wear and undressed. Fridaar talked to him and told him the local news. There wasn't much, there never was, but she always felt obliged to keep Newton up to date. When the water had been run, Newton kissed Fridaar, promised her he would be as quick as possible and went into the bathroom. He had been sitting in the water for less than two minutes when Fridaar joined him. She had stripped naked and as she stood in the doorway to the bathroom, Newton could not help but admire her beauty. She clearly looked after herself and Newton felt sorry that such a beautiful woman had been widowed at such a young age. She deserved to be happy.

'Would you like that I join you in the water?' She asked mischievously. She spoke perfect English but put on the phoney accent and faltering style whenever she was feeling mischievous. After two months without Newton she was feeling extremely mischievous.

'Okay, come on in. I could do with someone to wash my back.' Newton laughed back.

As he watched the Hungarian beauty step into the room he wondered whether one day he would ask her to come back to England with him. It was certainly a thought he had considered a number of times and each time they met his desire for her increased. Of all his female acquaintances across Europe, Fridaar was his favourite. He could live without the others if he had to, but it was the woman who now sat in the bath with him that he really wanted. Ganzagha was fiery and she was young but Newton knew she wanted him only so she could get away from her uncle and Yalvac.

Rebeka, the dark-haired Siren in Konya was a similar age to Fridaar. She was a good cook certainly, but she lived a simple life, a life that Newton could not appreciate. He felt the warm bubbles on his back as Fridaar rubbed them into his skin and felt he could live without Rebeka as part of his itinerary. Perhaps he should use this visit to ask Fridaar her feelings, to see if she would come to England to be with him. If so, then he could get out of the importing business and find something to do closer to home.

The redhead in Istanbul he could easily live without. Her fiery temper was a stimulant but she had on more than one occasion taken her temper out on Newton. He continued to visit her because he liked his comforts and she was a convenient person to be able to visit. Istanbul was a key stopping point for Newton on his journeys. He stayed there both on the outward journey and on the journey back home. Still, the woman was not someone he'd settle down with. Fridaar was still rubbing the bubbles into his back, but now she was using her nails and gently scratching him. She moved up to his neck and gently lifted the short hairs she found there. She knew it aroused Newton and she wanted him aroused.

Newton felt the tiny prickling sensations on the back of his neck and knew what Fridaar wanted. It was time to satisfy her needs. After all she had been very patient with him, waiting for him to relax. Newton had not made love to her in the bath before but now he did so, slowly, passionately and tenderly at first then with increasing vigour as their passion increased.

***

Simon Hart took his time with Sheera Ganzagha. He didn't want to cause her alarm or make her feel uncomfortable in any way. He stroked her, caressed her, and touched her in all the ways he knew she liked. After he had finished he rolled over and looked out of the window. The sun had gone for the day.

'I have an idea,' he said. 'Before we go for dinner, how about a drive around Munich to see it with all the lights on? They say it is quite spectacular in places.'

'Okay, Simon, that would be nice,' she replied dreamily, 'but I would like a shower first.'

Hart really was a very nice man, so much more refined than Newton. Ganzagha thought she was getting tired of Newton's ways with her. He lacked sensitivity, lacked the attention she delighted in when she was with Hart. Perhaps, she thought, she should have no more to do with Newton. After all, the man she was now with paid for her to travel to see him. When did Newton ever do that?

'That's not a problem. We're not in a hurry. Take all the time you want.' Hart tickled her back as he spoke. She was a good lover. AS things stood maybe they'd have a future but for now he was on a mission he'd planned meticulously and he could not let anything jeopardise the end result. Ganzagha was part of his plan, she had her role to play.

Hart rolled back onto the sheet and looked blankly up at the ceiling, distracted by the thoughts of the plans he had spent so long making, and what he was about to do.

'Have you ever thought about coming to England?' He asked her.

'What, for a holiday. Yes, it would be nice to see around London.'

'No, I meant to live there.'

'Well, no, I mean I don't know anyone there who I could live with.'

'There is always me.' He laughed gently as if playing a game with her.

'Simon, you are such a sweet man and yes I would love to come to England to stay with you sometime, but I don't know if I could make it a permanent thing, it would be such a change to what I am used to.'

'I see.' Hart understood the culture changes she would experience. Perhaps it was unfair to even think she might try to adapt.

Ganzagha turned to face him and placed her hand on his chest.

'Maybe it would work, but I cannot be sure. We have never spent more than a day or two together. I need time to get to know you before I commit to such a big decision as coming permanently to England.' Ganzagha looked at Hart closely. She had already decided that Newton would have been a good excuse to get into England but she would never have stayed with him. Hart was different. She could, perhaps, make a life with him, but she needed time to discover if it was possible.

'Okay, take all the time you need, but think about it.' Hart had put the woman at her ease. She would trust him now, do what he needed her to do. 'You'd better have your shower before we get into anything deeper.'

'Okay,' she smiled. She clambered out of the bed and went to the bathroom. Hart heard the sound of the shower, smiled and started to dress. The delectable Sheera Ganzagha was a part of the plan and the plan had to come first. If it didn't, five years of planning would have been pointless.

Twenty minutes later they were driving through Munich taking in the sights and sounds of the night. From there, Hart drove to the country house that had been converted into an upmarket restaurant. The meal was exquisite, beautifully presented and cooked to perfection. It added to the false sense of security Hart wanted to give the woman he was with. As they ate he looked into her radiant face and cursed himself for allowing his emotions to get the better of him. He ate slowly, pondering the days ahead. He would be busy and, if things went according to the plan, he'd end up very rich indeed, far more wealthy than he already was.

The meal over, Hart led the young woman onto the veranda and from there they strolled around the spacious gardens. Some of the other diners elected to follow their actions. They wandered along the flower beds full of blooms and came across a gazebo that was almost hidden beneath a huge creeper of some kind. Hart stood in the gazebo and pulled the woman towards him. They kissed passionately under the moonlit sky. Sheera Ganzagha was an extremely happy woman and suddenly the thought of living in England with Hart appealed to her.

'You know,' she said after a minute, 'I've been thinking. Why don't I come back to England with you this time, stay a while and see if things work out?' She kissed him again, the smell of the strawberry flan on her breath.

'Yes, it would be possible,' Hart started, 'but what about your folks back home?'

'They know I am with you here. I have told them all about you and they are happy for me. They know I have wanted to go to England for some years, so to go now would not be a problem. I could always go and visit them soon and take you with me. That way we could pick up my few possessions, if things worked out. Please say yes, Simon.'

'Okay, if you really want to.' The plan had worked perfectly but Hart could never let her know that. 'There is one thing, though. I have to visit Paris on the way back. There's something I have to do there.'

'Paris, I have heard so much about Paris. Can I come with you?'

'You'll have to if you are coming with me to England,' Hart smiled, 'but it will only be an overnight visit.'

'That sounds great. Shall we go back to the hotel, Simon? I have something I want to do for you.'

Hart took the hint.

CHAPTER SIXTEEN

Monday 29th June

Monday 29th June dawned fair and mild. Daniel Newton was an early riser. Today was the day in his journey he liked most. He would be across the border into Austria by late morning and would reach his favourite travellers lodge just south of Munich sometime during the late afternoon. In between he would pass through the breathtakingly spectacular views of the Austrian countryside. Newton had seen 'The Sound of Music' when he'd been a child and had always remembered the spectacular scenery. Now, every time he passed through the country, he longed to be a part of it. He longed to stay with the fresh Alpine air, the quiet and quaint Bavarian village life, the Bier-Keller and the freedom. Yet, as with every journey, his dream would last only a few hours. Still, he could savour it once again and think to the future. One day, he promised himself, he would do more than simply drive through this beautiful country.

Newton had spent the evening with Fridaar but she had left him for her own bed before they had turned in. Her decision to go home had left Newton surprised. Often she stayed the night with him but on this occasion she seemed to have something on her mind. He'd asked her gently but she had given no clue as to the issue that was weighing her down. Whatever the problem was, it had distracted Newton and he had failed to suggest she go with him back to England.

Simon Hart had spent much of the night awake. The woman beside him had quickly become an unexpected and significant part in Hart's life, even if such elevation might only be a temporary thing. Hart cursed his own emotions, the one thing he had not planned for, if he was honest with himself. Hart knew he'd have to take her into his confidence, there was no way he could execute the rest of the plan without her knowledge. It meant a complete rethink of the plan for the next few days and possibly even greater changes once they were back in England.

Ganzagha was still sleeping soundly when Hart turned on his laptop. He used his mobile phone to make the necessary connection to the world and in a moment was downloading the latest set of information. After a few minutes the screen was covered in figures, figures which made Hart frown.

'Bloody fool,' he muttered to himself quietly. 'Why the hell did he want to shift twenty grand straight into a UK bank account. Doesn't the fool know it will be traced? I've told him loads of times to be careful.'

'Told who, darling?' Ganzagha was lying on the bed, propped up on one arm, looking at Hart. He looked up from the laptop and smiled back.

'Sorry, did I wake you up?'

'No, not really, what is the matter?'

Hart explained what the matter was. He explained how he'd spent a small fortune funding a manufacturing plant in the East and how he made money on the Internet. He explained how he had built up this enormous secretive business to do it all and how important it was that the business remained secret. There were people who would not take kindly to him if they knew he was responsible for the business. There were others who were jealous of his success and would do anything to stop him as it would mean their own businesses would have a better chance of doing well. Then Hart had made some contacts and now one of them had just moved a rather large amount of money without thinking of the consequences. That was the matter.

'You see, Sheera,' he continued, 'the success of my business demands that my business affairs remain a secret to the outside world and now this idiot has moved the money. Well, he has put us at risk of being exposed. But I can stop him doing it again'

Exposed! That was the real problem so far as Hart was concerned. He knew already that the business accounts were being monitored. After all he'd been monitoring the activities of SB4 for four years, so he knew they were anxious to discover who he was. There were others who also wanted him out of business, if only because his demise would have the direct effect of furthering their own aims. Hart also knew about ATRIUM. His contacts were every bit as powerful as those who had set up that organisation. Yet, he had one big advantage, he knew about them all but they didn't know who he was. It thrilled him to think they wanted to know who he was. It challenged him and over the years made him more and more determined that his business would remain a mystery to them. Now, the stupid Jamaican, Pritwick, had committed the cardinal sin and risked the whole operation being exposed.

'Why is that such a problem?'

'Because my business plans will make us very, very wealthy. Now, there are people who won't take kindly to that, people who don't want to see others make a good living. There are people who will do all they can to stop me and that would be a shame after five years hard work.'

'And was meeting me part of your business?'

'Initially, yes it was. Let me explain. Some time ago I realised someone was out to jeopardise my whole business so I set about trying to find out who they were. I had certain people followed in my home country and then the pieces of the jigsaw started to come together. I followed one guy these people use. You must understand they have all built businesses for themselves in Britain and most of those businesses are fronts - they import certain kinds of goods from the East and the Arab countries for their shops, but their real business is done behind the scenes. Anyway, I followed this guy to Turkey and saw him meet you. Then something happened. I was told by a contact that the people who wanted to put me out of business were planning to bring something into the country that would help them achieve their aims. I figured they'd use their courier to do it so I set up a series of contacts across Europe to monitor his movements. You were one of those contacts and I think you will agree I have paid you handsomely.'

'Yes, you have paid me very well, for such little work and the chance to get to know you. I am very grateful. Tell me, Simon, is this business dangerous?'

'It could be, which is why we are here now. You see, this is the trip when the courier is bringing their consignment into England. You recall I wanted to know about some jewellery boxes; well the consignment is inside the boxes.'

'How can jewellery put you out of business?' Hart laughed as she asked the question.

'It can't, but the other contents in the boxes can. In fact they could literally kill off my entire business, which is why I'm here now, to intercept the packages so they cannot be used against me.'

'Are you sure about all this?' Ganzagha was sitting on the edge of the bed now.

'Positive. There were two dozen jewellery boxes, weren't there?'

'Yes.'

'Well I have well over a dozen establishments in England that form my business empire. The contents of each box can be used to destroy an establishment.'

'You mean there are explosives in the boxes?'

'No! I do not mean that kind of destruction. The boxes contain a tiny phial of liquid. The liquid is very dangerous and if spilled in a building would mean the building had to be sealed off and could not be used for several months. You see, my contacts know that my adversaries, those who would take my business away from me, simply have to close down my establishments and in a few weeks my business will be gone for ever. It is like that on the Internet these days. So they plan to make my establishments unusable and take my business away from me.'

'Can't you simply open up other places?'

'Yes, but it would take too long. We are talking several million pounds worth of hardware alone, let alone all the expertise and the time it would all take. These phials will be in Britain in a few days' time and then they will be delivered to my offices.'

'Does the courier know all of this?'

'No, I do not think so. He thinks he is simply transporting his usual items. If he did know he would be too scared to transport them.'

'So, what are you planning to do?'

'He will be arriving in Munich tonight. After he has gone to bed I plan to take the phials out of his van and replace them with dummy boxes, fakes, which I have brought with me. I hope then that he will drive to England without knowing they are gone.'

'What do you intend to do with the phials?'

'I have someone I can trust, someone who can deal with them and destroy them safely. You don't need to worry about that.'

'So, what can I do to help you? If I am to be with you I must be part of what you are doing.' It was what Hart was hoping to hear.

'You can help me this evening, to get the capsules away from the van. Then we will travel to Paris. We'll take the car to there and then we can catch the Eurostar to England – it is safer than flying.'

'Okay, but promise me we won't be in danger.' Ganzagha sensed adventure and she was looking forward to the kind of excitement she had often dreamed about while living in Yalvac.

'We are not in any danger, Sheera, trust me! Once I have the phials I will be able to pass them onto my contact in Paris tomorrow. Now, you are sure the boxes are the same colour and size as they have been for the last year or more?'

'I am sure. Uncle Saltig is not security conscious. It is easy for me to keep an eye on things. Okay, so what do you want to do today?' She walked over to Hart and draped her naked arms around his neck. Hart had been typing on the computer while they had been talking. Now he switched off the laptop.

'That will stop the fool moving any more money. I have changed the access code to the business account he had access to. If I can't trust him then he can't have access. Right, Sheera, first, I think we should get dressed and have some breakfast. Shall I order room service?'

'That's a good idea.'

***

Marshall didn't have much to go on. The mobile phone was pay-as-you-go and turned out to be unregistered. Marshall also had a brief description of Daniel Newton but, for now, he had no idea where Newton actually lived. All he knew was Newton was within striking range of Zussman's Reigate shop, but then for someone used to travelling the length of Europe he could live almost anywhere on mainland Britain. As Marshall had discovered, there were a lot of D. Newton's living in the UK. It would take far too long to check on them all.

At nine o'clock Marshall made the breakthrough he needed. He was sure Newton crossed the Channel by boat rather than use the train, because it was cheaper, so Marshall decided to see if he could find records of a Daniel Newton making a crossing in the past few weeks. He'd tapped into the ferry company's booking system. It was a simple enough system to hack into once you knew where to start and Marshall found a ticket issued for a Daniel Newton three weeks previously. The ticket had been sent to Newton's address, details of which Marshall noted carefully. He checked the booking system database carefully and found a similar booking sent to the same address a couple of months previously. Marshall closed the connection on the computer and waited to see what the Port Authorities came up with.

Newton's address was in Banbury, too far for Marshall to contemplate visiting on a whim, but close enough for one of Harding's men to take a look at. Marshall phoned Harding direct and asked the favour. For his part, Harding was keen to assist. As the new boy in the team's leadership he wanted to make some kind of impression, preferably not the kind made by his predecessor. Marshall put the phone down and knew it would take some hours before Harding would be able to confirm whether they were on the right track.

Marshall turned his attentions to the residence he'd followed Christine Matthews to a few evenings previously. The land registry had already told him the estate was owned by someone called Simon David Hart. Now, Marshall spent time looking for Simon Hart on the systems he had access to. There was nothing on the criminal records file, nothing from the drivers licensing centre at Swansea, other than Simon Hart did have a full driving licence and it tied in with the address he had followed Matthews to. Marshall did a credit check but gained little information. Hart didn't have a mortgage or any debt outstanding on his three credit cards.

The records at Companies House were checked and Marshall found nothing. It seemed almost as if Hart didn't exist in anything other than name. Then Marshall remembered his visit to Christine Matthews' house and the payslip confirmation from Braddock Holdings. He wondered for a moment what services she had offered the mysterious company and dismissed the notion that it would have been anything sinister.

The enquiries were taking up time, valuable time Marshall could ill-afford to waste. The interview with Zussman the previous day had been useful but it had opened up more lines of enquiry than it had closed. The fact Zussman had turned out to be a fake, a rehashed Syrian with a Jewish sounding name, was not of immediate consequence. People from that part of the world would, in times of need, resort to many tactics to gain entry into Europe and in particular Great Britain. Changing identities was just one of the tactics the intelligence services had come to accept happened. The fact Zussman was trading with a guy in Iraq was also of little consequence because it was hardly big business. What was of possible consequence was the appearance of the unidentified plant in the Syrian desert.

Marshall reclined in his chair and closed his eyes. He began to piece together a hypothetical jigsaw. What if the plant was sinister in nature? What if it was there to create weapons of mass destruction? What if those weapons were destined for the West? Newton was out there now picking up jewellery boxes from a supplier who came from Iraq. Could he be involved in something sinister? Were the targets simply waiting for something to be brought into the country, and if so, what? Marshall had been trained to think the worst, think around the 'might be' scenarios and formulate strategies to test out his theories.

Marshall began to focus his thoughts on the jewellery boxes. Certainly they couldn't conceal anything large but Marshall knew the most deadly of weapons were almost invisible. He knew various countries had developed viruses for which there were no vaccines. The Salisbury poisoning had been proof of that, if proof were needed. What if that was what the plant in Syria was doing? Certainly the boxes could conceal capsules of a reasonable size. Would they be large enough to allow whatever they contained to bring destruction on a large scale? Marshall didn't have the answers but it was a theory, one he would put to Preston later that day. Slowly he felt the jigsaw was coming together.

Certainly the contact between the targets and Zussman could be explained by the theory. Zussman was the middle-man, the vital contact between the Arabs and their groups in Britain. Newton was also part of the picture, he was the courier. That being the case, Newton would have to be searched on entry to the country, both from the current journey and subsequent ones.

Marshall already knew the kind of vehicle Newton drove and the index number. The people at Swansea had been cooperative on the matter and now the Port Authorities had the vehicle on their hit list. Whenever Newton came into the country by boat or by train, his van would have to be taken apart and searched with a fine toothcomb. If they found anything out of the ordinary then it would result in Newton's immediate arrest and confiscation of the suspected item. The orders were succinct and written copies would be faxed to the relevant authorities within a few hours. The call to the Port Authorities lasted nearly half an hour.

***

Dieter Zussman began his Monday morning routine as if nothing concerned him. He knew he was being watched both by the people who'd brought him to the country and by the authorities. At least he assumed the authorities were watching him now, so he decided to do nothing out of the ordinary. He opened the shop in Reigate as usual and called through to his other shop in Dorking to check all was in order.

He was sitting in the small back-office when the phone rang. His assistant, Sandra, had not yet arrived.

'Good morning, this is Zussman jewellers, how can I help you?'

'Dieter, it is Daniel, how are things with you?'

'Not too bad, Daniel, but it is cold and damp today and you know I hate that kind of weather.'

'Yes. Listen, Dieter, I'm travelling through Austria today. This is such a beautiful country.'

'Yes, I know, Daniel. How is the journey going?'

'Oh, fine. I should be home on Thursday. I'll stop off at Munich tonight, then somewhere in France the next day and catch an early crossing on Thursday. I should get to you early afternoon if all goes to plan.'

'And the goods are all safe?'

'Sure they are. They're all locked in the back of my van, packed carefully so nothing fragile gets damaged.'

'Have you checked inside the boxes?'

'No, but if the person who packed them was careful then everything will be okay. Do you want me to check each box when I stop next?'

'No, there is no need for that, Daniel. I'll see you on Thursday sometime. Have a safe journey home.'

'Thanks, Dieter, and you take care of yourself too. I'd best go now. It costs me a fortune to use the mobile phone for international calls. See you Thursday.'

The call ended and Zussman returned to the clock cleaning he had started the previous Saturday. It was a beautiful mechanism, in solid brass, but it had suffered from the years of neglect. Zussman knew he could restore the device to its former glory with a lot of care and patience. He continued the work from where he had left off and was engrossed in the matter when Sandra finally turned up.

'Sorry I'm late, but the crossing was down at the bottom of the hill and the traffic was stacked almost back up to the motorway.'

'That's all right, Sandra. It's just one of those things we have to live with, traffic. What do you think?' Zussman held up the grubby mechanism for the woman to look at.

'It'll look like new when you've finished. Are you going to strip it right down?'

'Yes, but oh so very carefully, and noting where each part goes. We don't want to make any mistakes with this beauty.'

***

Hundreds of miles away, Simon Hart had taken Ganzagha into Munich. He found the shops he needed. The hardware store was a good one. Of particular interest to Hart that morning were the mouse traps. Conventional spring-loaded traps were what he needed and he found them. He also purchased a roll of thin, metal wire.

The small hobby shop in a back street was Hart's next destination. There he purchased two radio controllers with servo motors. They were small motors and came supplied with gearing. They were ideal for his intentions. Next, and to Ganzagha's growing surprise, they visited a horologist's. The shop window was full with clocks and watches of many makes and designs. Hart purchased two small carriage clocks of a conventional design, with a wind-up mechanism and a complex set of cogs and other parts that allowed the instrument to tell the time. At the same time, Hart bought Ganzagha an expensive digital watch by a famous maker. It had eleven small diamonds down each side of the rectangular face and the black dial was inlaid with two further diamonds at the twelve and six o'clock positions.

Ganzagha was thrilled with the watch and intrigued by Hart's other purchases of the morning.

'What is all that stuff for?' She asked when she knew they couldn't be overheard.

'Well, the mouse traps are for catching mice, usually, but I have another use for them. The springs are strong enough to break your little finger, and the clocks and motors will be used so the springs can be released at a predetermined time.'

'I don't understand.'

'Don't worry about things you don't need to worry about. I think that might be a Buddhist saying, but I am not sure. Now, I think it is time we had lunch. Shall we find a Bier-Keller?'

'That would be nice. What do you want to do this afternoon?'

'I think we should go back to the hotel and rest. Remember we are going to have a busy evening and I have to see if I can make these devices work properly.'

'And will you have time for me?'

'Of course,' Hart winked at her, 'and you can help me make these traps.'

'Have you done this kind of thing before?'

'Yes, a few times.'

'So you know what you are doing?'

'Yes, I know what I'm doing.' Survival was something Hart was good at and the techniques he'd learned on a survival training course were going to come in very useful over the next few days. 'Now, you are worrying too much about things you don't need to concern yourself with. I'll explain more later on but now I fancy a pint and some food.'

After lunch they went back to the hotel room. Hart showed the woman how to assemble the traps and the clock mechanisms so that the trap would be released at a predefined moment, anytime up to twelve hours after the device had been set. He tested the effectiveness of both devices and when he was satisfied, he turned his attentions to the woman who had sat bemused and intrigued while he had stripped the clocks and made the preparations. If she had any inkling as to his real purposes she didn't show it, she was simply excited at the thought of going back to England.

When he'd packed the two devices into a bag she asked the question that had been on her mind for the whole afternoon.

'Why did you have to do that here? Couldn't we have assembled them when we got back to England?'

'I have other, more sophisticated, devices back in England. These are just to set a couple of traps on our way back, small things really, just to let the people I am fighting know that I have what they wanted and that I mean business. It is nothing drastic, just a statement of intent.'

'Oh, I see. Rub me just a bit lower, Simon, please. Ah yes, just there.' Hart was caressing her back and moved to the spot she indicated. She really was a lovely, warm, person and as attentive to him as he was to her.

201

The afternoon passed and evening drew in. As it did so, the white van driven by Daniel Newton pulled into the car park of the GastHaus he stayed at, just on the outskirts of Munich. As with every stopover, Newton extracted his bag from the foot-well in front of the passenger seat, slung the bag effortlessly over his shoulder and carefully locked the van. Ten minutes later Newton was running a hot bath and relaxing from the day's driving. The weather had grown noticeably cooler and Newton was grateful for the thick jumper he had brought on the journey. He planned to eat in the establishment's restaurant and then take a walk in the park that was just a short distance away. He'd had the window of the van open as he drove through the Inne valley and on through Bavaria, but the breeze had been mingled with the fumes from the vehicles on the road and Newton wanted to stretch his legs and enjoy the cool evening air as he strolled causally along the paths that were edged with beds of summer flowers.

At eight o'clock his meal was over and Newton set out from the GastHaus. He walked slowly to the park. At twenty past eight Hart and Ganzagha pulled into the car park. She identified the white van and Hart parked the rental car. He parked it so the car faced the van, giving them a clear view of the entrance to the building ahead of them. If Newton appeared then Ganzagha would simply sound the horn and Hart would be clear of the van before Newton could get there. Hart kissed her gently and exited the car holding a large, bulky bag. Sheera had not asked him what was in the bag when he'd placed it in the back of the car earlier that evening. Keeping her eyes firmly on the GastHaus entrance, Ganzagha did not see the ease with which Hart opened the back door of the van. In fact his dexterity was such that any onlooker would have assumed he had a set of keys, which was precisely what he did have. Some months previously one of his contacts had followed Newton to a public house in England. The contact had carefully removed the set of keys from Newton's jacket pocket and equally carefully made an impression of the key in a small tobacco tin filled with soft wax. Reproducing the key and having an extra spare key cut had been easy. Hart left the back door open as he worked on the small package of jewellery boxes. It took him two minutes to complete what he was doing, two minutes during which Ganzagha became more and more nervous.

Suddenly a man appeared at the doorway to the building. Ganzagha instinctively reached over to the steering wheel and held her hand poised to strike the pad that would sound the horn. She looked closely at the man for a few moments. He was drawing on a cigarette as he stood nonchalantly in the entrance. Ganzagha relaxed for a moment and was surprised when the driver's door opened and the bag was placed on the back seat again.

'That was quick.' Her voice sounded surprised and at the same time, relieved.

'Yeah, it was easy. Those crates are easy to break into and lucky for us, the boxes were right at the back.'

'Did you find what you were looking for?'

By way of reply, Hart held up one of the boxes.

'What did you have in the bag earlier?' She asked and reached up to take the box away from Hart. He moved the box out of her reach.

'Careful. What is in there is dangerous. And in answer to your question, I replaced his boxes with my own ones. They look the same, but they have only very cheap watches in them, though passable fakes for the genuine ones we have here now.'

'Why are expensive watches dangerous?' Sheera asked him.

'They are not dangerous, what is dangerous is inside the short cylinder that is used to support the strap of each watch. Each cylinder contains a small phial with some liquid in it.'

'What is it? Some sort of acid?'

Hart laughed.

'No,' he said, 'it's actually called Wipeout. It's a sort of bug and if you release it then it will make you very ill.'

'And that's what these people wanted to release in your offices?'

'Yes. They want to make all the workers sick and contaminate the building and hey, you put me out of business. Still, that won't happen now.'

'Surely they can get some more?' Ganzagha was still looking at Hart, not fully understanding what she was getting into. She would find out soon enough, but too late to stop her falling for the man who was still smiling confidently in her direction.

'It will take them time, too much time.' He said assuredly.

'We are safe, aren't we? I mean, they won't leak or anything, will they?'

'I shouldn't think so. The phials are encased in high grade plastic and the phials have been designed to take quite a bump before they crack. If they were going to leak I think our friend in the van might have become ill by now.' Hart decided not to reveal the plastic containers were in two parts that screwed together to enclose the phial within.

'Does he know about these capsules?'

'I don't know,' said Hart, 'but I doubt it. He wouldn't need to know so my guess is he doesn't. You've got to remember he's just a courier boy. Think about it. How many couriers actually know what's inside the parcels they deliver?'

'Not many.'

'Exactly, Sheera, now stop worrying and let's get back to the hotel. We have a busy day tomorrow and I want my evening meal.

Suddenly, Ganzagha grabbed his arm.

'Over there,' she muttered, suddenly afraid. 'It's Daniel.'

Hart looked in the direction she was pointing. Sure enough, Newton was just returning to the GastHaus, his walk evidently complete.

'Did you lock the van again?' She asked in a small voice.

'Of course I did. He won't suspect anything until he gets back to England, by which time it will be too late for him to do anything about it.'

'Do you think he noticed anything?' Ganzagha was trembling slightly, not from the cool night air but from fear. This was new to her, the adrenalin rush of adventure, and she had not learned to control the natural tendency of the human body to try to escape. She was frightened like a rabbit sitting in the middle of the road, trapped by the oncoming lights of a vehicle.

'No, he has noticed nothing. Look, he's going inside. Now, another minute he might have caught a glimpse of you as we drove past him but at this distance he wouldn't have seen anything at all. Come on, Sheera, relax, you're making me nervous.' Hart knew the smell of fear and he was used to the adrenalin, but the nervous woman beside him was unnerving him. He put the box back in the bag. Back at the hotel he had a small case that was lined with foam, into which had been cut twenty four cylindrical holes each of which were precisely the right size to contain one of the cylinders he had just taken from the white van. He would spend time that night, after Sheera had gone to sleep, carefully taking the cylinders out of the watch boxes, and transferring them to the holes in the foam that lined the small case. The watches could be disposed of at some point. They were of no use to Hart.

Hart started the car and drove back to the hotel.

***

Dieter Zussman knew the moment for his departure was fast approaching. His courier, Daniel Newton, was already in Munich which meant he had just less than three days before he would be in possession of the jewellery boxes. He knew also that a few hours after the boxes arrived he would be relieved of them. All he had to do was make one phone call to a number he had written on a piece of paper and the organisation that had brought him to England would swing into operation. He sat on the edge of his bed and looked at the silver picture frame. He picked it up and looked at the picture of the two boys before turning it over.

With great care he pushed back the six tiny retaining clips and the back of the mount was released. Delicately, with the touch of a man used to handling fragile objects, he prised the mount away from the frame. The slip of paper fell onto his lap. As carefully, Zussman replaced the mount and repositioned the picture on his bedside table. From now on he would carry the piece of paper in his wallet. He would have the telephone number to hand when the need arose.

He looked out of his bedroom window and watched the raindrops as they clung to the glass, sliding downwards under gravity. It was a miserable night outside and Zussman was glad he did not have to venture out.

Across the road the observer noted the usual pattern of movements from Zussman's abode and continued listening to the latest CD he'd had delivered a few days previously. The observer knew nothing about what was planned. His only concern was making sure Zussman did nothing untoward. The observer was bored. He'd been holed up for three months and still had another month to go before he would be replaced. His food and other needs were brought to him on a regular basis. Other than the occasional contact with his leader, and the music he loved to listen to, he had nothing to do with his time. He'd read a few books but got fed up with them. They were in English, a language he didn't speak very well and read even less well, so he was not interested in them. He had no idea why Zussman was so important to someone. It was not his position to know and the fact he didn't know didn't bother him. He was not entitled to be in the country anyway, so he was grateful for everything that came his way.

The rain was falling steadily and a strong breeze had come from nowhere. The sound of the rain pelting against the window made Zussman long even more for the day when his memories of the country would have faded. Before that day he knew there would be much to go through. Immediately he would have to handle the boxes from Newton. He only had a vague idea what they contained and he knew they were dangerous, but he had no choice.

Ahmed, his brother, would be released if all went according to plan and that was something Zussman wanted above all else. It was the only reason he was continuing to go along with the group that had brought him to England. They, or a close connection, held his brother in Syria, thus ensuring Zussman's cooperation. He could easily have settled down under his assumed identity and continued to grow his legitimate business. Indeed, he was planning the third shop when news of his brother's capture and his required cooperation had become known to him. At first he'd been reluctant to put his business plans on hold but he'd had no real choice. As soon as Zussman had seen the drawings of the capsules he'd realised what was going to happen, maybe not the precise nature, but at least the essence of the plans.

Now he sat in his bedroom and hoped the next few days would pass without a hitch, if only so he could make good his planned escape.

CHAPTER SEVENTEEN

Tuesday 30th June

Selena Preston looked out of her office window as The London Eye continued its relentless journey in the distance. The morning was fine but grey clouds hovered on the horizon and the forecast was for rain later on. Selena Preston was a troubled woman, something she was not accustomed to. First there was her relationship with Marshall to think about. Would it go anywhere? What would happen if it did? Then there were more pressing matters. The small matter of checking out Dieter Zussman's alternative identity had fallen to Marshall, while Harding had been tasked with checking out the address for Daniel Newton.

Deciding who to contact first for a progress update, Preston picked up the phone and dialled the number she needed.

'Roger Harding, how can I help you?' The man's voice responded after just two rings.

'Hi, it's Preston, are you secure?'

'Yes Ma'am, how can I help you?' Harding was suddenly very awake.

'How are you getting on with looking into Newton?'

'I was going to email you the report thus morning. I went to his address last night. As expected it was dark inside and locked up. I gained access fairly easily. The guy is not that security conscious. There are no alarms or sensors in the building and I spent about an hour going through the four rooms. Not much to report, I'm afraid. I found a file of papers, presumably for his tax returns as they are mostly invoices and receipts. It looks like he does the same trip to Turkey every three months or so, less frequently in the winter. The manifests indicate he usually brings back much the same type of products, so presumably he is acting as some kind of a courier for one or more shops here in the UK. The only thing I thought was a bit strange is the last year of trips he has always brought back exactly the same quantity of what are stated to be high-end watches, individually packaged in their own display cases.'

'How many, Harding?'

'Two dozen. Okay that could be to cover possible sales peaks and troughs, but everything else, the bracelets, necklaces and rings have styles and quantities that vary each trip, not by much, but they do vary. If I was paranoid I'd think the constant number of these watches is significant.'

'Thank you, Harding. Anything else?'

'Only that Mr Newton is on one of his trips at the moment. As Marshall discovered, he left the country for Europe by boat a few weeks ago. Looking at his usual length of trip I'd say he would be due back in the next few days but the return ticket is one of those open-ended ones to be used at some point within a number of days from the original ticket date. I did find a previous year's diary in his flat and the initial scan suggests he is usually away on these trips for four or five weeks maximum. Marshall told me he has already alerted the Port Authorities as to the type of vehicle and the registration number that Newton is driving and assuming they notice him coming through customs they will do a thorough search of the van and take it from there.'

'Good. I'm going to talk to Marshall in a moment. What with us talking to the jewellery shop owner on Sunday and discovering he is not who he has been claiming to be, and the fact he is the person who is importing the watches and other items using Newton as the delivery boy, I am pretty sure we have found our courier boy. The question is what is he bringing into the country if it is not just watches and other items of jewellery?'

'If you want an opinion Ma'am...'

'Yes, I'm asking your opinion, Harding.'

'I'd say it has something to do with those display cases. As it's the same type and quantity each trip, I'd suspect they have been practicing for something and for all we know, they still are. So, I'll bet the watches are legitimate and very possibly your jeweller has a stash of unsold items somewhere. If they are really high-end, unless he has an outlet in the right area of the country, he's going to find it hard to shift many of them in a month, every month for over a year, which is what the old diary I found indicates has been happening. So I'd focus on what else those boxes could be carrying. I know it sounds daft as it would have to be small but it would also have to be the kind of thing that would also not arouse suspicion if a box was opened at a border crossing for a cursory examination. That, Ma'am, is my opinion.'

'Thank you, Harding. Small as in drug packets do you think?'

'I doubt it Ma'am. The dogs would be sure to sniff that out. Assuming these are the usual box sizes, something like you'd get with say a Gucci watch, then there would be nowhere to hide any significant quantity of drugs with enough wrapping to fool the canine detectives.'

'Hmm, you have a point. Okay Harding, I have to press on. Good work. If you turn up anything else let me or Marshall know.'

'Will do, Ma'am.'

Preston ended the call and looked briefly over the notes she'd been making. Harding was thorough but he really needed to be able to précis his reports somewhat. It was something she'd mention when they next had a formal appraisal.

With her call to Harding over, Preston pressed the speed dial code for Marshall.

'Marshall, are you secure?' The voice was authoritative but friendly.

'Yes, Ma'am.' Marshall detected from the tone of her voice that this was business as opposed to anything else.

'Good, how are your enquiries going? I just need an update.'

'Harding has been checking out Newton.'

'Yes, I know, I've just been talking to him. Possibly he's a courier boy but I don't think he actually knows what he has got into.'

'I agree. I've been looking into Simon Hart. He owns outright the mansion I followed Christine Matthews to the other night. He also has other properties dotted around the country, including an apartment in London. His portfolio also includes a villa in Northern Spain on the Mediterranean coast. He has no debts, impeccable credit ratings, no criminal record and has a clean driving licence. His bank account shows up nothing untoward, just a current account in a major UK bank and a linked savings account. The only thing I can conjecture at this point is we know Christine Matthews is one of his customers and she is linked to Braddock. I haven't been able to tie him in but he just might be linked somewhere. Proving it could be next to impossible though. I think it might be worth putting him under surveillance but the airport systems show he's just flown out to Munich on a one-way ticket so unless we alert the Europeans we'll have to wait until he gets back. And before you ask the question, the mansion he lives in looks pretty secure to me so I don't fancy trying to gain entry unless we have a warrant and backup. For now, I can't think of a reason to get a warrant other than he is wealthy and uses the services of a local prostitute on a fairly regular basis.'

'Yes, not much grounds. Might make a judge blush with embarrassment if we approached them. What's your gut feeling on all this, Marshall?'

'For what it's worth, I think Newton is probably an unwitting courier for our Arab friends but if we look into it my guess is it will all look as if it is legitimate. He's been running this route for a number of years, been stopped and searched several times and nothing untoward has ever come up, and his paperwork is doubtless completely accurate. If he's involved in anything then either he doesn't know it or he is one of the best couriers I've ever looked into. That said I've given the Port Authorities a tipoff on his van so when he does come back into the country he'll be searched thoroughly, just in case.'

'Yes, Harding told me that was on the cards. And Simon Hart?'

'Until I can find out more about him I'd say he wasn't involved at all, and it's just a coincidence he is one of Matthews' clients.'

'Okay. Well, I must let you get back to work. Where did you say Hart went?'

'Munich.'

'Okay, thanks Marshall. Talk later.'

Preston terminated the call and went to her desk with her notepad.

***

Simon Hart rose early and completed the assembly of the two devices, carefully taking two of the phials out of his special attaché case and placing them in the devices. When the phials were in situ he set the clocks on the devices for six hours and six and a quarter hours delay and then took one of the devices into the ensuite bathroom. With a small screwdriver he quickly removed the grille of the extractor fan on the ceiling and gained access to the space above the ceiling. In less than two minutes the device was in place and the grille replaced. Hart then took the other device and put it in a small rucksack that had been in his suitcase. He packed the case with the few clothes he had brought with him and then decided to wake the peacefully sleeping Sheera.

'Breakfast time,' he said, 'and then we must make a move.'

'I just need to wash. Ten minutes.'

'Ten minutes then.'

Sheera went into the bathroom and Hart heard the sound of the shower. As Sheera showered, so the clock in the space above the ceiling continued its deadly countdown.

After breakfast, the couple checked out of the hotel and were soon sat in the hire car. It was nearly ten o'clock and the morning's business traffic had subsided, making the five kilometre journey to the hypermarket pass quickly.

'We have some shopping to do before we continue our journey. Then it's on to Paris on our way to England and from Paris we can pick up the Eurostar train.'

'That sounds fun. What do we need here?'

'Well, I want to get you some new clothes for a start and some jewellery, if that is not being too presumptuous?' Hart laughed as he pulled away from a traffic light.

'No, that is not too presumptuous. I am very grateful, darling. You do so much for me.'

'And you do far more for me than you probably realise. When we get to England I want to show you off to a few friends and as they believe I am quite wealthy, I want you to look the part. And this shopping mall we are going to I know has several concessions, so I hope we can find something you like there.'

'You are so kind, Simon, thank you.' Sheera reached over to her left and kissed Simon briefly on his cheek.

With the rental car parked up in the vast car park of the Grassvelde hypermarket, Hart picked the small backpack out of the boot and the couple strolled towards the shops. An hour and a half later Sheera Ganzagha had a new wardrobe of clothes and shoes, a new watch, and three other pieces of jewellery. They were about to return to the car park when Hart said he needed to visit the men's room. Leaving Sheera sitting on a bench with the half dozen or more carrier bags, Hart took the backpack with him and found the toilets he had reconnoitred the day before last. He found the cubicle he wanted was vacant and went inside. In a minute he had removed the four small screws keeping the grille in place over the extractor fan, and a minute later the device in his backpack was set, and in place. With haste, Hart replaced the grille and screws and noted the time on his watch. The device would go off in just three hours, minutes after the device in the hotel.

Smiling, Hart returned to Sheera and together they made their way back to the car.

'Paris, here we come,' said Hart as he backed the car out of the parking bay.

'But this is a rental car. Can you do that?'

'Sure, I've got an international rental agreement. I can hand it back anywhere in the European Union. All I have to do is take it one of their offices. It's one of the advantages of being wealthy.' Hart smiled and reached over to give Sheera a quick kiss. 'Which means we can leave this in Paris and take the train back to England and then get a private taxi to take us back to my place just outside Reigate. I think you will like it. Now it is just over 800 kilometres from here to Paris and that is a lot of driving. I reckon we should be able to drive about half way today. I know a hotel just outside Nancy, which is just inside France. We can make that before dark. Then an early start tomorrow will get us to Paris by mid-morning, leaving the day to shop and take in the sights. I have a room booked in a Paris hotel tomorrow night. The next morning we can catch the early Eurostar. I have to get home at a reasonable time on Thursday as I have a business meeting in the afternoon. But we will go out for dinner in the evening. Is that all okay with you?'

'It sounds good to me.' Sheera sat back in the seat as Hart began the five-hour drive to Nancy.

Three hours later, as they skirted the Swiss countryside, there was a small, almost inaudible sound of glass cracking as the phial in the roof space above the shower in the hotel room they had stayed in the previous evening was broken. The clock on the dashboard in the car showed Hart that the device had been triggered and he confirmed that by checking his wrist watch.

Fifteen minutes later they found a lay-by and Hart pulled in.

'I just need to make a couple of quick calls. Wait here, I won't a minute,' he said as he opened the driver's door. As he walked behind the car he pulled his mobile phone out of his pocket and dialled a number.

'Good afternoon. Is that the Hotel Gaswhitz?' A pause. Hart spoke in rapid, almost fluent, German. 'Could I speak to the manager please?' Another pause. 'You say he is busy with some guests who have just become sick? That is good. Please tell him that I know what made them sick. They will be dying soon and so will anyone else who comes into contact with the hotel. A small device has been set off in your ventilation system so within an hour everyone in the hotel will develop the same symptoms and in two hours you will all be dead.' A longer pause. 'No, there is nothing I want from you and this is not blackmail. It is a demonstration. I suggest you get your manager to seal the hotel to stop others coming into the building. For his information the sickness is caused by a rapidly spreading virus for which there is no cure. Goodbye.'

Hart terminated the call and dialled a second number and then spoke again in almost fluent German.

'Good afternoon, please can I speak to Herr Karl Swarztig, head of security?' A pause followed by, 'Ah good afternoon Herr Swarztig. I will make this brief. First this is not blackmail. What I am going to tell you is merely a small demonstration for something else that is about to happen. A few hours ago, a device was planted within your shopping mall, a device that has just been triggered. It has released a virus which we have called Wipeout, because that is what it does. Let me tell you what will happen. Within a few minutes people will start to feel unwell, no please do not speak, just listen. When they start to feel unwell they will sweat, and shake and vomit. As the device is planted in your air circulation system, within about an hour everyone in the mall will be affected. There is no natural resistance to this and there is no cure. Within two hours everyone in the mall will be dead. From the moment the device was triggered it became very unsafe to be in the mall. If what has been released manages to escape the mall then within a very short time people within a few kilometres will start to feel unwell and they will also die. And as the hours pass, people further away will also die. This could go on for at least twenty-four hours, I hope. We have tested the virus over a range of ten kilometres and it was entirely effective. Everyone died.' A pause during which Hart could hear the evacuation bells sounding over the phone. 'That was not a good idea. As the device has already been triggered you may have already let infected people out of the shopping area. That is for you to worry about. My suggestion is you lock the doors and accept the inevitable.' Hart looked at his watch. Another pause. 'I leave what happens in your hands, but do not underestimate what is going to happen, that would be very unwise, I think. If you want my advice I would seal your mall for at least forty-eight hours. There is nothing you can do to stop what is starting to happen. Now I must go before you can trace this call.'

Hart ended the call abruptly and returned to the car. As he walked round the back of the car, Hart muttered to himself, 'And now, my dear Sheera, we will complete our journey and prepare for the main event.'

'Is everything all right? Sheera asked as he opened the driver's door.

'Yes everything is fine. I just needed to check on a few things.' Hart smiled sweetly as he started the car's engine and they continued their journey into France and away from the emerging human carnage three hours behind them.

Within seconds of the phone call coming into him, Karl Swarztig had pressed the emergency evacuation alarms. Any perceived terrorist threat required one action, the immediate evacuation of the entire shopping mall. At the same time it alerted the local fire and police services to race to the mall as an emergency existed or was developing. It was only as Swarztig continued to listen to the caller that it dawned on him it was already too late, always assuming the caller was not just some kind of sick prank caller. With the call over, Swarztig opened his desk drawer and picked out a single sheet of paper with a list of phone numbers on it. He dialled one and spoke briefly, and in rapid German, to the person on the other end of the line. As he spoke he walked over to a control box on the wall of his office, broke the glass with the hammer that was hanging underneath it and pressed the large red button inside the box. Immediately two things happened. The alarm bells became silenced and instead a wailing sound filled the air. At the same time, all the exit and entry points to the entire mall were locked, all except one door leading from the main entrance to the customer car park. The only reason it did not shut and lock was because someone was holding it open while an elderly lady shuffled her way towards the opened door. Swarztig looked at the half dozen monitor screens on his wall, pressed a few buttons on his control panel and spotted the open door. In seconds he had his walkie-talkie in his hand and, interrupting the call he was holding on his mobile phone, he talked rapidly into the walkie-talkie. As he continued his conversation on his mobile phone he watched as two uniformed figures ran towards the door, and forced both the elderly lady and the male customer holding the door open, back into the building. The door swung closed and locked itself instantly.

His conversation over, Swarztig replaced his mobile phone in his pocket. Then he walked over to his desk and picked up the microphone. He pressed a button and in calm, clear German said, 'Ladies and Gentlemen, this is security control. We have been informed of a possible incident in the area of this building. For your own safety and until the incident has been checked out we have been ordered by the local police to place the whole mall in lockdown. I will update you again as soon as I receive further information. Meanwhile we will be providing free tea and coffee on the top floor in our restaurant area. Thank you for your patience and understanding as we work to resolve this as quickly as possible.'

The first police car arrived outside the exit road for the customer car park and blocked it. Within two minutes half a dozen cars, three fire engines, and ten ambulances had arrived on the scene and made their way to the main entrance to the mall. It was five minutes later when the first customers and staff who had been nearest to the men's toilets where the device had been triggered, began to feel unwell. Then the feelings of malaise began to spread quite rapidly. Within twenty minutes over four hundred customers were sweating profusely and coughing, vomiting and curling up in agony on the floor. Swarztig flicked through the monitor screens with growing horror on his face. Simon Hart did not know it, but the security centre had been designed with a possible terrorist attack in mind. It had its own ventilation system, with air coming through filters from outside the building. It was also a strong room, with inch thick steel walls and a hermetically sealed door when locked. There was also a small kitchen and bathroom area so the occupant could live there for a few days if necessary. It also had its own power supply system so any terrorist attack that knocked out the power to the shopping mall would leave the security centre unharmed. Only a direct nuclear strike would be likely to make the security centre inoperable. Its design had been considered advisable because of the proximity of the local airport and other grade 'A' targets in the area. It was a consideration Swarztig was now grateful for and one he was hoping actually worked. Below him in the mall a growing number of customers and shop staff were now retching as they lay on the floor.

The call was coming in from the head of the response unit outside. The German was rapid but controlled.

'Swarztig, this is Commander Brassmer, I need an update.'

'This is Swarztig. It is horrible. Everyone is sick. My own security people are sick. People are dying.'

'Okay, Swarztig. Can you open the door so we can get help in there?'

'The terrorist said if I did that then an area of ten kilometres would be devoid of human life in a few hours. From what I am seeing here I do not think he was bluffing.'

'Can you identify him, or give us any other information?'

'A male, he spoke in German, not quite fluently and he had a strange accent, possible English I think. The call was short but I recorded it. I can relay the voice file via computer. For now you must stay outside and the people in here must stay in here. We have to believe he is telling the truth. I have never seen anything like this, not even in the training programs.'

'Send the recording to Munich police headquarters. I will alert them it is incoming. You should be safe where you are and can start running through the CCTV of this morning to see if you can spot anything. I will arrange for our prime target list to be emailed to you so you can start looking for faces. If this is for real, we will not be able to reach you for some time yet.'

**

Daniel Newton started his day with a hurried breakfast before checking out of the GastHaus. He walked unhurriedly across the car park to his white van. He unlocked the back door, took a cursory look around and noted the bag holding the boxes he was taking back to Zussman was still there and locked the door again. Then he went around the side of the van, opened the driver's door, threw his backpack into the passenger well, and started the engine. Newton was in a good mood, it was his penultimate day on the continent before he would return to England, another trip successfully completed. Newton was also happy because the day had started out much cooler than the previous days, and he knew driving would be much more comfortable without the intense heat he had endured earlier in the journey home. His day would not be overly arduous as he planned to arrive at a small bed and breakfast hotel, a few kilometres outside Nancy sometime mid-afternoon. Then he could relax with the last of his European conquests, the delectable Marie. Actually, her full name was Jean-Marie, but she only ever used Marie as her name. The next day, Newton would cross France, arriving outside Calais in time to catch the Thursday morning ferry back to England. Newton had the radio on in his van, tuned to the BBC World service. He didn't speak any German, and very little French so he relied on the BBC World service to understand what news there was. Late that morning he listened with intrigue at the breaking news of a possible terror attack in Munich. News was coming through that indicated a shopping mall on the outskirts of Munich had been the target. Details were inevitably sketchy but it appeared a large police and ambulance presence had been called to the hypermarket and the complex had been sealed. The number of known injured was not known. Newton spotted the large white van speeding down the other side of the motorway and recognised the signing as being that of an international news channel. He continued on his own journey as the reporters in the other van raced towards Munich. Clearly they expected whatever was going on to be big news.

***

At about the same time as the white van raced past Newton, going in the opposite direction, there was a knock on the office door of Selena Preston.

'Excuse me Ma'am, the young man ventured, 'but there is something breaking in Munich, some kind of attack. It hit the news channels a few minutes ago and intel says it is big.'

'Thank you Rawlins, have we been notified officially yet?'

'We have a memo from the Germans, we should have it translated in a few minutes.'

'Okay, thank you.'

Preston rubbed her chin and picked up her phone.

'Marshall, are you secure?'

'Yes Ma'am.'

'Where did you say Hart had gone?'

'Munich, a few days ago. Saturday if I recall correctly. Why?'

'We're just getting intelligence of something going on in Munich. Might be worth turning your TV on – we're bound to get more from any local reporters initially than German intelligence.'

'I have it on now. Okay, breaking news is the Grassvelde hypermarket on the outskirts of Munich has been the target of what is believed to be a terror attack. Numbers of injured and dead not known but a huge number of police and ambulance vehicles have been called to the scene, as well as fire-fighting rigs. Still waiting for video footage, shouldn't be long I would think.'

'Okay, Marshall, I've just been handed a translation of an official memo from German intelligence. For once they are ahead of the news. The mall has been sealed following a very sudden and deadly outbreak of some kind of what they are saying is a virus inside the mall. They received a phone call from a mobile phone just as people started getting sick. The caller told them it was a

221

deadly virus called the Wipeout virus that had been released in the mall. He also told them if anyone who had been exposed to it was allowed out of the building then everyone in a ten kilometre radius would be dead in 24 hours. Christ! And because they saw people dying on the CCTV they believed him and have sealed the mall.'

'Any mention of a blackmail demand?'

'No. The caller said it was not blackmail but a demonstration for something bigger.'

'Anything else?'

'Not yet. The head of security at the mall is in the blast shelter they built, just in case it was attacked as it is so close to the airport. The airport and rail networks have been closed down to try and track the perpetrators but I suspect they are long gone. Anyone who planted a device like this, will have given themselves time to escape.'

'I agree Ma'am, this has been carefully planned. Hang on a minute, there is another news story coming through that a small hotel in Munich has also been attacked, people reported dead but no numbers yet. After the hypermarket attack, a 2 kilometre area around the hotel has been sealed off.'

'Which, if the mysterious caller is right, will be totally inadequate.'

'I agree Ma'am. First reports coming through of the phone call to the security centre of the hypermarket. Reporter on the scene is talking to the commander on the ground outside the hypermarket. Some kind of initial press conference, in German, which I can just about cope with. Seems like the caller was able to speak German but had a foreign accent, possibly British. Damn, I missed that thanks to the overlay by the newscaster. Something, I think, about a demonstration.'

'Okay, Marshall, this is not something we can do much about except gather information. I'll get onto the ministry and see what other information we've been made aware of officially. I guess social media is already buzzing – get someone to monitor that as well and see if there are any witness accounts. It could be coincidence that Hart has gone to Munich but it might not be. I know he's not there at the moment, but get his house put under 24/7 surveillance. I want to know the minute he comes back, if he does. Then get everyone who is watching our prime targets to report on what, if anything, they are doing right now. If this has any links to the UK mainland, someone is bound to be acting in a different manner to usual. I want to know the minute any of our targets do anything unusual.'

'Yes Ma'am. That news conference is over and there is another reporter at some kind of cordon presumably some way away from the hotel where something has been going on. I'll talk to you later Ma'am.'

'Okay Marshall.'

Preston ended the call. She had a feeling something was about to start happening, she just had to hope they were ready and that they had been following the right people.'

***

That evening, as Simon Hart and Sheera Ganzagha sat in their Nancy hotel bedroom after an evening meal at the hotel, Hart knew the TV would be filled with the details of the terror attack in Munich. So he was careful to keep Sheera away from the TV, spending the evening keeping her passions for him inflamed as he delicately caressed her body in every way he knew.

CHAPTER EIGHTEEN

Wednesday 1st July

Wednesday dawned fine and sunny in the region around Nancy. Overnight, news had been pouring out of the Germain intelligence agencies to their counterparts across Europe and the USA. Although it was too early to identify exactly what agent had been used in the terror attack at the Grassvelde hypermarket, it was evidently some kind of nerve agent or biological agent. Overnight the conversation between Hart and Swarztig had been listened to countless times. British Intelligence had been passed copies of it in the hope they could identify the voice. Mention of the name, Wipeout, had sent a chill through many people. The security guard trapped in the office at Grassvelde watched CCTV footage for the hour leading up to the attack but came up with nothing more significant than a few hundred people entering and leaving the complex. His superiors ordered him to go back an hour at a time. When he reached the fourth cycle, he saw Hart and Ganzagha enter the hypermarket and thought nothing more of it. They were just shoppers. Finally, he became too bored and tired to watch anymore. The past 24 hours of the CCTV recordings were sent over a Broadband connection to the local police headquarters. It would take many man days of effort to go through that amount of material. Without any idea what the terrorist looked like, to Swarztig it seemed a total waste of time. Swarztig spent more time thinking what job he would do next because after the events of the past twenty-four hours, he was determined to quit his post at Grassvelde.

The news was full of the events in Germany. All across the globe the latest terror attack was big news, if only because it was different to what had happened before and the deaths from the attack at the German hotel had begun to spread out into the surrounding area, raising concerns that it had not been contained within the hotel, and fears as to how far it would spread.

After a light Continental breakfast of croissant and other breads, Hart and Ganzagha began their journey to Paris. A few hours later they parked up at the offices of the car hire company, took their bags out of the car and Hart handed the keys back to the counter clerk inside the building, signing the handover documents. Then they took an open-topped bus on a four kilometre journey, alighting outside a grand hotel and entered it. Hart left Ganzagha sitting on one of the luxurious sofas while he checked in.

'Good afternoon sir.'

'You have a reservation under the name of Carlton, I hope.' Hart smiled affably.

'Ah yes. If you could show me your passport and credit card for payment, please sir.'

Hart, showed the clerk his passport. The young man thumbed through to the back page of the UK passport and noted the name, Brian Carlton, and the passport number. He then took the credit card and typed the number and other information into the computer terminal.

'Just the one night sir. If it is alright with you we can do an automatic checkout and charge your card when you have vacated the room.'

'That is fine with me.'

'I will just get the card key then sir. We have a card entry system. Your card will expire at ten in the morning.'

Hart thought the man spoke English well, though the French accent was unmistakeable. The young man returned after a minute with the card key.

'Enjoy your stay, Mr Carlton,' he said.

And that was the moment when Simon Hart ceased to exist in France, and Brian Carlton became his new persona. Adding Sheera as his wife was a gamble Hart had had to make a few days earlier. Obtaining a fake marriage certificate and a passport for her had not been a problem, not with his connections. Now he needed to explain who she was, though not his new identity. He did that in the lift to their bedroom. At first Sheera was shocked but then pleased as Hart (now Carlton) explained it was to allow her to enter Britain without question, so she could avoid the interminable interviews at Immigration and risk being refused entry.

Then they spent the rest of the day walking the Champs des Elysee, and taking in the usual tourist attractions of the Eiffel Tower, the Sacre Coeur and the impressive Arc de Triomphe. Sheera draped her arm through his and to all the world they looked like a happily married couple. By the end of the day both Hart and Ganzagha were tired. They dined in the hotel restaurant and ended up in each other's arms in bed by ten o'clock. After making passionate love, Sheera fell asleep quickly while Hart lay looking at the ceiling, pondering the days ahead, until his own tiredness overtook him and he too fell into a deep, satisfying sleep.

***

Daniel Newton rose early and drove to Calais. It was a longer drive than Hart and Ganzagha had to Paris and he was grateful when he arrived at the small country bistro just outside Calais. He confirmed his ferry connection and was given a sailing that was mid-morning the next day. It suited him, as he knew he would be able to get back to London mid to late afternoon, unload the cargo, and be home mid to late evening. The other customers he had been collecting for would receive their products on the Friday.

***

It was late afternoon when Newton phoned Zussman. Zussman had spent an anxious day in the Reigate shop, waiting to hear from Newton.

'Daniel, I hope you have good news for me,' he said as he breathed a sigh of relief when he recognised the number as his mobile phone alerted him to the call.

'Dieter, I do indeed. I have a ferry crossing tomorrow morning so I should be in Reigate by about three in the afternoon. I assume you can leave me space to park behind the shop.'

'Yes, I will put the cones out an hour beforehand to make sure.'

'Good. I will let you know if there are any delays.'

'Thank you and have a safe journey.'

Zussman ended the call and dialled a number he had long since etched in his memory. He waited patiently until the person on the other end answered him with a thick, Arabic accent.

'Yes, brother,' the voice was calm.

'The package will be here tomorrow.'

'Good. We will come and collect it at closing time.'

The line went dead. Zussman was perspiring and mopped his forehead with his handkerchief. Everything was suddenly very real, suddenly about to happen and Zussman was so glad he had planned his own escape from the inevitable.

Within one hour of the brief conversation, four of the ATRIUM team leaders started receiving reports from their surveillance teams that one of the targets they were watching had disappeared. Within another thirty minutes, Roger Harding received a surveillance report that a second 'A' list target in his area had slipped the surveillance team and disappeared. Harding, efficient as ever, was straight on his mobile phone to Preston.

'Ma'am, this maybe nothing but it could be significant. I've just received two separate surveillance reports that we have had two targets disappear. Both were out walking and both just vanished. We're doubling efforts to locate them but this is the first time they have made any attempt to slip past us.'

'Thank you Harding. I've just had three other reports come in via email to say other targets are doing the same. I assume you already have the bus terminal and the local railway stations covered.'

'Yes Ma'am.'

'Which targets have vanished, Harding?'

'Ali Benadir and Mahar Bin Aldre. Neither have a driver's licence but I doubt that would be a problem for them.'

'No, I don't think it would either. Keep a hawk's eye on the train station.'

'Already in place Ma'am.'

'Do you need additional resources at this time?'

'No Ma'am.'

'Okay, keep me informed.' Preston ended the conversation, sat back in her chair and looked out at the London Eye with a worried look, the look that said she felt something was starting to happen.

As soon as the call to Preston had ended two things happened. Firstly, Harding contacted the surveillance team who had lost Bin Aldre. They informed him that very possibly he had jumped on a bus into Newbury that had been at a stop just round the corner from where he had been walking. As they were some discreet distance behind him, they had arrived at the corner some moments later. It was not his usual habit to turn the corner as his usual haunt was further down the road, so they had been caught unaware. Secondly Preston called Marshall to warn him something was happening and to get a team to watch Zussman very closely but to make sure he wasn't aware of it. Marshall assured her that was what was already happening and updated her that Zussman had followed his usual ritual of going to the Reigate shop at the usual time.

Harding made a second call to the other surveillance team that had lost Ali Benadir. They too had been taken by surprise as their suspect had definitely hopped on a bus. Harding was shocked that both teams had succumbed to such a simple trick, but at least now knew both targets were heading to the middle of Newbury. He looked at his watch and estimated how long it would take the buses to get to the centre of the town then he called both teams back and ordered them to get to the railway station as fast as possible.

'Guv, we're on foot following targets. How do we do that?' Was the response from both teams.

'Call up support, back up, or whatever you usually do in this kind of situation. Use your brains. I'm going to drive there. Be there as soon as you can.'

Harding was already picking up his car keys and was locking the front door to his flat when he ended the call. He drove carefully into Newbury, and headed straight for the railway station car park. He pulled up just as a train was leaving the station, heading East for London.

Showing his security card to the station guard he asked to see the entrance hall CCTV for the past 15 minutes. It took the guard five minutes to check with his superiors and Harding was led into a small office.

'You know what to do?' The guard asked him. 'I have never had to look at this stuff so I can't help you.'

'I know, thanks.'

If Harding sounded exasperated, he was. He sat down, pressed the buttons to rewind the digital recording twenty minutes, and started watching on double speed. It took a few minutes for him to spot first Bin Aldre enter the concourse and then, a minute or so later, Benadir also crossed the concourse and headed for the East bound platform.

'Blast,' said Harding.

There was a knock on the door.

'You have company,' said the station guard who looked somewhat confused at what was happening on his shift.

'Thanks. Brown, Grafton, what kept you?'

'Taxis,' Grafton replied, 'and getting past this guy.'

'Okay, the targets are on a train bound for London. I need to alert Preston. From what I could see on the CCTV they weren't carrying anything other than bum bags. Okay, we're done here.'

Harding stood to leave and followed the others back to the station concourse. As he did so, he called out to the station guard, 'You might want to check that thing is recording – it could be important to someone one day. And thanks for your co-operation.'

Harding followed Brown and Grafton out of the station just as the other surveillance team of Harris and Caldermay arrived in a taxi.

'Well, you took your time. Anyone fancy a trip to London?'

There was no response, which did not surprise Harding. Moving several metres away from the others, Harding called Preston.

'Sorry to trouble you again Ma'am. The two targets of interest are on a train bound for London. I have seen the CCTV footage that shows them leaving Newbury a few minutes before we were able to get here.' Harding listened silently for a minute before replying, Yes Ma'am.' With the call over, Harding went back to the group of four men.

'Okay, instructions are to go back and support the other teams watching the 'A' targets. While you're travelling I'll call the team leaders and tell them to expect you. The London teams will handle our two escapees.'

'Guv,' said Caldermay, looking glum.

'And just make sure none of you lose anyone else.'

'Guv,' he said again.

As the men piled back into the waiting taxi, Harding made a few calls. Surveillance was going to be tightened. Harding didn't want any more mishaps on his watch, or on his patch.

***

Back in her office, Preston was having the busiest day she had experienced in a long time. After the reports of missing targets and now the certainty that at least two of them were coming to London, Preston had contacted the relevant police department to request surveillance assistance when they arrived. That request had met with a few queries on who would be paying for the extra work load. Preston quickly assured the commander it would not be a problem. No sooner had that conversation ended than she received a call that was directed to her from the anti-terror commander in Munich. The news was not good. The agent, now thought to be a fast-acting virus, continued to spread out from the infected hotel. CCTV showed that everyone in the Grassvelde hypermarket was motionless, and presumed dead, though no-one had entered the building as the risk could not be ascertained. Swarztig had decided to check on some cars that had been captured entering the carpark on the morning of the incident. He had so far identified a handful of hire cars and they had been checked. There was one of particular interest, which was the purpose of the call.

'So, Miss Preston, the car in question was hired last Saturday by a British man named Simon Hart. He arrived on a plane from England on Saturday afternoon and picked up the car at the airport. We have some not very good CCTV footage from the Grassvelde carpark of him and a girl he was with. They took a rucksack of some kind into the complex and returned about an hour later with a number of shopping bags. The car drove off and enquiries with the hire company indicate it is still out on hire. Hart did hire it for 4 days so we expect it to be returned tomorrow, though where he will return it to, we have no idea.'

'Thank you. Keep me informed please and let me know when you know where the car is. Also, please send my office any more information you get on the agent or virus that has been used.'

'We will. We are planning to enter Grassvelde tomorrow morning, so we should have more details later tomorrow.'

The conversation came to a close and Preston picked up her phone and used the speed dial option to call Marshall.

'Marshall, are you secure?'

'Yes Ma'am.'

'Good. Your man, Hart, who we know went to Munich, apparently visited that hypermarket that has been the subject of a terror attack, in a hire car, about 3 or 4 hours before the attack happened.'

'A coincidence?'

'Why do you think that, Marshall?'

'Because of the time lapse.'

'Possibly but we don't know the nature of the attack yet. What if he went there, planted something, and got out before it went off?'

'Yes, that's possible but we've not had that kind of thing to deal with since what, the IRA attacks decades ago. These days they seem to jump in a van and drive it at the crowds. More spontaneous, less to go wrong and still very deadly. Remember London, Barcelona and others.'

'I know, but this is a changing world, what if things are changing right under our noses?'

'I suppose we need to consider it. Any more news on the targets?'

'At least two are heading for London. I've got the police watching for them, to keep an eye on them when they arrive.'

'Will they be arrested?'

'No, it's not a crime to travel on a train unless you don't have a ticket. We could hold them under anti-terrorism laws but a good lawyer would have them out in under twenty-four hours as things stand, so all we would do is alert them to the fact we are watching them. The police will just watch where they go and keep me informed. Is the surveillance on your jeweller in place yet? We don't want to lose him as well.'

'Yes, Ma'am. He's in the shop as expected. The team will let me know the minute he moves and where he goes.'

'Good. If you need additional help just let me know.'

'Will do, Ma'am.' Marshall was a professional, able to separate business from pleasure and at the moment his mind was fully focused on his job. Any thoughts of Preston had to be business orientated right now. When things quietened down again, as they were bound to do in a few days, he could pick up where they had left off.

***

It was evening when the car hire company updated their systems to indicate the car Hart had hired had been returned to their Paris office. It was four hours later when that information finally filtered through to the German intelligence unit in Munich. Within five minutes they had issued a European arrest warrant for Simon Hart on suspicion of perpetrating a terrorist attack. That information took 30 minutes to filter back to the French anti-terrorism authorities and within another 30 minutes 4 cars and a tactical response unit were outside the office where Simon Hart had returned the car – about four kilometres from the hotel where he and Sheera were staying. He heard the sound of sirens in the distance as he lay in bed, smiling to himself as his plans began to come to fruition. He fell asleep knowing that in the morning both he and Sheera would have to adopt their new personae. For him it would be easy, it was one he was more than used to. He just had to hope Sheera would remember to be who he needed her to be though she could never know him as Brian Carlton.

CHAPTER NINETEEN

Thursday 2nd July

Selena Preston woke earlier than usual. Her mobile phone was ringing and it took her over a minute to respond to it.

'Damn,' she said as she accepted the call. 'Preston,' she said a second later.

'Sorry to call you this early, Ma'am, but there has been a development overnight you should know about.'

The male voice was not familiar to her.

'Who am I speaking to and how the hell did you get this number.'

'DI Lanchford. I called your office and told them it was important so they redirected me to you. I don't actually know your number.'

'All right, DI Lanchford, sorry for the shortness but it is rather early.' Preston looked at the alarm clock. 'Five o'clock early.'

'Yes Ma'am. We've just heard that your man Hart has left his hire car at the rental company office in Paris. Their anti-terror people launched an operation to arrest him after their German counterparts issued a European arrest warrant. They took over three hours to go through the local hotels looking for Hart and his companion, but there was no sign of him. So they have drawn a blank, which means he is on the run and probably headed back to the UK. We've alerted the ports and airports and they will stop him when his passport is scanned. We've instigated Operation Checkout, so all passengers coming into the UK will be scanned for the next 48 hours. After that we have to get a High Court judge to authorise its continuance. I was given instructions to call your office if anything happened overnight related to the Munich incident.'

'Okay DI Lanchford. I'll be heading to my office in an hour, if anything else happens please leave a message there.'

***

Brian Carlton and Sheera departed their luxury hotel at just on nine in the morning, after enjoying a Continental breakfast in their bedroom. Carlton's card would be charged an hour or so later, by which time the couple and their three bags were sat on the Eurostar train heading for the Channel Tunnel and England. They arrived in London after an uneventful journey and flashed their passports over the scanners at the terminal as they entered England proper. Carlton noted that evidently security had been stepped up as he had never had to scan his passport in the past. He smiled wryly as he wondered if he could be the cause of the heightened security.

As they walked away from the terminal, a siren sounded behind them. For a moment, Carlton froze, waiting to be called back, wondering whether to run just in case. Sheera certainly would not be able to run far, not in her shoes! After a moment the siren died and Carlton decided it was probably just a shop opening its shutters. He hailed a taxi outside the railway station and gave softly-spoken directions before sitting back with Sheera to escape the busy world of the city.

Ninety minutes later the taxi pulled up at the gates of what was evidently a substantial home, a few miles south of Reigate.

'One moment, I'll open the gates,' said Carlton as he opened the taxi door.

'Okay guv,' the driver responded.

Carlton pressed some buttons on the number keypad and the double wooden gates swung inwards. Carlton went back to the taxi.

'I'll close them from indoors after you have left.' The taxi driver nodded and took them up the sweeping drive to the front door.

'You live here alone?' Sheera whispered in awe at the size of the house.

'Yes, I like my privacy,' Carlton responded.

'Wow,' Sheera said. 'You never said it was this big.'

'You never asked.' The taxi stopped, they collected their suitcases and the attaché case from the boot of the vehicle and Carlton paid the fare, adding a generous tip.

'Thank you sir,' the driver said appreciatively. Here's my card if you ever need a lift again. It's not something we're supposed to do but a good customer is a good customer.'

'Why, thank you Mr Greivson, I'll bear that in mind.'

Carlton closed the taxi door and headed for his own front door, fishing the keys out of his jacket pocket.

'Wait here for one moment, Sheera, while I turn off the alarms. Won't be a sec,' he added as he opened the door. As soon as the door opened a fraction of an inch, Sheera heard the tell-tale beeping of the intruder alarm go into pending mode. She waited patiently while Carlton went indoors and did something with the control box that was hidden in a cupboard. After several seconds the beeping sound stopped.

'This is amazing,' Sheera stood in the hallway, hardly able to believe how luxurious the house was compared to what she was used to.

'Not bad, is it. Make yourself at home. We have a hot tub out the back, and you are welcome to use it. I'll show you how. Now, Sheera darling, I do have a bit of business to attend to later on, but I promise I will be back by seven o'clock and I have already booked a table at a restaurant I know for eight. I hope you won't mind being left on your own for a few hours.'

'I'll be fine. Who wouldn't be in a house like this!'

Carlton led her through the house, showing her the huge bedroom they would share, the ensuite bathroom and shower. Then he showed her the grounds, and how the hot tub worked. The tub was maintained regularly by a company he employed so it was always ready to be used. Sheera was open-mouthed with surprise for much of the time as Carlton showed her round his estate. Then he left her to unpack her case and made his way downstairs. Softly shutting the door to the study, he took his mobile phone out of his pocket and called a number.

'Hi Christine, it's Simon. Just coming back from my trip. I wonder, could you come over at about six this evening. I'm feeling really tense, so I will probably be upstairs in the gym doing some stretches.'

'Okay, Simon. Did the trip go well?'

'I think so, thanks. Anyway, if I do go up to the gym I'll remember to leave the gates open for you, and the door on the latch. I'll see you at six. It probably won't be a full evening but I need to unwind if you understand me.'

'Sure, Simon. See you at six.'

Christine Matthews ended the call and smiled to herself. Simon Hart was always easy money for her.

***

Daniel Newton boarded the mid-morning ferry at Calais, and the crossing went smoothly, bringing him into Dover just after noon. As he drove his white van down the ramp leading from the ferry a customs officer signalled for him to pull over to an inspection bay. If Newton was concerned or surprised it didn't register on his face.

'Random spot check, sir,' said the customs officer. 'Your passport and documentation please.'

As always, Newton was ready with the paperwork. 'Thank you sir. If you would just go into that office - leave me your keys, we won't be long.'

This instruction did slightly unnerve Newton. 'Can't I watch while you open the back door?'

'You can sir, if you want, but it will take longer to clear you.'

'Not a problem. I'd rather keep an eye on the van while it's unlocked, if you don't mind.'

'Not got something to hide?' There was a note of sarcasm in the officer's voice.

'I should think not.' Newton sounded serious. 'I make this crossing about 5 times a year and I've never had any problems to date.'

'Always a first time sir. Now, the back door key please.'

The officer raised a hand as he walked round the back of the van and was almost simultaneously joined by another uniformed officer. This one came complete with a fairly excitable Spaniel. The van door was opened and the Spaniel jumped up into the entrance and sniffed hard for a few seconds. Newton knew these dogs were trained to freeze and go silent if they detected anything. After a few seconds the handler was satisfied the wagging tail and occasional bark were enough.

'Nothing detected. Over to you Johnson.' He gave the Spaniel a tennis ball to chew on as its reward and took it off to search another vehicle.

'Well, that's one good thing,' said Johnson. 'Now, let's check what you have got in here. He jumped up into the van, checked the bag containing the two dozen jewellery boxes, picked one out and opened it for a moment, before closing it again. He spent five minutes rummaging around the back of the van and then came out again. 'All seems okay to me. So, if we lock this up and you come into the office we'll just check your paperwork and passport.'

Newton still had no idea he had been specifically targeted for the search. The passport and paperwork checks took five minutes and then he was cleared to continue his journey. He shut the office door behind him and the security guard picked up the phone.

'It's Dover Port Authority here, Inspector Johnson. You asked us to look out for a white van driven by a Mr. Newton. Well he docked about half an hour ago and we stopped the van. The sniffer dog found no trace of any drugs and the search revealed nothing suspicious. As requested I checked out a couple of dozen watch display boxes you said would be on board. The ones I inspected looked fine to me. To be honest I'd say they were pretty inferior watches, not high end ones and the boxes were a bit ostentatious for the quality of the watch. But that's only my opinion and the quantity and descriptions matched what was on the driver's inventory sheet. The rest of the van also looked to have on board what was on the inventory sheet. Mr. Newton stated he does this kind of trip at least five times a year so I guess he knows what he is doing. To be honest, sir, the problems we usually have are with the first-timers, not the professional courier types. He's now leaving the port as we speak.'

'Thank you, Inspector Johnson. Can you put that all in an email and send it to the office, just for the sake of filing a copy of your report?'

'Yes sir, I'll do it right away.'

'Thank you.'

The line went dead.

After being cleared by Customs, Newton began his journey back from Dover to Reigate, a journey which, with a comfort break, would take him the best part of two hours. Just before he left Dover he phoned Zussman to let him know he'd been delayed at the port but was now only a couple of hours from the shop, assuming there were no snarl-ups on the roads.

***

At two o'clock in the afternoon the news came into Preston's office from German intelligence. The attack at the Grassvelde hypermarket and the hotel some kilometres away had indeed been terrorist attacks and both had used some kind of biological agent to wreak havoc. The news left Preston dry in the mouth. Within minutes of the news coming through Preston was on the phone to Marshall.

'It's biological. They suspect it's a virus but who knows. The path to Simon Hart has gone cold. He can be tracked to Paris but then seems to have just disappeared

239

into thin air. So far there is no sign of him registering at a hotel overnight. I've already had checks done at airports and ports yesterday, but there's no sign of him coming back to the UK any time soon. The suspected courier is back in England, arrived at Dover a couple of hours ago. His van was searched and nothing was found.'

'I see, Ma'am. Well I have people in Reigate watching Zussman's shop. If he goes there we could always raid it if you want to. We might get lucky, but I'd want armed support and a warrant on hand especially if any of the targets happen to congregate round there. I've got a car sat just down the road from Hart's mansion. If, though it seems unlikely, he turns up there, we can always go in and arrest him. I assume you can get a copy of the European arrest warrant through to me or to the car that's outside his house. They have an onboard printer for such things.'

'I'll arrange both. You will have them in 30 minutes. And back-up on standby in Reigate.'

'Thank you Ma'am. As for this biological stuff, do you have anything else about it I should know?'

'No, the Germans haven't dared get too close to the scene of the incidents yet. Only thing, and it's not much use to us, is it doesn't seem to affect wildlife – at least not directly, but that might change if any wildlife got into the food chain. We'll know more about that in a few days' time though by then it could be too late for any of us. I have a nasty feeling about this, Marshall.'

'Me too, Ma'am. I know we've rehearsed this kind of scenario a number of times in the past but this has a feeling of reality about it that the roleplaying didn't, if you understand what I mean.'

'I do Marshall. And, I just hope to God the Germans are wrong and if they are right that it's not headed in this direction.'

'Right, I'll be on my way to Zussman's shop, just in case. I'll wait for you to send me the warrant and the

European arrest warrant on my mobile. When they arrive I'll get them distributed.'

'Good luck Marshall.'

The line went dead.

***

Two hours later Marshall had joined his team of two surveillance operatives parked in a nondescript red Corsa a couple of hundred metres away from Zussman's jewellery shop. A second team had picked up Newton's white van as it travelled up the M20 and they sat a few hundred metres behind it, keeping in mobile phone contact as their journey progressed. They notified the team in Reigate that Newton had reached the M25, which would lead round to Reigate Hill. That was the moment the warrants had appeared digitally and they printed off the copies that could be used. Marshall had been in the front of the red Corsa for less than fifteen minutes when the surveillance mobile phone rang.

'Just coming off the M25 and heading south on A217 into Reigate. Be with you in five minutes if the railway crossing is open.'

'Roger that, five minutes.'

Sure enough, five minutes later, Newton's white van passed the occupants of the red Corsa, went past the jewellery shop and turned left at the next junction.

'He's going to park round the back,' said Marshall. 'Adam I need you to run up there and carefully peer round the corner and call us to let us know what is happening.'

'Guv,' said the man in the back of the Corsa. Adam Wellman was an experienced surveillance operative, someone Marshall had used on a number of occasions, someone who Marshall knew was reliable. In seconds he was walking nonchalantly up the street, on the opposite side of the jewellery shop. He crossed over the road some distance from the shop and disappeared down the road the van had gone down a few minutes before. He was just in time to see Newton open the back of the van

241

and hand a couple of bags to the man he presumed must be the shop owner.

Back in the car the surveillance mobile phone rang.

'Just handed over a couple of bags to a short, balding guy. I guess that's Zussman.'

'It is,' said Marshall.'

'Okay, they've put one of the bags on the road for some reason. They're talking and Zussman is gesticulating. Something isn't right, I'd say. Now Zussman is taking one of the boxes out of the bag. He's opening it in front of Newton and...'

'Go on,' said Marshall.

'Holy shit, Zussman is not happy. He's shouting at Newton and he's pacing round, walking really quickly.'

'Why on earth would he do that? Can you hear anything?'

'Something about the wrong watches. Now he's opening more boxes. Each one he is getting more animated with and throwing it on the ground. Now saying they are worthless and he's a dead man.'

'Okay, make sure you keep cover.'

'Yes, Guv. Jeez, something has really got to him. Clearly whatever he was expecting hasn't been delivered.'

'Roger that.'

'He's now picking up the four or five boxes he's thrown on the ground. The van driver is shouting back at him that it's not his fault. He picked up the boxes in Yalvac and the van has been locked ever since. So maybe Zussman needs to call his people in Yalvac or wherever and sort it out for the next trip. Okay, the driver is closing the back of the van up, looks like he's going to be leaving soon. Zussman is red-faced but has picked up the boxes and is heading back into the shop. Wait, the driver is following him into the shop.'

'Okay, when he comes back to his van you need to get out of there. I want you and Richardson to follow the white van to wherever it goes. If he is anything more

242

than just a courier I want to know about it. I'll hang around here and see what happens with the shop.'

'Yes, Guv. Okay, the driver has just come out, looks like he's still putting his wallet back in his pocket, so maybe he's just been paid.'

'Probably.'

'Okay, I'm coming back. It's going to take him a while to turn the van round.'

'Roger that.'

Two minutes later Marshall opened the front door of the Corsa and got out to let Adam sit in the remaining front seat.

'In theory he's going to be heading for the motorway so try and keep with him.'

'Sure thing,' said Richardson.

As Daniel Newton valiantly manoeuvred his van in the tight alley, inside the shop Zussman, trembling and sweating, picked up his mobile phone and made the call.

'They are not here, the courier has failed. He has brought back rubbish, not the watches we were expecting.'

'How is that possible?' The voice on the other end of the phone was Arabic.

'I have no idea. We have been doing exactly the same consignment for two years and it has never gone wrong before. My guess is either the courier has been given the wrong goods in Yalvac, or someone didn't give our contact there the right goods, or something else has happened. But for sure, there is no point in anyone risking coming here.'

'We had a lot at stake on this trip, you know that. There will be repercussions, serious ones for all concerned. I will have to act quickly and a lot of people will be very upset.'

'Yes I know. I will contact the supplier and find out what happened. I will call you in 24 hours or sooner.'

'Thank you Dieter.' The line went dead.

The receiver of the call then spent the next thirty minutes relaying the bad news to his own people. Two of them had followed Newton on a number of the previous trips as soon as he had come back from England. They had followed him today from Dover and were waiting in a side road half way up Reigate Hill. As soon as the white van passed them, and then the red Corsa, they pulled out. They were in a small, nondescript blue Fiat. They were already at Junction 9 on the M25 when they received a call from their controller.

'Yes we are following him. If he does what he usually does he will stop at the service station in a few minutes. We can do it then. So the mission is put on hold, or aborted?'

'Until we know what went wrong, it is on hold.'

'Very good. I guess we will need a new and more reliable courier for the future.'

'This one is no good anyway. Even today his van was searched at the port. His use to us is over.'

The call ended and a few minutes later as they neared the junction with the A3, Newton pulled off at the Chobham services as usual. He parked his van in the usual corner of the carpark and went to the café for a break. He desperately needed coffee. The surveillance team in the red Corsa went to the exit end of the carpark, ready to pick up the trail when he decided to leave. They had coffee in a thermos flask which they used for these surveillance jobs. Unseen to the surveillance operatives in the red Corsa, the blue Fiat pulled up next to Newton's van just as he entered the café. It took one of the occupants of the blue Fiat exactly one minute to leave the car and bend under the white van. When he returned to the Fiat, the small package he had been carrying was no longer in his hand. The Fiat moved away from the van, by several parking spaces, and waited. They waited nearly thirty minutes until they saw Newton returning. Then, they pulled out, and returned to the motorway. They knew Newton's route home, so no longer needed to follow him. The traffic on the M25 was getting heavy, especially as they approached the M4 and Heathrow airport. The Fiat was still ahead of the van by several hundred metres when it turned onto the M4. Then the driver of the Fiat slowed somewhat to allow the van to get closer.

'Ready, I think it is time,' said the driver in some Arabic dialect.

'Ready. So we get revenge for Allah for he is the greatest. The passenger smiled, opened the glove compartment and pulled out the small black box with a red button on the top of it. He pressed the red button and two hundred metres behind them there was a brief bang, followed by a thunderous roar and bright yellow light as the van exploded and veered into the central reservation. Daniel Newton never knew what happened. The bomb under his seat killed him seconds before his van smashed into the barrier and the fuel tank added to the explosion.

Ahead of the carnage, the blue Fiat gained speed and continued on its journey. Behind the van, the red Corsa veered violently to the left as the van exploded.

'Shit,' said Richardson as he struggled to bring the Corsa under control and avoid the wreckage of the van they were rapidly approaching. He steered towards the hard shoulder, slammed on the brakes and prayed he was going to stop in time. He did, just.

'Urgent, urgent, urgent. This is Wellman, come in Marshall.'

'Marshall, what's up?'

'Thank God you're able to talk. The white van has just exploded. We're just on the M4 and it suddenly erupted. We've pulled up short of it. I doubt we can do much to help but Richardson is calling the fire brigade and police. They should be here in a few minutes. What are your instructions?'

'Wait until the police arrive, show them your security credentials and make statements. Don't say you were following it, just what happened. Then get back here. Something has obviously upset someone.'

'Roger that, Guv. Police arriving. We'll wait for them to come and talk to us. I'll let you know when we are moving again.'

'Okay. I need to call the boss.'

The call ended and Marshall phoned Preston.

'You secure, Ma'am, it's Marshall?'

'Yes Marshall. You sound unusually flustered.'

'Yes Ma'am. Something is going on. First, the courier was shadowed all the way back from Dover after nothing untoward was found on his van at the port. He came to the jewellers in Reigate as we expected. There was then an altercation between the courier, Newton, and Zussman. It sounds like whatever Zussman was expecting wasn't on the van. Anyway, eventually Newton carried on his journey. I sent the two people I'd been with to follow Newton. Apparently, his van has just been involved in some kind of explosion on the M4. Not got any more details on that yet, but the operative I talked to seemed to say it was a big bang on the driver's side so I think we can assume the driver is dead. The question is what we do about Zussman. Haul him in? Follow him?'

Preston sat silently for a full minute, thinking.

'What grounds do we have to arrest him, Marshall?' She said, finally. 'If we did, we'd only alert anyone else who may be watching him that we are onto them. If we continue to watch him then I think one of two things will happen in the next twenty-four hours. Either he will carry on as if nothing has happened or, and I think this is more likely, he will try and get away. If he tries to do that, arrest him on some terrorism charge or other. If what he was expecting on the van wasn't there then we need to focus our attentions on what he was expecting, and where it could have got to. I doubt he's going to be willing or able to answer either of those questions. So, I suggest we just sit and wait and see what happens next, but we keep our eyes and ears open.'

'Yes Ma'am. I'll call you later and update you with any further news.'

'Thank you, Marshall. Where are you, by the way.'

'Sitting in my car in Reigate watching Zussman's shop.'

'I suggest you go home. We know where he lives and my guess is that is where he will go after work. I assume you have people watching his house.'

'Yes, Ma'am.' Marshall sounded tired, he was.

CHAPTER TWENTY

At four o'clock Carlton said goodbye to Sheera and left for the short journey to his other home. He had reckoned on it being under surveillance by now. After all, it had already been watched by someone a few days earlier and he was damn sure that person would have checked the house was owned by someone called Simon Hart. It had been a useful persona for the past five years, ever since he had managed to steal the identity of the real architect named Simon Hart. The genuine Simon Hart was a wealthy man, the owner of eight properties in the United Kingdom, though he only knew about seven of them. He had no idea about the house Carlton was driving to. A fifteen-minute drive through country roads from his home south of Reigate, heading west towards Dorking. Taking the side roads he loved to drive down, Carlton was in his black BMW X6. He passed the surveillance car parked just before the corner of the road before the mansion he was driving to.

'Fools,' he muttered as he passed them. He knew they would register his car, but they could not see the wrought-iron gates opening. He drove past the gates and turned the BMW round, driving back to the mansion's driveway, and carried on into the property. The gates closed silently behind him. To those watching in the car it would later appear that someone unconnected with the property had driven past it and carried on with their journey. Probably they wouldn't even check the owner of the vehicle.

Once Carlton had gained access to the home he had acquired as Simon Hart, he worked quickly. The gas cylinders had been stored in his garage for some weeks. Now he connected them together, opened the cylinders and placed the mobile phone with its detonator on top of them. He left the garage and locked the door to the house. Some time ago the garage doors had been altered to include rubber seals, thus making it a sealed container. Carlton reckoned the cylinders would need about an hour to release their high-pressured gas into the room.

He had just returned to his study when the CCTV monitoring the gate showed a car had pulled up. The silver Mercedes looked almost brand new.

'Hi Simon, I'll just let you in.' Carlton pressed the button on the control panel at the side of his desk and the gates opened. As soon as they did, Carlton pressed another button on the panel. It had the effect of deleting the recorded history from the camera.

'Brian, good to see you again after all these years. Nice place you have here.' The man was in his forties, about the same height and build as Carlton and he carried with him an A3 folder.

'It's not bad but I want to make some changes, always assuming we can get planning. Which is why I wanted to start with getting you involved. You did a great job with my former home near Reigate so I'm hoping we can do the same here. At the moment I'm essentially using a bedroom as my gym but what I want to do is build a complex out the back which will include an indoor pool, spa or hot tub, whatever you want to call it, and then have changing and showering facilities, a sauna and space for a moderate sized gym. I don't know if that's possible.'

'I presume there's nothing out there now.'

'Only a lawn leading to a tennis court. I sort of expect the court to more or less follow on from the new complex.'

'It's not going to be cheap, you understand?'

'I figured it wouldn't be. I'm planning to get married next year. My girlfriend, or should I say fiancée, is a real sports fanatic, so I figure having everything here, that is possible to have here, would be a good idea.'

'Well, congratulations, I guess. So how big does the gym need to be?'

'About twice the size of the one upstairs. I'll show you it, if that would help.'

'Okay, lead on. I'll take some measurements and then we can rough out some plans. What size pool do you want?'

'Say twenty-five metres, and three or four lanes wide, whatever looks reasonable and doable. I'll show you where I want it after we come back downstairs. How long do you reckon the plans will take to draw up?'

'Not long, maybe a fortnight, maybe less. The difficult part is usually getting planning permission but you are pretty much secluded here so hopefully that won't be an issue.'

'If it helps, we could dig down and basically just have the roof above ground so it isn't too visible.'

'I'll hold that idea for now. Okay, where is the gym?'

'Top of the stairs, second left. After you.'

Carlton followed the real Simon Hart up the stairs. About halfway up he put a hand in his right trouser pocket, as if he was looking for something. Carlton opened the door to the gym using the number pad on the wall to release the magnetic lock, and stood to one side while Hart went inside one pace. Carlton was right behind him. Hart barely felt the sharp prick of the needle in his left buttock cheek a few seconds before he started feeling dizzy.

'Whoa, I must have climbed the stairs too quickly,' was all he said before he fell unconscious onto the floor of the gym. Before he did anything, Carlton pulled on a pair of medical examination gloves. Then Carlton removed what looked like an epi-pen from his pocket. He carefully placed it just outside the door to the gym and then proceeded to haul Hart onto the weights bench. He undressed his upper body and lay him flat on his front on the bench. By the time he had done this, Carlton was breathing heavily from the exertion. He was a fit man but Hart was heavy. Carlton found the keyless fob to the Merc in Hart's jacket pocket. He took the jacket with him. Leaving the door ajar, Carlton set the automatic closer at the back of the door to close next time the door was pushed open. He picked up the epi-pen and went downstairs. He hung the jacket on his coat stand in the hall, and put the A3 portfolio case underneath it. He put the pen in his attaché case and checked his watch. He switched off the CCTV camera monitoring the gate, opened the gates and left the front door on the latch. Then Carlton went outside and moved the Mercedes to the side of the house so it would be hidden from view to anyone coming up the driveway. He turned the BMW round so it was ready to drive back to the gates. Then Carlton went back indoors and put the keyless fob to the Merc back in Hart's jacket pocket before retreating to his study and shutting the door.

A few minutes later, Christine Matthews drove down the road past the car and its occupants who were monitoring Hart's mansion, and turned into the driveway. The surveillance team noted the registration plate on her car as she passed them but could not see her enter the driveway. Matthews drove straight up to the house, saw the note pinned to the front door and read it as she went inside.

'Dear Christine. I am in the gym, please close the front door and come straight up. I am waiting for you! Simon xxx'

Christine smiled, shut the door, straightened her ultra-short black skirt and almost skipped up the stairs. She had another client booked for 9 o'clock and she knew Simon would be more than content by then. She opened the door to the gym, which was in darkness and saw the man lying on the weights bench.

'Hi Simon, it's only Chrissie. Now, where would you like me to...ARRRGGGHHHHH!' She shrieked as she touched the body and immediately realised it was not the Simon Hart she knew. At the same moment, the door to the room closed behind her, the magnetic lock sealing her in the room with whoever he was. She found the light switch next to the door pad and turned the lights on. Then she returned to the man. She shook him but there was no response.

Somewhere in all of this she thought she heard the front door open and close downstairs and then she heard the sound of a car starting up. That sound, through the double glazing, scared her more than her own predicament.

Downstairs, as soon as he heard the door to the gym close, Carlton opened the front door for the last time and softly closed it behind him. He jumped into the black BMW and started the engine. Driving down to the gates he turned right, away from the people watching the house. A kilometre down the road was a layby. Carlton pulled into it, applied the handbrake and picked the mobile phone out of his pocket. It was a pay as you go phone, almost untraceable. Carlton dialled a number. Back in the garage of the house he had left a few minutes earlier, the mobile phone rang and vibrated. It vibrated twice before the detonator was triggered. There was a small bang as the detonator exploded, followed a moment later by a much more massive explosion as the gas-filled garage erupted. The sound of the explosion reached Carlton a moment later. It was probably loud enough to be noticed by everyone within a kilometre of the house. It certainly was noticed by the surveillance team watching the house. Not only did they hear the deafening roar of the explosion, they saw the massive fireball that engulfed the house in seconds.

'Jesus, what was that?' said the man in the passenger seat.

'Dunno, but look at that,' said the man in the driver's seat, pointing at the burning house they were watching.

'Oh shit,' said the passenger, picking up his mobile phone.

'Yes, emergency, we need fire, ambulance and police attendance at what looks like a major gas explosion and fire. The address, oh yes, and he read the address details to the control centre operator. My colleague and I are sat outside the house. We're going to go and see if there is anything we can do. Yes, we will wait for the police to arrive.'

Meanwhile the driver was calling Marshall. He told him the same story that his colleague had just told the emergency services.

'Okay, I'm on my way. At this time of day it will be about 30 minutes or so. Stay where you are until I arrive.'

Marshall plugged his mobile phone into his Bluetooth headset and talked to Preston as he drove. When he arrived at the scene, parking just outside the wrought iron gates which were blocked by two police cars, the two surveillance officers pointed him to the senior police officer and Marshall introduced himself and showed his security credentials. The rank of Detective Inspector was intended to impress. It did.

'Does that make you in charge of this, sir?' the Detective Sergeant asked him.

'No, it's your case. My only interest is who is in there, assuming there is someone in there. What's your name, by the way?'

'Charles Crawford,' he replied. 'Detective Sergeant.'

'Thank you, DS Crawford. I just need to know for my own report.'

'Not a problem. There is a car in the driveway and what looks like it was a silver Mercedes just in front of what was the garage. We're not going to be getting very close for a while, the whole house is going up.' Inside the gate, Marshall counted two fire engines, an ambulance and two more police vehicles. The house was indeed an inferno.

'Too early to guess what caused this?'

'For media release, yes far too early. But seeing as you are who you are, and the fire crews will have to confirm it, I'd say this started in the garage. The door and roof have all blown out and the Mercedes has been badly burned out. It could well be a gas leak. Although we will have to make our own enquiries, I presume from your presence, you know already who lives here, sir.'

'Yes, a guy called Simon Hart. I've done some research on him for our own purposes. He's got a European arrest warrant out for him in Germany in connection with the two terror attacks in the Munich area a couple of days ago. Actually, if he has come home and slipped past customs we could have a big problem. Come to think of it I need to talk to the fireman in charge urgently. Whose car is that in front of the house?'

'Not had a chance to check yet but it's some kind of black Saab sports car. The Merc I have already identified as belonging to someone called Simon Hart.'

Marshall winced at the mention of the black Saab. 'We need to be very careful. If that belongs to who I think it belongs to then we are all in very great danger. Can you run a check on the registration plate?'

'Yes, sir. It will only take a minute.' The Sergeant was on his police-issue phone requesting a number check. Marshall heard him read the registration number and paused. Finally, the Sergeant thanked the operator on the other end of the phone. 'Car is registered to a Christine Matthews, sir,' he said. Marshall felt his stomach cramp up at the name.

'Damnit, she's a prostitute used by Hart on a number of occasions. You don't need to know how I know that, but we've been interested in Miss Matthews in connection with our own case. Okay, we have to clear this area now. There is very likely something in that burning house that is potentially going to do exactly what happened in Munich a few days ago.'

'The fire chief needs to make that decision, sir. Until the fire crews declare the area is safe it's their case.'

'Then I need to talk quickly to whoever is in charge.'

'Yes sir. Come with me.' The Detective Sergeant led Marshall down the driveway at a run. They arrived at the second of the fire engines, slightly out of breath.

'Who's in charge?' Marshall shouted.

'Who the hell are you. Get back, this place is dangerous.'

'Yes, far more dangerous than you'd believe right now.' Marshall held up his security card and demanded again, 'I said who is in charge. It's urgent.'

'Okay, Bill, I'll deal with this. Fire Chief James Marchmont, who are you?'

'Travis Marshall, ATRIUM – to you that is anti-terrorism. I haven't got time to explain everything but you have got to get everyone out of here, right now. The car there belongs to a prostitute. The DS has just identified that for me. She has a regular client who lives here called Simon Hart. He is a suspect in the recent Munich terror attacks. I assume as she is here, then he must be as well, though we have no idea how he slipped back into the country yet. If he's in there, then in all probability he has the same devices in there as were used in Munich. If just one of them goes off then everyone in a 10 kilometre area will be dead by the end of today. I'm not exaggerating. I need you to give up on saving the house and get your men and women clear now. Same goes for the police cars and ambulances. Chances are, if anyone is in there then they are already dead, from what my operatives told me about the initial explosion.'

'I agree with that, sir, but we have a duty to put the fire out, though I'd say it's a foregone conclusion the house will collapse before we do that, judging by the ferocity of the fire when we got here.'

While Marshall was speaking, his mobile phone rang.

'Sorry I have to take this, it's my boss.' Marshall walked a few paces away from the others and spoke softly. 'Marshall,' he said out of habit.

'Hi, have you arrived at the scene yet?'

'Yes, a few minutes ago. House is burning ferociously, looks like some kind of explosion that started in the garage area. There's a silver Merc in front of it. The police have identified that as belonging to Simon Hart. There's also a black Saab that belongs to Christine Matthews. My guess is they are both inside. Whether we ever find enough evidence to identify them I don't know. What bothers me is if Hart really was involved in Munich and he is here now, does he have any more similar devices with him and if so, could they be in the inferno I'm looking at.'

'Which is why I called you. The German scientists have done some work. It is a virus and it is incredibly powerful and quick acting but it has one weakness, which may be to your advantage. It can be easily killed by heat – extreme heat, such as you get when something explodes. I'd suggest you get them to let the house burn to the ground, contain the fire within the house if necessary. Then wait 24 hours for it to cool down and start the investigation. If there is any of this stuff in there, then if it gets released I reckon the heat will kill it off instantly.'

'Thanks, Ma'am, that's worth knowing.

'Glad to be of assistance, Marshall. Do you want me to talk to anyone or can you handle it?'

'I can handle it. I'll update you later on.'

The call ended and Marshall returned to the DS and the Fire Chief.

'That was my boss. The Germans have discovered that what we think Hart planted in Munich was a virus, and though it spreads faster than anything we have ever seen before, like it can cover a radius of ten kilometres in

24 hours, it has a weakness. And that weakness is it can be killed almost instantly by intense heat, at least in a laboratory. My boss recommends we let the house burn to the ground, just containing the fire so it doesn't spread. That way if there are any devices inside, and they get set off, the heat from the fire will kill the virus. Then we let it cool down for 24 hours or so before we start sifting through the debris for bodies and anything else. And, we will be sending in our own units to do all of that. They are specially trained to handle what we think we might come up against. Any questions.'

Marshall sounded authoritative and with the information he had revealed the others seemed relieved the responsibility for dealing with the situation had passed from them to a government agency. Just as Marshall finished speaking his phone rang.

'Travis, the press is here. What do you want to do?'

'Nothing. I'll let the DS make some kind of statement when we come back up to the gates. For now this is a crime scene and highly dangerous so no one, and I mean no one, is going to go past those gates.'

'Yes, guv.'

The phone went dead.

'DS Crawford, we have already gained some press interest. They are being held at the gates for now. Maybe you need to put out a holding statement. Area highly dangerous, trying to get control of the fire. Not sure if anyone is in the house – can't get near it due to the raging inferno inside. That kind of thing. Absolutely no mention of Simon Hart or what we think he is involved in. Is that understood?'

'Yes, sir.'

Marshall and the DS had been walking back to the wrought iron gates. When they got there, they opened the gates manually and stepped out of the property before pulling the gates closed again. As the DS talked to the two media reporters standing just down the road beyond the police cordon, Marshall briefed his own surveillance officers.

Over the next hour the fire continued to burn ferociously and after the hour the roof collapsed. By now there was a small group of people standing on both sides of the road which had been closed by the police a hundred metres either side of the gates. Once the roof collapsed the fire started to subside until after three hours it was all but extinguished. All that remained were blackened walls and a wholly burnt out interior.

***

By seven o'clock, Carlton had returned to Sheera and by seven thirty they were ready to go out for the evening. The restaurant was small, private and secluded. Not far from the Epsom Downs race course, it had a very rural feel to it, just a half dozen tables and a host who was very attentive.

'We have the table by the window for sir and madam,' the Maitre'd said as soon as they entered the front door.

'Excellent, a view over the fields, absolutely perfect,' said Carlton, the events of the evening appeared to have had no effect on him.

'And would sir and madam like to see the drinks menu before you order.'

'Sheera, darling, they have a really nice vintage Chardonnay, or we could do a Champagne if you prefer, or maybe something first?'

'I'd love a gin and tonic actually.' Sheera was wearing a figure-hugging black dress, one they had acquired a few days earlier in Munich.

'In which case make that two, and when we are served the meal I'd like a bottle of Dom Perignon, please – whatever you have that is a good vintage.'

'Of course sir. I'll fetch the drinks and come back to take your order.'

The host left them and was gone for several minutes. While he was out of their hearing, Carlton reached forward across the table and met Sheera half way. They kissed before Carlton told Sheera he would take her into Kingston as he knew how much she liked the shops.

'That'd be great, Simon,' she reached forward a bit further and kissed him.

Carlton almost corrected her but caught himself in time. Just so long as he could keep up the double identity for another couple of days, his plans would be executed perfectly. The drinks arrived and the food was ordered.

'So this is where they run the Derby?' Sheera had heard of the famous race but never imagined she would be sitting down for a meal in a restaurant so close to the course.

'It is,' Simon smiled sweetly.

'And do you like horse racing, Simon?'

'I have to confess it's not a sport that interests me much. I used to be into football when I was younger, and then rugby, but horses actually scare me a bit.'

Sheera laughed politely. The food arrived after a while and the happy couple set about the task of enjoying their repast.

***

While Carlton and Sheera dined, all hell was breaking loose elsewhere in Surrey. The fire at Simon Hart's mansion had started to die down. The roof and two walls had collapsed some time earlier in the evening. It would be at least 24 hours before anyone would start to sift through the debris. Meanwhile Marshall had interviewed the two surveillance operatives who'd been monitoring the property. He'd taken their notebooks, copied down details of the car registrations that had passed them in the two hours before the explosion and had started to run some traces. There were only a handful of vehicles and the checks showed a car registered to someone called Brian Carlton had passed them at just after 4:15 pm. A couple of cars had followed in the minutes after – and Marshall had them checked and noted their registered owner's details. They'd all have to be checked out, of course. It was the fifth enquiry that attracted Marshall's attention. At just before 5:00 pm a silver Mercedes had passed the surveillance team. They'd noted its registration number as required. It appeared to drive rather quickly but that was just a note on the notebook one of the team had been using. Marshall almost knew what the DVLA check would reveal, and he was not surprised when the car came back as belonging to Simon Hart. At 5:50 a Black Saab had passed the surveillance car. Marshall knew this had to be the car owned by Christine Matthews so was not surprised when the check with DVLA confirmed that a few minutes later. Those checks confirmed what had been found at the scene of the explosion. It appeared Hart had arrived home from the continent a short while before the prostitute he seemed to favour had arrived and then something had happened and as their cars were still outside the house, Marshall had to assume from the ferocity of the explosion and the subsequent fire that they had both died in the conflagration.

Marshall returned to the police officer in charge of the scene.

'When it's safe to go in there,' Marshall said to the officer, 'I think we are going to find two bodies at least. One I suspect will be the owner of the Merc, a Simon Hart, the other will be a female who we believe is Christine Matthews. But, before anyone goes near that house, they need to be in full protective gear and I mean bio-hazard protection suits. I want no-one to take any chances. We'll send our own team down tomorrow to make the initial entry and investigation.'

'Yes sir.'

'Good, when they get here, get the person in charge to call me immediately. This is my card. I cannot stress enough that it is imperative no one disturbs anything unless they are in full protective gear. We have no idea what is actually in there but after events in Munich over the past few days we can't take risks especially as the person who we think has died in there is the person the Germans are interested in.'

'Yes sir.' The officer took Marshall's card and added the details to his own notebook.

Having done what he could for the moment, Marshall told the surveillance team to call it a day and to go to the local police station the next morning to file formal statements. As he walked back to his own car, he called Preston.

'Marshall, are you secure, Ma'am?'

'Yes,' Preston had been waiting in the office for news.

'I've done what I can at the scene of Hart's house for now. It's still burning but now under control. The roof and two walls collapsed so it's going to be the devil's own to find any remains and anything else that might be in there. I've arranged for our bio-hazard team to come down in the morning. Meanwhile the police are imposing a two hundred metre exclusion zone round the property and there will be a guard there overnight, and the fire service will be on site until they are sure it's all safe.'

'Sounds like you have the situation in hand.'

'I hope so. The only other thing I think we should do immediately is pull in Zussman for questioning. After what happened on the M4 and now this, I think firstly Zussman knows who is behind the events on the M4. From what Wellman described earlier, I'd hazard a guess that Zussman was expecting a delivery of something this trip, but it didn't arrive. Now, it's a bit of a stretch at the moment but we know Simon Hart was in Munich a few days ago and that Newton's van was in the same vicinity. It could be Newton gave Hart whatever he was supposed to deliver to Zussman. It could be coincidence but I have a feeling about this one. I think Hart and Newton were in this together, somehow. So Newton gets back to the UK and passes the Customs check because whatever he was carrying was no longer in the van. So I think Zussman knows what he was expecting to receive and as he hasn't got it, I'd say he is in danger from whoever he is involved with.'

'Interesting,' said Preston. 'There's something you won't know yet but the Germans have made progress with their own investigations. First the hotel that's been attacked. It appears a certain Simon Hart and a female companion by the name of Sheera Ganzagha stayed there the night before the event. We have no idea who Ganzagha is other than she flew into Munich from Ankara on 28th June.'

'She met Hart in Munich?'

'Yes, CCTV from Munich airport has picked up the moment she got off the plane and the person she met up with in the Arrivals lounge. Also, Hart had a hire car he'd rented for a few days. That was clocked entering the Grassvelde hypermarket on Sunday 28th and then again on Tuesday 30th. On the 30th it left the carpark about two hours before whatever happened there and a couple of traffic cameras clocked it on the Autobahn heading to France. We also have Daniel Newton registered at a GastHaus on the outskirts of Munich on the night of 29th. He stayed there quite a lot and was known to the house owner – seemed like it was a part of travel itinerary whenever he was on the continent. So it's possible he met up with Hart at some point in Munich. The Germans are continuing to investigate that line of enquiry.'

'Hmm, there is another possibility,' said Marshall slowly.

'Go on,' Preston sounded tired but intrigued.

'What if Hart knew what Newton was carrying and decided to steal it. Maybe we have a whole new terror outfit here in the UK we know nothing about? It's just a thought.'

'Yes, and a pretty sinister one too. It's possible, but he'd need a whole load of people working for him to know just when and where Newton was staying.' Preston's line of sight caught the London Eye, it's gondolas lit with yellow light.

'He wouldn't need that many people. Where did you say Ganzagha came from?' Marshall spoke softly, his mind thinking fast/

Preston found the sheet of paper she was looking for after a few seconds.

'Ankara.'

'That's pretty much where Newton used to travel to from what I recall from Harding's team visiting his house a few days ago. So all Hart would need is someone watching wherever Newton travelled to. If they'd already been watching Newton travel across Europe they'd know how long it took him to do so and where he stayed. My guess is Newton is a creature of habit and the GastHaus registrations kind of confirm that. So all Hart would need is someone at the pick-up point to let him know when Newton was starting on the journey back and you know what, I think I know who that person is.'

'You do? Go on.'

'Sheera Ganzagha.' Marshall may have been tired but his brain was working quickly.

'Could be, but not necessarily.' Preston needed convincing.

'Yes, necessarily. She is part of whatever is going on, part of Hart's or whoever's plan. So she meets up with Hart in Munich to identify the van, or more likely Newton. I'll bet Hart has no idea who Newton is. So Ganzagha comes to Munich and identifies Newton and then Hart somehow gets hold of whatever is coming to the UK.'

'Which may be an issue then, because somehow both Hart and Ganzagha managed to slip into the UK after disappearing from somewhere in France. The hire car was returned to the hire company in Paris but Hart never registered at a hotel overnight and the French have checked all the local establishments already.'

'Or at least he didn't use the name Hart.' Marshall yawned silently to himself.

'True, but that may not be relevant. Remember from this evening it looks like he's dead in the burned out ruins of his own house, and we already know his favourite prostitute's car is in his driveway so it's fair to assume she is also in the rubble. Which creates a problem because I doubt Ganzagha would be overly pleased to come all the way to England to then have to put up with Hart spending time with a prostitute. So the question is, where is Ganzagha, if Hart is dead.'

'I have no idea Ma'am. Maybe Ganzagha found out Hart was not exactly loyal and she found a way to get rid of him. Until we know how many bodies are in the ruins we can't be sure. We should know more tomorrow.'

'True, Marshall, but until then we have to face the possibility that neither Ganzagha or Hart are actually in that house and if they're not and they still have whatever they brought back into the country, then they are potentially extremely dangerous.'

'Agreed Ma'am. I'll get onto the specialist unit tomorrow and see how quickly they think they can start work.'

'Okay, Marshall. Meanwhile about ten minutes ago you asked if we could pull in Zussman for questioning. I think we could do now. I'll get a warrant sorted and a team to pick him up first thing in the morning and get him taken to Redhill probably.'

'I'll make myself available there in the morning to question him then'

'Thanks Marshall. Call me when you've had a talk with him.'

The line went dead, and Preston put in place the necessary arrangements to haul Zussman in for questioning and then, as Marshall called it a day, Preston turned off the light in her office and made her way to the car that was waiting for her in the underground carpark.

***

Dieter Zussman, badly shaken by events of the evening, drove back to his house as usual, unaware of the explosion on the M4 but nevertheless convinced it was time to run, not from the authorities but from the people who controlled him. So he drove home as usual and parked his car in the driveway. Keeping to his usual ritual, as he was sure he was being watched, he went indoors and waited. He waited until ten o'clock and started his usual routine of locking up before retiring for the night. In the darkness, and using a small flashlight, he removed the screws holding the floorboard in his bedroom in place and removed the contents beneath for the last time. His small suitcase was already packed and it took Zussman only a few minutes to recover his personal identity papers, his passport, and a few other items. Meticulously double-checking everything, he pulled the simple mobile phone from his pocket. It was a small and simple device with a Pay As You Go SIM in it. That suited Zussman fine as he only planned on making one phone call with it. He turned the phone on and placed the call. In under five minutes the taxi was booked for four in the morning. Zussman paid by card and closed the call before turning off the phone. He would not sleep that night but sit up in the darkness waiting for the clock to slowly approach his hour of departure.

A few minutes after sitting in his armchair, Zussman felt the first chest pain. A moment later he felt his left arm go numb as his right hand reached up to his chest and he let out a loud gasp of pain. The constriction in his chest grew and grew until Zussman let out a bone-chilling gurgle and slumped back into his chair, dead. The heart attack had been sudden and massive.

At four o'clock the taxi pulled up outside his house and the driver knocked on Zussman's door politely.

Then the driver rang the bell and knocked again. The house was in darkness. The driver pushed open the letter box and could hear nothing. Early morning calls were annoying and often resulted in no fare being ready for him which was one reason the company he worked for took credit card payments in advance for such journeys. Cursing his luck at a wasted journey, the driver turned on his heels and in a few minutes the taxi pulled away as the driver called in the no-fare.

At ten to six, there was more activity outside the house where Zussman lived. Two black cars pulled up and four plain clothes detectives alighted. The officer in charge went up to the front door and banged on it whilst he shouted the single word, 'Police'. Unexpectedly the front door of the house next to Zussman's opened.

'I don't think he's there,' said the tired male voice as he exited the door.

'No. Why do you think that?'

'Cos a vehicle pulled up about two hours ago and I'm pretty sure it was a taxi, seeing as we got woken up by his door being knocked on and his doorbell ringing. Who wants to know anyway? Sorry, but you can't be too careful these days, so I assume you have some ID so I don't have to call the police myself.'

The officer proffered his warrant card in front of the neighbour as he walked over to the dividing low-level fence.

'Perkins, can you see anything? Do you have a key to this place sir?' The officer in charge asked the neighbour who was standing outside in pyjamas and a dressing gown.

'No, never really knew the guy even though he's been here a while. Kept himself to himself if you know what I mean. Until this morning I don't think we've ever heard a peep out of him. What did you say his name was?'

'Dieter Zussman is on the warrant.'

'Doesn't ring any bells to me.'

'And your name sir, if you don't mind. We may need a statement at some point.'

The neighbour gave the information requested.

'Guv,' the officer called Perkins walked up to him and spoke softly. 'I think I can see someone in the lounge sitting in a chair. I'd say he's slumped, but I can't be sure. Permission to break the door down, guv?'

'Yes, do it.'

Perkins returned to the others who were standing near the front door.

'Doesn't look too solid to me. A good kick might do it.'

'Yes, should do.' The tallest and bulkiest of the men took up position and aimed a good kick just below the main lock. It took three hits before the door gave way and splintered. Two more shoves by two of the officers had the door opened enough for them to gain entry.

'Police. Come out and show yourself.'

Nothing happened.

'Perkins, take the downstairs, we'll go upstairs.'

Perkins opened the lounge door, flicked on the light switch and smelled that all too familiar smell of – death. Recent death, not death that had been masked for days, but death, nonetheless.

'Male occupant in the lounge, deceased. He's blue and white and cold.' Perkins preliminary examination was perfunctory and told him there was nothing that could be done for the man. Upstairs his colleagues found nothing.

Perkins continued to call out his findings as the officer in charge entered the room. 'Suitcase on the floor, passport, currency and what looks like a travel visa in the internal pocket of his suit. No sign of a wound or anything. Probably a heart attack or something but we'd better get the duty pathologist to take a look before we move him.'

'Agreed. Can you do that Perkins? I'd better get onto the people who ordered this.'

Ten minutes later Detective Sergeant Wilkins had been connected to a bleary-eyed Selena Preston.

'Sorry to disturb you Ma'am. I'm Detective Sergeant Wilkins. I gather you are behind the execution of a warrant to detain a certain Dieter Zussman,' and he read off the address where he was standing. 'I'm afraid we're too late Ma'am, or at least I think we are. We have just had to gain entry to the dwelling and there is a single male in the living room who is deceased. It looks like he was about to go somewhere, suitcase packed and a passport, currency and a visa in his suit pocket. According to the neighbour there was a taxi turned up at about four this morning but the neighbour was asleep until the banging on the door woke him and he doesn't know if the taxi left with or without his fare.'

'Thank you DS Wilkins. I take it you have the duty team on their way. I will be sending my own man down as this is a matter of national security. His name is Marshall. Please make sure no one touches the body or his belongings until Marshall arrives.'

'Very good Ma'am, and sorry to have had to disturb you so early.'

'That's not a problem DS Wilkins. I was expecting a day in the office anyway.'

Preston ended the conversation and called Marshall.

'Marshall, it's Preston. Sorry for the hour but this is important. It appears Zussman is dead. The guys executing the warrant this morning found a body in the lounge of his house. I told the DS, a guy called Wilkins, that you are on the way. Also the duty team are on their way, so the doctor may be able to tell you a preliminary cause. Main thing is I want you to get the paperwork and so on and start working out where the hell Zussman was going and if he was going alone.'

'On my way, Ma'am.'

'Any developments overnight, Marshall?'

'No Ma'am. I'll call the team who are at Hart's house when I'm on route but I doubt there will be any more news there until this afternoon at the earliest. Even if the rubble has cooled down enough to gain access, it's going to take a while for the fire service to make the place safe and that's even before we can start looking for bodies.'

'And in the meantime we have no idea if Hart or what was her name, Ganzagha, are alive or buried there. It's a mess, Marshall and I don't like mess.'

'No Ma'am. Right I'm on my way to check out Zussman. Can you meet me at my place in a couple of hours, please. We have things to deal with that are best not discussed over the phone.'

The meeting was agreed and both Preston and Marshall went to work.

Marshall made light work of his journey to Zussman's house. As he drove he confirmed there were no developments overnight at Hart's property. As he turned into the road where Zussman lived he could not help but notice the three police cars and the forensic team's van pulled up in front of it. Marshall parked up and walked up the road to the temporary police cordon that had been set up.

'DI Travis Marshall, anti-terrorism,' Marshall showed the officer at the cordon his ID card and was allowed to pass under the tape. 'I'm looking for DS Wilkins.'

'He's in the house, sir,' the officer spoke smartly.

Fishing the blue, plastic overshoes from his jacket pocket, Marshall approached the house, pausing at the entrance where the front door had once been to pull the overshoes over his own boots before entering the property.

'DS Wilkins?' Marshall called and attracted the attention of a man in his mid to late thirties. 'DI Travis Marshall, anti-terrorism. What have you got for me?'

'Body is in here, sir, together with a suitcase. My officers went upstairs when we first got here but only checking for people so we haven't touched anything up there. The kitchen is through there and likewise we haven't opened anything. If you don't mind me asking, why are anti-terrorism involved, sir?'

'I don't mind the question Wilkins. This guy, if he is who we think he is, has been under surveillance for a while, which is why you had a warrant to execute this morning. It's possible, just possible, he has attempted to import something that is extremely dangerous. My aim here is to confirm he is the person we've been following and to determine if this place is safe from the agent we think he was trying to import. Shall we get started?'

'Sir.'

Marshall led the way into the lounge and took a quick look at the dead man sitting in the armchair.

'That's Zussman, no doubt about it. We had a preliminary chat with him here a few days ago. Has the doctor been?'

'No sir, he's due any minute.'

'Okay, absolutely no one is to touch that case for now. If you have the pictures you need, I'd rather remove it to a place of containment before it's opened. I have a recovery team coming shortly.'

'Yes sir. What do you think could be in it?'

'Clothes, probably, but until we're sure we need to be careful. Right, I'll just go upstairs while we wait for the doctor.'

Marshall left the lounge, rubbing his chin thoughtfully, and climbed the staircase. His examination of the upstairs rooms was quick. The wardrobes were empty, and what few possessions Zussman had were probably all in the suitcase in the lounge. Marshall scanned Zussman's bedroom, and noticed the few possessions he'd seen before had all disappeared. It really did look like Zussman was leaving and never coming back. After what had happened on the M4 the previous day, and not being sure of Zussman's real allegiances, Marshall did not blame Zussman for trying to get away from whatever, or whoever, had been controlling him. Marshall was back downstairs a minute after the doctor arrived.

'Mark, what can you tell me?' Marshall asked as he re-entered the lounge. Mark Cavendish, one of a team of Home Office Pathologists who worked in the area, was a man who Marshall had known for several years.

'Male, deceased. I'd say sometime early this morning. No obvious trauma wounds. Position of arms and hands would be in keeping with cardiac arrest but I'll know more when we do the post-mortem which we may get done today. We don't know who he is, do we?'

'You'll know him, if he's on record, as Dieter Zussman, but he is actually from the Middle East – and there he had the name of Mohammed Ali Burgansa. I'll leave you my card and I want to know the minute you know anything more, time of death, cause and so on.'

'Okay.'

'Thanks Mark.'

'DI Marshall, your team have arrived.' Wilkins reappeared in the doorway to the lounge.

'Thanks Wilkins. We'll need just a minute and then your usual team can do whatever needs to be done. Ah, Hennessy, you have things ready?' Marshall added as he spotted the man appear behind Wilkins. Hennessy, wearing a blue jumpsuit, special boots, gloves and a facemask that fed him oxygen from a cylinder on his back, entered the doorway and nodded.

'It's that case Hennessy.'

Hennessy nodded again and picked the case up before wrapping it in a roll of plastic he had brought with him. The plastic was then taped up before Hennessy picked up the case and started carrying it out of the building. Outside a vehicle that looked like an armoured truck, because that was exactly what it was, had pulled up. Hennessy placed the case very carefully in the

271

airtight back of the truck and then removed his face mask and other protective clothing.

'We'll deal with that shortly, sir and I'll call you in an hour or so. Anything else you need us for?'

'Not right now Hennessy. We can talk later.'

Marshall turned back to DS Wilkins and said, 'it's all yours now Wilkins to determine if there is anything untoward going on. One thing, I noticed it as I arrived and I also noticed it when we talked to Zussman last weekend, the people living at number 42 across the road seem to have a habit of twitching the curtains in the upstairs room. If I was paranoid I'd say they were watching Zussman, so that might be something for your enquiries. No, don't look up there now, he's just moved the curtain again.'

'Yes sir, I'll get some back up and see what's going on.'

'Very good. Now regrettably I have to get back to my superiors and then find time for breakfast. Call me if you find anything interesting.'

'Yes, sir.'

CHAPTER TWENTY-ONE
Friday 3rd July

It was just after the rush hour when Carlton opened the up and over garage door. Inside were two cars, the black BMW X6 and a less ostentatious silver VW Golf. Carlton backed the Golf out of the garage and then closed the garage door.

Returning to the front door of the house, he called inside.

'Come on Sheera, we won't have much time for shopping if we don't get cracking.'

'Alright, Simon, I'm ready.'

'Good,' said Carlton locking the door behind Sheera as she walked to the car.

'You have a silver car as well?'

'Yes, this is more functional and the car I use to leave in multi-storey carparks. It is nowhere near as precious as the BMW.'

Sheera laughed as she found the passenger door and sat down in the car. A few minutes later, with a small black rucksack stowed carefully in the boot of the car, Carlton began the drive to Kingston. A short while later they drove up the A217, through Reigate and crossed the M25, taking the A217 towards Burgh Heath. Turning left at a parade of shops, Carlton drove past the ASDA supermarket and then after a few minutes they passed the NESCOT college and the growing conurbation next to it. At the roundabout, Carlton headed away from Epsom and headed for Tolworth. The traffic was moderate and Carlton was careful not to trigger the numerous yellow cameras that were designed to catch speeding motorists. From Tolworth he headed for Kingston and a short time later located the Seven Kings carpark. With the car parked, Carlton took the small rucksack out of the boot and headed, with Sheera, to the shopping area.

'It's the best shopping centre, I think, leastwise if you don't go into somewhere like Oxford Street in London. So, it's time for you to get a few more clothes, my dear, and I want to get you a necklace and bracelet set. I know of a good jewellers I've been to before, if I can just remember which floor they are on.'

Sheera and Carlton spent the next few hours happily walking around just about every shop that existed. Sheera seemed amazed by the experience and slowly the number of carrier bags she and Carlton were carrying grew. When they got to the second floor, Carlton made Sheera sit down on a bench opposite the book shop and said he needed to go to the toilet. He took the little black rucksack with him and was gone for nearly ten minutes. Once in the men's toilet, Carlton found the cubicle he had noted a few months earlier and in a few minutes had secreted the small package he'd brought in his rucksack behind the false wall that hid the toilet's cistern. He washed his hands and came out of the toilets smiling.

'Do you need to go?' Carlton asked Sheera when he came back to the bench. Sheera took Carlton up on the offer and left him guarding the bags for a few minutes.

When she came back, Carlton had a mobile phone next to his ear and seemed to be listening intently.

'Okay, Roger, the signal in here is not good. We're about to go to Chessington so I'll call you back from the carpark there.' Carlton appeared to end the call. 'Ready?'

'Yes, but where to next? You know, you don't have to show me everything in one day!'

'I know, but we have a theme park in Chessington, just a short drive away, and it will be a lot less busy today than at the weekend, so we won't spend hours queuing for rides.'

'Okay.'

'I assume you know what a theme park is?'

'Not really, but it sounds interesting.'

'I think you'll love it.'

'I hope so.'

And so, Carlton and Sheera made their way back to the carpark and were soon on their way to Chessington World of Adventures. Behind them, in the third men's cubicle on the second floor, the hidden package waited for the signal to activate.

Just over half an hour later, at twenty past one, Carlton pulled the silver Golf into the car park at Chessington World of Adventures. He parked the car and paid the fee. Then, he told Sheera he just needed a few minutes to call his colleague back. She sat in the passenger seat while Carlton walked a discreet distance away, picked a mobile phone out of his pocket and pressed the buttons to make the connection. He waited patiently for the phone to connect and then spoke softly.

'Good afternoon. Am I talking to Detective Chief Superintendent Selena Preston?' The voice sounded distant, distorted in some way but still understandable. Preston guessed correctly that the caller was using some variation of a small voice changer to disguise their own voice.

Preston was on her personal mobile phone and was instantly shocked and taken aback. She was sitting next to Marshall on the sofa in his lounge, having nearly completed their hastily-arranged meeting, when the call came through.

'How did you get this number?'

'One of your operatives was a bit careless with a prostitute we share in common. She took the number off him a few weeks ago and let's just say I took the number off her.'

'I see. Would you identify who you are please?'

'Who I am is not important. This is a prepaid phone and will be destroyed long before you can trace it. Now, I am going to say this once. This morning a package, similar to the one left in a hypermarket in Munich, was planted in the Bentalls shopping centre in Kingston. It will be triggered in two hours if you do not follow my instructions to the letter. I assume you appreciate the consequences will be similar to those in Munich. Similar devices will also be planted at other locations around the country in the next day or so unless you follow my instructions. First though, I imagine you will take more notice of my request after I have proved this is not some kind of hoax.'

Preston signalled to Marshall who had been listening in on the conversation. Silently, Marshall stood and left the room, picking up his own mobile phone as he did so.

'You have about two hours,' Marshall said softly, 'to evacuate the whole area, and I mean everywhere. Actually you need to seal the centre once everyone is out, and no one is to go back in there. And while you are doing that get a trace on the call coming into Preston's mobile number at the moment.'

The short conversation over, Marshall silently returned to the lounge and picked up the end of the ongoing monologue.

'Three days ago a white van was broken into in a carpark in Germany. The van belonged to a man called Daniel Newton who you doubtless know was working for a group of IS members. He was a courier for a number of those people in this country. Many of those people are under my control though of course Mr Newton does not know that. Actually none of the people on his lists knew I was in control. From the back of his van, two dozen watches and boxes were removed and replaced with trash. The original boxes each contained one phial of a highly dangerous virus which goes by the non-scientific name of Wipeout. While in Germany one of the phials was compromised in a small hotel and another at the Grassvelde hypermarket. The remaining phials were brought back to the UK by a separate team of people headed by a man called Simon Hart. Mr Newton is now dead. A third phial is now inside the Bentalls Shopping Centre.'

Carlton continued to issue his monologue to Preston. 'If you wish to avoid a disaster then you will deposit the sum of twenty million pounds into a Swiss numbered account, which I will text you after this call. If the money is not deposited in 2 hours then I will trigger the device in the shopping centre and a further demonstration will take place later today without any further warning. Once the money is deposited you will be told where you can collect the remaining phials and make them safe. Do you understand all of that?'

'I think so, but how do I know you are capable of doing what you say?' Preston was stalling for time, time she hoped would be enough for the call to be traced.

'You will find out in two hours if I am bluffing when people start dying in Kingston. Now, to avoid the risk that you might be able to trace where this call was made from I will hang up. The device I have used will be triggered in exactly one hour and fifty five minutes. Goodbye DCI Preston.'

The mobile phone went dead and thirty seconds later it beeped as an SMS text message arrived.

'Marshall, we've got a bank account just arrived.'

'Do you think he's genuine?'

'If he's not then he knows a whole lot of information about what's been happening. He knows about Alan Green and his proclivities and his lax attitude to security. I don't think we can take the chance.' It was the first time Marshall had seen Preston looking shaken.

'I agree. The Kingston police are on their way to evacuate the town centre. I suggested they put up a kilometre exclusion zone. I know it's not far enough if this guy is real, but it buys us a bit of time, and is probably more than they can achieve in two hours. I pulled rank on a few people to get this to happen – I hope you don't mind?'

'No, if it saves lives. And a call trace?' Preston looked hopefully at Marshall.

'They were trying. I'll call in a minute to find out if they got anywhere. What about the demand?'

'We never have, and never will give into terrorists, Marshall.'

'Understood. So we can expect this phial to go off in a couple of hours.'

'I expect so.' Preston sounded subdued.

'Which doesn't give us long to find the device then. Do we have any intel on what he did in Munich.' Marshall was pacing up and down the living room, thinking as quickly as he could.

'Not much other than the deaths seemed to start in the vicinity of the men's toilet and the floor above them, so I assume that means some kind of ventilation shaft.'

'So,' Marshall continued, 'we have to hope this guy is using the same M.O. (method of operation). Get the bomb squad to go to the men's toilets and rip it apart. They will be looking for something small and I guess with some kind of phone attached to act as some kind of trigger. I doubt he's simply put a timer on it, as he'd have no way of stopping it if we paid up.'

Preston was already connecting with a contact she had at the very top of the bomb-squad as Marshall spoke. Marshall's own phone rang and he answered it immediately.

'Yes, any luck?' Marshall asked.

'Okay, well that's better than nothing. I suppose there is nothing more you can do to get a more accurate fix? No, Okay, I'll let my boss know.' Marshall ended the call and waited for Preston to complete hers.

It took her less than two minutes to explain the situation and then as she listened, she smiled. When she put the phone down, Marshall asked, 'why the smiley face?'

'According to Brigadier Keene, our would-be terrorist has made a bit of a mistake. Like several of the more modern shopping centre constructions these days, the centre in Kingston has a state-of-the-art phone signal jamming device installed. It's a military system that has been put into various buildings to stop events such as these from happening. He's still going to send the unit, but our two hour time limit just got a bit longer. Once the evacuation alarms have been sounded the jammer will automatically kick in. Did they manage to trace the call.'

'Not entirely. They got two points but they needed a third to triangulate from land masts. They are going to see if they can pinpoint something from GPS but they are not hopeful. Another minute and we'd have known. So the best we know for now is somewhere in the Chessington area that covers about a five kilometre area between the two masts. I hate to put a downer on it, but the guy did say there would be another event today and more in the days to come if he didn't get paid.'

'I know, but the jammer capabilities buys us time.' Preston was thinking hard. 'We have to make some assumptions. The partial trace indicates he is well clear of the shopping centre by now. So, did he come in on a train or drive? If he came on a train then he could still be on that heading to God only knows where for the next demonstration. If a car, maybe he's parked up in the Chessington area somewhere, so we may have time to check on the CCTV at the three main car parks and maybe spot something. Get your team over there and start checking the cameras. I'm going to authorise the Opus Protocol. You know what that is, Marshall?'

'Yes, it's the protocol we can put in place in the event of a terrorist attack to check any vehicle we want to check without a reason. Are you seriously thinking of tracking maybe a thousand cars? And my team are already on their way. The first ones will be there in ten minutes or so.'

'So, you have been swatting up for promotion! And no, we don't need to track thousands of cars. We just need to start with any that went into and out of the carparks after the morning rush and up to the point where he called me, that was about one twenty. As it looks like he drove some distance before calling me you can probably stop tracking after one. So that gives us a four hour slot. Actually, thinking on it, it might be quicker to start with if we just monitor cars leaving the car parks.'

'It's a start point,' agreed Marshall. While Preston used her phone to activate the Opus Protocol, Marshall contacted his own team to issue instructions. 'Work back from one o'clock and get checks done on every car leaving the carpark. Report back anything you find that is of interest. No we don't know what we are looking for but I'm hoping something will come up we can use. If you get back to nine and nothing has shown up then call me. I'm with the boss for now.'

'All set?' Preston looked up at Marshall.

'All set. I could go and help them but it'd take me an hour to get there and I don't think they really need another set of hands. I've got a team going to each of the carparks. One person can go back through the CCTV and the other can handle the checks. If I get called, I'm ready and waiting to go.'

'So all we do now is wait?' Preston looked anxiously at her watch.

'I don't think there is much else we can do until something happens. When will the squad be there?'

'About twenty minutes, they have a unit in the area on standby for events such as this.'

Marshall's phone rang. He answered it, said 'Okay' and hung up.

'First team has arrived at the Seven Kings carpark. They're in the security office and starting work. The other two are five minutes away. Coffee?'

'Sounds like a good idea. And I need the little girl's room.'

'Be my guest.' Marshall went to the kitchen to make coffee.

***

After concluding his monologue with Preston, Carlton smiled and returned to the silver Golf.

'Right, that's all done and dusted, as they say. The rest of the day should be ours with no more interruptions. This, my dear Sheera, is Chessington World of Adventures. Shall we go, and I am so sorry that took longer than expected.'

Sheera smiled, and got out of the passenger side of the car while Carlton fetched his black rucksack from the boot of the car. He carefully took the two drinks bottles and sandwiches he'd purchased at one of the delicatessens in the shopping centre earlier and put them in the top of the ruck sack. Then, hand in hand, they walked the length of the large car park to the entry kiosks.

'Two adults, please, and express passes,' Carlton said to the attendant behind the glass. As he did so he extracted a credit card from his wallet and waited for the attendant to tell him to place it in the card reader. In a minute the transaction was paid for and Carlton and Sheera had gained access to the park. 'And now, we should decide what rides to go on. I don't much like rollercoasters, no head for heights, but there is a lot to do so at some point if you want to go on a ride that doesn't appeal to me then I can sit it out and wait for you.'

Sheera was struck by the sheer number of people in the park, the queues for the rides and the general ambience of the place. More than that she was so happy to be with the man she knew of as Simon Hart. They joined the almost none-existent express queue at one of the rides and a few minutes later were sat down as they started the ride. And thus they started an afternoon of apparently carefree fun together.

***

The same could not be said for those responsible for the mass evacuation taking place in Kingston, nor for the anti-terrorism teams stationed at each of the three main carparks. As those teams worked as quickly as the

CCTV systems would let them, Marshall and Preston sat waiting nervously for any information.

'I keep thinking,' said Marshall once the coffee cups were empty, 'what his next move could be. He must know deep down that we won't pay up, unless he is totally deluded.'

'Which he may well be, but go on?'

'Well, lets assume he has a plan. From his call earlier it looks like he had twenty four phials of this stuff he called Wipeout. He released two of them in Germany and has presumably left one in Kingston. That leaves twenty one unaccounted for. Which means he must have a plan for them. Both where he plans to let them off, until we do pay, and more importantly how to get in, plant the device and then get out again undetected. This has taken a lot of planning in my view, and right now I'd say he is several steps ahead of us. Even though the call looks like it came from the Chessington area, we don't yet know what we're looking for, so we could put a hundred officers into the area and draw a blank.'

'Agreed, but where are you going with this?'

'I'm trying to out-think him. He went to Kingston this morning, probably by car, or at least I assume that for the present. He did whatever he did, and we could take a few days going through the CCTV in the shopping centre and probably still not identify him, and then he left. Sometime later, thanks to Alan Green, he called you on your personal number. Which also shows planning. As does the whole way he has got hold of the watches and the phials. So, I think that call to you came when he had parked up wherever he went to from Kingston, at least ten kilometres clear I would guess. If he plans to let more of these off in the days and weeks ahead, or until we stop him, he must have planned for the likelihood we wouldn't pay up at the first demand.. Question is where did he go in the Chessington area? There's golf courses, common land and of course the World of Adventures.

We could put teams in place at the likely locations, but we could just be wasting man power.'

'You know this part of Surrey far better than I do,' said Preston. 'He mentioned another demonstration later today. Do you want to start moving people into the area we think the call came from.'

'Not much point until we know what we are looking for. We need to find that bloody car, and fast.'

'Or we're sunk if he is using public transport. He'd be miles away from Chessington by now, if he is.'

'Let's hope he isn't.' Marshall's mobile phone sounded and he answered it. 'Yes, it's Marshall. You have and, no way. Good work Richardson. Now, get onto the authorities, we need to try and track where it went. Start on the road out of Kingston to Chessington. We think he went that way.' The phone went dead.

'They've found it.' Marshall sounded almost exuberant. 'At least they think they have.'

'What? How come?' Preston was confused.

'Silver VW Golf left the Seven Kings carpark at ten to one. Registration number belongs to a guy called Simon Hart .'

'So, there must be hundreds of Simon Hart's in the country.'

'Very probably, if not more. Only this car is registered to the address that burned to the ground yesterday. Which makes it kind of unique.'

'So are you saying Simon Hart was not in the house when it burned down? I thought his Mercedes was in the driveway, and the car that belonged to his prostitute friend, what's her name?'

'Matthews. Well it could be he set her up somehow. Perhaps he needed to silence her for some reason. I wouldn't put it past the bastard to have a second car we knew nothing about and he simply left his house in that.' Marshall had that dry taste in his mouth, a taste he often got when something wasn't quite right. 'Something's bugging me though.'

'How do you mean?'

'I'm not sure, just something intangible that doesn't quite add up for now.' Marshall paused for a few seconds. 'Got it. The car left the carpark at ten to one and he called you at twenty past from somewhere in the Chessington area. So I reckon he drove straight to wherever he placed the call, and it's about a half hour drive. From my memory of driving in that area my best guess is he's gone to the World of Adventures – it's a massive carpark and he could easily hide in the crowd.'

Marshall's phone rang again and he put it on speakerphone as he answered it.

'Marshall.'

'Richardson, guv. The VW Golf picture is coming your way right now, and we've managed to spot it on the road from Kingston to Chessington. I'll know more precisely where it went from there in a little while.'

'Okay Richardson. I have the boss here so we'll start driving towards the Chessington area. Let me know when you have it.'

'Okay, guv.' The call ended and a minute later the mobile phone pinged to alert Marshall to the arrival of a message. He opened the message and clicked on the picture to make it full screen.

'Well, that's something we didn't have before.' The picture was a full front image of the Golf, the registration plate and the two occupants. 'I guess,' Marshall continued, 'that is our terrorist and beside him the person we know as Ganzagha.'

'She looks young, Marshall, don't you think?'

'Yes, maybe twenty, quite pretty. I wonder what her role in all of this is?'

'Care to speculate?'

'Skin complexion indicates somewhere East, possibly Turkey or Syria or somewhere out there. Other than that and what I've discussed previously, I don't know where she fits in. Just got to hope they can find the car now. Any word from the bomb people?'

'Not yet but I just checked the news channel and the top story is the evacuation of Kingston which the press are saying is due to the discovery of an unexploded World War 2 bomb on a riverside building site.'

'Well, they got the unexploded bit right. About par for the course with journalism these days. Just so long as the real reason doesn't leak out.' Marshall was back to walking holes in his lounge carpet. 'I think it's time to head to Chessington.'

'Fair enough. Your car?'

'Yes.'

Five minutes later they were on the road heading for the Chessington area. They had no sooner set off than Preston's phone rang.

'Yes, yes, I understand. And where is it going to? Okay, I'll talk to them in a bit. Good work by the way. I think once the forensic people have done their work we can remove the blockade and put out a press release that says the bomb has been dealt with and the area is safe. That should satisfy the press pack that must be there behind the cordon by now.'

Preston put the phone down.

'That was the bomb squad commander. They located the device. This guy obviously likes men's toilets. Having an intact device is going to be very useful in the coming investigations. For now, the trigger device, a brick mobile phone, has been disconnected and the whole thing has been put in a lead-lined container which is even now on its way to Porton Down. They can hopefully tell us more about the phial's contents in a few days' time.'

'So once news of this hits the airwaves, and assuming our wannabee extortionist come terrorist, is listening in, we can expect another attempt by him.' Marshall sat in the drivers' seat for a moment, pondering. 'I know it's too late now, and it would probably have been impossible, but I wish the press were kept totally in the dark over things like this. Having it exposed just makes things more difficult.'

'Hart, or whoever he may be, might not be listening in. We can but hope, but I agree, today isn't over with yet. Now, the question is, where exactly is that blasted silver Golf?'

CHAPTER TWENTY-TWO

It was nearly 3:30 in the afternoon when the call came through to Marshall. He and Preston were still on route to Chessington.

'DI Marshall is driving at the moment. This is DCS Preston. How can I help?'

'DS Richardson Ma'am. We have a trace on the silver Golf Ma'am. A series of cameras have picked it up heading for Chessington. We followed it all the way through Surbiton and down the A243 and here's the funny thing. Well, Ma'am it's not funny but the car pulled into the car park just before the World of Adventures. And so far there is no sign of it leaving.'

'That is incredibly good work Richardson. Marshall, we need to get to World of Adventures, and fast. Richardson, get your teams out of Kingston and down there. And get me an armed response unit there as quickly as you can.'

'Yes Ma'am.'

Even before the call was ended, Marshall had turned on the blue lights hidden around his unmarked car, something he rarely did.. With his foot to the floor he sped up the A24, joining the A243 outside Leatherhead and was in sight of the World of Adventures park when he saw a solid stream of marked cars heading from the top of the road to the same destination. As he pulled into the carpark, he muttered, 'all we have to do now is find the damn car.'

'The uniform will do that,' said Preston. 'It won't take long.'

It didn't. Two minutes after entering the carpark the VW Golf had been located. A quick inspection showed it was empty and the doors locked.

'So we have to assume the occupants are in the park,' said Preston to the group of ten officers standing around her. 'The park closes in just over an hour. I don't think if we even sent a hundred people in there with his identity we'd find him in that time, unless we got lucky. Our best bet is to pick him up when he comes back here.' Preston paused as if seeking a response from the group gathered round her.

'Yes, Ma'am,' a few voices concurred.

'So we lie in wait. A couple of cars on the exit, a couple parked up in both directions outside. I want two unmarked cars parked as close to this as possible and the armed response unit hidden out of sight but ready to jump at a moment's notice. Who's in charge of that.'

'Me Ma'am. Detective Sergeant Andrews. I have my partner, DC Stoneman with me. What are we supposed to be on call for? The instructions were vague but the centre said it was terror related.'

'This car, or rather its occupants, are the cause of the mayhem in Kingston earlier today. There are two occupants. A male who is roughly in his forties, and a younger female. Unless they have walked away to God knows where, they are in the park at the moment. We don't know if either of them is armed, or what is in the car. We can find that out later on. For now I need you as back up in case they are armed.'

'Yes Ma'am. I suggest we go park down the far end of the carpark and then come back up and wait over there. We won't be visible from here and can get here if needed in just a few seconds.'

'Agreed. Right, everyone take up your places. Marshall, we'll wait in your unmarked car here.'

'Yes, Ma'am.'

***

In the park itself, at the time the flotilla of blue flashing lights arrived at the carpark, Carlton and Sheera were on the sky train. Carlton spotted the lights in the distance, rubbed his chin thoughtfully for a moment and then smiled to himself. A few minutes later the ride was over.

'I really want to do the rollercoaster. Have we got time?' Sheera asked. The day had been a big adventure for her and she didn't want it to end, even though Carlton had told her the park would be closing soon.

'You can go on it, but I don't really like that kind of ride so if it's alright with you I'll sit this one out. I'll wait over here on the benches for you.' Carlton showed Sheera where the ride entry point was and where he would be waiting.

'See you shortly, Simon,' she said and disappeared into the queueing area for the ride.

Carlton sat down and pondered the situation. It was not part of his expectations that he would have been tracked so quickly to the World of Adventures. He had intended that the theme park would keep Sheera away from any television or radio news of the carnage that he hoped would be developing in the Kingston area. He fished inside his pocket and pressed the button on the small black box he had hidden there. Smiling to himself at the thought of what was just happening back in the men's toilets in the shopping centre, Carlton stood up. He opened the black ruck sack and extracted the wrappings from the sandwiches they had eaten earlier. Hiding the small black box in the wrappings, he deposited them in the nearby waste bin. Thinking quickly, Carlton then moved away from the area, headed for the exit where visitors could pick up a bus or a taxi and before Sheera had completed her ride, he had hailed a taxi and was heading away from the theme park. As the taxi gained access to the main road, two police cars with blue flashing lights pulled into the area reserved for taxis. Carlton commented casually to the driver, 'Seems like a lot of police activity round here today.'

'Not surprising really,' said the driver, navigating his way through the traffic lights.

'Why's that?' Carlton continued with his pretence.

'You not heard?'

'Heard what. I've been in there since about ten this morning. I've been in a business meeting most of the day.'

'Oh. Well there was some big deal going on in Kingston, a bomb or something I heard on the news. Seems like they cleared whatever it was about an hour ago, but the whole area has been crawling with cars ever since lunchtime.'

'Oh, right. Well I'll have to watch the news this evening. Sorry, I've got a call coming in, must take it.'

Carlton fished his mobile phone from his pocket and looked at the contact. It was Sheera. He ignored the incoming call and instead texted her back.

Come to the car. I had to take a call and the signal in the park was bad.

As the taxi headed towards Reigate, so Sheera unwittingly walked out of the theme park and into the carpark.

'That's her,' said Marshall as soon as he spotted her walking down the road leading to the silver Golf. But where is he?'

'Gone to the loo perhaps,' offered Preston. 'Okay, we take her and clear the area so he doesn't suspect anything. Get unit 1 to move in and arrest her quickly.' Marshall obliged.

A marked police car drove straight towards the unsuspecting woman. The car was nearly with her when the brakes went on, doors were opened and the two officers rushed towards her.

'Sheera Ganzagha?' One questioned her as they approached.

'Er, yes, I'm Sheera.'

'Sheera Ganzagha you are under arrest on suspicion of acts of terrorism. You do not have to say anything but it may harm your defence if you do not mention when questioned something which you later rely on in court. Anything you do say may be given in evidence. Do you understand?'

'Err, yes, but what am I supposed to have done.'

'We'll deal with that down the station. Now I need to handcuff you. Are you carrying anything on your person that you should not be carrying such as a knife, or any drugs.'

'No, of course not. I have my mobile phone and some coins, that's about it.'

'Are you with anyone here today?' The officer asked her as he cuffed her wrists.

'Only my boyfriend.'

'And his name?'

'Simon Hart. Why? What am I supposed to have done?'

'In the back of the car, Miss. We'll deal with that down the station. Is your boyfriend still in the park.'

'I think so but he texted me to come back to the car so I don't know.' Sheera was only too willing to co-operate, her eyes filling with tears as the situation dawned on her.

'And which car is that, Miss?'

'The silver Golf just down there.' Sheera tried to point down the road with her cuffed hands. As she did so the officer opened the door to his car and helped her into the back seat.'

'Tango 1,' he spoke into his shoulder phone, 'target detained. Taking her to the station to process. Second target believed to still be in the park.'

'Good work Tango 2, we will wait for target number two to appear.'

'Roger.'

With Sheera handcuffed in the back of the BMW X5, the blue lights flashed as the car sped away from the area.

'And now,' said Marshall, 'where the hell is Hart, or whoever he is? And what is he planning next?'

'Good question,' replied Preston.

'A second demonstration, perhaps? Should we order the park be evacuated as a precaution.'

'I don't think so. If he was going to do anything here then he'd be long gone I think. No, this isn't what he's planning next. The park closes in 20 minutes or so, so we'd only cause panic and take even longer to close the park if we got the staff to follow evacuation procedures. If he's still in there, he can't be long and we have more than enough manpower to handle him when he comes out. What we don't know is what else he has in the car – and that means we don't go near it or open anything except under strict quarantine conditions. From what I heard of the arrest of Ganzagha she clearly thinks he is Simon Hart. If that's the case then the team at the burned out house aren't going to find much.'

'Possibly, but I still don't understand how he could have got away from such an inferno, assuming he was in the building when whatever it was exploded.'

'Any word on the investigation there?' Preston asked.

'Nothing's come through yet. I'll call Patterson and see what's going on.'

Marshall did and spoke for a few minutes.

'The fire service damped the building down overnight and declared it stable enough for our team to go in. We've got people in there now but so far there's no news.'

'Okay. The sooner we discover what happened there the better,' said Preston. 'Looks like it's leaving time,' she added, as the trickle of people leaving the theme park had noticeably increased as they had been talking.

'I think we're in for a long wait,' said Marshall, rubbing his chin thoughtfully.

'Why?'

'I smell a rat. Why didn't Hart come out of the park with Ganzagha? What was it she said to the arresting officer – something about a text telling her to come down to the car. Something to do with a lousy signal and he had a call to make, wasn't it?' Marshall looked questioningly at Preston.

'Pretty much. The officer's report will be more detailed but we have to wait several hours for that.'

'If he was coming out to the car park, why isn't he here? You know what I'm beginning to think, Ma'am. I think our man has planned this all along. The girl is a decoy to throw us off the scent. She sounded surprised at being arrested and wasn't hiding anything. I don't think she has much of an idea about what is going on. I'll be surprised if she does. If I'm right we'll be waiting here in the carpark all night for the driver to return. Possibly he is holed up in the theme park somewhere waiting for the cover of darkness but I think he's already gone from here, some planned escape route. Possibly a bus or taxi before we ever got here.'

'You could be right. I suggest we call recovery now,' said Preston. 'I don't like the thought of what might be in the Golf and by removing it to a safe place we can mitigate any potential risk. We'll need them anyway if we arrest him. We should start forensic recovery of the car and form our own conclusions as to where he's gone if he doesn't appear in the next thirty minutes or so. I think, if he doesn't turn up, we should go and have a chat with the woman. I'll come, for moral support, but you can interview her.'

'It's been a long day. Would it not be better to interview her tomorrow?'

'Tomorrow may be too late. Remember his threats of another demonstration today?'

'As he's been rumbled here I don't think he'll be doing much more today. I would think he's more concerned about what his girlfriend is telling us – and if he planned to hand her over and make good his escape then that is what he will be spending his energies on right now.'

'Fair enough, I hope you're right.' Preston was keeping an eye open roving over the growing number of people returning to their cars. After 30 minutes the carpark had all but emptied, just a handful of cars remained.

Marshall had walked up to the kiosks and flashed his credentials, and then stood there waiting for the staff to lock the barriers. Then he called Preston.

'Ma'am, the gates are locked. If the recovery team are here I suggest we leave them to it and leave a car here and the armed backup just in case he appears but I don't think he will, though God knows where he has gone. I think it's time to go and interview the woman. I'm coming back to the car as I speak.'

'Agreed, Marshall. Once you've sorted out the manpower needed here we'll stand the others down. The low loader has arrived. This is going to take a while as they have to wrap the car for forensic purposes before they move it. Our time would be better spent talking to Ganzagha.'

Preston had just finished her conversation with Marshall when her mobile phone pinged, indicating the arrival of a new message. She looked at the screen for a moment and said one word – 'shit'.

The message on the screen was stark:-

You were foolish not to obey my instructions. I still have enough of what I left in Kingston to destroy every major city and town in this country, and that is what I am going to do. There will be no more demands. From tonight it will just be a matter of watching the bodies pile up. Today you got lucky, but you won't from now on. And the girl you have just arrested has no idea who I am or where I am. She was just a useful decoy, expendable.

Preston read the message a few times and then showed it to Marshall when he returned.

'We need to find this maniac and fast,' said Marshall.

'Agreed. Where do you suggest we start?'

'Well, it's clear he's not around here anymore. I can try and get the SMS to your phone traced but that will only give us a rough idea of where he went and, in my opinion, he's smart enough to know that's what we'll do, so by the time we've done that he will be long gone.' Marshall was looking back up the road to the entrance area.

'I agree. But if he left this place, how did he leave. On foot, bus, taxi?'

'Taxi probably. On foot would be too risky and by bus would be the same.'

'Okay, get someone over to the taxi area and check on CCTV – anything in the last hour.' Preston waited for Marshall to place the call that would start the process of getting the CCTV checked. 'And if they spot him, track the taxi and find the driver.'

'Yes Ma'am,' Marshall said in an impatient sounding voice.

***

While the CCTV was being checked by members of the ATRIUM team, Marshall and Preston set out for the police station where Ganzagha had been driven and processed. She had demanded a duty solicitor be present and one had been summoned.

'DI Marshall,' Marshall introduced himself to the desk Sergeant as he showed him his warrant car. 'You have a Sheera Ganzagha booked in on suspicion of the terror incident in Kingston earlier today. I'm here to interview her on behalf of ATRIUM.'

'Never heard of ATRIUM?'

'Well Sergeant, you have now. If you want I can get my DCS here to call your boss and clarify things?' Marshall phrased it as a question but it was intended to go unanswered. The Sergeant looked at a pad on his desk.

'No need sir. They have already called down to let you through. I'll buzz you in and then if you wait in the foyer I'll get the detective in charge of the case to come and collect you both. Ma'am if I could just verify your Id please.'

Preston showed the Sergeant her own credentials as the buzzer on the door sounded and she and Marshall gained entry to a waiting area. They were not kept waiting long. A young, slightly grey man with dark rings under his eyes appeared from another door and ushered them inside.

'DS Barton,' he introduced himself. 'From the point of view of the investigation I've been put in charge of handling the suspect. From my own position, I know you are in charge and yes, I have heard of ATRIUM before. I think it was about three years ago so I understand who you are. But I would ask for the sake of things that I am involved in the interview, in a back seat so to speak.'

'Granted,' said Marshall. 'And thanks for your understanding. Is her solicitor here?'

'Yes, they're having a discussion at the moment in the interview room. Been here about twenty minutes. Right authoritarian she is. Name of Sandra Ashton from Peasbody, Lake and Undermeyers. She's already twitchy about the arrest procedure and reasons. One of those. Also the suspect has declined an interpreter. I'd say her English was very good, actually.' The DS had referred to his notebook to provide the names.

'Thanks for that. Do you have an interview room where proceedings can be watched without anyone being the wiser? DCS Preston would like to observe from outside if possible.'

'Yes we have that. I'll take you there now and then I'll fetch the suspect and her brief.'

Five minute later, Marshall and Barton were sat on one side of a table, while Sheera and her brief sat on the other. Formal introductions were made and Barton went through the formalities and started the recording device.

'I would like to start,' said Marshall, 'by clearing up a matter of your identity. 'According to immigration information I received an hour ago, you registered at a hotel in Munich on 28th June as Sheera Ganzagha, a Turkish national, but your passport was scanned on entry to this country as being Sheera Hart, a British citizen. Which is correct?'

'It's Simon, he made me change my name. My name is Ganzagha and I am Turkish. Simon told me it would be easier to come to this country if it appeared I was his wife – he already had all the paperwork when we met up in Munich so I could hardly argue.'

'I see, and for the avoidance of confusion, what is Simon's surname?'

'Hart.' If Sheera was nervous she was masking it well.

'And how long have you known Mr Hart?'

'Several years. He came out to Yalvac, where I live, when I was a teenager. We have met a few times and he has helped with my education as my father is dead and my uncle is not wealthy. In return I simply call him every now and then to let him know when certain things are being collected by couriers who are going back to this country.'

'So your uncle is responsible for supplying goods to this country. Does he have an export licence?'

'I think the courier dealt with all that. My uncle just collected orders in his garage for the courier to collect.'

'And what happened for you to go to Munich?'

'Mr Hart invited me to. He wanted me to identify the van that the courier was driving. He told me it was because there were things in the van he needed to obtain before they were brought back to this country, because people here would use those things to close his business down.'

'And that made sense to you?' Marshall was watching the young woman closely. He had already decided she was either a very good actor or she knew nothing about Hart's real intentions.

'It made sense at the time.'

'So what happened in Munich?'

'We did some shopping, had meals in restaurants and then he took me to a place where the van was parked. I identified it and he went to the back of the van. Whatever he did only took a few minutes and we were about to leave when the driver returned. I recognised him as the person who had dealings with my uncle.'

'Go on,' said Marshall evenly.

'The next day we drove to PAris and dropped the hire car back at the company Simon had rented it from. We stayed overnight in a hotel and came back to this country yesterday morning. We came back through the tunnel on a train to London. Then we got a taxi to his home. That evening he had a business meeting that lasted a few hours and then we went out for a meal.'

'And what is the address where Mr. Hart lives?' Marshall had guessed what her reply would be – Hart, or whoever he was, was not stupid.

'I have no idea. I know we were in the area of Reigate, I think it was. I saw a few signposts with that name on it, but I really have no idea what road the house is in.'

'I see, and where did you go after the meal?'

'Back to his house. As I said, I don't know the address, and by the time we got back it was dark, but it had a big gate in front of it with a device you press buttons on to open the gates.'

'I see. And tell me about today?' Marshall may have raised his eyes at her previous reply but if he did it didn't register with the young woman.

'Today we went to Kiston…'

'Kingston perhaps?' Marshall offered in a friendly voice.

'Yes, Kingston, and did some shopping. It was a very big shopping centre. After that we went to the place where I was arrested, after I had been on some rides. They were exciting. I really do not understand why I have been brought here.'

'I am beginning to believe that could be true,' said Marshall. 'When you were with Mr Hart, either in

Germany or this country, did he show you what he had taken from the van, assuming he took something.'

'He showed me in Germany when we got back from the van. They looked like jewellery boxes, or watch boxes. I had seen them before, on several occasions, when they were delivered to my Uncle, so I was not surprised.'

'You said, several occasions. So this was not the first time you had seen these boxes.'

'No. My uncle has been sending them with the courier for over a year now. Always the same number and size if I remember correctly.'

'And have you ever looked in the boxes.'

'Of course not. They were sealed with tape but my uncle told me they were expensive watches.'

'Did Mr. Hart say anything about the watches?'

'Only what was in the boxes was dangerous to his business and for me not to go near them, so I didn't.'

'And did you see him do anything with the watches?'

'No. He did tend to stay up later than me as I was tired from the travelling and the excitement of shopping and so on. It was all a big change for me.'

'I see. When Mr Hart came back from his business meeting last night, did he appear at all anxious or was his behaviour any different to normal.'

'Not that I noticed. Why?'

'Well, Miss Ganzagha, I'm afraid I can't tell you that right now. Now, one final question, well two actually. First, do you have any idea why Mr Hart deserted you at the World of Adventures earlier today, and second do you have any idea where Mr Hart is at the moment?'

'The answer to both questions is no, I don't know. Maybe he has gone home?'

'Maybe, but the problem with that is a house we know he owned was burned to the ground last night, so unless he has another property, or he has another name you have not told us about, he can't have done that.'

'But we went back to his place last night after eating at a restaurant and we stayed there all night and I can promise you, there was no fire.' Ganzagha smiled weakly.

'And do you remember the restaurant name and roughly how long it took to drive there?'

'Not the name but it did overlook the race course where the famous race is run, Epson, or something like that. And the journey was about fifteen minutes I would say, maybe a bit longer.'

'So one more question. I take it you went to the restaurant in the silver Golf we found at the theme park, the same one you went to Kingston in?'

'Actually, no. Mr Hart also has a black BMW. It's one of those big ones. Before you ask, I have no idea what the registration number is.'

'Thank you Miss Ganzagha. That's all for now. Interview is terminated. The Sergeant here will have the interview transcribed into a statement which you will need to sign as being accurate. You will, I am afraid have to spend the night here for two reasons. First we may need to ask you more questions tomorrow after making some more enquiries and then we have to ascertain whether you have a right to be in this country or whether to charge you under our anti-terrorism laws. You can have a minute with your solicitor before one of the officers will take you back to the cells.'

Marshall and Barton stood up and left the room, the door automatically locking behind them.

'Well Barton, what do you think?'

'I think she's probably here illegally but I doubt she knows what Hart is involved with, or even if that is his real name. I think at best she's an unwitting party to it all. I doubt we're going to get enough evidence to convince a jury of much. We might get enough for conspiracy to commit an act of terrorism, but I really don't think she had any idea what Hart was up to.'

'I have to say I agree. What's your opinion Ma'am, having listened into it all?'

'She's either a good actor, which I doubt, or she has about as much idea of what Hart is involved in, as would the average person on the street. I suggest tomorrow we hand her over to the immigration people. What they do then is not our problem, but maybe after today we suggest they put it to her that she should go back to Turkey immediately and we leave it there. I could see if I can pull some favours in. That would put a fair bit of distance between her and Hart. Main thing now is to find Hart and quickly. If he's still got the other phials of that stuff he used in Munich and tried to use in Kingston, then he could strike again at any time and any place just as he promised in the text message earlier.'

'I'll go back to the restaurant, Ma'am and see if I can get any more information from their bookings. I think it's a long shot, and if we're looking at a fifteen to twenty minute journey from wherever Hart lives to it, that's too big an area for us to cover. I'll drop you at your car on the way, Ma'am.'

'Thank you Marshall. Well, Barton, thank you for accommodating us today. Marshall will call in the morning if he wants to interview Ganzagha further but if you don't hear from him by mid-morning then you can hand her over to immigration.'

'Yes Ma'am.'

'I'll call you regardless,' Marshall said as they left through the foyer door.

They were back in the carpark when Marshall's phone rang. He took the call which lasted less than a minute and then closed the call.

'That was the team going over CCTV at the theme park. They have a taxi of interest that left the rank just after we arrived. Single male got in the back, not a great picture, but it could be our man. They also got the

301

registration of the taxi and are trying to get hold of the driver to see where he took his fare. The only problem is he's gone off duty and has switched off his mobile. So we will have to wait until a car has gone to his address and they've talked to him. I have a couple of guys on their way right now, but he lives down in Crawley so it might take a while.'

'Okay, well we may as well head away from here, back towards your place so I can get my car.' Preston looked at the message on her mobile phone while Marshall backed the car out of the parking space and drove out of the station carpark, and then said, 'This guy has to be stopped even if we have to work round the clock to find him.'

'Yes, Ma'am.'

***

The taxi completed the journey back to Carlton's Reigate house just before quarter to six. Carlton paid the driver at the gate and watched as the taxi disappeared up the road. His escape from Chessington had been a close run thing and Carlton was somewhat rattled by it. His meticulous planning had gone wrong, but the situation could be recovered. Sheera, Carlton expected, was in custody, and as he pressed the buttons on the control box to open the double gates t the driveway, he was glad she did not know his real name, though he could not be sure she had not observed the address of the driveway he was now walking up. He would need to act quickly. The case containing the deadly phials was already stowed in the back of his black BMW in the garage, together with a suitcase containing all the clothes he had had in the wardrobe of the house. Although Sheera didn't know it, the house was a cover, a six month rental that Carlton had prudently taken out as a bolt hole. It came fully furnished and to a specification that provided Carlton with the same air of opulence that befitted the persona of Simon Hart. James Sneddon, the owner of the house, was away on business somewhere in Japan, so Carlton understood. The tenancy was almost up, the six months past.

Carlton entered the house, switched off the alarm and did one final sweep of the property, ensuring he cleared out all of Sheera's belongings from the bedroom and bathroom as he went. By the time he'd finished he had almost filled three black bin liners with her belongings. He planned to dispose of them later that evening. Finally he was sure he had removed all his personal belongings. Not worried about fingerprints as he was not on any police register, Carlton reset the alarm and went back to the garage. He tossed the bin liners in the boot of the car and backed it out of the garage onto the driveway. After turning the car round, he went back, secured the garage and then drove out of the property. Ten minutes later the keys to the property, in a white envelope stuck down with tape, were pushed through the night-safe box of the property agent he had rented the building from.

With his tracks covered, Carlton began his journey to the New Forest. He already knew it would take just over two hours to get to his destination, which meant he would check-in at about 8:30pm.

**

Preston was on her way back to her own home after collecting her car from Marshall's. Marshall was contemplating writing up a report of the day's activities while they were still fresh in his head when his mobile phone rang.

'Marshall,' he said almost without thinking.

'Guv, we've got an address from the taxi driver. A short talk with him confirms it's Hart alright, and we now know who Hart really is. The house the taxi took him to is actually owned by someone called James Sneddon.'

'Good work, Richardson, and the driver is absolutely sure?'

'Yes, we showed him a picture of the driver of the silver Golf we got from the carpark in Kingston. The taxi driver recognised the man instantly and had no doubts. His onboard dashcam confirmed the address he dropped Sneddon off at.'

'So, where are you now?'

'Just coming out of Crawley. We can get to the address in about twenty minutes if you want to strike tonight.'

'I don't think we have much choice. I'll call the boss and make sure we get an armed response unit there waiting for us. I'll be on my way in five. Text me the address.'

'It's already on it's way. See you later.'

Marshall closed the call and immediately called Preston.

'Ma'am I need a favour. We know where the taxi dropped Hart and who owns that property – a guy called James Sneddon. The taxi driver was very co-operative. Richardson is sending me the address right now and I'll forward it to you once it arrives. I'm just on my way to the address to meet up with Richardson and Wellman. I could do with an armed response unit or two to meet us there in say twenty minutes.'

'Consider it done but don't raids like this usually get done at dawn?'

'Yes Ma'am. The point of going now though is he won't be expecting us and if we left it to a dawn raid he might well be another step ahead of us.'

'Fair enough. Be careful, Marshall, he may have a lot of very nasty phials on him.'

'Understood. Let's hope this is the last sortie for today. I'll call you later.' Marshall closed the call and was about to start driving when the address pinged on Marshall's phone and he forwarded it to Preston. Then he typed the postcode into his navigation app and started driving.

Twenty minutes later, Marshall drove slowly past the house where the taxi driver had dropped his fare off earlier. He spotted Wellman standing in the shadows opposite the open gateway, looking as if he was talking innocently on his mobile phone. It was evident that Richardson and Wellman were waiting for armed backup before walking up the driveway.

A hundred yards beyond the house sat a marked police car with its lights off. In front of it sat a smaller car in which sat Richardson, who was waiting for Marshall's arrival. Marshall pulled up and was greeted by one of the police officers who was now dressed in body armour and carrying what looked to be a semi-automatic weapon.

'DI Marshall,' Marshall showed his warrant card to the officer. 'And I assume by now you've met DS Richardson and DC Wellman who is standing up by the gate keeping an eye on things. Good idea that, Richardson.'

'Thank you guv,' Richardson commented. 'No sign of any activity in the house, according to Wellman. There's no sign of any lights on inside either.'

'Yes, they introduced themselves.' The armed officer replied. 'So what's going on here?'

'The house back there about a hundred yards, the one with the open gates and with one of my team standing opposite it. The chap we believe is in there is known to us and most of Europe as Simon Hart, but his real name we now believe could be James Sneddon. We believe he is responsible for the attempted act of terrorism in Kingston today. He's also responsible for at least two acts of terrorism in Europe in the past few days.'

'And how can you be sure?' the officer was just inquisitive.

'First we have his partner in custody and though she is foreign and only arrived here yesterday, she described the gates and control box and had a rough idea where the house was. Second a taxi driver identified dropping his fare here a few hours ago and we have CCTV of that fare being the person we know as Simon Hart. Third we believe he has a number of phials of a very deadly substance in there. It is vital we disable him before he has a chance to do anything with them, so we need to go in quietly and very quickly. I expect the house is protected but we need to get through whatever we find and arrest the occupant as quickly as possible.'

'Yes, sir. And I assume you have a warrant. We have another unit on its way, no lights or sirens. They should be here any moment.' Even as he spoke a second marked car pulled up and the passenger window was wound down. It was evident the passenger was already dressed and ready for an armed response.

'Where do you want us, guv?' The passenger officer asked the armed officer.

'Yes I have a warrant," Marshall reached into his inner pocket and pulled out the printed document.

'You may as well park up here and we'll go and see what's what,' said the officer.

Three minutes later the four police officers were all in body armour and armed. Together with Marshall, Richardson and Wellman they walked up the driveway to the house. At the front door the armed officer in charge banged loudly on the door.

'Armed Police,' the officer who had been standing next to Marshall shouted loudly.

There was no reply. The officer bent down and pushed the letterbox open.

'It's dark inside,' he said and then more loudly, 'Armed police. Open this door now, or we'll break it down.'

Silence.

'Harrison, have you got your big red key?' The officer in charge asked one of his colleagues.

'Yes, sir. Two minutes.' The junior officer turned and ran back down the drive. Two minutes later he returned holding a large red, heavy-looking device.

'The big red key,' said the officer to Marshall. 'It opens most doors.'

And sure enough, it did. The wooden door splintered on the third time the device was swung against the door, and on the fourth swing, the door gave way. The air was instantly filled with the sound of the alarm beeping, indicating it had been triggered.

'Wellman, when we're inside, find the control box and turn that damn thing off,' ordered Marshall.

'Guv.'

'Armed Police, come out now with your hands up.' The officer called out into the house.

Nothing moved.

The officer found the light switch, turned on the downstairs lights and the four officers did a quick sweep of the ground floor. Not surprisingly they came up with nothing.

'Secure the upper floor,' the commanding officer ordered his three colleagues. 'Okay, sir, you can come in now. I suggest looking under the stairs for the control box.'

'Got it,' said Wellman as the full alarm system started ringing around the house. Twenty seconds of deafening noise later and Wellman had worked his magic and the noise died.

'Well, if he was asleep upstairs that would have woken him up,' the officer said sagely to Marshall.

'No one up here, guv. We just have the attic to look into. Won't be a minute.

'Guv,' said Richardson coming from the kitchen, holding an envelope. 'Something you should see.'

'What is it Richardson?'

'A letter I think, only it's addressed to the boss.'

'Really?'

Marshall realised Richardson was wearing blue surgical gloves. Evidence preservers they were called in the business. He took a similar pair out of his own pocket before Richardson passed him the envelope. On the front was the addressee in simple, evidently-disguised, handwriting –

For the attention of D.C.S. Selena Preston

'Attic's empty,' the voice called down the staircase. 'Property is empty.'

Marshall held the envelope in front of him as if bemused. Instinctively, with his free hand, he fished his mobile phone out of his pocket, photographed the envelope and then called Preston. She answered almost immediately and a few seconds later Marshall was instructed to open the envelope and read her its contents.

It took Marshall several seconds to carefully peel back the seal on the envelope and extract the single piece of folded paper. On it was the simple message:

Close, but not that close.
Better luck next time.
Simon.

'Damn it, Marshall, he's playing games with us now. Okay, check the garage. According to the woman he had a black BMW. If it's gone then we know he's on the run. So we should put out an all points alert for what was his name, Sneddon?'

'Yes Ma'am, James Sneddon.'

The garage door was not a problem for Wellman, who opened it in under a minute. Even as the door opened it was obvious the BMW was not there. The bird had flown.

EPILOGUE

It was mid-morning on the 4th July. The German intelligence people had contacted Preston with news that the virus appeared to have lost its potency after the first forty-eight hours, and she had relayed that information to Marshall when he had met her at the office in London. There had been no luck tracing or apprehending James Sneddon. The property they had broken into the previous evening had been searched thoroughly. Nothing untoward had been found, certainly no phials. There were, of course, lots of fingerprints. Some would, in the days ahead be associated with Sheera Ganzagha, others would remain unidentified but kept on file, possibly for ever.

Preston looked out of the window at the London Eye. It was a sunny morning but her mood was anything but good. She and Marshall both knew that out there somewhere was a terrorist waiting to pounce.

***

Brian Carlton woke early. He had never stayed in a treehouse before but out in the New Forest was the perfect park where he could go unnoticed for days on end. He'd stayed at other Centre Parcs villages before but never in their grandest of accommodation. He'd picked Centre Parcs for one reason, and one reason only. He knew he would not be searched on arrival, which meant he could take anything into the park in his car, park up next to his accommodation and take it into the accommodation unchallenged.

He sat on the balcony between the main accommodation and the games hut, sipping hot coffee and eating freshly baked croissants. Next to him sat a small case, closed, locked shut, ready and waiting.

THE END